WAVES

C. L. Paur

C. L. Paur
www.clpaurauthor.com

Printed in the United States of America

First Printing: Aug 2018
Kindle Direct Publishing

ISBN-978-0-692-15987-3

*For my husband and daughters who
provided inspiration and love.*

For whatever we lose (like a you or a me), it's always ourself we find in the sea.
—FROM *MAGGIE AND MILLY AND MOLLY AND MAY*
E.E. CUMMINGS

CHAPTER 1

Welcome." I looked up to see a casualty from the seventeenth century glowering with muddy-colored eyes at me, or more precisely, the dead Catharine Zimmer.

As our glances seemed frozen upon each other, my body descended slowly down, down, down. "Am I going to Hell?" I screamed.

He shook his head and held out his hand, which felt like a rubbery, wet eel. "No, Catherine. We're on a beach, and the sand is wet."

Once I felt more secure (though how does one feel secure when one is dead?), I looked again at the man. Breeches and a waistcoat, probably black in their day, had faded to gray. Tattered muslin hung in place of a shirt. His forehead towered like a snowdrift blunted by a plow. A long greasy rope of a braid hung down his back. Red torn stockings exposed most of his toes. Bile rose up in my throat when I glimpsed at the grime layered under his toenails.

Cold and damp distracted me from the visage in front of me, and the desire for warmth soon consumed every thought. "I'm dead! Why can't I get warm?" I complained.

"It is part of the condition you've embarked upon. We all must endure it. My Christian name is Radulf." He bowed gallantly. "You are to begin your journey here."

"By the ocean? Is this the ocean on earth or somewhere else? Are we on another planet? What is this place called?"

"Shush, Catharine, listen and watch."

"How long have you been here?" I asked him taking another hard look at his shabbiness.

"About an hour."

"No, I mean wherever you call this, this..." It looked like earth, but it didn't look like earth. "Place."

He whisked a lock of hair off his forehead. My lips pursed on their own accord. I tried figuring out the math of this man's apparent sentencing. He probably died in the 1600's so he probably had been roaming for a good 400 years. My body trembled even stronger as I contemplated whether my demise would be the same or even worse.

"We're caught betwixt the cosmos as our punishments mete out our intended sufferings. Anguish and I have been companions these last three-hundred and thirty-four years."

I gasped. Though I barely comprehended his high English, I understood. Tears sprung out of my eyeballs. "You mean I'm to be here for that long?"

"Some are here even longer." He pulled out a leather pouch, and unwrapped it to reveal a clay pipe and dried leaves. His grubby hands stuffed the pipe and it lit as if from some invisible lighter. Inhaling and puffing, his expression grew thoughtful. He could have been having a casual smoke before dinner. Though his clothing looked ancient, I figured he must have died only in his fifties or sixties since few wrinkles marred his countenance.

"Are you my guardian angel?" I had always figured my guardian angel was less than exemplary, and this man seemed aptly dressed for the part.

He guffawed. "Hardly. Haven't you seen pictures of angels?"

Sure, I've seen paintings of angels by Michelangelo, Raphael, even Leonardo da Vinci, but we were always taught angels didn't really look like the images in art. In fact, one teacher said they didn't even have bodies, yet sometimes appeared in human form as messengers to us.

"So, if you're not my angel, why are you here? Or is this just where you do all your time here, like prison, and occasionally someone, like me, pops up and interrupts your, whatever you call it?"

"Watch!" He pointed as a wave carried into shore a sunflower starfish curling its tentacles. Back into the ocean, the weakened water retreated, and the starfish relaxed its arms. Whoosh, another wave washed in, pushing the echinoderm closer to me. I bent down to retrieve it, but the next wave snatched it away from my grasp. I stood up and the man stood watching me. He waved his arms up into the air as if beckoning some far off person. As quickly as the starfish disappeared, we were transported to another beach. Whoosh, the ocean coughed up the same sea star. I recognized it because of the black line, like a minus sign, at its center.

"The ocean has many lessons to teach," Radulf said. "You ask how we're connected. My uncle left me a tidy fortune, allowing me the luxury to sail and write about my experiences. As a child I was lured into composing words onto paper, yet as I grew, it waned. Like you, I squandered the gold."

"It seems so preposterous." I was still reeling from the heavenly court proceedings where the stories of a dictator, nurse, and movie director somehow had something to do with me. How could the gaps in my own life create such craters in the histories of others?

"It does? You, in your century, flick on lights instead of burn candles, drive horseless carriages, and fly in the belly of steel birds, and yet you cannot conceive how the ideas or the words of one person can change the course of history, even for one?"

I shrugged and shook my head. Where was he going with this? I had nothing to do with automobiles, electricity, or the Wright Brothers.

From inside his vest he procured a book. "Read this."

"It's a novella." I grew hopeful. "Will I enter my eternal rest when I finish reading it?"

"Catharine, you're not living up to your lineage." He backed away, his face beginning to fade. "You may use any of the ideas for your opus."

"What?" Gone before he could answer.

My earthly journey was finished. It was no longer feasible to write. What did he mean?

A craggy bank had long since backed itself away from the ocean's assault. I climbed over huge boulders and perched myself on one. Old English filled the pages inside the worn leather covers. Rain spattered down, poking into the ocean like hole-punchers. The dampness increased the chill in my body. Worse, droplets poured into my eyes, making it difficult to read. I wiped my face repeatedly, but the words were blurry. Still, I tried. Reading Shakespeare was like reading a different language, but *The Travels of Radulf Langley* transported me to another universe, one in which I couldn't decipher its language. I set it down and looked around.

A cherubic-looking black woman, with wiry hair that formed a cloud around her head, was walking toward me. She glowed in a white tunic, golden sandals, and wings, taller than she. Like a duck, she was impervious to the raindrops.

My angel? My guardian angel? I had spoken often to her, yet as I matured, I could no longer hear her responses.

"So. Catharine, do you like my angel costume?"

"Are you my guardian angel?" I asked for the second time that day.

"Age hadn't completely diminished your intelligence, I see." She touched my shoulders, and the rain disappeared.

"What?"

"You would tell me everything, then one day it all stopped. The other angels told me that is how it often happens."

"We were told to stop talking to our imaginary friends," I said, wiping my face with her proffered handkerchief.

"There was nothing imaginary about me." She looked down at the book by my side. "Humph, giving up is still your specialty." She stooped down and handed it back to me. "Try again. A mother giving birth finds the final act of pushing out her child one of the most difficult aspects of the delivery. If she gives up, the child will die."

"Not if the doctor performs a C-section," I glibly responded.

"Read!"

Only my elementary teachers could garner such an instant reaction like the one my angel elicited at that moment. My face flushed, and my eyes averted downward and remained. I pretended to leaf through the booklet.

"What shall I call you?" I asked.

"I will return when you're finished," was her answer.

I lifted my head when she disappeared but noticed the tide climbing higher and closer. About fifty feet away stood a higher embankment in which I climbed to avoid drowning, though I was dead, wasn't I? Could a dead person drown?

Some of the rocks crumbled away as I stepped upon them, forcing a collision with my knees to their jagged surfaces. My dead knees bled! I tried to recall the Giant's edict for my purgatorial existence. I would carry the weight of humankind with no joy, hope, or happiness to buoy the spirit. Even a simple scrape upon the knee burned with an intensity never before felt on earth.

As the water rose higher and higher, I climbed until it seemed as if the tide began to subside. I sat on a flattened stone and opened the book.

"Written by Radulf Langley," I read again. "Dedicated to my parents."

Once I deciphered his penmanship, a world of sea monsters, pirates, and crashing storms, colored the stories. At the conclusion he wrote, "All these events are true."

"Radulf fought pirates and weathered the wily sea? Interesting, but I don't see any connection," I thought.

"You've finished?" She reappeared.

"I don't understand," I stuttered.

"A simple little book. The author would have never achieved fame or glory, but his words would be like a torch for you, Catharine. Do you recall the name Langley?"

"Langley, Langley," I repeated in my mind. Why did that name seem so familiar?

"Family tree, Catharine, family tree."

"Langley! Yes, it's a name from my mother's side of the family. I can't tell you how far back it went."

"Sixteenth century. But Radulf wrote this in the seventeenth century."

I was right. He was from that time era. "That's nice." I didn't know what to say. The book was interesting, but sea monsters and Catharine Zimmer?

The angel waved her hands, and before her stood the oak, hand-carved trunk that had stood at the foot of my parents' bed. As a young girl, I would run my hands along the carvings and the leather fasteners. What intrigued me most, however, were the family artifacts Mom stored inside its woody scented interior. Wedding pictures, embroidered wall hangings, old shoes, and linens were among some of the treasures. I'd spend hours looking through the trunk even though I had looked at the antiquities numerous times.

"This belonged in here," the angel set Radulf's book inside. "But it was never written for you to read."

"It's only an adventure story, not my favorite genre," I spoke smugly.

My angel shook her head. "You have grown too pragmatic, Catharine. As a child you had woven fanciful tales in your mind. As you let practicality in, your imagination bolted." Her lips curved in a sardonic frown.

"I don't know what to say. I still don't understand what Radulf had to do with me."

Our beings were transported to an old, quaint, city square. Situated in the center of the plaza stood an ancient cathedral. Cafes, bistros, banks, and shops sprouted like little patches of grass around the redwood. Tourists, people everywhere, were smiling, talking, and snapping cameras. The voices swirled together like one wave of sound.

In a moment, a bald man appeared with a cello. A girl of about five dropped money into his cello case, which had the effect of turning him on. Back and forth, he pushed and pulled, the strings obeying his movements by producing the opening chords of *Ode to Joy*.

More musicians joined him. A conductor, wearing a polo shirt, moved to face the performers and quickly waved his arms up and down and sideways. To his right a little boy waved in an attempt to mimic the conductor.

My heart raced, tears stung my eyes. My favorite hymn. I was in the middle of a Flash Mob. My great nieces and nephews had told me about these, but I myself had never experienced one. I was alone with this symphony. For a split second joy trembled expectantly, trying to enter into my being.

"Do you know the date of Beethoven's life?"

"Somewhere in the 1800's, I guess."

"1827 was his death. Do you know the time period of this Flash Mob?"

"The 21st Century."

"Do you think Beethoven inspired others?"

"Well, of course, he was famous, he was brilliant."

"Perhaps this wasn't a good example," the angel said more to herself than to me. We then were transported to a small house. Inside there was a man, in a wheelchair, writing at his desk. His arms and legs were shorter than normal.

The angel touched him, but he must not have felt it because he continued writing. "It's a letter to his niece. She wants to quit college."

All this made no sense to me.

"Look at the letter."

My eyes scanned the heartfelt words, which explained to the niece how the man had let his disability keep him from pursuing his dreams. He regretted that decision, and had hoped that she wouldn't let the challenges of college keep her from finishing.

"He wasn't famous, but his words inspired her to finish."

"Did she?"

"She became a scientist, one who has discovered many cures for various diseases."

"But Radulf's book? It's just a little book of adventure!"

"Written by one of your long, lost relatives, from the pages of history."

"So?"

She handed me Radulf's novella. "Read it again. Read it as a child would read. Read it as if you're young Catharine Zimmer, inside your house on a rainy day, sitting on your window seat."

She disappeared.

This time the words cavorted and caused my heart to race. Radulf fought off a pirate, but not without sustaining an injury that left a scar on his right arm. I envisioned the ship, the shiny hilts, and the blood dripping onto the wooden deck. The whales that sputtered and swam under their vessel were more real than the whales I had seen off the coast of Boston. Worms and lice teemed among the words; I cringed in disgust. I began to understand how Radulf's words would have triggered an even greater inspiration for Catharine Zimmer to write.

"Did I make my point, finally?" My angel returned.

"Yep! Now may I go to heaven?" This was much easier than I thought.

She rolled her big brown eyes and shook her head, the wiry curls bouncing. "Catharine, don't add more to this journey than is already set before you."

I tried a different approach. "But the book was never written!"

"That is correct. That is why Radulf traveled for centuries atoning for his misdeeds and in this case, omissions."

"So," I was afraid to ask, "those books I started in the closet? Do they have anything to do with all this?"

"Yes. Catharine, what seems so insignificant to humans, is very significant in this realm. Come follow me."

"Where are we going?"

"A funeral."

I trembled. "How long will I..." I couldn't finish. Inside myself I had sensed this journey would take longer than centuries, perhaps even a millennium.

"It all depends upon you, Catharine."

CHAPTER 2

She looks so natural," Hillary said as she peered into the casket. Why was Hillary at my funeral? Oh, yes, the free lunch to follow. She had lived right next door to me, but Hillary was the dog, and I was the cat.

"Hillary von Münchhausen. You have more lies to your credit than cells in your body." I finally had the guts to tell Hillary what I felt about her. Did it matter that I was dead?

"Yes, she does look very natural," replied Laurel, my neighbor to the north. Her father, Earl, lived with her. Earl was like that bill collector calling during dinnertime. If I was lucky, I'd spot him in my picture window and hide before the doorbell rang. Sometimes I wondered if he watched my house because he'd usually shamble over as I was climbing into my car. It didn't matter the day or time.

"I'd love to chat, Earl, but I'm late for work." I would close my car door, crank the ignition, make sure he wasn't directly behind me, and roar off. Unfortunately, he often grabbed my door handle before I could escape.

Earl wore the same clothing he wore when he had been 275 pounds. When he knew I couldn't escape, he would release his grip on my car door, hike up his blue slacks, and monologue about his amazing daughter, her travels, and of course her books. Huff. Puff. His words clipped by the effects of emphysema.

"Then her oxygen," pant, pant, "level," pant, pant, "hovered near empty. I almost," pant, pant, "lost her in the death zone."

Nile River. "The crocs there," pant, pant, "are deadly. Watch this." He flashed his phone into my face. He almost lost his slacks that time. I grimaced as I went from looking at him to a team of crocodiles chomping into an antelope.

Laurel swam in the Amazon River and almost became piranha bait.

I turned toward my angel. "Will part of my punishment include meeting up with Earl? I think five minutes with him here should suffice."

"He's already in his eternal glory."

"What? Earl?" Disgust dripped through every pore of my non-porous specter.

"Earl was lonely. He decided to help out at church and he often let people who needed a bed stay in his extra bedroom." She shook her head. "This is your judgement Catharine. You don't have to worry about anyone else's."

Mom had once asked me if my travels had anything to do with Laurel.

"Sounds like you're trying to keep up with Laurel," Mother said. "Wish you had that same drive for your writing."

That pinprick stung. "I could fly to Mars, and I'm sure Laurel would fly to Jupiter, collect some rare gas, and win a Nobel Prize for science."

"Jealous?"

"Not jealous. But let's face it, no matter how hard I try, Laurel will always exceed me."

"Are you living for you or for others to approve?"

To be fair to Laurel, it was her father, not Laurel, who bragged. Laurel genuinely listened to my stories. She also was my little voice of conscience.

"Have you done any writing?" she'd ask almost every time I saw her. It was like the doctor asking if you had scheduled your colonoscopy. There were times I had spotted her in the grocery store and I would run to a different aisle just to avoid contact. I would then berate myself for letting her look at any of my writing.

"Nah! I gave that up." Or, "It just wasn't for me." Or, "The store keeps me so busy. I am a manager now." Looking back, I shudder at my lassitude.

Laurel persisted. "You are very good, Catharine. I could even pass along some of your stuff to my editor friend."

My ego appreciated her comments, but the rest of me ignored her requests. Laurel wrote twenty-seven books. Catharine Zimmer, zero. It was like a spelling bee, where the winning team spells Chiaroscurist with ease, while the losers don't even bother trying to spell D-O-G.

Laurel's books were just non-fiction travel, I had told myself to assuage my guilt, *not the great American novels I have in mind.*

I left the chatting women standing next to my coffin to stroll through the beige carpeted, sound-controlled atmosphere. Who else came to bid me last respects? Fifty, I counted them. Fifty people, including Hillary and Laurel, stood around at Catharine Zimmer's wake. Where were the rest of my nephews and nieces? I had twenty-three of them, but only six showed up. How about the residents of Snug-Haven nursing home?

"They're being quarantined," my angel appeared next to me. It was unsettling to have her pop out and then pop back in.

"Do you think you could warn me when you're coming back into my view? You're scaring me to death," I quipped, thinking I was quite humorous.

She had her own clichés to mete out, "By the way, my deepest sympathies. You're in a much better place now, and I know how you feel."

"Right. And look at me! Who did my makeup job, Medusa? And where is the rest of my family?" Chagrin tainted my words.

"Too busy, I suppose."

Perhaps I had a few delusions of my State-style funeral with tolling bells, gun carriages, and a weeping cortege.

"Does anyone care that I died?"

"I've been to many a burial with no attendees," the angel said. "Face it Catharine, you were a very old lady. Most of your family and friends had passed away. It's tough being the last one to go."

"My sister is the last. Look at her. She's not even crying."

"She did, Catharine. But she's very stoic and wants to put on a strong face. You were her favorite, you know."

"I was?"

"You were all your siblings' favorite."

"I was?" We left that scene and moved to another. "This isn't my funeral. Where am I?"

"Your Brother John's funeral, the one you didn't attend."

"I don't drive at night."

"Didn't drive? Why?"

"Bad eyesight, I guess."

The angel handed me a medical form. "20/20 vision," it said. My name was sprawled over the top of the form. We seemed to be traveling on a cloud.

"A different funeral?"

"Your Uncle Fred."

"I wasn't there either."

"I know."

"Who is that?" I pointed to the corpse sinking into the sateen lined box.

"Your brother, Patrick. He enjoyed all your postcards."

"He lived so far away."

"But the Great Wall was right next door?"

"Angel, may I return to my funeral?"

We returned to a church hall, with about ten tables decked with paper table coverings, and silk-flower centerpieces. I found myself next to Hillary again and I watched her savagely gnawing on a chicken leg, the fat dripping down her chin. I tried grabbing a napkin from the table to wipe her awful face, but my hand went right through it. I left that grisly scene to watch my sister.

Claire sat alone, pensively. She was dressed in black. Claire's children and their spouses chatted amiably.

"They're sure happy I'm dead."

"People do that at funerals. But you wouldn't know that."

"I went to a funeral or two."

"Two. Your mother's and your father's."

"I was very busy. And most of them were out-of-town. I sent mass cards!"

"Mass cards are good. But they're even better when hand delivered."

I glided over to the Catharine Zimmer photo board. I scrutinized each picture.

"Yee gads!" I shouted.

"What?"

"Look at that! I have a carrot stuck in my nose, and I'm wearing a bandana. And look at that!"

"All these pictures were taken when you were very young. I don't see any of you past middle age. Did you ever go to any family functions after you grew up?"

"They moved away, not I. Gas prices were ridiculous."

"You were very beautiful," the angel complemented.

"I was. But it all slipped away so suddenly."

We turned to listen to my nephew, Gregory, talking to a small group.

"I remember Auntie Catharine asking me to buy her some hair dye," Gregory began telling the group around him. "I told her to buy it herself. She said she didn't want anyone knowing she dyed her hair."

Chuckles.

"Very funny," I snapped.

Hillary spoke next. "Did you ever see her on the treadmill? She looked like a clucking chicken chasing her babies. She'd move her neck, throwing her face forward in rhythm of the machine." Exercising was a private affair for me. Hillary should have never seen me, but one day she let herself into my house because she had run out of toilet paper.

"Why did I ever give that woman my house key?"

"Because you kept locking yourself out," my angel answered.

"A chicken? Did you hear that, a chicken? I can't believe those children are listening to that old hag."

"They're all adults, now, Catharine." My angel smiled, but it looked more like a sneer. "I wouldn't be calling people hags while you're in this state. Might add more time."

"Chicken legs, that's for sure. Skinniest legs I'd ever seen!" Another obnoxious voice popped up.

One silly comment after another I had to endure. All about my looks. I had prided myself on preserving some modicum of beauty, but it was all just a joke to them.

"May I have a piece of my own chicken?" I asked the angel.

A bucket of the ambrosial crispiness appeared. I sank my teeth into a drumstick. No crispiness, no fat dripping down my chin. Just a piece of cardboard. Would my taste buds depart from me as well?

"This is terrible," I said.

"Also part of your present condition."

"No joy or pleasure is to be had?" I asked, hoping for some reprieve.

"Eternity of joy awaits you. Oh, and fried chicken."

We returned our attention back to my funeral. Hour after hour it seemed I listened to the life of Catharine Zimmer. No one took me seriously. I was just a goofy old woman.

"She wanted to be a writer," Claire interjected. "She wrote beautiful poetry."

"Auntie Catharine a writer?" They all laughed hysterically. "Comic books?"

"No, novels," Laurel came to my defense. "I didn't' know about the poetry, but I read some of her writing while we were still neighbors."

"I found four boxes," Claire interrupted, "of novels that were started, but never completed. She hid them in the back of her second closet."

"Could the books still be published?" Gregory asked.

Claire shrugged her shoulders and sat down.

"I really wanted to be a writer! Listen to me!" I shouted. Wasn't it enough I had to be humiliated during my trial? At my funeral too? I had thought my deceit was well hidden. No one had known about Dad's money, but they knew I had not finished my job on earth.

"Catharine," I turned to see my father speaking, with Mom at his side. They were in the realm with me, but I knew they were not here to share my sorrow. "We know what you did," Dad said, his voice solemn.

What could be worse than being the guilty child brought before her parents? I was dead, yet the pangs of shame burned as if I pressed my face upon the grille of an electric heater.

"So much potential." Were there tears in Dad's eyes? He and Mom shook their heads. "But you took my money to use it on a cruise."

Pretense, that was what my life had become, yet I had fooled no one, except perhaps myself. The delusion kept me from the life I had aspired to live, one full of love, heroism, and greatness.

"I was afraid," I simpered like some chastised puppy.

"We didn't teach you fear," Mom answered.

"Catharine, I don't envy you your journey," Dad said, speaking as a father to a daughter. "We can no longer be with you." He kissed my forehead, and Mother hugged me. They didn't yell, but the disappointment swelled and seemed to radiate to me. They disappeared.

"Your aunt was a very sweet woman," Father Swerik approached the group, plate in hand. "She made me laugh all the time."

"Yes, we loved her very much," Claire smiled. "I will miss my Little Chicken."

Little Chicken, that's what she had always called me. Tears welled up in her eyes as well as mine. The Giant dolling out my sentence was right. Alienation pulled at every nerve ending in my body, leaving only bitterness and loneliness. I wanted to embrace my loved ones, but this realm held me captive.

"Angel, please may I go now? Angel? Where are you? Please answer me."

CHAPTER 3

Did I fall asleep? Where was I? *America.* I spun around, staring at the rows of marble and cement markers. Holy Cross Cemetery - the burial ground of my family. Where was my body laid to rest?

"We are not here to look at your gravesite." Her words carried heaviness, and I felt a sense of foreboding. Like Dickens' Ghost of Christmas Yet to Come, she pointed toward a stone.

I shuffled over to it and gasped. Gregory Sinclair! Gregory? Claire's son? What happened? He was laughing and telling jokes at my funeral.

"Suicide." Grief wove itself into the angel's words, like black thread in a bright tapestry.

"But, Gregory? He seemed perfectly fine just a moment ago. Didn't you just hear him?"

"That's often how it is. How much did you really know your nephew?"

"He would visit me every Wednesday evening for supper. We talked all the time. He had never given any impression of..." The words cemented themselves inside my lips.

"Did you listen to his stories or blab on about your own life?"

I watched as elderly Catharine Zimmer placed a platter of slices of meat on the table. She sat down next to Gregory. They prayed first, then ate. Catharine Zimmer liked to talk about herself. Not one second was spared to ask Gregory anything whether it was about his job or things he liked to do.

"And you complained about Laurel's father talking all the time!" The angel whispered the words as if the two in front of us would hear.

"Gregory seemed to enjoy himself when he came for supper," I said. "Besides, I was a lonely, elderly lady. He was just showing his respect."

"Yes, he loved you deeply, but he was hurting deeply too. Self-doubt coursed stronger through his veins than his own blood."

"I was Gregory's god-mother. Why didn't I see this coming? Was I so consumed with my own life that I failed to notice?"

"Worse, Catharine. Timidness is never a good role model. He wanted to be a writer, yet, like you, its neglect weakened his desire. Despair rules over Gregory now. Hope has vanished."

"Why haven't I met him in death or wherever I am?"

"Because there is still time." Gone. *There she goes again!*

"Angel, don't leave me! Where am I?" I was no longer Catharine Zimmer, but a different woman. An intravenous tube was taped to my right arm. I tried lifting my limbs and pulling myself forward, but I was the prisoner of a wheelchair. Only my eyes were free to move.

Claustrophobia! I felt trapped as if in Houdini's Water Torture Cell, unable to breath in this body. I wanted to scream, but only guttural grunts escaped from my lips. I heard the flush of the toilet. Out came Gregory, with my bedpan.

"Gregory," I choked, but it was a crude growl.

"Hey, are you talking?" He said. Though he was in his thirties, he still had that boyish charm I loved so much about him.

"Gregory, Gregory. What can I say?" I thought, but couldn't verbalize. "You were such a beautiful baby, and grew up into a wonderful man. Can't you see it? Everyone around you sees it."

"He can't hear your thoughts. You must convince him." My angel spoke inside my mind.

"Convince him? Like this? I can't even talk," the thought, like a meat mallet, pounded in my head.

Gregory was going to leave this hospital tonight and kill himself, and there was nothing I could do about it. The sting of tears blurred my vision.

"Are you crying?" Gregory peered down at me. "What's the matter, Laureen?"

A nurse popped her head into my room. "Gregory, your shift has been done over an hour ago. Why are you still here?"

"Look at Laureen! She's crying. I think she's sad," Gregory said. "Do you want me to stay?"

Tug of war. I was ten-years-old, and it was the girls against the boys. Our teacher stood on the sidelines cheering us on, telling us to pull, pull, pull. Harder, harder, harder. Burning muscles overwhelmed all my senses. I wanted to release the rope, but I heaved and heaved.

Harder, harder. Pull, heave, strain. Talk, talk.

"Yes!" The grunt was so painful. Every nerve, every muscle screamed in defiance, but I spoke. I began to wheeze as if I had run a marathon.

Gregory's eyes lit up. "She spoke. That means I must stay. It's a sign."

The nurse arched her eyebrows in derision. "I guess if you want to stay, suit yourself. She doesn't get any visitors anyway."

After the nurse left, Gregory pulled a chair next to me. His blue eyes searched mine.

"Laureen, I know I can tell you this because I trust you. My Auntie Catharine died. I miss her. Tonight would have been our dinner date, but she's gone. For some reason I knew I couldn't do what I had planned to do with her still around. But, when I go home tonight, I'm...." He hesitated. My body trembled.

"Laureen! What's the matter? Are you okay?"

"Gregory, Gregory. What are you doing, my sweet baby! So many people love you. Your family, your friends. Don't do this. There is so much to live for." No sounds emitted from these thoughts, just tears and shaking. I felt so useless, so foolish.

Gregory grabbed a tissue and gently wiped my eyes and face. What woman wouldn't love this man?

"I've thought about it, and I've decided my life has no purpose. I work every day. No one really appreciates what I do. This really isn't what I wanted to do with my life. A writer, that is what I wanted to do, yet who makes a living as a writer? I just found out my Auntie Catharine had wanted to write. My mom found four novels that she had started, but never finished. I wonder why. It was sad to see those boxes. I asked Mom if I could keep them, instead of throwing them out.

"Not only is my professional life a mess, my personal one isn't much better. I don't have a love life. Who wants to marry me? I hardly make enough as a CNA to support myself." He took my hand and squeezed it. I wanted to squeeze it back, but my limbs were limp.

"Gregory! Stop this thinking. It will lead to your demise." Again, no words, just grunts.

"Laureen, you're really talking to me. But what are you saying?" He jumped up and peered into my eyes.

Tears, only tears.

"Let's change the subject," Gregory said. "Let me tell you about my Aunt Catharine. I thought I knew all about her, but her novels tell a different story. I assumed she was just some cute little old lady, but there was real depth to her. I wish I had the chance to know her when she was young."

Gregory patted my shoulder and walked over to the window. He pulled opened the curtains.

"You gotta look at this," he returned to wheel me over the white tiled floor. Across the river the setting sun filtered through the thick grove of pine trees, forcing their reflection upon the river. Night would soon drape over the image. I grunted in pleasure.

"Like that? I tried to get Aunt Catharine out of her apartment, but she became somewhat of a recluse. I would drag her from the living room to look out the backyard. I must admit, I had often dreamt of being with a younger woman besides Aunt Catharine."

I grunted in displeasure.

"Oh, Laureen. You are making me laugh. Before Aunt Catharine got sick, she always had a huge meal, with dessert waiting."

I looked at the whiteboard, with the doctor and staff names scrolled on the board for the patient's benefit. Wednesday, August 20, the date on the tombstone.

Gregory would bring flowers every Wednesday. Not the cheap flowers you'd pick up at the grocery store for a last minute bouquet, but roses, gardenias or orchids. I'd prepare some roasted meat, potatoes and dessert. Gregory would eat everything with gusto and gratitude.

I did manage to stop talking about myself to ask him the same question every week. "Gregory, have you found a nice woman yet?"

"Aunt Catharine, have you found a good man yet?" He was teasing, but it pinched my soul.

He looked into Laureen's eyes again. "You're smiling, Laureen. Did you know my aunt? She had this awful red hair."

"What do you mean, awful?" I grunted.

"When she was young, it was beautiful. She was beautiful. She never married either. I don't want to live like that, though."

It was as if he stabbed me with those words. Never before had I fully considered the consequences of my life. The stories of Aleric, Ursula, and Adrien during my trial had given me a glimpse, but I had no idea the pain I had wrought was so close to home.

The brightness of joy had faded. Why hadn't I noticed it during his visits?

I continued looking out the window, and he sat on the bed. "She took all her nieces and nephews once to Fun Country, you know that place with roller coasters and rides? She stood and waited for us, not willing to ride anything! I challenged her to go on a roller coaster, but she refused.

"She always would say to me, 'Gregory, you should face your fears,' and yet I'm finding out she never did. I can't blame Auntie Catharine. I think it's a myth people want to perpetuate when they say 'Follow your dreams.' I'm starting to think it's just a few of the chosen that really find success."

"No, no!" I shouted my grunts. I wanted to cover my face in shame, but my arms hung limply at my side. "Gregory! Don't follow my path! You must..."

He pulled out some sheets of paper. "Rejection letters! 'Dear Mr. Sinclair. Thank you for your submission. Unfortunately, your article doesn't fit our editorial needs.' Listen to this one, 'Dear Gregory Sinclair, We regret to write that we are not interested in your book proposal. All the best.'" Bitterness contaminated his words.

Did he carry these around? Why would anyone do that? Keep them, maybe, hide them, but when you have wild success, bring them out and burn them in joy, but don't carry them with you. Oh, I wanted to speak those words of wisdom, but I looked haplessly at my nephew, crying.

Then his failure pointed to my guilt. At least he had rejection letters. I hadn't even gotten to the point of reaching out to publishers. The most I had done with my work was to show it to Laurel.

"Gregory, Gregory. What have I done?" The words seemed to repeat themselves over and over.

He folded up what must have been at least ten letters, and crammed them into his pants' pockets. "I'm sorry Laureen, I'm upsetting you. Would you like me to read the newspaper for you? Near the end, when Aunt Catharine's eyes grew bad, I would read to her."

Gregory pulled out his laptop, pressed whatever he pressed, and scanned his eyes over the screen.

"Hey, get a load of this. The newspaper is having a writing contest. A short story. Hmm. Probably wouldn't win anyway. Those letters don't lie. Sure, they were trying to be nice, but what they were really saying was don't even consider yourself a writer!"

I groaned through searing pain.

"What are you saying, Laureen?" Gregory leaned to listen.

"Writing contest. Writing contest!" I said, but it was just more pig grunts.

"Should I try the contest?"

More blubbering. "Yes! Yes!"

"Wait a minute, the deadline is tomorrow. I can't write a story that fast."

"Yes, you can! I remember how you could devise a story in two minutes."
Snorting, tears, moaning.

"Do you want me to write about you, Laureen? What is your story? What secrets do you have hidden behind your sad eyes?" Gregory leaned so close. "Maybe I'll write about my Aunt Catharine who never finished writing her novels. I wonder if there's a story there."

Suddenly the same nurse, and another woman showed up.

"Hi Laureen, time for bed. Gregory, why are you still here?" she asked.

"We've been chatting," he said.

"You could talk to a tree," the other woman said. She had chestnut colored hair and sea green eyes. Gregory seemed to blush at her comments. I checked her left finger. No wedding band.

I wondered if Gregory liked this woman.

"Most women talk too much, so I usually can't get a word in edgewise! Laureen, here, knows how to listen." Gregory joked. "Here, let me help you."

Gregory rolled the wheelchair closer to the bed. He stood next to the young woman. Her nametag said Patty. She smelled as pretty as she looked. Nice name. Patty and Gregory, I rolled around in my thoughts. I wanted to smile, but only drooled. Patty gently dabbed my chin with a tissue. She smiled, one of her front teeth slightly ahead of the other, yet warmth and beauty emanated from it. This was the woman for Gregory, I was sure of it, but he needed confidence.

The nurse left after checking my vitals. Patty looked down at Gregory's laptop

"Writing contest? Are you entering the newspaper's writing contest? I saw it a few weeks ago. Deadline's tomorrow, you know."

"I just found it tonight. Not sure I have the time to get it in."

I wiggled and grunted. They both looked at me.

"I think she wants me to enter."

"I didn't know you were a writer!" Patty said.

"I'm not. Well, I would like to be, but I don't know. Too many rejections."

"How many?" She challenged.

"Uh, maybe ten." He shrugged his shoulders.

"Only ten? Really? You can start complaining if you get one hundred, not ten! I've heard your stories," Patty sounded determined.

Gregory hemmed and hawed.

She wiggled her eyebrows. "Dinner Friday if you enter!"

Clever way to get a date. I really like this woman! I smiled, but no one decipher my actions.

"It's impossible!" He shook his head.

More grunting.

"Listen to Laureen. Two smart women can't be wrong. Get going Gregory! You can even pick out the restaurant."

The cleft in his chin appeared when he grinned. "Do you think the hospital would mind if I stay here and write? Laureen inspired me," Gregory said.

Patty was erasing the white board and scrawled in the new staff for the night. She would be the night nurse. "In the dark? Laureen needs her sleep."

I grunted such a fierce grunt, they both looked at me.

"Do you want me to stay?" Gregory asked.

"Of course!"

"That's her yes grunt," Gregory said.

"Well, we'll see." Patty wasn't convinced. "I'll check on you in a little while."

I must have dozed. When I awoke, it was three o'clock. Gregory was pacing back and forth.

"Why did I say I'd enter this? All to get a date with Patty? I've been wanting to ask her out, but now she won't even want to talk to me if I don't do this. Laureen, look, I have nothing. It's three o'clock. I have to be in to work at seven. Only four hours to go!"

"Pray," I grunted, but there was no way he'd understand my garbled utterance.

"Pray!" Once more I uttered.

"What?" He stared, trying to decipher my grunt. Unsatisfied, he did the one thing most desperate people do. "God, you know I'm not a praying man, and I feel like a hypocrite asking, but could you give me a little help here?"

Within minutes, he was back at his computer typing. It was 6:30 when he lifted his head back up.

"Done, sent. Shower and back to work! Laureen, you're a doll. Thanks! You know what? I don't even care if I win. I'm so happy to be going out with Patty."

Gregory kissed the crown of my head and left. My guardian angel appeared.

"Time to go, Catharine."

"What happens next? Does he win the writing contest?"

"I'm not privy to reveal the future. Suffice it to say that Gregory did not kill himself tonight. Patty will take up where you left off."

"All that and I don't get to know?"

"That is part of your current condition."

I felt gypped. So much energy. It was like being in a competition, winning, then being whisked off before you could enjoy the accolades.

"Is this what my voyage will be, setting it all right?" Catharine the problem solver.

"Nope." She dashed all hope. "Only a few will be like this. For most you will only submerge yourself in the misery you had created."

Misery I had created? I had worked, played, rested, went to church, and repeated those actions like a wheel churning on a bike. Father's sermons challenged me, but once I had left church, it was on to my own pursuits, unaware of the eternal consequences of my delusional laziness and comfort. Did I really create all that misery?

Her words poked me and I sought solace and comfort. Since I had hoarded them in life, however, there were none left in the bank account.

CHAPTER 4

How many years of this was I to endure? Loneliness marched over my soul. Bodies surrounded me, but they existed in a dimension where bonds of friendship could never form.

I was in school, but this time I was sitting, tightly squeezed in a too small desk. I was back at Assumption High School. There were the chalkboards, dusty with chalk remains. A large, round clock hung over the door. A globe and encyclopedias stood on a shelf. To my left were the windows that spanned the entire east wall. Behind the desks was a wall-sized, packed bookshelf.

Sweat poured down my back. It was late summer, a terrible time for school, especially with no air conditioning. For some strange reason I didn't feel like Catharine Zimmer. My arms and legs were chubby, not how I remembered my limbs. My hair was cut short, never the style for me. I looked ahead, and there I was, Catharine Zimmer, seated in the middle of the class. She chatted with students around her.

Who was I? My angel appeared holding a gilded hand mirror. She thrust it in front of me.

"April Morris? I'm April Morris?" I asked as I peered at the acne studded face before me.

April Morris committed suicide at twenty-three. My mother called me at work to give me the terrible news. I didn't know how to respond to my mother because I had barely known April Morris.

"You had never bothered to get to know her," my angel answered. "Now you get to really meet April Morris."

"Why?"

"Why not?" She disappeared.

All traces of Catharine Zimmer left my consciousness, and were replaced with April Morris, staring intently at the beautiful, popular Catharine Zimmer. I envied her long, red hair while I, April, picked at a pimple. My stomach growled. I stared at the clock, 10:35.

Lunch! When will it be lunch? I couldn't get food off my mind. Then I stared at Kerry Colgorski. "Kerry, I love you." I played back and forth in my mind.

Kerry's last name was ugly, but he was beautiful. Brown, wavy hair went below the typical preppy style of the day. Kerry played football, basketball, and baseball.

Kerry and Catharine were an item this month. When will Kerry and April be an item? I wondered.

I scribbled Kerry all over the inside of my notebook. Then I colored hearts around his name.

Finally the lunch bell buzzed. My classmates raced out of the class. I waited until they left, and then carefully heaved my body out of the tight desk. Mr. Bleecker's eyes arched above his glasses as he watched me struggle.

"Miss Morris, perhaps you should try a diet." He then continued staring down at the papers on his desk.

My cheeks flared red. I picked up my books and rushed out.

"I won't eat lunch! That's it, I'll skip lunch." I threw my brown bag into the garbage. I stood there. "What am I doing?" I scrambled into the garbage and tried to retrieve my lunch.

"Hey, fatso, can't get enough food, now got to scrounge in the garbage?" Carson Atherton sneered. He pushed me, and I fell into the container. I was stuck.

"Help me! Get me out of here!" I shouted. I could only hear more voices, more laughter.

"Look at her! She's where she belongs!"

"April Morris is garbage! I could have told you that a long time ago."

Strong arms pulled me out. Mr. Bleecker's eyes, again peering over his glasses, bore holes into me.

"Miss Morris, we do have a cafeteria. Perhaps you should buy yourself a salad." He brushed off his hands and returned back to his classroom. All the students around me laughed even louder, their jeers echoing over and over in my head. I scuttled to the bathroom. Catharine Zimmer was brushing her hair.

"Hi," I said to her, hoping she'd talk to me.

"Hi, April," was all she said. She grabbed her book bag and left the bathroom. Catharine was never mean to me. She was never really friendly, but at least she never said a cruel word to me. If she ever did speak to me, it was all about herself, but I didn't mind. She at least had given me some attention.

I dreamed of looking like Catharine Zimmer. Long, red hair, beautiful eyes and complexion. Thin and fantastic looking in the cheerleading outfit. The only thing wrong with Catharine Zimmer, they said, was her long neck. I didn't think it was long at all. It was slim and graceful, not stocky and short like mine.

"Why, oh why am I cursed looking like this?" I stared hard at my face. "Why was I ever born to live this horrible life?" I hated me. I hated April Morris. I didn't want to be April Morris.

Catharine Zimmer and April Morris split bodies. The angel was with us.

"Catharine, how does it feel to be April Morris?"

"I didn't know she suffered so much."

"And you have only been April while at school. Wait until you go home."

Catharine became April once more.

Excitement and fear intertwined themselves as I walked to my house. I knew what my parents would say, but I couldn't believe that Father Cowan had just asked me to try out for *Our Town*.

As I squeaked open the back door, I heard the hum of the television. I would wait until their favorite program was over to tell them the good news. I found some chips and cookies and sat down to eat my snack.

"April? Is that you? Come and get the remote control for me," my mother shouted.

"Mom, Dad, Father Cowan said I should try out for the school's production of *Our Town*," I blurted as I handed Mom the remote.

Dad hiccupped at my news. Mom stared. Mother had stopped smiling a long time ago.

"Really? Miss Fancy Pants wants to strut around on stage? And who do you think will do the work around here?"

"What part do they want you in?" Dad slurred. "I hope they have a costume that fits."

"She ain't going to be in any stupid play!" Mom screamed. "We got ourselves enough problems without adding to it!"

I ran to my bedroom and plopped onto my bed. I didn't cry. I knew that was the response I would get. Why did I ever bother? I went back to the kitchen. Every day it was the same. First I would wash the breakfast and lunch dishes, then vacuum and dust. Around four o'clock I'd start supper. After supper, I'd clean up the kitchen while my parents watched television. I would slip into my bedroom, with some candy or cookie, and do my homework. When I finished, my favorite part of the day would arrive - poetry. Stanza after stanza filled pages of numerous notebooks all hidden beneath my bed.

When I was younger, they were happy poems about the sun, flowers, bugs, grass, worms, Jonny, or just about anything. Then as my life changed, the poems decomposed like the dead flowers in fall. I'd write, cry, write some more, cry some more. I even wrote poems about Jonny leaving. Those were the poems that hit me the hardest. He didn't really leave, he just ceased to live. I wasn't really angry with my parents. They just didn't know how to cope with me killing their son, their favorite child.

Jonny was five and I was seven when it all happened. We were playing outside. Mom was inside washing the kitchen floor. Daddy was still at work. We threw a ball back and forth. I threw it too hard. Jonny ran out into the street without looking. I can still hear that horrible crash, then the squeal of brakes. Mommy ran out and picked up Jonny. He hung limp like Kitty, my old stuffed cat.

Images and smells of the funeral ironed themselves onto my little brain. Heavily scented flowers draped over the casket. It was a box in my mind, and Daddy held me as I tried to crawl in with Jonny.

"Why is he in there? What are the flowers for?" I kept asking.

"Stop being a baby and act like a seven-year-old!" My aunt yelled and pulled me away from my father. "Your parents don't need you to be a baby right now. You need to be strong!"

There was no one for me. Everyone seemed to console my parents while I sat and watched.

"Oh, Jonny, I miss you so much. Please come back. Just be a bad dream," Every day I wished Jonny back into my life. No one talked to me. I was alone, like some strange bystander who watches the living, but remains dead on the sidelines. Only my poems listened to me, recording the words from my brain onto the white paper.

Days melded into weeks, which morphed into years. This was my life. My only oasis was poetry. No one hurt me. I was important.

Home meant Mother screaming and Dad drooling and laughing. School meant isolation and loneliness. Each morning I looked inside the medicine cabinet. Inside was the solution I craved, yet I could not bring myself to its completion.

April, April. I didn't know. I didn't know any of it. I am sorry.

I tried to disengage my soul from April's body, but my angel appeared with her hands stuck on her lips and her head shaking with derision. "You didn't know or didn't want to learn more about an overweight, acne studded girl who hid away in the crevices of the school? Tell me, what was it?"

My hands burnished my face trying to disguise my shame. When I first met April, she probably weighed about 200 pounds, and red blotches mottled her fair skin. All my girlfriends were thin, had clear complexions, and shopped at the fashionable stores. She just didn't fit my notions of what a friend should look like.

"It's interesting," my angel grew thoughtful. "We often avoid the people who would positively impact our lives all based on superficial motives. As April, you had a chance to read her poetry."

I nodded, grimacing as I recalled my own feeble attempts.

"You and she could have ignited a renaissance in literature. Catharine, there is more." April's consciousness once again overtook mine.

"Let her go," my father insisted. "If she can't get a date to prom, at least let her help at the dance."

"Thank you, Dad. I'll make it all up to you, I promise."

Dad's eyes searched mine. He was trying to tell me something, but I couldn't read his look.

Aunt Mimi bought me a midnight blue dress. "It don't matter if yur ain't goin' with a boy, yur's still gotta look beauteeful."

Beauteeful, that's how she said it. I smiled.

"I got it at one of those second hand stores, yur know."

"Aunt Mimi it's so beautiful. Look at my face! It's all cleared up! I've been doing what you told me to do."

"I see you've dropped a few pounds, too. Not that I thought you was fat or anything."

Aunt Mimi loved me for me. She had moved into the neighborhood about a year before.

"Can you believe it? That house is now being rented out," my mother complained. "Who knows what kind of trash will be moving in?"

"People are not trash," I said. I was getting bolder speaking up to my mother.

"Listen to you!" She tried to crush me, but it wasn't going to work.

"I'm going to bake a pie and give it to our new neighbor," I said.

"Not with my ingredients!"

"Fine. I have babysitting money." I had lots of babysitting money because that's all I did on the weekends was babysit. I didn't have any friends at school, but I had so many young friends who played and talked with me. And I made good money doing it.

I made a blueberry pie and took it over one Saturday. I nervously knocked on the door. An African-American woman, probably in her seventies, answered the door. A black band pulled her springy gray hair off her smiling face. Lids, tired from age, hooded her brown eyes, which were hidden behind wire-framed glasses. She wore a pale yellow sweater and brown tweed skirt. I towered above her and resisted the urge to crouch down to her level.

"I'd like to welcome you to the neighborhood!" I shoved the pie into her arms.

"How sweet. What kind is it?" she asked as she unfolded the foil. "Blueberry! How did yur know it's my favorite? Do yur have time to join me for a slice or two? Everyone calls me Aunt Mimi. Yur can too."

I sat at her kitchen table and watched her bring out a carton of whipping cream to the table. She poured some into a bowl and whipped it into a froth. All that energy coming from such a tiny woman. Then she sliced the pie and dolloped the cream on top.

"I is diabetic, yur know. I shouldn't eat this, but oh, it's so good."

"I'm sorry. I didn't know. Oh, I feel terrible, now."

"Honey, relax! Yur done a good thing. Don't stress so."

I sat in her kitchen for three hours. Aunt Mimi and I were like old buddies. On that day, and many after, she would listen to my woes.

My mind returned to my bedroom as I looked at myself in the mirror. The dress transformed me from a dud to a daisy. Aunt Mimi pinned up my hair, applied makeup, and sprayed a little perfume on my neck.

"Look at yur! A beauty." Aunt Mimi smiled.

"A floozy if you ask me." Mom came into the bedroom.

Aunt Mimi rolled her eyes. "Come on girl. Let's go."

"April, is that you?" Catharine Zimmer stopped and actually talked to me! "You look amazing! Who are you here with?"

"I'm just on the prom committee. I don't have a date."

"That's okay, my date is a dud. Kerry and I broke up."

In an instant, I became Catharine again probably to experience this memory. April Morris, I couldn't believe how beautiful she looked. No one had paid attention to her before prom, but everyone stared and smiled in admiration. I must admit, I was feeling a little jealous of April. Kerry even asked her to dance. His date from Whitney High watched, furious, as he and April danced.

Back into April's body I returned. Her memories flooding my thoughts.

"Would you care to dance?" Kerry! Kerry! He was asking me to dance! I had never had a boy's arm around me. My body tingled with excitement.

"Thank you! This is wonderful. You look great. I hope your girlfriend isn't mad. I should be serving punch..."

"Hey, slow down. I didn't know you talked!" Kerry laughed. "She's not my girlfriend, just someone I know from Whitney High. Catharine dumped me."

"Everyone said you dumped her."

"Whatever. Let's talk about us."

I laughed, and then the dance was over. We smiled at each other.

"I better get to work! Someone needs to serve punch!"

"They can serve themselves," Kerry said, putting his arms around me for another slow dance. *All My Life* played as the disco ball swirled above our heads. There was no one but Kerry and me. This was my dream come true. As we danced, I envisioned our marriage and kids, and even grandkids. I smiled.

"What's so funny?" Kerry asked.

"Nothing. I'm just enjoying myself."

The dance ended too quickly. I turned toward the kitchen since I was there to work, not play. Then anguish assaulted me as I spotted Aunt Mimi trudging toward us, a grim expression over her usual happy face.

"Honey, I'm sorry, but yur gotta come home this instant."

Though Aunt Mimi drove in worried silence, my mind was still on the dance floor with Kerry. When we arrived, an ambulance and police cars scattered themselves all over the lawn and driveway. Flashing red and blue lit up the black night. The commotion took me back to Jonny.

"No, no, no," I shook my head. "I can't go in there."

"Honey, yur gotta. Come on, lean on me if yur need."

Suicide. Dad committed suicide. Couldn't deal with his life, so killed himself. Not too many people at the funeral. Kerry didn't show up. None of my classmates showed up.

It wasn't like Jonny's funeral, with my parents in the receiving line for six hours. For Dad's funeral, Mom and I met with the few visitors. Aunt Mimi stayed with us, and brought us bottles of water, tissue, and coffee. Aunt Mimi's entire family showed up from Chicago. Five boys and one daughter. They all stood very tall, unlike tiny Aunt Mimi.

"My late husband was a big man. They all took after him," she told me after I commented on her children.

After Dad's funeral, Mom didn't say much of anything. Often she never left her bed in the morning.

"Mom, you have to get up. You have to live your life." I tried to coax her, though I honestly preferred she would stay in bed so I did not have to listen to her moan or yell. I told Aunt Mimi. She told her daughter, Evelyn, who was a psychiatrist.

Doctor Evelyn stopped by the house one day.

"Mom, there's someone here to see you," I said, popping into her bedroom.

"Tell them to go away."

Evelyn sat in the kitchen with me for several hours. She listened even better than Aunt Mimi listen and seemed to ask all the right questions.

"I have an office about an hour from here. I would encourage you to visit, or see someone that can help you." She handed me her business card.

"What do you mean?" I asked.

"You've been through so much. Sounds like you need to sort things out."

When she left, Mom came out of her bedroom. "Trying to drum up business for her shrink shop, huh? People always having to talk about their problems. Weaklings!"

"Was Dad a weakling, Mom? Was he?"

"Shut up!"

"He needed help. We all need help, but you won't take it!"

"All families have their problems."

"Not like this," I said.

"The problems with April Morris were too deep for little old Catharine Zimmer to dig out." I said as I returned to myself.

"Little pieces of dirt are all some people need to plant a seed." My angel's eyes glistened in tears, making them into beautiful glass orbs.

I refused to carry the guilt of April's suicide on my conscience. "I couldn't be expected to save her."

"All those beautiful pyramids you made in cheerleading. Take away one person at the base, and all you pretty girls come tumbling down." She refused to relent on the charges. "Tell me, Catharine, does one person matter?"

Since I had no answer, I once again became the wretched April Morris

CHAPTER 5

Senior year actually improved somewhat. At least the teasing stopped. Kerry and I never dated, but at school, he was friendly to me. I was afraid to make friends, didn't want them to know about my home life. I did not need to worry, however, since no one pushed to become my friend. I was relieved but lonely. Aunt Mimi taught me how to drive. Having my license was handy for Mom. I ran all the errands, such as grocery shopping.

I graduated number two out of a class of ninety-eight. With a 4.25 GPA and an ACT score of 34, St. Norbert College offered me a full scholarship. I grabbed it and headed away from my home into college life to double majors of Philosophy and Political Science, with Theatre Studies and English minors.

"What the Hell kind of job will you get with those degrees?" my mother demanded.

"I want to be a lawyer," I answered back. "I'll need to go to law school."

"How do you expect to pay for that?"

I didn't know and didn't care. I just saw myself as Rachel Dawes working with my Batman.

Everything I hated about high school, I loved in college. Friends, teachers, music, and drama. A new world existed from my dreary life at 729 Monroe Street.

"You're in what play?" Mom screeched.

"It's called *Fat Pig*. I'm the lead female role, Helen," I was so proud.

"Fitting, I guess."

That was Mom's typical response to anything I did. After that phone call, I disowned my mother. I survived without her maternal love while growing up. I did not need her ruining my life any further.

Aunt Mimi did not approve.

"She's yur family, girl. I knows she not the bestest of mothers, but yur gotta respect her."

There was too much pain. I couldn't go back. Why couldn't I have been born in Aunt Mimi's family?

On campus, I hung out with Bethany, Mary, Steve, and Dan. If we were not in class or working, we were all together in one of our dorms playing cards or board games. Morons wasted their time on these diversions my mother would say, so at home closets were empty of game boxes. College was different and wonderful. The games were a new experience for me. I didn't even care if I lost. Sometimes we would stay up until two or three in the morning. It made it tough going to classes, but when a game finished I begged everyone to play again.

Recreation was for my parents only. After Jonny's death, I wasn't permitted to watch television. I had almost missed my favorite television show, Gruber's Garden, as much as I missed Jonny. He had loved it too. As I grew up, the students would talk about their favorite shows, but they were meaningless to me.

Holidays and birthdays had also been forbidden. That first year of college, I decided not to return home for Thanksgiving break. I would stay on campus. The cafeteria was hosting a Thanksgiving dinner for those college students that were stuck on campus. Mother wouldn't know the difference. I was happy with these plans until the Wednesday before the holiday Mary knocked at my door.

"Hey, you can't stay here all weekend! Come on. The car's running."

"What?" I asked, dazed. Did she want to invite me home?

"I should have asked you earlier, but I was so busy getting that paper done for World History. Mom insists you come home with me."

I jumped off my bed and scurried around looking for clean clothes to pack.

"Take dirty stuff. We can wash it at the house. Leave your pillow. We have plenty of that stuff."

In that fall, trees were reluctant to release their crumpled leaves, and they rattled when we stepped outside the courtyard. Mary's rust speckled Dodge Colt waited along the curb, rumbling with its tired muffler. Mary tossed my bag into the back seat, and as I sat in the front seat, heat enveloped me like a sauna. I pulled off my jacket. Two steaming cups, with Maggie's Coffee Shop labels, rested in the cup holders.

"Thought you'd be ready for a pick-me-up. The drive is sort of long." She shifted into drive, and the car heaved forward. "Good thing we weren't holding our cups or we would have had coffee all over the place."

Our chatter and laughter filled the hot car as Mary drove from the east toward the west. As we neared La Crosse, hills erupted from the flat land. The bluffs were the closest to mountains I had ever seen. I vowed I would climb them as soon as possible.

"Can we drive up one of them?"

"Do you mind if we just head home? Our farm is on a hill. It looks over the Mississippi." Mary said. "Look, there's an eagle!"

Perched regally on a piece of driftwood sat the bird. It turned toward us as if he knew we were talking about him.

My jaw ached, and my voice was hoarse when Mary finally pulled up the long driveway to the farm. I spotted a bearded silo alone amongst the trees.

"That's my hide-a-way," Mary said. "Let's check it out."

As we were leaving the car, someone came out of the back door onto the porch.

"Hey, where are you going?" A handsome young man shouted. "You have to peel potatoes!"

"I'm showing April around! You go peel them!" She pulled on my arm. "That's my oldest brother, Ted. He and John Paul are the only boys in this family. The rest of us are girls! And we always get stuck with the housework!"

We ran to the lonely stone cylinder. Birds crowned the edge. They were chirping as if they were in a choir. As we approached, they remained stationed in their formation. An opening had been carved out of the structure.

"This silo has been here since my great-grandfather built this place. My daddy cut out a door for us."

Daddy, she said daddy. After Jonny died, I could no longer use the endearments Mommy or Daddy.

"Mommy," I remember saying one day.

"Mom," she corrected me. "You're almost eight. There's no need to be such a baby anymore."

"Are you okay?" Mary tapped my shoulder.

"Just thinking," I said and sighed.

"Are you sure?"

She took me around to the other buildings, and then pushed through some brush. There, rolling down toward the south was the Mississippi. Across were more bluffs. Eagles were dipping into the water.

"May I sit here longer?"

"You'll get cold."

My life had always been just home, school, back to home again or school. I had gone to other houses to babysit, but that was it. My family never took vacations, and Mom banned school field trips. Those days were the worst. I would sit at my desk and watch my classmates load onto the busses. Some of them would look back at me. When they returned, no one had asked me how my day was.

Mary rubbed her upper arms and stamped her feet. "It's getting cold. Let's go inside!"

"A few more minutes, please?" I had reacted in the same way when Dan drove me to Lake Michigan. I had never seen a lake, sand, or seagulls. "This is like the ocean!" My shoes were off and I ran and ran.

"Hey, slow down!" Dan had shouted.

I sighed and stared hard trying to soak up as much as I could. Boats chugged merrily in the Mississippi while cars drove along the bridge connecting Wisconsin to Minnesota.

"I could stay here forever," I sighed.

"And starve to death! Come on, I'm cold."

Mrs. Drexel was rolling out piecrusts, while the stand mixer swirled some concoction around inside the metal bowl. Ted peeled potatoes and tossed them into a twenty-quart stockpot.

"Ha ha," Mary tormented her brother. "You got stuck with the potatoes this year!"

"Yeah! Thirty pounds of starch!" He stuck out his tongue. "I'm sure Mom will find something equally unpleasant for you to do. BTW, the garbage needs emptying."

Mary shrugged her shoulders and pulled an apple out of a fruit basket cast aside on a counter. "Help yourself." She chomped down. I quickly shook my head no.

"Put your stuff away and come back to set the table," Mrs. Drexel said.

Inside the bedroom were two bunkbeds with a large window set between them. Flecks of paint curled up and down the wood. My eyes once again were drawn to the verdant images beyond the windowpanes. I burned it into my subconscious.

The dresser creaked opened, and Mary spoke, "You can have the top bunk." I just kept staring. Finally, Mary tugged at my arm. "Mom's not going to be happy if we don't get downstairs." She laughed. "You act as if you're in a palace or something. This is just the old Drexel homestead."

I continued staring, transfixed. "It is a palace to me."

Ted continued peeling in the corner.

"Poor Ted, still peeling," Mary mocked her brother.

"Someone could take over," he muttered.

Mrs. Drexel brushed her hands down her apron when we returned to the hot kitchen. She squeezed Mary into her arms, "Welcome home, darling. We missed you." She then turned to me. "We like to hug around here. May I hug you, too?" I nodded, and we embraced. She was soft, not hard like my mother. The scent of cooking and baking surrounded her. Classical music competed with the motorized whir of the mixer. She turned the radio dial down.

"I'm April Morris," I stuttered.

"Hi, April. Welcome to the Drexel castle."

"Mom, she just told me it was a palace."

"Palace is not regal enough." Mrs. Drexel winked at me. "Call me Mom. Everyone does. Dad and John Paul went to get pizza for supper."

"Where is everyone else?"

"The important one is already here," Ted smiled. "The other ones don't count."

"Keep peeling," Mrs. Drexel directed her gaze at her son. "It's taken you almost an hour. Mary would have been done by now."

"She can finish for me." He jumped out of the chair.

"Practice, practice, oh exalted one." Mary bowed.

Off went the mixer. Mrs. Drexel lifted up the top and scraped off the paddle. "Patrick had to work late, so Kathy's family won't be coming until nine or ten. I hope the babies will be able to sleep when they get here. Rosie is taking a nap..."

"That's why it's so quiet!" Mary looked at me. "Rosie makes the most noise. Just wait until she plays her Elvis music."

"Felicity and Ana are at the grocery store picking up a few more items I had forgotten. Felicity called to say the stores are packed. They might be stuck there forever!"

Just then, feet stomped on the outdoor mat, and the door creaked open.

"We're home," a young woman's voice shouted. "Come and help us get the groceries!"

Ted grinned. "Ah hah! The exulted one is too busy with potatoes to help!"

"Get outside, Ted," Mrs. Drexel said. "Your sisters have peeled a lot more potatoes than you have!"

"My fingers are turning into prunes."

"Boo hoo," Mary said. I followed her outside, and we began unloading bags and bags of food. Where will they put it all? We were still unloading when Mr. Drexel and John Paul showed up with five enormous pizza boxes.

"Do you think we have enough?" Mr. Drexel said as he entered.

"Put them in the dining room. I have leftovers if they're still hungry," Mrs. Drexel was standing on a step stool.

I laughed at all the happy chaos, another new experience for me. With all the helpers, however, we finished quickly. Generally, I shopped, put away the groceries, and cooked meals for my mother. I was never permitted to shop over the dinner hour. Once I had dallied at the market and didn't return until close to five. Mom was standing at the door, waiting.

"What took you so long?" she asked.

"There were a lot of people there," I lied. Grocery shopping was my escape. Most find it a mundane chore, but I looked forward to it like someone looking forward to going to the theater on a Friday night. That night after unloading the groceries and making dinner, Mom sent me to bed without supper, though I was 17-years-old!

"Who is making all the racket?" A plump woman, probably in her thirties, appeared in the doorway. She wore her hair in tight, red curls. A limp, blue teddy bear hung from her right hand. She spied me, so decided I should be someone she should meet. "Who are you?"

"April, April Morris," I stuttered.

"April is a month," she answered.

"Rosie!" Mary exclaimed.

"April is a good month," Rosie rectified. "Can we hug?"

She squeezed me for a long time. I couldn't breathe.

"Rosie, let her go!" Mrs. Drexel said. "You know what your teacher taught you."

"Meet my husband," Rosie thrust the bear into my face. "Herbert is his name. Herbert Drexel."

"He has the same last name as you." Ted appeared carrying two bags of groceries. "You're supposed to take on his name."

"Nope, he takes on Drexel," Rosie was adamant. "Can we eat now?"

"Not until you help put away groceries," Mrs. Drexel said.

Rosie was smart. "The pizza will be cold."

"Not if you work fast," her mother handed her a pack of toilet paper. "Put this away."

Rosie sighed and left with the toilet paper.

Mary spoke. "Rosie's the oldest but acts the youngest. Mom, how's her new job going?"

"Great," Mr. Drexel answered. "They love her at work. She's actually not as lazy there as she is here."

"I heard that," Rosie shouted from another room.

I gorged myself on pizza, like everyone else. How anyone could eat with all the laughter and chatter I marveled at, but we did. After cleaning up, we helped Mrs. Drexel with some of the final touches for tomorrow's dinner. She let me make a blueberry pie.

"You actually make your own crust? I do have packaged ones," Mrs. Drexel said. "I just don't think it's worth the effort."

"If you taste her pie, you'll think the effort was way worth it!" Mary said.

"Aunt Mimi loves my blueberry pie," I said.

"A relative?" Mrs. Drexel asked.

"No, Aunt Mimi was the nicest person April knew before go to college," Mary answered. "She's so funny. She was April's mother for Family Weekend."

"I should call her tomorrow," I said.

"What about your mother?" Mr. Drexel said.

Mrs. Drexel glared at him. He shrugged his shoulders.

"Dad never gets all the details," Mary laughed.

Rosie grew bored of our conversation. "When is Kathy and the babies coming?" she asked.

"Soon, honey. She called an hour ago and they should be here around ten," Mrs. Drexel said.

"The babies will be asleep," Rosie complained. "Let's dance." She pulled my hands.

She pressed her music player, and Elvis crooned to Hound Dog.

"Dance," she commanded.

It was Rosie and me. The other siblings stayed in the kitchen to clean up. They had probably danced with Rosie hundreds of times, and were happy to share that chore with a guest.

"You're nothing but a hound dog," Elvis bellowed.

Elvis wasn't my favorite, but I could see no way to extricate myself from this, so I wiggled and jumped, and did all sorts of strange moves. Rosie laughed. I probably danced to Hound Dog at least twenty-five times. The rest of Rosie's siblings finally appeared, and I fell into a chair, panting.

"Keep dancing," Rosie demanded.

"Rosie, give her a break," Mary said. "The boys can dance with you."

"Nah! They're terrible dancers."

Mrs. Drexel walked to the television and flicked it on. "No more dancing. I want to watch the Waltons' Thanksgiving."

"Mom, we watch that every year!" Ted complained.

"But it's a tradition. Besides everything on T.V. is Christmas stuff." She turned my direction. "You're our guest. Is there something you'd like to watch?"

All eyes turned toward me. I didn't know what to answer since I hadn't watched much television. I had never heard of the Waltons. Watching them would be a new experience. "The Waltons sound nice to me," I answered timidly. "I have never seen it before."

Despite their obvious derision of the folksy show, all the kids remained in the living room and found their favorite chair. Rosie insisted I sit next to her on a couch covered with her special blanket. Husband sat between us. The boys commented frequently, but I was mesmerized by the show set in the 1940s. The cuckoo clock struck ten. On cue, car lights flashed into the bay window.

"They're here," Rosie heaved herself off the chair and headed outside. I wasn't sure if I should follow the rest of the family or remain in the living room.

"Come on," Mary said. "Meet my older sister and her family!"

What a commotion it all became. I held back, watching the eldest sister, her husband, and children scatter into the farmhouse. Mary introduced me, and Kathy shook my hand haphazardly. Her husband carried in a sleeping infant tucked into a car seat. Mrs. Drexel pulled out gallons of milk, cookies, and chips. We squeezed ourselves around the dining room table to hear the stories of their trip.

"This buck stepped into the road, and luckily I braked." Patrick took a gulp of his milk. "He then waited for me to drive on before running across."

Kathy shuddered. "Anthony was crying so much I had taken off my seatbelt to turn around and hold his pacifier in his mouth. Just think what might have happened if Patrick hit that buck."

We chatted. The family even talked to me and asked questions about my life. They seemed genuinely interested. At eleven, Mrs. Drexel stood up. "I want to get to mass tomorrow. It wouldn't hurt any of you to join me."

Everyone settled into his or her bedrooms by 11:30. All seemed quiet, so I headed to the bathroom to purge myself.

A knock on the door, and Mrs. Drexel's voice seeped through the wood. "Honey, are you okay in there?"

"Yes, yes. I probably ate too much pizza."

"We all did, dear. Can I get you something?"

"No, I'm fine."

I quickly wiped up my face and returned to bed.

Mary had awakened. "Hey, are you okay?"

"Just too much pizza, I guess. I feel great now," I said. All those terrible calories evacuated from my body.

"You sure have been losing weight fast," Mary whispered. Why did she mention that now? I wondered. "Are you sure you're feeling alright?"

I rolled over onto my right ear, the better one, to avoid Mary's inquisition. "Yeah, yeah."

I still heard the next question. "You're not on one of those eat and vomit diets, are you?" A hole in one - Mary never missed.

"Really? Me dating a pre-med student doing something so stupid?" My body began its nervous quake. I rotated onto my back and tucked my arms under my body.

"Stupid, yeah, but I know you have a lot of pain in your past. It can make you do stupid things."

"I'm really tired. Can we just go to bed?"

I left April's body and watched her quaking body. She covered her face with the pillow. All her life she had hungered for beauty, the wonders of the world, and love. This day with Mary's family was like feeding a starving child an entire chocolate cake and expecting her to digest the rich confection. I reached out to touch her, but the difference in worlds prevented any contact.

"It's too late to comfort her," my angel appeared. She floated from the bedroom down the stairs, and I followed her, the rancid flavor of vomit tormenting my taste buds. How come I couldn't taste the pizza or root beer of earlier?

"You know the answer, Catharine." My angel stopped in the living room, where Rosie and I had danced to Elvis music. I noticed four non-matching chairs cinched in the four opposite corners. The couch, in which Rosie and I had sat, might have had noble beginnings as a beige hide-a-bed. It now slouched, speckled with stains, against the north wall. Three fabric pillows, with bright orange and gold paisley designs, seemed to have fallen into the sinkhole at the center. A red crocheted afghan rested over the sofa's right shoulder trying to muster up a little bravado.

Unwilling to allow anyone to press its ivory keys, an upright stood between two of the four chairs.

"Dad won't let us get rid of that monster," Mary had said earlier. "It's from his grandfather, but it doesn't even work!" She pressed on the keys; they held firm.

"It's pretty," I, or April had said. Someone had carved oak leaves in the front façade.

"What good is pretty if you can't play it?"

My angel touched the keys, and they released their stubbornness. She played a soft, but vaguely familiar sonata. "Aren't you worried about waking up the family?" I looked to see if Rosie appeared.

"*Nocturne Two*, Chopin," she answered with the notes obeying every strike of her long fingers. Nobody appeared, so I stepped into the dining room. Earlier I had been so engaged with the family that I had never taken in the surroundings. Large sections of wallpaper were stripped of its whimsical designs. In one section, hung a one by two foot wrought-iron grate disguising the small section missing paper.

"You might have been a guest here," my angel said. "But, hanging with the likes of April might have tainted your reputation."

"She was a junior when I was a senior."

"Good thing because she would surely have ranked higher than you." She tapped her chin like a child deciding what she wanted for Christmas.

"Am I finished being April?"

"You're just beginning," she answered.

"No, please. April's early life was terrible. The pain I feel when I am she is unbearable. Tonight, eating with Mary's family, I nearly exploded into tears.

To her body I was to return, the sobs tearing at her stomach, her face drenched in tears.

"Wake up!" Mary was shaking my shoulders. "It's nine o'clock already!"

"Finally, the college sleepy-heads," Mr. Drexel said as we entered the kitchen. "I think they saved you some breakfast."

"Where is everybody?" Mary asked.

"Church," he answered, sipping his coffee.

The aroma of turkey baking filled my nostrils. I was hungry, again.

"Why didn't you go with them?" Mary asked.

"I didn't want you two being alone when you woke up. Here have a bagel," he said.

"No thank you," I said. "I want to save my stomach for turkey."

"Are you feeling okay?" he asked. "I heard you last night."

"Just eat a piece of toast and some fruit," Mary said. "You shouldn't be starving yourself. Are you going to call Dan?"

"Nah, he's so busy with his family. I might call Aunt Mimi."

I was in the bedroom talking to Aunt Mimi when I heard commotion downstairs. Aunt Mimi heard it over the phone. "Sounds like a party is about to begin. You better get going."

"Okay. I made blueberry pie."

"I did too! The kids are doing the rest. Most came yesterday and helped clean and get ready. I wish they'd dun that when they were younga." She laughed. "Bye, my dear." She hesitated. "Make sure yuse eating."

"What?"

"And no puking it all out."

She knew my secret! How could she know? She visited me during Family Weekend. We ate together, but I thought my trips to the bathroom meant nothing to her. I could not deny it because Aunt Mimi had told me she hated liars. I needed her love.

"Are yur still there?" Her strong voice pushed through the phone.

"Yes."

"Honey, I love yur, and the world has so many wonderful joys waiting fa yur. I just don't want yur to miss out."

We said our good-byes. Outside the window, gray dappled itself over the landscape. The river, the sky, even the landscape bore an ashen expression. Most of the oaks in the yard joined in the blah feelings except for one that still wore its coppery leaves. It waved as if encouraging me.

Downstairs I found both sets of grandparents with a cadre of aunts and uncles at their stations stirring, carving, or scooping food. Cousins swirled around me.

Mrs. Drexel shouted, "Not in the kitchen. Take all that energy outside!"

I laughed as I watched the crew of children march from the kitchen to the outside. Mary was zipping up her jacket. "Come on! We'll let the big people get dinner ready!"

Mrs. Drexel finally clanged the triangle dinner bell ending our game of tag.

I asked, "How many are here today?"

Ted answered, "Forty-seven, counting the babies."

Food and tables were everywhere. A line formed along the dining room buffet laden with the beginnings of the feast - turkey, potatoes, gravy, cranberry sauce, and stuffing. A card table rested next to it with rolls, vegetable casseroles, roasted sweet potatoes, and salads. Dessert would come out later. Despite the exorbitant calories, I promised myself I would keep this meal inside of me.

"My, you eat like a bird," Kathy looked at my plate. "And you know what happens to some birds," she pointed to the pile of dark and white meat resting on the large platter. Unlike Mary's untidy red hair, Kathy's was blond without any stray hairs out of line. Her makeup lent her a cosmopolitan look though she was a harried mother of two and a part-time nurse. She gently touched my stomach, and then my forehead. "Are you feeling okay? I heard you last night."

Who hadn't heard me? Were there speakers in the bathroom?

I smiled nervously. Healthcare professionals had a way of figuring out things you didn't want discovered.

She scooped some green bean casserole onto my plate. "I made this, and I don't want any leftovers."

Mary scowled. "Stop forcing your food onto my guest. Come on April, we're going to eat in my special hiding place."

"It's not so special if we all know where it is," John Paul spoke up. He rarely said much in this talkative family.

"Too bad, I called it!" Mary rushed out. I followed.

"Is your mom going to mind if we take her dishes outside?"

"She probably has a hundred place settings of this stuff. She bought so much so she could divide it up among us girls." She curled her lip, which crinkled her nose. "This stuff makes me feel like I'm at a diner."

It was a white, shiny glazed plate with fluted edges. It was something you might see in a cafeteria, but it was better than the paper plates we used every day, even on holidays. Actually, there were no holidays in the Morris household. The days, the months, the years had been smeared into one dreary black image created by a despondent artist.

I compared the meal I was looking at to what might have been served at the Morris house on the fourth Thursday of November. Sandwich and maybe some chips. There could be no mention of turkey. I had made that mistake when I was ten.

"Mommy, all the kids at school eat turkey. Why don't we?"

"Do you want to make the damn meal? I hate turkey!" Mom screamed.

I must have winced at the memory because Mary quickly asked, "Are you okay?"

"I don't remember ever celebrating Thanksgiving, or any holiday for that matter." Tears tingled. I did not want to cry, but the tears were shouting, "Let us out, let us out."

"You can cry in here, no one will see you. This is my secret crying space. Here is where I hid after all the times my heart was broken." She stopped, a look of shame on her face. "I'm sorry. This sounds so shallow."

"No. Don't apologize. I am happy to share your, what should we call it, Crying Silo?"

We laughed and continued forking food into our mouths. I was hungry and I wanted seconds and thirds and fourths... I never wanted the meal to end, but it had to.

"Are you ready for dessert? I cannot wait to try your blueberry pie. The boys better have left me some."

"I don't know if I'll have room for pie!"

"No one has room for pie, you just make it!" Mary scraped her plate.

We were about to exit our domain when we heard Rosie. "Mary," Rosie shouted. "Mary, where are you?"

"Shh, don't say anything or she'll barge in on us," Mary whispered.

"I don't mind. I like Rosie."

"Yeah, but she always has to be the center of attention."

"She's hiding in the silo," John Paul shouted. "Let's go get her!"

All the little cousins, Rosie, and John Paul squeezed themselves into the silo. Mary almost dropped her plate. I soon understood the term packed like sardines.

"Hey, watch it." Mary wiped her pants.

"No big deal, you don't like these dishes anyways," John Paul said, his mouth full.

"So? I don't want to be sweeping up the millions of china chunks that will fall between the cracks!" She squeezed out and ran toward the house. We all followed like ducklings.

I scooped up more stuffing and a piece of cranberry-apple pie.

"Don't forget the whipped cream," Mr. Drexel said. "I made it!"

"Woo hoo!" Kathy said. "Dad made one thing!"

When we returned to the silo, Eddie, who was three, watched three barn cats licking up potatoes from his plate. A little Tufted Titmouse, perched on the rim, watched and waited for the leftovers.

"Hey, Eddie, what are you doing? Scat!" She gently shooed the felines away. The mouse had long disappeared. "Don't give your food to the animals. They'll get sick."

"Potatoes yucky," Eddie said and scampered away.

The entire family joined in helping with cleanup, and then went outside to play Hide-and Seek, Kick-the-Can, flag football, and Red Rover. The grandparents watched on lawn chairs. By six o'clock, we ate again, and stayed inside to play charades, cards, and other board games. I pressed my cheeks; they had a workout today. Though I was tempted, trips to the bathroom did not include the purge. I wanted to feel the wonderful sensation of fullness.

The relatives started leaving by eleven, which rolled into eleven-thirty as we all stood outside talking a little more before each family drove away.

Back in the bedroom, I checked the phone and played back Dan's voice mail.

"Hello, My darling. Hope you are having a great time. We are at the hospital. Stevie fell and broke his arm. They needed to do surgery to set it. I had to drive them, since my sister and her husband were wrecks. I hope we don't fall into a heap if our kids get injured! Stevie is in recovery now, and we should be able to still eat turkey! Have you been flirting with Mary's brothers? According to Mary, she's trying to get you to marry one of them so you can be her sister. Love you! Can't wait to hug you."

"He's right, you know. Though I really wouldn't want to put any decent woman onto my brothers, if you married one of them, we could be sisters."

Mary's brothers were charming and handsome, but Dan had stolen my heart. He was the first boy whom I dated and we fell in love immediately. Mary said it was all hormones and I needed to date a lot more boys than Dan. I wondered if Mary was a little jealous, but I never said anything.

When we returned back to school, exams and papers kept me occupied. Ed's Diner on campus hired me. Since coffee was free for employees, it replaced all my other liquid sustenance. It seemed to curb my appetite, or maybe because of the heartburn I didn't feel much like eating.

Dan usually picked me up after my shift. We would walk for what seemed like hours. That is if we didn't have homework.

"I've been watching you," Dan said.

"That's good," I laughed.

"No, I mean, I noticed you haven't been eating when you're around us."

"I eat. Can't you see how fat I am?"

"April, you're starting to waste away. I mean it."

CHAPTER 6

Dan, you worry too much. I'm fine. I'm eating. I'm just eating less and more healthy foods, not the garbage they serve on campus."

How could Dan say that? The image in the mirror was fat and ugly. I hated the image and could not understand how Dan could love it. True, I was down to a size four. I had always been a size eighteen. A size four, but I was still too fat, too ugly for anyone, especially for Dan.

One day, at the end of gym class, Coach Robinson told us we'd have to weigh in.

"Weigh ourselves?" I panicked

"Yes. We can do this privately," he said. "Ladies, go over to Miriam. Guys, come on, we'll go in the locker rooms."

"Ninety-seven pounds." Miriam impassively wrote the weight down.

"Too fat, too fat. I cannot believe I'm ninety-seven pounds. Too fat." The urge to run struck me. I suited up, but as I ran out of the locker room, I crashed into Coach Robinson.

"Hey, whoa! Where you going?" he gently grabbed my arm. "I want to talk with you. Got a minute?"

"I was going to go running."

"That can wait."

Miriam stood next to Coach's desk as I sat on his stiff vinyl couch.

"April, we're very worried about you. Today you weighed in at 97 pounds."

"So?" My heart began to pound. Was he going to scream at me?

"You're five feet, nine inches tall. That's not enough to sustain your body frame."

I began to laugh. "All my life I've been told I'm too fat. Now I'm too skinny. I'm never going to be just right. Never, never, never!"

The dam busted loose. "Never, never, never..." I repeated like an alarm clock that keeps beeping into your dreams. "No, please don't take me home. I want Jonny. Jonny, come back." I blathered on and on. Tears I should have shed years ago tumbled down my face. I made no sense, even to myself. Miriam sat at my side and tried to comfort me.

"Honey, let's go to the hospital. Let's get you checked out. It'll be fine."

"No, I can't go to the hospital. They will say I'm too fat. They will yell at me. No! I can't go! I have a test tomorrow."

"It's Saturday," Miriam tried logic, but it failed.

"I have a test. I know I have a test. I won't get into law school if I don't take this test."

"What test?" Miriam asked.

"My spelling test."

Miriam and Coach looked at each other.

"Why don't we take you, and we'll tell the doctor that you have to be back tomorrow for your spelling test."

"I have to study tonight."

"What words?" Miriam continued talking to me as if I made perfect sense.

"Hat, cat, bat, rat, sat, mat, fat, fat, fat, fat, fat, fat, fat, fat."

"Stop! Come on. Lean on me. I'll walk you to the car. Is there anyone I should call?" Coach held my arm and led me out of the gym, along the corridor, outside to a small car.

"My Daddy. Jonny. Call Daddy and Jonny. Don't call Mommy. No, she will yell at me. I can't go, no."

A nurse ushered me into what appeared to be a storage room. I shivered it was so cold. Miriam sat in the chair next to the bed.

"What do you want us to do?" A blond, attractive doctor entered.

"I think she's dehydrated," Miriam answered. "She hasn't eaten since Tuesday."

"I've been drinking coffee," I said.

"Yeah, sure," offhandedly the doctor replied. "For her insurance to cover this, we have to run some preliminary tests to make sure this isn't medically indicated. A nurse will be in to run an I.V."

Miriam kept looking at her watch and the clock on the wall. Finally, she stepped out of the room and hailed a nurse.

"I'm sorry. I didn't know anyone was in our overflow room. There have been no orders yet."

Miriam sighed. "Could someone get her a blanket? She's freezing."

Dan arrived around noon when an aide was bringing me a tray. Miriam had to get back to the college. Mary, Bethany and Steve showed up a little later. They all stepped out of the room, and I heard them whispering, but couldn't decipher their words.

Mary returned and eased herself onto the bed, "April, they think you're physically fine, but want you to go to Winnebago..."

"Winnebago! That's for crazies. I'm not crazy. I'm fat. That's all!"

"Can we call Aunt Mimi? Isn't her daughter a psychologist?" Mary asked.

"No, no. Don't bother her."

Dan squatted down and looked at my eyes. "She loves you and would want to know."

I vehemently shook my head. "You are making too much out of this. Take me back to school."

Dan gently pushed the hair off my face. "April, when you get a bad cold or sore throat, don't you go to the doctor's?"

I shook my head no. "Mom never took me."

"Well, your brain is not feeling very well. We need to get it better."

"I'm fine. I can't miss any school. No I won't go."

Another doctor appeared. He was older than the female physician was. He rolled his chair up to my face. Doctor Lynn, I read on his nametag. He was probably in his forties; gray blended in with his white-blond hair. His ruddy complexion contrasted with his blue jay colored eyes. "Ms. Morris. You will feel so much better if you spend a little time there."

"No! I won't go."

He looked at my friends, and with his eyes, he motioned them out of the room. More whispers. Dan returned, alone.

"Honey, would you consider going for me, for us?"

"Get me out of the picture? You have another woman? Mary? I knew you loved her better than me. Could it be Bethany? No one can compete with her looks. They're both much thinner than I."

"Stop!" Dan shouted. "You are the only one for me. Always have been. Don't you remember our first meeting?"

Yes, I did, but I still couldn't believe he said I was too skinny to play the role. "We're going to have to stuff you a bit. Better yet, let me take you out to dinner."

"Me skinny? No one has ever called me that!" I laughed. Dan was the assistant director of the play. Pre-med student and theater, what a combination.

After that dinner, we were inseparable, except for classes. By the fifth date, I was resolved to reveal the history of April Morris. He didn't run. I knew he was the man for me. We held no secrets from each other, though compared to my life, his was a Norman Rockwell painting. At this moment, he wanted to send me away to a place where they did frontal lobotomies and put you in a white room with strait jackets. That's what my mother always said.

"No. I can't go there."

Dan sighed. He left the room again, and the rest returned, glum.

"Hey, I'm feeling better!" I said. I actually ate two meals today! I am sure I just flipped out because I hadn't eaten."

"Young lady, you better make sure you eat and keep up your strength. I have written an order for you to see our nutritionist. Please call her and make an appointment. Also have this to give you." He handed me a card. Lakeshore Associates. "Give them a call. They can help you, but only if you let them." The doctor stared at me for a long time as if drilling into my mind the importance of following through with his directions.

"I will. I will," I lied. I already knew what I was going to do when I left the hospital. "Thank you. I'm feeling really so much better."

That experience made me realize what a burden I had become. Dan deserved a better, more stable woman. Mary and Bethany were more like my shrinks than my friends.

I dressed with new resolve. Dan drove; he with his thoughts, me with my plans.

All the other dorm mates had left for the weekend. "Do you want me to stay?" he asked. "I'll sleep on the couch in case you need anything."

"Everyone is overreacting. All I need is a good night's sleep."

Dan kissed my forehead and stared hard at me. Did he guess? "It's only six o'clock. I think we need to get some dinner."

"No, no. I am so tired; I need to get some sleep. Just let me go."

That was my good-bye. I pushed him out the door and quickly bolted it. He pounded on the wood. "April! No. Let me in."

I grabbed my purse. Inside were all the pills I confiscated on my trip to the bathroom. Since I was in a storage room, I had to walk through the ER to use the rest room. I passed a dispenser filled with different meds. No one watched as I scooped up the little packages and hid them in my gown. Back in the broom closet, I stuffed them into my purse.

I dumped the contents onto the sink, and began to rip open all the packages. Quickly, before I changed my mind, I gulped down the pills. I choked, and the pills popped out of my mouth. I scraped them out of the sink, and tried again. One by one, they bulleted down my throat. Should I dress for the occasion? Too late, my head hit the toilet as my body slumped to the floor.

Death unleashed April Morris' grip on Catharine Zimmer, yet I was gripped in a paroxysm of sorrow. I groaned as my body cramped up like a Charlie horse.

"She was twenty-one, not twenty-three," my angel reappeared. "The newspaper had it wrong."

In answer, a scene appeared back in high school. April's locker stood next to mine.

"Catharine, do you want to come over tonight? Listen to some music?"

"I'm busy. Sorry, April." That night I had read a book alone in my room. No thoughts of rejecting April had even entered my consciousness.

Another scene - chemistry class: April and I were lab partners. "Catharine, I loved your article in the newspaper. You're a great writer. I have a bunch of poetry. Someday I'd like to have you read it so you can give me some feedback."

"I'm really not into poetry," I lied. My disdain had already opened up the pill bottles.

"Do you need to see more?" my angel asked.

I choked back the tears of guilt. Perhaps I would not have stopped April on her destructive path, but my treatment of her surely hastened it. My hands covered my face.

Oh, Catharine, what a dreadful woman you were.

CHAPTER 7

My angel brandished her arm. "There is more."

"I can take it no longer." I turned away, shame piercing my soul.

"But you must." She pointed my head toward the image of emergency personnel, followed by Dan, breaking down the door. They rushed through the rooms and then halted by the bathroom. They pushed, but something or someone jammed the entrance. For several minutes, they worked to unhinge the door. A male EMT fell to the ground and began resuscitation efforts, a woman began an I.V. Dan watched sorrowfully.

Then the funeral, the head shaking, the confusion on faces. Then her mother standing passively next to the pine box awaiting burial. Then friends mourning. Then the solemn good-bye of Dan, alone with the casket. Then Catharine Zimmer.

"I wasn't there," I corrected.

"You're right. You weren't there at all. Your reputation was more important than this poor girl's life."

"I was only in high school," I retorted.

"You never changed, Catharine. First it was April, then it was Cheri, then Bruce, then..."

"Stop!"

"Why? Too painful? Do you even understand the misery these people experienced? Isolation, rejection, despair? And their loved ones? Have you ever felt the agony of losing someone to suicide?" Tears welled in my angel's eyes. She whispered, "It is unbearable."

I stared back at the image of Dan weeping over the casket; this time his suffering became my suffering. The hammer struck my heart releasing soul-wrenching grief that could find no solace.

A cyclone hit! Terror replaced the sorrow. I was vacuumed up like some obscure speck and violently tossed around in a tornado, which then dumped my body onto soggy earth. Dewy, inky fog enveloped me. Figures, ambulating like zombies, closed in around me, and we squeezed forward as if in a subway tunnel.

We marched for miles on a path flanked by a wrought-iron fence. I wrestled myself free from the group, but the corpses' automaton movements shoved me up against the metal barrier. My hand melded onto the gate, reminding me of a boy in school who froze his tongue on the flagpole. I pulled, but it burned. It wanted me to see something. My eyes squinted as I stared at the finials, which were not the usual pineapple shape, but were instead stone hearts pieced by swords.

Beyond the bars green hills poked into misty, gray clouds. In this melancholy land, the rain gushed without ceasing. People, frowning, stared out, the rain pouring into their eyes, but they did not blink. They pushed their arms through the slats in an attempt to grab one of the robotic figures.

I heard what sounded like a bird trilling some low lamentation. Yet there were no birds, no living things in this land of wretchedness. Eventually, I decoded a chant: "*Why? Why? Why?*" A question with no answer. They were all there, April's friends and family, joining in the chorus of *whys.*

Before too long, the frozen gate released me, not to freedom, but to the macabre care of the zombies. I, too, became blighted, moving like Frankenstein's monster. My arms raised up on their own accord; my legs stiff, fell hard on the trampled surface below me. No time existed as desolation conjoined itself with my body. Despair chased away all my private thoughts and memories.

I am pathetic. I am filthy. I am disgusting. I am rotten. I am useless. I am unlovable. I am a reject. I should have never been born. I am stupid. I am wretched. I am pathetic. I am filthy. I am disgusting. I am rotten.

Self-loathing crawled its slithery hate inside and outside of me. It lusted for the complete annihilation of my mind, body, and soul.

An opening drew us into its folds, leading us to a dark, open sea. As if obeying a command, I drifted to a skiff, stepped inside, and it floated out into the water. Millions of others joined me, but we were alone. If we stretched, we could touch each other, yet an invisible barrier gripped us in alienation.

The mental pummeling continued hour after hour, leading me to believe it would never end. I beheld the landscape around me. We were animals caged in some cinereous aviary, bobbing on some murky water, with a slate dome above us. No other life apart from the despairing souls seemed to exist.

I moved freely in the small space without tipping over. I tried to throw my leg over the side, but an unseen power held me inside. I sat down, but the movement unleashed more self-loathing.

My parents despise me. My siblings hate me. I can't do anything right. Life would be better if I was dead. Who would care if I died? Everyone hates me. I'm a loser. I'm not good enough. They're all talking about me. They're plotting against me.

The paranoid cacophony reverberated endlessly. One calamitous thought replaced another. I was already dead, but the discord supplanted any logic. I searched on the empty boat for any object to end the misery -- a gun, a knife, poison. Nothing. Only discorded thoughts strung oddly together, their only fruit - misery. My hands reached for my throat. Perhaps I could strangle myself. Even in that, I failed.

Strangely, sleep overtook me or more accurately, consciousness left me. I can't even tell you for how long because time, as I understood it on earth, was only a fleeting memory in this trepidity. A bell would ring, awaking me back to my sordid rituals of self-flagellation.

One day a mirror appeared, interrupting my mental anguish. I stared at the obliterated image of Catharine Zimmer. Bedraggled red hair projected from my scalp, as if I was in a museum's static electricity science exhibit. It looked as if a painter smudged dirt over my face. Shards of fabric hung on my emaciated form. Sad, dark, gibbous moons hung below shadowed bloodshot eyes. What frightened me the most was the desperate glower that said, "*Kill me.*"

A blast, as from a foghorn, shattered the crippling anguish. A golden frigate cut through the sea. It was almost blinding to look at its ethereal majesty. Rays of sunlight projected out from its every corner. Three pure white sails fluttered on gilded masts. Figures floated from the ship and alighted onto the various skiffs. The white figures, probably angels, touched the captives, transforming them into heavenly beings. They ascended together onto the large ship.

I watched with longing, though misery pounded me down.

"Take me," I shouted, realizing I was not shouting alone. "Take me, take me," the forlorn millions continued, their arms outstretched.

I glanced at the boat next to mine. There, April Morris ascended to the ship. Radiant, beautiful, and at peace. She was complete. My body crumpled into a heap. In life, I had played a trick in my mind, convinced myself that April Morris was irrelevant. The rejection of April reproached me with a contempt that held no impunity. I neglected to share her sorrows in life, thus in death, April's torment consumed me.

My angel appeared and gently brought me to my feet. She turned me toward the mirror. Catharine Zimmer had returned beautiful, yet not luminous like April.

"Will I go with them?" I pointed, the desperation slowly evaporating.

"No, you are not ready for that. Your journey isn't complete."

"I don't know how much more I can endure."

"You have experienced the worst - the most deadly of all emotions."

"I thought hate was the most deadly."

"It is despair that prompts men and women to hatred. Despair that the rancor will never cease. Despair that enemies can never be friends. Despair that forgiveness can never heal."

I pondered her words and remembered all the failed relationships in my life. My angel was right. Despair clamped around our hearts convincing us that forgiveness and healing were impossible.

"Are you ready?"

"No, I need to do something first." I crawled out of the small boat and walked on the water. In the next craft stood a young man. I fell to my knees. "Forgive me," I begged. From boat to boat I apologized to the grim figures. Each time I hugged one of these souls, it released them from their torment. They, too, ascended, but not in a ship, but into a white cloud.

"Now I'm ready." I turned to my angel. "Is there more sorrow to come?"

CHAPTER 8

In answer, I found myself in a sea of dirt. Dry clay encrusted itself all over my body and coated my teeth. I groveled on the ground. I clawed at my scalp and was rewarded with grime stuck between nails and fingertips. *Cleanliness was next to godliness* I had often quoted to myself. Until I grew sick, I showered daily, sometimes twice, to rid myself of any sensation of sweat or urine. Would this condition be worse than being in Laureen's body?

Something was pulling at me. A naked child suckled at my shriveled breast. He was like those starving children you see on the posters and television ads. The child reminded me of an arthropod with his jointed elbows and knees. His chest was a washboard of ribs. It was an image I had turned away from when those posters or ads appeared. I had donated and felt comforted for a while until the images appeared again.

What was that pain pulsating in my gut? This child was taking from me what I myself did not have. I looked down to count my own ribs. He was not my child, yet he was my child. Finally he released his grip on me. I scratched the ground, searching for a blanket, something to swaddle the boy and a top for me. There was nothing. I crossed my arms over my bare breasts. Suddenly, other people seemed to appear, or perhaps I began to notice their presence. No one was dressed above the waist. All around me, bodies heaped themselves against any solid frame that would hold them.

"There was much left undone by your life, Catharine," the angel appeared.

"What is my purpose here now?"

"To languish in the misery of your fellow man."

"Can nothing be done?"

"That was your job when you were alive."

"But Gregory. He went from the precipice of suicide to choosing life. Surely I can do something here. It can't be too late."

"Your village is dying, Catharine. There is no food. There is no water. The pangs of famine will encroach upon you, and anguish will fuel your demise with more pain than you had experienced with your own death."

"This child. He will die too?"

"One by one the disregard of others will separate you all from life."

"I don't understand."

"Neglect. Too busy. Too afraid. Too political. All those excuses mankind uses to rationalize starvation."

"Surely we couldn't have been expected to feed the entire world? Often war and droughts are the cause of so much suffering, or worse war and evil tyrants. Furthermore," do I dare ask the question? "Furthermore, why did God give so much to some and nothing to others?"

"Once upon a time the parents gave their two boys each a truck and some sand. They didn't have to share. One day the oldest brother took away the younger brother's truck and sand. Was it the parents' fault?"

Into the air she left. Our conversation ended. I tried to pull myself forward so I could stand, but an invisible force gripped my body in sheer weakness. I slumped back. The boy child, eyes huge in his cavernous face, gazed at me as if waiting for another feeding.

"I can't let him die. He must live," I struggled to tell myself.

With an energy I knew came from somewhere else besides my debilitated body, I heaved myself up, using the tree for leverage. The villagers glanced my way, which was all they could muster.

I staggered to a small grove of trees. Surely the soil would be softer here. I fell on my knees and cleaved a hole that might have been a centimeter deep. This was slower than I had recalled seeing in the movies. A large stick jutted out near the depression. I clasped the frail wood and began hollowing the ground again.

The hum of the villagers' voices faded as I concentrated on my task. Suddenly I hit upon something hard, and before I knew it, a glove of beetles sheathed my arm. I screamed. Some villagers surrounded me.

One of the women quickly scraped the insects into a basket and dropped to her knees to capture the ones fleeing from their nest. This woman wore a bright cloth on her head. Starvation had not attacked her so vehemently. Her skirt matched the scarf, giving her a cheerful appearance.

"You find us food," she smiled. "We will eat today."

I brushed my arm repeatedly, trying to expunge the tingling feeling of tiny, crawling claws. What other horrors awaited me? I hesitated, afraid to return to my digging. Another villager carried the child to me. He was hungry, yet I had nothing to give him. I sat down and tried to nurse.

As the boy nursed, I looked up and noticed an elderly man, his mouth carved into a smile. Each line on his face was curved in an S pattern. His black hair was closely shaved to his scalp. Only one tooth remained rooted into his pink gums. I nodded in acknowledgment. He nodded back.

"Stay strong. You will find water."

How did he know that? I had told no one. Why didn't he tell anyone else to go dig for water? Perhaps they wouldn't have listened to him.

Dusk approached quickly. Maybe I had dug down a foot. Within me a battle between my body and my will raged. Exhaustion, hunger, and some unknown fear begged me to quit. Determination demanded I continue what seemed like a futile pursuit. One of the younger men crawled over to me and grabbed my digging tool.

"What are you doing?" It was not English I spoke, but some foreign dialect.

"Fire. I need stick for fire, or we will be attacked by lions. Come closer or you will be eaten."

"Let her dig," the old man yelled back.

"Ah, you're crazy like she's crazy," the younger one replied. He tossed the stick into the fire.

I returned to the group, and again the child grabbed onto my breast. We all sat staring at the glow. Around the fire a woman was cooking something in a clay pot. I leaned over to see the beetles that had crawled up my arm that morning sizzling, their shells crackling like popcorn.

Beetles? My trip to Asia revealed that people will eat almost anything, scorpions, cockroaches, mice. I never took advantage of those delicacies. Starvation, however, knew no boundaries. She scooped some onto a large leaf, and I crunched them, almost gagging, but I managed to swallow them.

A joke in my family was we'd say everything tasted like chicken. Once, I ate frog legs. I told my sister they tasted like chicken. My nephew, when asked what his thumb tasted like replied, without taking his thumb out of his mouth, "Chicken." In my current condition, these beetles didn't have the luxury of tasting like chicken, but had the suggestion of garbage left outside on a hot day.

The meager repast lifted our spirits. I began to learn some of their names. Akachi had been the man who stole my stick. He assumed a leadership position amongst the people, but I sensed his position was tenuous. Ebele was the women wearing the bright cloths. Anuli was frying up the beetles. The elderly man's name was Ndidi. My name was Nkechinyere.

"I watch fire. Go to bed," Akachi commanded. Everyone listened, found a rock, and fell asleep. My child, Chibueze, snuggled up to me.

"Hot, hot, hot," my unconscious mind said in my dreams. "Zzzz," buzzed around me, but I was no longer sleeping. My eyes flew opened and I tried to swat a swarm of bees, but only succeeded in angering them. My hand blazed in reaction. Ebele staggered to one of the trees and pulled off one of its leaves. When she returned, she ripped it opened to expose the sap. Within minutes the swelling had stopped.

"Thank you," I said.

She smiled, but I didn't feel as if she felt any warmth for me. When she stepped back to her place, Anuli approached and whispered in my ear. "She thinks you took Akachi from her."

We were all starving to death, but we were still worried about who was with who? I said nothing to her and felt my scalp. There would be no shower with shampoo and soap. *Would this child get off my breast?* I was hoping to dig before it grew hotter; I stood up carefully balancing the boy in my arm. Akachi grabbed my shoulder as I was leaving the group.

"Why do you dig?" he asked.

"Water. Water deep, deep down," I answered him.

He threw his head back and laughed.

"Nkechinyere says water below. Foolish woman! She knows nothing."

"She knows more than you," Ndidi said. "This woman comes from God."

Uncertainty painted itself on the villagers' faces. Should they follow their leader or listen to wisdom? An uncomfortable laugh broke out.

"You think you're our leader, but no one gave you that title," Amadi, another young man, stepped forward.

"My father led all of you," Akachi lifted his chin.

Azubuike, a tall middle-aged man, also stepped forward. "The lions ate him. It was a sign that he was not to lead any longer."

"You hated my father," Akachi replied. "You were glad he died."

"He was my friend," Azubuike answered. "How could you say that?"

"This fighting will get us no water," I interjected. They turned, shocked that I spoke.

"She is right," Ndidi's carved smile remained even as he spoke. "Besides, what harm can it be?"

"She will unleash only evil," Akachi said. "No good will come from it."

Anuli looked up. "She found us food. How can you say that is bad?"

I stormed away from them and searched for the hole I had begun. In daylight I realized my digging yesterday had produced only a cranny, nothing more. My heart sank, yet I had to find water. In I plunged my hands, still stinging from the bites. One scoop, two scoops, three scoops. Twenty-seven more scoops I counted, then stopped. This digging demanded all my brain power.

Akachi tried to follow, but the other men stopped him. They all watched as I worked. I wanted to tell them to come over and help, but thought they'd end up arguing. So, I worked alone.

Switching my position, I brushed up against a bush. Instantly some creature slithered from its depths. I stared face to face with a coffin-head mamba poised to strike. I had seen one in a zoo once before, but it had been coiled around itself in a secured glass box.

This snake glared, his head swaying, its forked tongue pulsating in and out of its mouth. He was no more than a foot away, I could reach over and run my fingers along his mosaic skin. Adrenaline tainted my taste buds with a metallic flavor.

Pounding from my heart deafened me to any other sounds. Terror's grip clamped down on my body, molding me into a statue.

The mamba glowered for a few more minutes and then lost interest and slithered away. Akachi walked, his face frozen into a zombie stare, toward me and my hole.

"I was right, only evil will come from this!"

Azubuike interjected, "Ndidi said you were a god. You must be powerful to chase away mamba. I dig too."

"God is powerful," I said.

"Snake god powerful," he answered.

"Shut up! She is evil, I tell you!" Akachi paced back and forth. "Stop!"

The other men ignored Akachi and began to dig. One carried an implement similar to a trowel. He made the quickest progress. *Why hadn't he brought that yesterday?*

Ebele was carrying Chibueze, "Your baby needs you."

Once he finished nursing from the nothing I had, I returned to the tree with the sap in the leaves. I opened them up and tried to scrape away the dirt on his body. It was primitive, but worked. The women watched me curiously. Some went to the tree and repeated my steps, washing their babies and children.

I returned to the hole, which was growing. Akachi sat alone in a corner, crooning some unintelligible words. Evening soon approached. We would have another supper of beetles. Ebele served me, breaking from their tradition of feeding the men first.

"I eat first," Akachi stormed forward. "She gets nothing!"

The villagers clicked their tongues against their cheeks in a sound of disapproval.

"She nursing mother, she eat first," Azubuike stared Akachi down. "Bad for men to eat first."

First in line for beetle buffet wasn't my choice. I tried to smile my appreciation while chomping on the hard shells. The nice thing about beetles is they don't get stale and soggy. We finished eating, with Akachi brooding again. He decided he wouldn't eat because the beetles were tainted.

Around the fire, I began humming "*Row, Row, Row Your Boat.*" I sang the words I remembered, but they came out in a different language. The others joined me, cautiously at first, then jovially. All but Akachi laughed.

That night was cooler than the night before. I shivered next to Chibueze as sleep evaded me. Each tossing and turning of my body meant a different rock or stick poking into my neck, shoulders, back, head, or legs. There was no comfort in this harsh, makeshift sleeping arrangement. Chibueze slept peacefully. Finally, I resolved to lay on my back. A canopy of stars twinkled in the sleepy black sky of the African savanna. I reached as if to touch them. Sleep finally arrived.

A dragging sound awakened me. My eyes opened to discover Akachi, his spear pointed at my heart.

"What are you doing?"

"You enchantress. You plot against me and convince my villagers to do the same."

"I am only here to help, not hurt you," I tried to sit up, but he plunged the spear closer.

"Snake charmer! I saw you talk to that snake."

He pressed the point into my flesh.

"Ow!" The pain radiated from the point of entry out to my entire chest. "Stop this minute!" He pressed harder, piercing the skin and exposing blood.

"Your husband killed my father."

"No! My husband is dead too. The lions ate him." How I knew this information, I don't know, but it came when I needed it.

I yanked at the blade, and Akachi tumbled to the ground. I scrambled to my feet and raised the spear over him. I wanted to stab him but restrained myself. He was stronger than I was, but I held the weapon with authority. We stared at each other, the animals of the night howling and chirping in the background. The racket increased proportionally to the tension. Akachi stood up.

"You reign over the animals too," he said and disappeared into the darkness.

I tried wiping the blood off my chest. It wasn't a deep cut, but it hurt. A leaf would have to do, I thought. I noticed dew on its leaves and licked. Water, sweet water. I crouched under the leaves and gently shook dew from the leaves into my mouth. I didn't want to shake too hard lest I waste any precious drops. I had to wake the others before the sun burned off the dew. Before I knew it, the villagers were pushing and shoving to get to the tree.

"There is more," I shouted, pointing to the other trees. They scampered to the other leafy plants, laughing joyfully. I grabbed Chibueze and poured the tiny droplets into his dry, caked mouth.

"What happened?" Anuli pointed at my chest.

"Nothing."

Amadi picked up the spear. He touched the point. "There is blood here. Where is Akachi? Did he do this?"

What point would there have been to incriminate Akachi? I felt he would not return. "He left," was my only answer.

"We must find him," Azubuike said. "He must face justice."

"Let him go," I said. "He will not be coming back."

"Did you kill him?" Ebele, this time. I felt as if I was in court.

"No, I did not. But he left for good."

The answers satisfied them. Several of us continued excavating the well. I began to have doubts about finding water, but there was nothing else to do. Some of the men decided to go hunting.

Azubuike handed me a spear. "You watch over other women and children."

"I will be digging," I said, unwilling to protect everyone from wild beasts.

"You can watch too."

The morning and early afternoon were quiet. We were resting when the earth began to shake. A bloat of hippopotamuses charged toward our camp.

"Get up!" I shouted. "Take the children to the water hole!" It was wide and deep enough to hold several children. We crouched behind them in the bushes. Swirling dust and rocks, resurrected by the racing of these mammoth creatures, buffeted our faces and necks. We had to turn or our eyes would become targets.

"Ebele! Give me a spear! We will kill one for food!" I screamed. What was I thinking? They'd be gone before I'd be able to lift the weapon into the air. But I seized it, threw it from an energy that hadn't existed in this realm before, and hit one of the smaller beasts. It fell, but was not dead. It waved its legs and groaned, sounding like someone blowing on a kazoo. Anuli handed me a primitive looking scythe. I plunged, and within a few moments, the animal was dead.

A spider in Catharine Zimmer's bathroom would have sent me to the neighbor's for help. Now I was killing wild beasts. I stared at it, but the women appeared out of hiding and began butchering it. It was about this time the men returned emptyhanded.

I chewed endlessly on the rubbery, tasteless hippopotamus meat. The others ate with gusto. If only I could have a glass of Merlot or Cabernet.

Chibuez, not used to eating meat, began gagging. The villagers shouted and pointed. I threw down my steak and pulled out the chunk from his throat. I had fed myself with no thought of this child. I found a sharp implement and hewed out tiny pieces and fed him from my own hands. I thought of my siblings with kids. Chop up the grapes, the hot dogs, or anything that might choke a child. Once I put a large wedge of watermelon on my niece's highchair tray. Fortunately, my brother knew the Heimlich maneuver.

"Good job, Catharine!" Claire had chastised me. "Almost killed your niece."

It was painstaking feeding Chibuez. When I finally returned to my hippo, it was cold and the flat flavor was replaced with rotting flesh. I spit it out, some of it dribbling down my chin. Having no napkin or cloth, I wiped my face with the back of my arm. I shuddered to think of what I had become.

"You think you're better than these people because you used napkins to wipe your face?" There she was again, my angel, to share her noxious attitude with me, her suffering charge.

"It just feels terrible," I replied. "Isn't there anything I can use?"

The angel handed me a leaf. Apparently leaves were the remedy for everything around here. I dabbed my face, then Chibuez. The villagers watched and copied me.

Sleep came quickly that night, and in the morning, more dew awaited us. I tried setting the clay pots under the leaves, but the pottery absorbed the water that fell inside. Despite this, the villagers were beginning to liven up. Some of the women tittered in a corner and exchanged knowing glances.

"Why do you laugh?" I asked.

Azubuike stepped forward. "Akachi left village. I now take over. Your husband is dead, so I will wed you."

"Marry you?"

"Yes. You god; I am now the leader. We marry."

"But you have a wife," I said.

"Five wives," he corrected me. "But you best wife."

This was worse than starvation. I had to get out of here before the nuptials took place. Was this God's joke? Marriage avoided me in life, now I was to be wife number six for Azubuike?

"I can't get married," I said. "I am leaving soon."

"You go back to gods?" he asked.

"No, I am not a god. I am only human." I didn't tell him I was dead already. "There is only one God," I tried again, remembering the stories of missionaries I had learn of as a child. "He is the creator of all things."

"He created you, and we get married!" Azubuike's eyes lit up.

My arms immediately went to cover my breasts. "I go dig now." Back to the trench. It had become so deep; we had to surround the hole with stones to prevent anyone from falling in. This made it more difficult to dig.   Someone would crawl down and scoop dirt into one of the pots attached to a rope. We would pull up the full pot, empty it, and then send it back down. Slow and painstaking. I started wondering if we were just wasting our time. Then I thought of how the children were able to hide when the hippos ran through. They could use it as a shelter if no water bubbled up.

Azubuike followed me.

"We dig this later. Now it's time for our wedding. Besides water grows on trees."

"That is only for a short time. I know there is water down here," I lied. Despite the famine these people were living, Azubuike must have managed to find food. Extra flesh rippled around his arms and legs. "Only a few more feet, and we'll find water."

"Ceremony will be soon." He turned and left.

I peered into the dark depression in the earth. I climbed down the makeshift ladder. When I landed, my feet touched water.

Water! Finally, we found it! I wanted to shout, but there was no way they'd hear me. I stepped onto the ladder to climb out, but it fell into the well. I lifted it up, and twisted my wrist, spinning the ladder like a lasso around my head. I tossed it, but it slapped my face and landed back with a thud next to my feet. I repeated this several times, and each slap stung more than the previous one. In my feeble attempts with the ladder, I failed to recognize the water gaining in depth. Before I knew it, my calves were soaking, and the water was rising quickly.

My worst fear, drowning. One of the reasons I rarely went swimming was my fear of water filling my lungs, suffocating my very breath. Even my bath water had to be very shallow. Once filled, I'd jump into the tub, wash quickly, and crawl out.

"That must have been relaxing," Ceil joked once when we took a girls' weekend away. "How long did that take you, five seconds? I thought you took swimming lessons?"

I felt foolish at the beach wearing floaters. No amount of swimming lessons healed my phobia.

At that very moment my fears crowded me like an angry mob reaching to kill me.

"Help!" I screamed. "Help, help, help!" Nothing, just the sound of rushing water edging closer and closer to my upper body.

I continued screaming, but my voice grew hoarse. I prayed someone would realize I was gone and search for me. Suddenly Chibuez appeared. He grunted then crawled away. Water reached my chest.

"No! Don't go!" My voice was barely a whisper.

Within minutes, the rest of the villagers appeared.

Azubuike fell on his knees and peered down into the darkness. "You are a god," he shouted.

"No! No. I am not! Please don't say that!" I shouted.

A rope appeared, and I wrapped my arms and legs around it as they pulled me up. They then lowered their pots into the water and brought them up, full of cold, fresh water. Azubuike put the pot to my lips. In this realm, however, it did nothing to quench my thirst.

After the villagers had their fill, I spoke up again. "You must keep a wall around this to prevent yourselves and the children from falling in."

That night we ate more hippo, and the villagers danced around the fire. Relief at avoiding the wedding filled me. They all fell asleep, content. Sleep evaded me, but I knew the reason. My heavenly travel agent would send me on my next vacation. I looked at the sleeping villagers who had become my friends. In life, they had not existed; but in death, they materialized, forcing Catharine Zimmer to acknowledge their value as human beings.

"Are you ready?" I wasn't sure if I should smile or run when she finally appeared.

"I helped them," I said. *Catharine Zimmer the hero!*

"Did you?" She smiled. "What did you learn?"

As I walked next to her, I didn't want to reveal that these people had meant nothing to Catharine Zimmer while she was alive. They were just images on a flyer asking for a donation. I said nothing, figuring she could read my mind.

"Are you ready for your next adventure?" She smiled brightly.

"Do I have a choice?"

CHAPTER 9

I found myself alone on a school bus. It was parked next to a cream-colored brick two-storied building, butting up about two yards from the street. A six-foot metal fence encased the entire property. Children and teachers strode into the green metal doors.

Jefferson Education Complex. Welcome back to school. Today's lunch; Black Bean Tacos with Soy Smoothies.

I cringed at the marque. School? It wasn't even a school I had attended as a youth. Why, I had wondered.

"Here you go," my angel, who was the bus driver, said as she swung opened the door. "Ms. Catharine Zimmer, seventh grade teacher."

"Teacher? I've never taught anything in my life."

"You're dead, remember."

"Funny."

"Don't forget this." She handed me a black tote bag, filled with books.

I cautiously descended the deep steps of the bus and found myself merged into human traffic. My body flowed along with the pushing and shoving, back and forth as we all seemed to squeeze ourselves into the metal doors. Inside was more of the same, pushing, shoving, this way, that way. I tried to discover where I fit. Finally, there was an office. I walked in to discover a woman standing on the third rung of a ladder.

"Yes?"

"I'm Catharine Zimmer." After the words escaped my lips, her eyes squinted in consternation. Maybe my name was supposed to be different. I looked inside the book bag, but there were no clues to my identity.

She scratched her head. "Oh, yeah, the replacement. Hand me that bulb, would you? You're in room two-forty-seven. Good luck."

I climbed the terrazzo steps. The room at the top of the stairs was unmarked. Down the hall I counted the rooms, but they were not in any sort of order. Two-hundred-fifteen was followed by two-hundred-seventy-three. It was like being in a library with books scattered on shelves with no sense of alphabetizing. Surprisingly I found room 247 and entered. Inside became the outside grounds of Assumption High School where I had graduated in 1978. There I sat, on a bench watching, as Gary Odell, a senior, pounded on Mike Brandt, a sophomore.

"Where's my paper?" Gary shouted. "I'm not going to graduate without that damn paper! You're not going to live if you don't get me my paper." Punch in the gut. Mike, a greasy-haired nerd, clutched his stomach in pain. Gary kicked him and punched him again. Catharine Zimmer, a senior too, shoved her schoolbooks into her brown, leather backpack. She stood up and walked away.

"You didn't even go tell a teacher what was happening," my angel appeared. "Nothing. It was as if you had a slight itch on your arm, scratched it, and forgot about it."

"Gary was so dangerous. Everyone was afraid of him!" I said.

"Really? After you walked away, you missed the best part of this show."

Natalie Ribone, a classmate, hobbled to the boys. She used canes to help her walk. Natalie stood about four feet, seven inches - at least two feet shorter than Gary. Whack went one of her canes.

"Not my method," the angel said, "but it worked."

Then I was in the school cafeteria, watching as Gary and his buddies threw soda at Danielle Zitler, who sat in the corner, alone. Brown liquid oozed down her dress. She looked out at us students, imploring someone to do something. We stared and did nothing, except for Natalie. She stormed up to the boys, waved one of her canes, and glowered. The boys scooted out of the cafeteria.

"I was in high school!" I said. "My judgment goes as far back as high school?"

"Have you forgotten April Morris already?" my angel asked.

My head hung down in shame.

"Should I show you all the school dances, the football games, gym classes? I counted thirty-seven incidents of your active participation of just watching, not helping, not saying anything, just watching. I can't tell you how it broke my heart."

"Angels don't have hearts."

"Angels feel pain when their charges sin."

"I didn't do the bullying."

"You didn't do anything."

Then I was transported to the sales floor of the department store. Catharine Zimmer, probably in her thirties, stood behind her register watching as Rawley Hawkins mocked Daley Rose. She manned the Stationary Department. She wore pilot rimmed glasses that were tinted brown; her short-cropped hair gave her a mannish appearance; and she suffered from eczema and chronic sniffles.

"Hey good looking. Bet ya got a date tonight, honey." Rawley would start.

"No, no," she'd say.

"Wanna go out?" he'd ask.

"You want to go with me?" She'd push up her glasses and sniff.

"Nope. No way I'd be seen with an ugly chick like you. Gotta go." Rawley headed back to the shoe department.

Daley sniffed again, but I wasn't sure if it was her sinuses or tears. I walked away, not mentioning how much of a jerk I thought he was. I was in my own little world. Rawley was annoying, but I had too many other things on my mind to concern myself with Daley.

"Catharine, I thought you had so much spunk, so much compassion for others, but that was only in your imagination," my angel pushed through my thoughts. "I heard in your mind all the ways you had planned to right all these injustices, but your self-preservation had won out." She shook her head and disappeared.

Would I get the chance to make it all right? I froze as I found myself in a classroom. A boy crashed into me.

"Whoops," he laughed.

"Whoops, is right! Sit down, now!"

"You can't tell me nothing."

"You can't tell me anything," I corrected, but it went over his head. Chaos! Utter chaos. I could have been Godzilla and no one would have noticed.

I slammed my black bag onto the desk. Some of the students jumped, but most just ignored me. I whistled, loud. Students swung around, and eyed me coolly up and down.

"You're a hot mama," a freckled, redheaded boy cooed.

"You like her cuz she has the same color hair as you," a boy, wearing his baseball cap backwards, said.

"Take off the hat," I said.

"Make me," he said.

I grabbed it and threw it into my bag. Chuckles ensued. "Up to the board, and write your name, twenty times."

"Ah! I ain't doing it."

"Give me that," I grabbed his cell phone.

"You can't do that."

"I just did. Now get up there and write your name." The other students watched, wondering who would win this battle. I had no leg to stand on, but mustered as much bravado as possible. I had hoped they wouldn't see me trembling.

"Justin Bieber," he wrote twenty-times. Tittering from the class.

"What's so funny?" I asked.

"You don't know who Justin Bieber is?" A girl asked. She had brown, wavy hair, braces and glasses.

Justin Bieber? I had died so long ago, but even before death, I didn't keep up with the latest trends or superstars.

"Ah, Justin Bieber. Yes, I forgot. Very funny. Now I want you to write, 'I love Justin Bieber' fifty times."

The class roared. I laughed too, proud of myself. The boy wrote, and I began to pull out my books.

"My name is Ms. Zimmer."

"I'd say, 'Hottie,' if you ask me," the redhead continued with his one-track mind.

"There's room next to the board. You can write, 'Hottie is a degrading term for women, and I will not use it again,' seventy-five times."

"My hand is gonna cramp up. How am I gonna throw a football at practice today?"

"You won't be going to practice if you don't finish writing."

Jeremy persisted in his protesting. I found the detention slips. "See you after school," I smiled as I ripped it off the pad and handed it to him.

"I'm going to miss football practice," he whined. "Please," he thrust his face into mine, fluttering his eyes, "let me off this one time."

"No can do. Attendance first." I pulled out the attendance chart. Thirty-three students on the list, but only twenty-one in class on the first day of class. What kind of school was this?

"Let's say the Pledge of Allegiance," I said, my right hand over my heart.

They stared at each other in dumb silence.

"You don't know the Pledge? I'll write it on the board, you copy it down, and memorize it. Whoever memorizes it by tomorrow will win ten bucks!"

"Yeah!" they all shouted.

"How are you going to come up with that kind of money?" Daniel, the boy with the cap, asked.

"Pretty sure most of you won't even bother," I replied.

At lunchtime, the kids scooted out to the cafeteria, then on to the playground. *What middle school kids have recess?* I wondered, but was happy to have the break. I marched to the teachers' lounge and listened into an already established conversation.

"Can you believe that kid?" Mr. Walert, the fifth-grade teacher said. His gray hair was cut in a crew style, and he wore a cranberry shirt. His eyes were tiny balls of black, like bullets pushing out of the wrinkled folds of his face. He stopped speaking when I sat at their table.

Mr. Walert and the other teachers turned their heads toward me, and glared for a full sixty seconds. Then they turned their attention away and continued talking. No one had bothered to introduce himself or herself to me. I only knew their names because of their nametags. I ate as if alone. I hung around trying to get someone's attention, but I faded away much like the brick walls.

In my mind, I returned to a different breakroom, the one I had spent so many years in while working at the department store. This time Daley was sitting, alone, while many of us sat at a different table talking and laughing, oblivious to Daley or anyone else.

Back to Jefferson Education Complex. After recess was history class. The students groaned when I told them to pull out their history books. A few minutes into the lesson, some of them looked ready for a nap.

"Let's jump up and down," I said.

"That's for the little kids," one of the students shouted.

"I know, but you all look very tired. I'm not sure history is a good class after lunch."

Surprisingly they did what I had asked, but it was difficult to get them to return to their seats.

"Alright! Settle down. Take your seats." How did teachers manage? "Who can tell me about the Reign of Terror?" I asked.

Amanda, the young girl with brown, wavy hair, raised her hand.

"It was a terrible time during the French Revolution when people got their heads cut off," she said.

"Hey, can we make a guillotine?" Jeremy asked. "That'd be so cool." The class broke out in chatter.

"Quiet! Class! I might just have to bring one to school and cut off your heads!"

"Neat!" Jeremy said. "There'd be heads rolling all over the place."

I stared hard at him. "Yours would be the first."

Silence. Probably not in a teacher's manual, but it worked. For the rest of the hour we discussed Maximilien de Robespierre. The kids even acted out a skit. From history, we went to math, not my strong suit, but in that realm, I was almost as smart as Einstein. The final class was literature. Another bad decision, since the kids were so restless. I decided to talk about Victor Hugo since we were already talking about the French Revolution.

I was ready to fall asleep at the three o'clock bell. Jeremy scooted out.

"Jeremy, get back in here, now!" He backed himself in, bumping into departing students.

"Here's the list I have for you," I handed him a sheet and then looked down at my lesson plans for the next day.

Jeremy swept the floors, washed the boards, emptied the garbage, and sorted papers. By five, he was ready to take the activity bus home.

Alone in the classroom I wondered where I lived. My angel appeared.

"There's a car out back that's yours. Here are the keys. Here is your address. The GPS will tell you where to go."

"GPS?"

"You have been dead a long time, haven't you?"

I drove up to a two-story, white colonial, with tightly squeezed-together red shutters. They tried to look cheerful, but only succeeded in looking garish, like a woman with misapplied red lipstick. I parked in what was probably once a horse barn.

Into the door lock I inserted a key into the backdoor knob. It fit, but like a wrong jigsaw piece of a puzzle. I tried another key. Finally, a copper key fit and unlocked the door.

Country cottage welcomed me; floral wallpaper, shiny parquet floors, hardwood window frames, fluttering curtain, and vases filled with the same flowers from outside. It was a scene from a magazine, yet it held no warmth. Each chair I sat upon was too hard, too soft, too tall or too short. There was food in the refrigerator and cupboards, but like a dollhouse, it was all for display purposes only. I hoped Goldilocks's three bears would not show up.

Not knowing what I should do, I went to bed. The pillow-top bed was too soft, and the comforter suffocated me. Finally, an alarm clanged to tell me to stop tossing and turning.

"Rise and shine, sunshine!" My angel, sporting a tennis outfit, appeared.

"Why are you dressed like that?"

"I like it. The human body has its limitations, to be sure, but one thing I miss without a body is wearing outfits like this."

"I thought you wore a choir gown with wings," I said.

"Of course not. We're spirits. I'm only in human form..."

"Yes, I know, you're only in human form for my benefit. My fifth grade religion teacher told me all about angels. What is my purpose here? Will I get the children to straighten out? Do I need to show them the value of an education?"

She chortled in glee. "Catharine, Catharine. You will wish it was so easy," she said, pulling outfits out of a closet.

My angel selected black trousers, with a short-sleeved black jacket. Under it I wore a sleeveless white blouse, and completed the look with a gray jabot. I slipped on a pair of low-heeled pumps.

"Somewhat severe," I commented, looking at myself in the mirror.

"Yes. You'll need these as well," she hooked on a pair of black-framed, square-rimmed eyeglasses.

"Oh, yeah. Here's your lunch. Garbanzo bean arugula salad on the school menu today."

"Whatever happened to chicken nuggets and mac'n' cheese?"

"Killers."

"What's in here?"

"Egg salad. Have a good day. I think you're going to need it." Gone.

I was alone again. Something sinister simmered beneath the surface. I waited until seven-twenty before getting into the car, which propelled me, against my desires, back to Jefferson Education Complex. Up the stairs, down the hall, to the right. Dust closet! Went too far. I walked backwards to my classroom.

Two large boot-clad feet rested on my desk. They were connected to an ape of a man, around thirty-years-old, leaning back in my chair. His black hair was made even blacker with styling gel. His brown eyes and groomed eyebrows sunk behind a flat nose ending with flaring nostrils. Though young, his forehead took on an appearance of a crumpled shirt. A cleft in his chin completed the high testosterone image.

"Get your dirty feet off my desk," I crashed down my book bag, something that was becoming somewhat of a habit.

"Ms. Ms. Ms." He pronounced the 'S' like a 'Z'

"Zimmer," I finished for him.

"So glad to make your acquaintance." His size twelve feet remained resting on my desk.

With a strength I hadn't known I possessed, I yanked the chair back, and his feet dropped, almost toppling him over.

After composing himself, he unfolded his six foot, three inch body and hedged it next to me. I backed away and stepped over to the windows, opening the blinds.

"I'm Derek Hairball," I heard him say. "I'm the football coach."

"Nice. Don't you have to get your classroom ready?"

"I see your classroom is nice and clean. Must be because you kept Jeremy from football practice yesterday."

"Jeremy kept himself from football practice." I snapped down the world map.

"Can't a boy recognize a good lookin' woman when he sees one?"

"Recognize, yes. Degrade, no." Markers and paints were extracted from the cupboard. I set them on the art table.

"Touchy, touchy." He strode over to me, bent down. Reflexes jolted my face away from the blast of halitosis. "That kid is going somewhere with his football talent, and I don't need no puritan teacher gettin' in the way."

"Listen Hairball..."

"Coach Hannibal," he corrected.

"You tell your little boys that to be real men means to respect all people, starting with girls and women. Hairy muscles prove nothing. If they don't respect me, or their classmates, they are not going to play football. Furthermore, if you come in here again trying to intimidate me, I'm filing a complaint with the EEOC."

He laughed in contempt. "EEOC? I can do whatever I want with you. Just watch your back."

"Are you going to leave, or do I need to call security?"

"Security! Hah! You are delusional. I ain't done with you little lady."

He left, but the stench of his odor lingered. Some men think that cologne disguises the fact that you haven't bathed. Hairball was one of those people. I found some air freshener and sprayed down the room. Little puddles of the aerosol pooled onto the desks. Then I opened the windows. I didn't care if the air conditioner was on.

Why did he scoff me when I said the EEOC? I still didn't understand what all of this meant. One thing for certain, Coach Hairball and his cronies were not done with me yet. Or maybe I wasn't done with them.

CHAPTER 10

The temperature outside was eighty-seven, but inside the teachers' lounge it felt like thirty-below. I sat on a vacant orange chair, and extracted my egg-salad sandwich from my lunch sack.

"Do you think we'll have much of a football team, this year?" Mr. Walert asked while boring his bullet eyes into me, my body shivering stronger.

"Not if certain teachers keep students from practice," said Mrs. Ferensi. She looked about fifty years old and strained her body frame with more weight than it could bear. She wore a pale green, polyester dress that clung to every roll on her body. Her gray hair hung lankly down her round back, and whiskers formed a light gray beard on her chin.

"Don't you think some people are a little touchy? Kids will be kids, and sometimes they say stupid things," said Mr. Jalensky, the other seventh-grade teacher. His hairstylist must have been the same one that Mrs. Ferensi visited for his brown, greasy locks slumbered on his head.

"One thing for certain is things are going to get real ugly for someone if she keeps handing out detentions." Mr. Theodin, the sixth-grade teacher. I had heard in passing that he was the reason the seventh-grade students were incorrigible. Mr. Theodin scratched a scab on his right arm. It began to bleed.

What were these teachers saying? They couldn't have been on Coach Hairball's side. Teachers defending a sexist student and coach? What kinds of school was this?

Three teachers shoved their unfinished sandwiches into their lunch bags, stood up, and walked away.

I scraped back my chair and stood up. "You are despicable," I stammered out.

"Sticks and stones will break my bones, but words will never hurt me," they shouted in unison. "Sticks and stones will break my bones, but words will never hurt me."

It was as if I pressed the "on" button to a machine, but couldn't turn it off. I scrambled out of the lounge, the echo following me back to the classroom.

The students that afternoon behaved as poorly as they had in the morning, though in the afternoon they had decided to play Pickle-in-the middle, with my book bag as the ball, and me as the pickle. Some of the kids purposely lobbed the bag at my head.

"Get it! Keep it from her!" They would shout. "Pickle, pickle, get the pickle."

After several minutes of this torment, I stormed down to Doctor Theodora Wilkins, the principal's office.

"Those kids won't behave," I said.

She continued looking down at her paperwork. "Kids will only respect you if you give them something to respect," she answered.

"They should respect their elders!"

"Kids will only respect you if you give them something to respect," she repeated.

I stood up. "Angel! Really, angel. Where are you?"

"Ms. Zimmer," Doctor Wilkins finally looked up. "Is there a problem? Are you hearing voices?"

"Only the ones that tell me this place is filled with crazies."

The doctor stared hard at me. "Your words, Catharine, watch them. What may I do for you?" she asked.

"The students are playing Pickle-in-the middle, led by Jeremy Black."

"You sure have it out for that boy, don't you?"

"No, I don't."

"You marched in here all ready to get that boy in trouble."

"He was causing all the problems."

"Ms. Zimmer. I suggest you leave Jeremy Black and Coach Hannibal alone. You could get into all sorts of trouble tangling with them."

"What are you trying to tell me, Doctor?"

She laughed. "Really, Ms. Zimmer. I'm only trying to tell you that Coach Hannibal has developed the football program and put our little school on the map."

"And you don't care how the players treat the other students?"

"I think people are too sensitive these days."

I left the school not caring what happened to the students. They were just a figment of my imagination, or something like that. Back at the dollhouse, I hopped into the shower trying to scrub away the verminous feeling crawling over my skin. I was toweling my hair, when my angel appeared, looking at the silver-bangle watch on her arm.

"School doesn't end until three."

"What school? I can't teach there!"

"But are you learning anything?"

"Learning? Sure am. People can say and do whatever they want, and there are no consequences."

"Has anyone come to your defense?"

"No! You should have seen it! Teachers defending Coach Hairball. Even the principal was on his side."

"How does it feel?"

I knew what she was getting at. Catharine Zimmer had done nothing to protect the Mikes, Danielles, and Daleys of this world. I had watched them being tortured, but did nothing. Angel was right, self-interest had won out. I was afraid of getting hurt, or worse, being bullied and tormented. Kids can be cruel, very cruel. The less I had said, the better. That mindset had a price tag, a very high price tag, one that needed to be paid.

The bed was no comfort, so awake I remained again. My body felt like a leaden weight, but there was no way I could force it to sleep. Anxiety of the next day acted like a quart of caffeine on the system. What would those students do? Worse, what would Hairball and company do? It was a terrifying night, each noise igniting my nerves. Sleep finally shaded my eyes and my consciousness.

I awoke to darkness, but it wasn't the black of night, but the veil of storm clouds. My heart pounded as I drove toward school. Even the hallways were overshadowed by impending gloom. Inside the classroom, I flicked on the lights. Calm before the storm.

Students trickled in, like the few drops that began to fall from the sky. By eight-fifteen, all the students that were coming to school that day were in their seats, whispering secrets.

How menacing can seventh graders be?

"Class take out your notebooks," I began. Instead of complying, however, the boys stood up and barked like seals while marching toward me. They encircled me and pushed me from one boy to the next, my body flopping in a vertiginous motion.

"Stop! Stop it this minute!"

What difference did my shouting make? Our classroom was at the back of the school. Only the dust closet and empty classrooms, all mismarked, would hear the screams. Then the girls stomped forward.

"Kill her, kill her," they chanted.

They took turns kicking me or yanking at my hair.

"Stop it!" I sobbed. "Please stop." It only inflamed their passions.

Pins, compasses, anything with a point, stabbed me repeatedly like I was some voodoo doll. My head swirled. Fainting failed to rescue me.

"Students!" A voice louder and with more authority shouted. "Students go to your seats at once!" Dr. Theodora. I drooped like a leaf. "Ms. Zimmer, I see you're not fit to teach. Report to my office at once!"

That was it. No rescue from these monsters. No reprimand for their deleterious behavior. I was the one to blame. I had to pay.

"You won!" I shouted, and they burst into a loud cheer. I ran out of the school and jumped into my car. Did I run a red light? Did I hit anyone? Did I drive over the yellow line? I don't know. All I could recall from the ride home was the reset button being snapped on, and the tortuous event in my brain replaying itself.

As I neared my temporary home, however, instinct tolled warning. Red gashes appeared on the white clapboard. I couldn't distinguish it because I was still about a block away. As I neared, I read, "SLUT," scrawled about twenty times across the front facade. A few neighbors stood outside, gaping.

"Do you live here?" a woman asked.

"Yes," I said, racing up the steps to go inside.

"I'll call the police if you want."

Inside was worse. Slut and whore, written in red paint, covered the walls and furniture.

"What do you think of our artwork?" Coach Hannibal emerged from behind the armoire. He grabbed my shoulders. "Heard you're nice and easy." His lips began covering my face.

"Stop it!"

"Come on baby, give it up!"

My knee crashed into his groin.

"Ouch!" He released his grip and I ran to the powder room and hooked it locked.

Thunder roared above, while Coach Hannibal crashed against the door, trying to force it opened. Suddenly, more voices, boys' voices.

"Let's get her!" My brain reenacted the scene from the classroom.

They slammed against the wood, and the door splintered.

"I get her first! No, I do. I do. I do. I do!" One after another, deciding like little children, who gets to play the game first. It wasn't a game, however, but predator versus prey. My body wilted to the floor.

"Bang!" A gunshot exploded in the air.

What's going on out there?

Chaos ensued judging from the shouts and scrambling of feet. Then silence.

"Are you okay in there?" A woman's voice. "It's okay now. They've all been taken away."

"I'm not sure," I whimpered.

"It's okay. Did they touch you?"

I retched into the toilet, remembering Coach Hannibal's wet lips on my face.

"Do you need to go to the hospital?"

I wiped my face with the back of my arm. "No."

"Can we call someone for you?"

"I have no one, no one, no one," I sobbed. "No one! My family is all gone. My friends are dead. I'm dead too. There's no one. Get me out of here. Please won't you get me out of here?"

"Ma'am. I can only help you if you open the door."

When I opened it, my angel stood waiting, holding out her arms. I rushed into them and began sobbing.

"That was horrible!"

"That is how many people live. Children, sitting on the school bus, blood pressure escalating in fear, wondering who will bully them or when will the bullying begin again. Playgrounds, intended for joyful romps, become premises of terror. And in other countries, the attacks on the innocent is even more heinous. All these people living in terror with no one to help them. No one, Catharine, no one. Not even you."

"Am I done here?"

"Yes, Catharine, but I assure you that even though you're living out your punishment, this experience will not fade easily from your memory. Though it will be far away, you will often wonder when it all will happen again."

"Is that how it is for all the victims?"

"Yes, some go on to lead successful lives, but the scar never leaves. Sadly, many are unable to climb out from it."

Toughen up was the motto I had lived by. I had assumed these people were just babies asking for trouble. Worse, I assumed they should have fought back instead of taking the attacks. Because they had done nothing to defend themselves, they didn't need Catharine Zimmer to step in and save them.

"Was this worse for me because of my judgment?"

"Catharine, some people have it far worse than you did." My angel patted me on the shoulder. "Toughen up! It builds character."

CHAPTER 11

Angel, am I finished yet?" I asked as we continued walking. I cannot describe the path because fog enveloped us within its damp folds.

"No, Catharine. Your words had deepened the trench of sorrow for many."

"Words? 'Sticks and stones can break my bones, but words can never hurt me,' I was always taught."

"Parents trying to salve their children's feelings with that little fictional phrase. You know words hurt, Catharine, ones spoken directly to you and others spoken behind your back."

We stopped next to a large television with two chairs in front of it. The angel sat down, and motioned for me to join her. She pointed her finger like a remote control, and instantly I watched seven-year-old Catharine sitting at her family's kitchen table, crying. My father, down on his knees, wiped my cheek with a tissue. I had just come home from Brownies.

On my walk home, Doris Schlick, eighth grade, had shouted, "Hey clown baby! Where did you find that ugly red wig?" Then she rode off on her bike like Almira Gulch, the nasty woman in the movie of *The Wizard of Oz* who had tried to steal Toto, Dorothy's dog.

The screen changed to reveal the lunchroom of where I had worked. There I watched two of my work friends eating and chatting.

"That Zimmer thinks she's something, doesn't she?" Brenda Limmers spoke with a straw between her lips. I watched in shock. Brenda and I played volleyball together. "I wish she'd quit the team. She's awful."

"So you wasted your time playing a useless game?" my angel queried, eyebrows arched.

"I was okay," I stammered.

"But the recruiters passed you by. Hmm, that shake in her hand looks tasty." Suddenly one appeared in my angel's hand and she slurped loudly. "We better pay attention."

"I can't remember the other woman's name."

"Charlene. Shh, I'm trying to listen." Slurp went the shake up the straw.

Charlene fussed with her ponytail as she spoke, "As far as Catharine Zimmer goes, she's a terrible department manager. She thinks that just because she got accepted into the manager training program she can boss us around."

"She certainly wasn't complaining when she ate all my food and drank all my drinks at my Christmas parties," I said wryly. "How come I didn't know these two disliked me?"

"Keep watching."

The television switched channels. There was Catharine Zimmer, sitting in the lunchroom, with her co-workers. Charlene and Brenda were among the group.

"You've been dead for so long, I'm not sure you will remember this incident. You probably don't remember a lot of your lunch room drivel."

In five minutes, Catharine Zimmer managed to inculpate a slut, thief, and child molester while munching on her egg salad sandwich.

"I don't trust Harold. His drawer is always off. I also noticed certain items missing from his department.

"Oh, yeah, her outfits are tacky. But she has to attract the men, you know. She's a loose one all right."

I covered my mouth in shock.

"Don't ever let your children near him. I've suspected he was a child molester."

I threw slurs as casually as I would sprinkle salt on my popcorn. At the time, saying those things had elevated my stature in my own mind. Watching them at that moment was like swirling in contaminated sewage. This wasn't the only conversation. For two hours, Catharine Zimmer entertained listeners while disgracing anyone who ever had had contact with her. I was reporting the news, all right, just the wrong kind. Somehow the comments made by Charlene and Brenda paled next to mine.

"Why didn't this come out during the stories?"

"Would you want Aleric, Ursula, and Adrien to see this?"

Humiliation scorched my cheeks.

"Let's see the fruits of your labor," she leaned back in her seat.

I gasped. On the screen were Harold, Bianca, and Ralph. I had worked with them, but never learned of their private lives. Harold was married with two children, one with cerebral palsy. Bianca was a divorced mother of one. Ralph lived alone with his junk and helped at his church.

Harold was fired for stealing. Store security escorted him out of the building. There was Catharine Zimmer, whispering to Elaine Loomos, the store's controller. After his firing, I had to watch him struggle to find a job, deal with the bill collectors, and finally take his family to a homeless shelter.

"He was guilty! I just knew it," I said.

"Nope. The criminal was Richard Spicuzza. Your lunchtime gossip inspired Richard to plant the money in Harold's locker."

The next victim was Ralph. I watched as he went to work, then puttered around in his home. He often spent long hours at his church repairing equipment, painting, or cutting the grass. Ralph's fate turned with a visit from his pastor.

"Ralph, there's been talk around church. There are some people saying you've been messing around with their kids."

"It's not true," Ralph put down a cast iron pan. "I love those kids as if they are my own."

"We can't even have the slightest suspicion," the pastor said. "Sorry, but we gotta let you go." Poor Ralph left the church, never returned, and took to the bottle.

"How did I have anything to do with this?"

"Melanie Zinzer."

Oh, Melanie! She often sat with me at lunch and she went to the same church as Ralph.

"Melanie heard your prattle and shared it with the pastor."

"I can't believe it!"

"Why not? Gossip is a billion, or even trillion dollar business."

"That's for celebrities."

"People love to hear of others' problems. It distracts them from their own failings and sins. Catharine, you were so good at filling in all the details. That talent was meant to be used for your writing, but instead you used it to defile the reputations and even endanger others."

I watched Dino, the shoe salesman, walk out with Bianca. They were the last to leave the store. The parking lot was empty except for their cars. He pushed her against her tan Nissan.

"Hey! Heard all about you, willing to give it to anyone." Dino spattered kisses over her face. She turned her head from left to right, right to left.

"Turn the television off!" I shouted. It went black. "I didn't intend for any of this to happen! Harold was always so nervous. He just seemed so guilty to me. He'd stutter and sometimes drop the cash bags when he carried them to the back office. He had tried to talk with me, but I had always made sure I was busy."

"Yes, you were very good at that."

"I didn't know Harold had a disabled son. Ralph worked in maintenance. Talked with anyone, but he almost seemed too nice, especially around children."

"Yes, you were also very talented at judging people," my angel said.

"Bianca was gorgeous but wasn't very friendly," I wanted to muster up some justification.

"Wasn't friendly or just not interested in listening to Catharine Zimmer drone on and on about the lives of others?"

I shook my head in shame remembering. At the time, gossiping was as enjoyable as drinking a glass of wine or perusing a magazine. The more sordid the details, the more frenzied my words became. I had especially relished the large crowds that would gather around the lunch table to listen. My ego had become the sow that was fattened with this slop.

"How are you feeling now?" My angel was clutching an overstuffed feather pillow.

"Like a murderer, thief, adulterer, molester."

"That pretty much sums it up. Come, follow me." I touched her hand and we were on top of the old stone lighthouse perched on San Francisco's Telegraph Hill. "My old friend, Phillip, taught me this." She ripped open the pillow and waved it. A blizzard of feathers swarmed, then dissipated throughout the 239 square miles of the city. "Now I want you to go retrieve every feather." She captured one before it fled away. "Here's one to get you started."

One thousand, seven hundred and seventy-five days, or about five years, earth-time I roamed, searching out the feathers. Each feather returned would result in my angel responding, "Only one thousand, three hundred, and thirty-three to go. Only nine-hundred seventy-two more..." and so forth.

The first feather fell in front of a small cottage. I reached to pick it up when the front door opened. Father Cordoba! I hadn't seen him since childhood.

"Father! Father it's me, Catharine Zimmer. But I'm all grown up!" I was dead, too, but everyone in this realm was either dead or sent here for a purpose.

"Sí, sí. Niña! But I am no longer a priest. They chased me away."

"Why?" I remembered the whispered conversations between my parents. Then one Sunday he wasn't there. He wasn't going to come back. I was too young to put the pieces together.

"The priest they wanted, I could not be," he said, hanging his head.

What did he mean? Who didn't want him?

"First they no like the way I speak. They no like my sermons, too tough. They say I no take care of the church money the right way. Finally, they accused me of molesting a boy."

"But you didn't – did you?"

"Never. I know some had problems with that, but I didn't."

He was dead in in this realm, would he lie to me?

I decided he was innocent, so asked, "Why didn't you fight?"

He crumpled a piece of paper in his hands. "Words crush the soul. I could not arise from the rubble. Your parents defended me, only."

"Where did you go? You never said good-bye." He was just our parish priest, yet I felt like my father had abandoned me. We were supposed to be strong. Move on. But it niggled at my heart every so often.

"Come, see."

He pulled a ceramic tile. In the center was the crucified Christ, with St. John on his left, and the Blessed Mother on his right. One by one, Father lifted a sculpture or a painting from his stock. "I spent the time traveling."

"Father, were you finally exonerated?"

"The world did not want to see."

I looked down to see Father placing a feather in my palm. "More feathers await."

I had a strange sensation that I had just gone to confession, and he was giving me absolution, but it was he that confessed. He vanished.

Feathers everywhere, yet only one at a time. It was like the "find the image in the picture" game in my favorite children's magazine. I'd be walking along a road, a street, or in the woods, and I would spot a feather. Each revealed a secret, one I may have known already, but never understood. For most of this journey my angel was absent, until I had captured what I had believed was the very last feather. I handed it to her.

"Thank you, Catharine."

"Am I done?"

"No, Catharine. Gossip is one of the world's greatest sicknesses," the angel said. "So easy to do, slip of the tongue. Expose a secret. Perpetuate prejudices. Malign innocent people. All to make ourselves feel important or ignite fears."

"I know that already. I had seen what happened as a result of my words."

"Of course. Those people had suffered, but you had not."

"What do you mean? I roamed for years searching for feathers."

"Only five. Most people suffer the consequences for life." She placed her hands on her hips, unsure of what to do with her charge. "But did you suffer pain and humiliation?"

At that, I was inside a buzzing newspaper building: voices, the clacking of computer keyboards, chairs scraping back and forth, the hum of printers vomiting paper. There was only one man with me inside this bustling office. He wore his red hair in a ponytail. I was dismayed to see it was the exact red as mine. Precise creases ran down the center of his pants, but no other indentations marred the silk, black suit. His black jacket he wore buttoned, contrasted with a white square above his left breast. His image was an oxymoron of sorts. Greasy and slippery on the inside, smooth and polished on the out.

"Hey, get a load of his face!" The leisure suit wearing a Brioni beckoned me over to his computer screen. "What a man will do for sex."

I looked at the photo. "That's not true! I know him."

"Yeah, baby, all the women want to know him."

"That's his mother. He was trying to help her," I pleaded.

"Since when did you get so high-minded?" the man asked. He pushed up his black, rectangular glasses.

"This is all lies! Adrien told me his story. He was in Chicago trying to find his mother."

"I don't care if it's not true." He rubbed his thumb along his fingers. "I can get lots of magazines sold just with this picture on the cover. Old ladies will skimp on their groceries just to have this five-dollar magazine with Adrien Inveres' image on the cover. And to think in a week it'll be thrown out or used for kitty litter." He guffawed loudly; spit splashing on my face.

"Where am I?"

"Catharine, you know where we are. It's second nature to you." Again he pushed up his glasses, a habit he couldn't control. "I need you to camp out at a little place out in Martha's Vineyard. Seems like the Secretary of State has a little love interest going on over there. Pictures. We need lots of pictures."

"No! I won't do that!"

My shouting made no difference as I landed in a hydrangea bush. I peered into the five-paned bay window. The Secretary of State, wrapped in a towel, embraced a younger woman, clad with much less than a towel. I shrunk away from the prurient spectacle.

"Angel, this is horrible. Please!"

"Are you going to take the pictures?" She appeared.

"Of course not. It's revolting."

"He's cheating on his wife. The entire country thinks he's an upstanding citizen. Don't you think they have a right to know?"

She was right. He posed with the children's and church groups, and he spoke often on family values.

I scrambled out of the bushes and onto the doorstep. I bulldozed the doorbell. Footsteps, and suddenly I was standing face to face with the Secretary of State. He must have had a robe handy.

"I work for the *Daily Rag* and I was sent here to take pictures of you and your mistress. I suggest you stop this affair if you don't want it splayed out for everyone to see." He shut the door, and within minutes, the woman was dressed and scurrying out of the home.

When I returned, Mr. Feculence, the name I gave him, asked, "Did you get the pictures?" He was almost salivating, while the office still hummed, loud and invisible, like grasshoppers on a hot summer night.

"Nothing. Nothing happened," I lied.

"What? My source is never wrong. Benny saw everything. He's sending over his pictures right now."

"I don't like this job. I finished finding all my feathers. Where is my angel?"

"Your angel isn't going to help you now." He stood up. I fell back.

His silk suit split opened, revealing crimson flesh. Steam escaped from his pores like a smokestack. Horns jutted out from the shocks of red hair, and the fabled fork-tail snaked around his body.

"Catharine. This is where you belong. Your tongue is as forked as this tail. We can have an eternity together."

"I've been judged already!"

"Yes, but doesn't this look so much better? It's what you did so well while you were alive."

"No! No."

"Oh, yeah, baby." He snaked over to me. "You were so easy. Just a little whisper and you went with it. You were my little helper."

"Never!"

"Always! One little word from sweet Catharine Zimmer meant another lost soul for me."

His hand seared my arm as he grabbed me. Wailing and moaning greeted us as we descended into a cavernous pit.

"Hell?"

"No. The Abyss of Remorse," he hissed.

"Forever?"

"Do you want it to be?" His eyes filled with glee.

Harold, Bianca, and Ralph waited, my judges.

"Aren't you proud of yourself, Catharine? Beautiful work. Couldn't have done better myself." He roared in laughter. "Catharine," his voice sizzled like greasy burgers on a griddle. "Don't you remember all your wonderful Tuesday nights? Penelope's Cafe? You were more successful there than at work. And all done for the sake of the church."

Could my face burn more in that heat? It did. After our parish board meetings, some of us hung out at Penelope's. For two hours, no more, no less, we'd insinuate, suggest, and scandalize any parishioner who piqued our interest that week. Pity the person who botched up running the festival, suggested new ideas, or seemed too holy for us.

"Can you believe Shannon Gordon is running the festival this year? She can't keep her house, how will she run a festival?"

"Yeah! And she wanted to move the festival to a different location. That will never work."

"She was supposed to mail out the raffle tickets by now, but no one has gotten them."

"She and her drunk husband probably lost them."

We'd sip our coffee, pay the bill, and leave. Next week it would be another victim.

"Ben and Isabel. Do you think their marriage will last?"

"No! He's working all the time, and she's a helicopter mom. She needs to lighten up."

Another meeting, another night out.

"She died of cancer, by the way," the Devil interrupted.

"Who?"

"Isabel. No one knew it. No one cared." He chuckled. "That's what I crave - isolation and loneliness. You were a master!" His eyebrows wiggled up and down.

Then a new family joined our parish. Home-schoolers who dressed funny.

"Annabella Rogers. What kind of mother teaches at home?" I said. They belonged on the Prairie a hundred years earlier.

"Those kids are going to revolt, mark my words."

"Did you see how those kids were dressed?"

"They're Jesus freaks."

Sharon, Annabella, Ben, and Isabel all left the parish, or stopped attending. No one bothered to find out what happened to them. Others left, too. We blamed our priests because they were either too opinionated or too boring; the church because it was irrelevant or too strict; and others for all their stupid blunders. All the deficient people finally departed. We had the perfect parish. But it was too small to stay open.

"My greatest destruction is right in the church," the Devil's voice was as animated as a used-car salesman about to seal the deal on a lemon. "When Father Cordoba fell, there was much rejoicing."

"No one looks happy here," I said.

"Except me!" He shoved me up against the dank wall, scorch marks flared upon my flesh. Chink, my arms were locked into a metal bracelet. "Soon, you'll have a delightful taste in your mouth. It's what you've been craving all your life."

Putrid sulfur tainted the thousands of taste buds hiding within my tongue. Gray smoke poured out of my mouth. Beautiful Catharine Zimmer became a smoking dragon. Shame and humiliation coursed through my veins as if I wore a scarlet letter upon my breast.

"Stop! I'm sorry. I'm really sorry." Smog consorted with the sound waves.

"I know you're sorry, but you have to pay, baby." He winked. "I'll mail you a thank you card!"

One by one, in the moldering dungeon, a victim of my tongue materialized, handed me a feather, and faded away.

"I thought I had collected all the feathers," I moaned.

"There were tiny, tiny feathers that were also dispersed by your words." My angel appeared.

The numbers were staggering. I had no idea my tongue cleaved so much destruction.

My last visitor triggered an eruption of tears in my eyes. In life, he had been the object of most of my scorn and derision. I had often wondered why I had paid so much attention to the life of a far-away movie celebrity. One little newsclip about him was all it took to consume my every thought for that day. After my judgement which included hearing his story, I realized what I had been missing, and why I had been obsessed with him.

I twisted my face so he wouldn't see or smell the effluvium emanating from my mouth. He too, held a feather.

With his hand, he turned my face toward his. He gently and sweetly kissed me, not on the forehead, but on my foul smelling lips. Roses tinged my taste buds dispersing the sulfuric flavor. The feather became a white rose. Adrien handed it to me. He leaned up against the wall, lifted up his arms, and the bracelets clinked around his wrists.

"It's my turn," he spoke, fumes releasing themselves from his lips.

I didn't want to leave him, but my chains fell away.

"Get out of here." He motioned with his head. "I have much longer than you. Much, much longer. Don't make this any more difficult."

I bent and touched his lips.

"Good bye."

"Don't say it like it's forever."

I smiled for the first time in a long time. Even in misery, he could make me laugh.

My angel arrived and took my hand.

"That was fun." I frowned.

"Wait until your next adventure." She was not smiling.

"And that is where?"

CHAPTER 12

In reply I found myself squatting on a three legged bar stool looking at torn wallpaper, large gashes in the walls, and a sink filled with dishes. I held a discarded newspaper and noticed several want ads circled in red.

Wanted: Office cleaner: Five nights a week. Apply in person.

Wanted: Cook: Weekends a must. Good starting pay. Send resume to Blind Box 470, Fairhope, AL 36532.

A resume for a cook? I had never had formal training but I could whip up an omelet or two. *Where was I?* I suddenly wondered. Why was I looking for a job? I was dead. My thoughts were interrupted by two little children busting through a splintered kitchen door.

"Mom! Tell Timmy to leave me alone!" A tiny girl spoke about her brother standing next to her. Both were dirty from head to toe.

"Get lost," I growled. The telephone jangled. "Don't pick it up!" I shouted, but too late. Timmy handed me the earpiece.

"Yeah, yeah, yeah. Hey, I hardly have money to feed my two kids, let alone try to pay you back. Hah! Take my kids, cuz you ain't getting nuttin'." Slam went the phone.

Who was I? I knew I wasn't Catharine Zimmer anymore. My angel appeared.

"Welcome to the world of deadbeat mothers."

An image appeared. Beautiful Catharine Zimmer sat at a restaurant pontificating on the evils of welfare.

"Did you see Moment to Moment last night? I knew there were a lot of deadbeats on welfare, but not that many. I'm sick of paying for all those losers that bilk the system." Catharine, I, said.

Then I appeared behind a mother with two small children paying for her groceries with food stamps. My eyes scanned their designer outfits and the expensive cellphone of the mother.

"Must be nice having your groceries paid so you can afford designer clothing and that phone," I said to her. The sales clerk nodded her head.

"I bought my clothes at a resale shop, and my parents paid for my phone," the young mother answered.

"She sure put you in your place," my angel said.

"They were cheating the system," I defended myself.

"Perhaps. But, did you do anything to change the system? Did you try to help people who were stuck?"

"Stuck? Stuck? They chose to live like that."

"Maybe."

"And the other ones made poor life decisions that got them in the mess that we taxpayers had to pay."

"We're not here to discuss the morality of a system that you refused to help change. Only one person, Catharine. You were only asked to help one person."

The recording of Catharine Zimmer's life rolled again to reveal me stepping into our church narthex to bump into Meredith Brand. We began chatting, small talk mostly about her five children. Then she paused for a moment.

"We need some instructors downtown to help with the literacy program. You can pick the day or night, we're so desperate for teachers."

"Oh, Meredith, I'm just so busy right now. I'll think about it, okay?"

More of my pitiful life rolled on again as I watched myself play volleyball at the tavern, bowl at a different tavern, attend book clubs with nice, clean, middle-class women, and attend wine tastings with more upstanding citizens.

Then the camera shot changed to the Huerta Center for Cultural Studies where Meredith, her husband, and some of their children taught people to read. It was a dismal building, or more like an abandoned warehouse. Bright pictures painted in different cultural designs tried fervently to brighten the mood. Chairs, probably picked out of the garbage, were cobbled around equally forlorn tables. The teachers and students wore their winter coats during instructions. Then Meredith took a group of families to a different room where boxes of food waited.

"These were all illegal immigrants coming into our country. Of course they couldn't read English!" Catharine Zimmer, her own defense lawyer, tried a different tactic.

"Look again. The skin tones vary."

Sure enough, there were people from all different heritages. "Could I help it our school systems failed our own people?"

"How many times did you volunteer at the schools?" My angel blinked her eyes rapidly, reminding me of a teacher I had in first grade. I called her Mrs. Blink.

"I didn't have child…" I stopped. I didn't have children because I didn't take my father's money for college, didn't meet the man of my dreams, and on and on.

More blinking for angel; more recrimination for Catharine Zimmer.

"Now you'll get to be one of those losers who probably won't be invited to a wine tasting party." She disappeared once again.

Someone tugged at the hem of my shirt.

"Now what?" I yelled.

"There's a rat in the shower!" The little girl moaned.

"What's your name?" I asked.

"Mommy, you don't know my name? It's Megan." She began to cry. "I wish Daddy was here. Why did he leave?"

"Because he don't love us anymore," Timmy answered. He had a baseball bat in his hand. "I'll kill the rat." He solemnly left the kitchen, and crashing and banging filled the tiny confines of the apartment. I didn't wish to see the murder take place yet I didn't want Timmy using the bat on anything besides the rodent. When I entered the blood bath (yes, pun intended) I heard a squeak from the victim and then silence. Blood, like some macabre painter, smeared itself all over the walls and floor as well as the tub.

"I suppose you want me to clean it up," I stated impassively. "You killed it, you clean it up."

Megan grabbed the remains by the tail, threw it in the trash bucket, and ran the shower water. She took the garbage bin and carried it down the apartment steps. Timmy scrubbed every surface in the bathroom. I looked outside to see Megan's head and torso lost inside a large green dumpster, and then resurfacing. This was a ritual they had performed frequently and with aplomb. Me, Catharine Zimmer? A tiny mouse sent me scurrying up furniture and screaming for help. Discomfiture at my cowardliness in contrast to their staunchness niggled at me like some pesky gnat that hovered in front of your face.

The phone clanged again. *I am going to hate this phone, I just know it.*

"Holly, this is Mrs. Jones from Trenton School. Are Megan and Timmy feeling okay?"

I looked at the fissured clock in the kitchen - nine-thirty. "No, they're not sick. We just had a rat in the bathtub. Where's the school?"

"What?" she asked, sounding perplexed. "You've been here dozens of times."

"I'm not feeling good. Just give me the damn address."

"Fourteen twenty-two Roger Street."

"Yeah, yeah. I'll get them there." I looked at Timmy and Megan. "Hurry on and get yourselves cleaned up."

"We've never done that before!" Timmy said.

"You will today. Megan, you first. Let's see what clothes you have." Rag upon rag filled her tiny dresser. I wouldn't have used them to wash my car, let alone dress a child. I found some bathroom cleaner and re-scrubbed out the tub, even though Timmy had done a decent job. I filled the tub and found some shampoo to make bubbles.

"Mommy, we've never had bubbles!" Megan said joyfully. She wore a bubble beard while I scrubbed and washed her hair, then patted her dry with two thin towels. She hugged me so tight, "Oh, Mommy, I love you so much!" *What was stirring inside of me?*

"Timmy, you're next."

"The water is gray!" He complained.

I pulled the plug, rinsed out the tub, and watched as the faucet poured in fresh water. "Do you want bubbles, too?" I asked.

"Can I?" his eyes lit up.

I let him play in the water while I braided Megan's hair. I searched for an iron to press out all the wrinkles from the one dress I thought was somewhat presentable. Nothing. I would have to go shopping, I thought.

Finally, they were ready. "Where's your lunch?" I asked.

"Mommy, you're so silly!" Megan laughed. "They feed us at school."

"How do we get to school?"

"The school bus left a long time ago. We could take a city bus," Timmy answered.

"Okay," I said. We hiked down the stairs. We walked to the bus stop and waited. Ten minutes later a bus appeared. The door swung open. We stepped on.

"Where ya headn'?" the bus driver asked.

"Waldon School," I answered.

"That'll be $3.00, ma'am. And step it up, people are trying to get on."

Money? I didn't have any. How could I have forgotten about money? My angel stood behind us.

"I'll pay their fare," she answered.

An image appeared before me. Young Catharine Zimmer impatiently standing behind an elderly woman, who apparently didn't have the right bus fare.

Catharine Zimmer scowled. *Why didn't she check her purse before getting into line?* Impatience seized me after a few more minutes. "Some of us have to get to work!" I spoke indignantly.

The image stung. I remembered it all very clearly. My car was at the shop, and I hadn't planned for the extra time it would take to ride the bus. I was running late for work. This woman had no concept of time, as she wasted mine. I recalled pushing her as I squeezed passed, put my money in the till, and plunked down on the closest seat. The man behind me paid the woman's fare and stared harshly at me as he moved toward the back of the bus.

"Move to the back," the bus driver shouted. "Young lady, move to the back. The front is for the elderly and handicapped." I blushed in embarrassment.

My thoughts turned back to Timmy and Megan. They rushed to the very back seat, and I followed with my angel stepping on the back of my shoes, flipping them off. I sat, and so did she, too close, and I scooted tighter toward the children.

"Why aren't you two in school?" she asked.

"None of your business," I answered.

"You must be a welfare mom," the mockery tinged her voice as she whispered in my ear.

"Very funny. How do I get money for some clothes for these poor kids?"

"Money goes for utilities and to pay back all your debts. You'll need to go to St. Vincent for some clothes." She handed me some more cash. "Use it wisely. Don't forget, you have an appointment today at Human Services." At the next stop, my angel seemed to float off the bus. Megan noticed.

"She reminded me of an angel," she said.

"Yes, she did," Timmy replied back. "She was our angel because she paid our bus fare and gave Mommy some money."

Angel? Humph. Jail warden, yes, but angel, no.

At the school, a woman waited outside. It was Paige Simmons, school psychologist. She wanted to talk with me. I followed her to her office, a spacious, tidy room, with windows to the outside, and windows to the inner office. We both sat in our respective chairs. In front of her desk, her name was etched in calligraphy onto a brass plate. Next to it, a solar flower bobbled back and forth.

"Your children have missed a lot of school this year," she said, peering over her glasses.

"Yeah, so what? All they learn is a bunch of crap anyhow. What good does it do?"

"I hardly call reading and writing crap, Ms. McDermot. They're the foundations for doing well in society."

"Yeah, right. And what if your husband ups and leaves you for another woman? How do you prepare them for that?"

She fumbled with the papers on her desk. "I'm sorry. I didn't know." More fumbling with the papers and then she looked back up at me. "Have you checked out Social Services?"

"Hm. Yep. Right. Jump through their little hoops to get a little cash flow into the house. What about getting my deadbeat husband to start paying child support?"

The door swooshed opened. Megan clutched her abdomen. A stout woman who stood about six feet tall, stood beside her.

"Ms. McDermot, I think Megan is having an appendicitis attack. She needs to be checked right away."

"I don't have a car. I can't take her on a bus. Can't you call an ambulance?"

At the triage desk, I flashed my Medicaid card to the receptionist. Megan rested on the stretcher with an EMT waiting next to her.

"Oh," the receptionist looked at the card and spoke, her words flat and lifeless. "Wait over there," she pointed to lonely chairs in a waiting room.

"We brought her in an ambulance!" I exclaimed. "I think she's having appendicitis."

The EMT, pushing an unconscious Megan toward us, "She needs immediate help now. Open the damn door."

Gone! But what I heard overhead chilled me. "Code blue! Code blue, ER room 8C. Code blue, ER, room 8C."

Carts and people rushed into the emergency room and I followed, watching people poking and pressing devices all over my daughter's body.

"What's going on here?" I shouted.

"Your daughter's heart stopped." Someone said as he rushed into the room.

I could only stare at the curtain as I listened to the urgency the behind the curtains. Beeeeeeeeep. Flatline. Television taught me that. No heartbeat. Was Megan dying? Why? This was horrible. Someone tapped me on the shoulder. I turned to see a man with a clerical collar around his neck.

"Come, let's go in the family area."

"No, no, no," hysteria swelled, enveloping me in some strange bubble. "She's dying!" I screamed. People stopped and stared. The cleric tried to lead me out of the area.

Suddenly a woman appeared. She looked like an older version of my angel, but she was heavier, and there were streaks of gray in her black hair.

"Honey, let's go with the good pastor. You can't do anything for your baby right now."

She touched my elbow and walked alongside of me into an enclosed room with soft couches, soothing lights, and tasteful artwork on the wall. *The Bad News Room.* Every hospital has at least one on each floor. They give it a euphemistic term, such as family conference room, but it is always the same. I had sat in one with my friend Amelia. Her son, Jonathan, had been in a car wreck, and Jonathan Senior was out of town. I didn't want to be the substitute, but there was no one else to go with her. Sometimes it's the Good News Room, but on that night it wasn't. Jonathan died from crashing into a tree.

"Honey, come out of it." The kind woman touched my arm. "It'll be all okay."

She sat her body next to mine. "May I hug you?" she asked carefully.

I nodded absentmindedly. Her arms engulfed me and we rocked sideways. It was soothing, until the door opened. Grim faced, minus the look of death, a woman, with surgical scrubs sat down across from us.

"She is a fighter. Your daughter has endocarditis, which is an infection of her cardiac system. Has she ever been diagnosed with any congenital heart defect?"

"No, why?"

"This usually occurs when there's some history of cardiac disease or dysfunction. Your daughter is very, very tiny for her age. We'll have to admit her, get her infection cleared up, then I'd like to run tests."

"I'm not sure we can afford it."

"Your only worry right now is to get your daughter better."

"Praise Jesus!" the woman said. "The Good Lord has mighty things for your baby to do!" She stood up and handed me a business card, which read, "Naomi Liner, God's Big Angel on Earth." There was an image of a round seraph along with phone numbers and email addresses. "You just call me any time or email me and I'll be there. I come to the hospital every day, so if you don't mind, I'll visit."

Doctor Carmichel and Naomi hugged. "Thank you, Naomi." Naomi left and the doctor spoke, "Megan's in ICU. I'll take you there."

For several weeks, we lived in the hospital as they prodded, poked, and examined every aspect of Megan's body. Doctor Carmichel was correct. Megan's final diagnosis was ventricular septal defect, which meant nothing to me, except that there was a problem with her heart.

I tried calling the phone number of the children's father, but it had been disconnected. The woman from Social Services appeared one day and told me she had no luck reaching him, but they were working on it.

"Unfortunately, we're so bogged down with parents not paying child support," she said. "Do you have parents or in-laws?"

"Nope. They're all dead. I had no siblings and neither did my ex."

Timmy's third-grade teacher organized rides for him to get to school as well as meals for our family and chores done around the house. Megan's first grade class visited her, and the entire school sent her cards. The room was wallpapered with childish images of flowers, balloons, little girls, and rainbows.

Open heart surgery, rehabilitation, and three weeks later Megan was finally discharged. Doctor Carmichel said that was a record time for healing. As we wheeled Megan out of the hospital, there was a car waiting for us, with a man holding up some car keys.

"Hi there. I'm Mark Klein from Klein Auto Sales. Heard about your dilemma and thought a car would help you out. Hope you don't mind it's pre-owned, but one of the best on the lot."

Megan and Timmy clapped and cheered, but I gawked. He placed the keys in my palm, his hand warm and friendly. "We got you insurance and a bunch of gas cards. Should keep you going for the year."

I drove in stunned silence as the two chattered in the back seat. This realm presented some type of fairytale where extreme kindness abounded only to serve as a chastisement for my earthly indifference.

"This all happened, Catharine," my angel said. "All these kind people, very busy people, took time and money to help this family."

"Really? I have never heard of car dealers giving away free cars!"

"Catharine, I thought you prided yourself on being media savvy. In your lifetime, free cars were given away frequently."

"In contests."

My angel's curls bounced when she shook her head. "In charity."

Back in the apartment, more surprises awaited. It was freshly painted with new furniture and wall hangings. On a bookshelf rested a frame with Timmy and Megan hugging each other. All traces of the earlier indigence had been replaced with good taste and lots of love. Mrs. Timperand, the third-grade teacher, stood self-consciously in the kitchen. Timmy hugged her.

"I hope you don't mind we took some liberties with your home. Do you want to see the children's and your bedroom?"

We were in one of the television shows where the family walks through their new home for the first time. The children's rooms were brightly painted and had new bedroom furniture. Mrs. Timperand opened the dresser drawers to reveal new clothing and undergarments. "The families and the school wanted to help in some way. The Porters donated all the furniture. Nice, huh? We contacted some of the local department stores, and they donated the clothes for all of you."

"Me?"

Mrs. Timperand laughed, "Of course. Let's check out your room."

I fell onto the bed and began to weep. A small community came together to help one family. They pushed and strained their capacity and found they had so much more love to share. How stingy I felt being so cooped up with the life of Catharine Zimmer that I had no time for anyone else.

Megan had been home for two months when the angel appeared. Though we received large donations of money, I had struggled with bills and collectors and continued searching for a job.

"Have you learned anything?" She asked.

"Yes."

"What?"

I knew that was coming. "Never criticize a man until you've walked in his moccasins."

"Catharine, I've seen that quote on countless mugs. You're a writer, come up with something more creative."

I thought for a few moments. "It was awkward being Holly. Bill collectors calling every day! Not finding a job, and then having to be so dependent upon others for help. When I was alive as Catharine, I had always worked and supported myself. I paid for everything..."

"Everything? You paid for your Caribbean cruise where you didn't find the man of your dreams?"

Should I respond? I ignored the jab and continued, "My life was my life, I created my own opportunities and depended upon no one to scrape me out of trouble.

"The most humbling aspect, however, was being the recipient of all the donations from the school families and the community. People aren't all hardened and consumed with themselves."

"Are you referring to a certain hardened red-headed woman?" She popped a chocolate into her mouth.

What made my angel so obnoxious? "I'm going to miss the children. I hope they can make something of themselves."

"Do you remember Naomi Liner from the emergency room? She too had been a, what you call, welfare mother, but someone helped her out. She married a pastor of a church and took over visiting people at the hospital after her husband died."

"She never told me her past," I said. "But I sure loved when she visited us, especially when she brought us her homemade donuts."

"Her life inspired Holly, who eventually went back to medical school and became a nurse practitioner. Timmy went into biomedical research, and Megan specialized in pediatric cardiology. Remember that good-looking car dealer? He and Holly married. You see, you can't judge a book by its cover."

I groaned at her cliché, but clichés contain truths. Living as Holly revealed to me that the outer core of people reveals only a tiny fraction of the real person. For Holly, she looked like a mother making all the wrong choices for her children. Inside, she struggled with the loss of the man she loved and the father of her children. Maybe she married poorly, but she also didn't have the advantage of loving parents to guide her.

I still wasn't completely convinced. "Angel, a lot of people who have had great advantages make terrible choices affecting so many people. Was I to show them kindness?"

"Prayers, Catharine, are sometimes the most you can do in those situations. Unfortunately, you'll learn that lesson later."

What did she mean?

"Don't trouble yourself now with this. You have many more experiences before you meet your nemeses."

"Angel, I believe I'm done here."

"Great, you'll get to meet another woman. This one you have met before."

CHAPTER 13

We approached a park bench, and my heart pounded at the sight of the woman waiting for us. Blanche Patch. The angel said I would meet my nemeses later, but I would not have described Blanche as a bosom buddy. She had bullied me so many times on the park bench that experience suggested I visit a different garden. Grown women don't bully others, do they? I had wondered. Why did Blanche harass Catharine Zimmer?

On warm and dry days, I would take my lunch break at Wilma Allibates Community Gardens, which was across from the mall. I would watch strollers, joggers, and skaters roll pass me as I'd eat my egg salad sandwich. In June, the rose bushes around Wilma's copper statue would bloom in reds, whites, pinks, and lavenders. Sometimes the gardeners would be trimming, and if I was lucky, they'd give me the excess roses. Those were delightful lunch hours. A few years later, Blanche Patch started intruding upon my tranquility. I'd be sitting on the bench eating my lunch or drinking coffee, when she march up to me and begin to yell, "Get the hell off my bench!"

Afraid for my life, I'd acquiesce and move somewhere else, to which she'd follow. There were only five benches in the park, and when Blanche showed up, they all belonged to her. That was only if Catharine Zimmer was there also. I had never seen Blanche chase anyone else off a bench. I wondered if I reminded her of someone. The people at work said she was probably jealous of my youthful beauty. I didn't believe them, but Blanche looked like a refuge from a chemotherapy camp.

Her body had so many sharp edges she looked like a jagged cliff. Shampoo rarely touched her locks, and the hung limp and gray over her shoulders. Her face revealed every wrinkle life had etched into her face, and each line dove downward giving her a chronic grimace.

"Blanch Patch? What does she have anything to do with my life? She should have to learn of the torment I suffered because of her bullying."

"She has a story to tell, Catharine. Sit and listen."

I turned back to see a girl of about six or seven. The towhead thin hair fluttered with the wind. She had brown sad eyes. The hem of her plaid dress had unfastened itself in different places, and brown spots marred her once white Peter Pan collar. Her bobby-sock had faded to gray, in which her Buster Brown shoes revealed through large holes. She turned and smiled, her front tooth missing.

"Are you here alone?" I asked. "How old are you?"

"I'm seven," she replied. "Mommy is sleeping with the baby."

"Shouldn't someone be watching you?"

She scooted closer to me, touching me as she leaned in. "Are you going to kidnap me?" Her eyes registered excitement, not fear.

"No," I laughed.

"Oh, then let me sit here for a while." Disappointment laced through her words. "Then you can escort me home."

We sat silently when suddenly a squirrel scooted at her feet.

"Charlie, you've come back," she said. "I don't have any peanuts today."

Charlie tilted his head to the right, then to the left, and then scuttled up the tree next to us. A robin scooped up a pink ribbon from the grass and flew it to its nest. An occasional chipmunk would peek out of its hole. Women, wearing dresses, and men, in suits and fedoras, strolled past us. Some of the women pushed prams, with their children tottering behind. The leaves were beginning to unclench themselves from their tight buds. Lilac fragrance put the season somewhere in late May or June.

"Could you lift me up to look inside that nest?" the girl asked.

"Where?"

"Over there," she pointed to a pole tree; its bows sheltered the tiny nest. I lifted her up.

"Oh, ah! There are three tiny blue eggs in here."

After I set her down, I stretched and peeked at the eggs as well. A tiny fissure streaked across one of the eggs.

"I hope they all live," she said. "I saw a broken egg near my house the other day."

She reached out her hand to me. "Can you walk me home?"

I smiled at Wilma and marveled at the gleaming copper reflecting the sun's rays. The rose bushes looked freshly planted.

"Bye, Wilma," the little girl said. "She talks to me, you know."

My eyebrows arched. "Hm. What does she say?"

"She says she had a hard life too. Actually, we learned about her in school. We got to go to the dedication ceremony last year. The mayor talked. He was boring. The best part was they gave us ice cream."

I had never taken the time to learn about Wilma Allibates. By the time I attended school, she had slipped out of the community's notice. Once there was a campaign enacted by the Historical Society to repair the statue and polish off the green.

We walked the streets that looked familiar yet unfamiliar. The cars parked or driving past us were from a different time era. I guessed the 1950s, long before my birth. People, sweeping their front stoops or walkways, watched us curiously. I looked down to see myself wearing a full skirt, white blouse, and saddle shoes. I had worn this getup at a Halloween party one year. One generation's wardrobe, another generation's costume.

Where was she taking me? Over the bridge we crossed and the houses on this side bent and hovered as if ready to pounce. "How much farther?" I wanted to break our protracted silence.

She said nothing, so we continued walking past forgotten factories, taverns promising something they couldn't deliver, and rows of cream-brick buildings darkened by age. She stopped and looked up to a window, missing panes, on the third floor.

"That's where I live."

"Don't you worry about bugs coming into the house?"

"Mom said that's the landlord's problem."

On the first floor landing a trash can vomited garbage down the stairwell. At each step my shoes stuck. I discreetly tried to cover my nose.

The child gently pushed opened the apartment door. A woman slumbered on a sofa. Squeezed next to her was an infant, squirming. Puss was oozing from his eyes, and flies landed on his face. I fluttered my hands shooing away the pests. Bottles littered the living room. Seventeen I counted -- seventeen empty Old Crow flasks.

Piles of laundry stacked up on a chair. Cups and dishes were strewn on a coffee table. The baby began to whine, so I scooped him up. His diaper was heavy.

"Where are his diapers?" I asked.

The girl took me to a small bedroom with a crib and a bed squeezed together along with a three-legged dresser that leaned against the wall. She rummaged through a drawer, but no diaper. I followed her as she led me to the kitchen, where square cotton clothes hung on lines. I reached for one, but it was still damp. The baby whimpered.

"Let's give him a bath," I said. "Maybe the diapers will dry by then."

I ran the water. A crimson rash ran all the way down his tiny bottom.

"We never formally met," the little girl said. "I suppose you should know our names if you're going to give Junior a bath. I'm Blanche."

I stared hard trying to find the old bully that harangued me at the park. Where was she hiding in that smooth complexion and fragile demeanor?

Junior laughed through the entire process and cried when I lifted him out. I hugged his toweled body tight. I inhaled hoping to partake in the fresh smell of baby, but in my circumstance, nothing but old mothballs assaulted my nasal passages. *Humph, I can't even enjoy the smells of a baby? I suppose if he pooped, that smell would be stronger than ever!*

I could imagine my angel smiling in mockery.

"Do you think he's hungry?" I asked while I toweled and diapered him. I set him in his metal high chair. The tray was sticky like the kitchen table and counters. "Blanche, do you know how to make him a bottle?"

She expertly performed the task and handed the warm bottle to him, and he grabbed it. She climbed a kitchen chair and found a jar of baby food. When he set down his bottle, she dutifully spooned the mush into his mouth. I began cleaning, starting with the kitchen table and counters.

"Are you daddy's mama?" she asked. "You look just like the picture."

"Nope, just a helper."

Three hours Blanche's mother slept. Three hours I cleaned the tiny apartment. Junior fell asleep in Blanche's arms. I was warming another bottle in the kitchen when I heard a voice crack.

"What's going on here? Where's my bottle?"

"Mommy, look, the house is cleaned!" Blanche innocently replied.

"What did Mommy tell you? You must never dirty your hands from cleaning. That's why we have hired help."

Hired help? They were not getting their money's worth if they were paying someone. I hid in the kitchen not trusting my response to this woman.

"A nice lady cleaned! Lady, come on out. Meet my mother!"

I crept in as Blanche spoke.

"Finally coming to see your grandchildren!" The woman spoke in surprise.

What did I look like? There was a mirror next to the woman on the couch. It didn't really matter, but I felt younger than a grandmother.

"I'm not a grandmother." I said.

"Blanche is always picking up strangers. I tell her one day she's going to get kidnapped. She don't pay me no mind." Her arm strained for a newspaper, which was only about five inches away from her. "Honey, help your mother and get the newspaper."

Blanche, swinging Junior in one arm, ran over and put it onto her mother's lap. Junior wiggled and almost escaped.

"Blanche! You're going to drop the baby! Be careful."

She had been beautiful, once in her life, but indolence and liquor are bad companions. Her stomach and hips swelled along with her neck and chin. Even her nose had grown fat and wide, and seemed to slumber in the puffy pillow of her face. She noticed my stare and reached to smooth out her over-processed blond tresses.

"Not everyone can look like Herman's family," she retorted. "Blanchie, what did you do with your hair? Come to mama. Let me fix it. Where's the ribbon?"

"It was too tight. It's part of a bird's nest now." She grinned widely. Junior laughed.

"Those ribbons cost good money! Look at you. Wild animal" Her mother scoured her scalp with a metal brush. Blanche cringed but didn't complain. Quickly her mother wove the ends together in a braid. "There! Now you look presentable."

"Mama, we are all out of milk for Junior."

"Oh! You weren't drinking it, were you?"

"No. I drink water like you said to. This lady offered to buy some milk and other food. Can I go with her?"

"Of course not! Why would I let you go with a stranger?"

Blanche pressed the right buttons when she began crying. Junior joined in the fray, and her mother shouted, "Stop! Okay. But what is the lady's name?"

"Catharine Zimmer," I answered.

"Cath-a-rine Zim-mer," she prolonged each syllable in mock formality. "My name is Gwendoline. I am sure Blanche failed to tell you that. I used to perform at the Willgate Theater downtown. Vaudeville."

The old theater had burned down before I had ever seen it. Restoring it was another historical committee effort that lost to no funding.

"I do have a grocery list," she ruffled the newspapers and a little slip of paper fell out.

My eyes scanned the list. "I made a list already." I pulled out my slip of paper and held it authoritatively.

"Couldn't you just grab, you know."

"It doesn't become you."

Her head pulled back and her legs swung off the couch. "Fine! I'll get my own."

Talking an alcoholic out of their habit was a futile effort even if it destroyed everyone and everything around them, so I just said, "Suit yourself." I squatted on my knees and looked into Blanche's eyes. "Honey, you stay and watch Junior."

"You're coming back, aren't you?"

"I am your mother," Gwendoline whined. "You can come with me!"

"Who is going to watch Junior?"

"I'll take them both, of course."

Go and let them wander the streets with their mother, or stay and watch them, but they don't get food? What awful choices. Then I thought I'd go shopping when the mother fell asleep. That made perfect sense until I realized I was back in the 1950s when most businesses closed by five.

"Fine, you go to the store, but I'll watch the kids. You know it's getting dark."

We glared at each other, but Blanche pulled on her mother's skirts and begged to stay with me. Gwendoline seemed relieved and soon left. I figured she wouldn't be back until very late.

"Come on, kids, let's meet some of your neighbors," I said when I noticed it was already nine o'clock. Junior had been crying for a good two hours, but I had nothing to give him. I shoved my ears up to the apartment doors on my floor to see if anyone was stirring inside. A door opened when I was doing this and a petite elderly woman smiled at me.

"Come in! Do you want to see my teacup collection?" Junior was still bawling, but Blanche nodded. I had not seen her eat anything all day, but she didn't complain.

"I'm sorry for coming so late this evening, but we're out of groceries, and I just wondered if you had some milk."

She tottered over to her kitchen and opened the refrigerator that stood just a few inches above her. "Oh, you answered a prayer. My son bought me too much milk the other day, and it's going to go sour. I also have bologna. I could make some sandwiches."

Adeline Schubert regaled us with her teacup collection as the children munched on their supper of sandwiches, crackers, cheese, apples, and cookies. As I tore the food in pieces I remembered my African experience.

"My, those poor children. Suppose their mother is out doing you-know-what."

Though Adeline was probably right, I felt I a need to defend Gwendoline, especially in front of her children. "She went grocery shopping."

"This late? Oh, well, none of my business."

The children were bathed and tucked into bed by ten. At eleven-thirty, Gwendoline staggered in without groceries. "Where are the kids?"

"Sleeping, of course."

She tromped to their bedroom and began shouting. "Blanchie, wake up. I want to watch you dance! This is the only way you'll be famous like me."

The child blinked her eyes sleepily when she entered the living room.

"Blanchie, come on baby, dance for Mama."

"I'm tired."

"You can always sleep, but to be a star..." Her eyes looked into some imaginary stage. She plopped junior, who had awakened, into his playpen. "Come on, Blanchie. Show the lady your stuff."

Blanche pushed the hair out of her eyes and began to sing.

For nobody else gave me a thrill. With all your faults, I love you still. It had to be you, wonderful you. It had to be you.

Blanche stopped, but her mother demanded, "Keep singing! Don't stop."

Finally, someone from the apartment below pounded on the ceiling. "Be quiet up there! Don't you know what time it is?"

Gwendoline's face fell. "Okay, time to brush your teeth. All starlets have pearly white teeth!" Gwendoline sprinkled baking soda onto Blanche's toothbrush.

"We already brushed the children's teeth," I said.

"You can never brush enough!" Gwendoline brushed as if sanding away rough wood.

"Ow, Mommy. That' hurts." Blanche pushed the brush away.

"No, no. You're not done yet!" Gwendoline sprinkled on more baking soda, shoved the toothbrush into Blanche's mouth, and scoured. Blood pour out on both sides of her mouth. Blanche cried. "You don't want rotten teeth. No one wants a toothless starlet."

After torturing the teeth, Gwendoline applied facial cleaner onto a cloth and scrubbed Blanche's face. Then she applied a purple paste around her eyes and lips.

"Don't want wrinkles!"

Finally the braids were removed and Gwendoline applied one-hundred strokes to Blanche's hair. She scooped Junior out of his playpen and dropped him into his crib. Both children fell asleep instantly.

I kissed them good-bye, then Gwendoline watched me leave the apartment. My angel stood waiting.

"Wow. What a terrible childhood," I said. "Okay. I think I understand Blanche, now. She suffered."

My angel nodded, but spoke no words. She pointed and the apartment became a large television screen. I watched Gwendoline slug down more booze and shook my head. Around midnight I heard a door creak open. There stood Uncle Herman, removing his coat and cap. We had never met, but I knew him from the family photo of my great grandmother and grandfather and grandpa and Uncle Herman.

"Who is he?" I asked my grandmother one day.

"Your grandfather's youngest brother. He hasn't seen him in years. They don't talk. Grandpa has no idea where he even lives."

"Has he ever tried to find him?"

Pain washed over her face. "Once, but Herman told him to get out of his life. It made your grandfather very sad."

Blanche and my ties were stronger than a park bench. She would have been my father's cousin. Herman and the rest of his family were dead for all we knew. We lived our lives like people in revolving doors. We were together, yet separated, one going in, one going out.

"About time you showed up," Gwendoline slurred.

"Yeah, you're drunk all the time anyways. Where's the kids?"

"Asleep, you dodo!"

Herman went to Blanche's room. "Honey, it's me, Daddy. Wake up!" He then went to Junior's crib and picked him up.

"Nice, real nice. Wake the kiddies up so you can have some fun. Don't you know they need their sleep?"

I let out a gasp of shock at her hypocrisy. She had just woken them up probably an hour earlier.

"They can sleep anytime! What's this purple crap on her face?" He strode over to the bathroom and returned with a wet rag. He scrubbed Blanche's face. "She's only seven!"

She looked at her mother, then her father.

"Some lady came today. She reminded me of Grandma. She was wonderful."

"Couldn't be my mother," Herman swiped his lips with his arm.

Blanche rubbed the sleep from her eyes. "She cleaned."

He set Blanche down and looked at Gwendoline. "What's the kid saying?" Gwendoline shrugged her shoulders. "I don't know what that kid says half the time."

"Well, was someone here? The house looks decent."

"Some do-gooder, I guess. She did look an awful lot like your mother, but she was way too nice."

I winced hearing those words about my great-grandmother. Grandpa had never talked about his family too much. When I asked my father about it, he explained that not all families were as happy as ours. This little vignette revealed more than I wanted to learn.

"Surely not Mom. She'd come for my funeral, and she wouldn't be crying, but to see the grandkiddies, forget it. You gotta stop letting strangers in the house."

"I didn't bring her in," Gwendoline retorted. "Blanche brought her home. She brings people in like they're strays."

"She was so nice. We went to Mrs. Schubert's apartment. She fed us supper.

Herman rolled his eyes.

"What? Gwendoline, didn't you use the money I gave you the other day for groceries?"

She shrugged her shoulders.

He turned from her and set Blanche on his lap. "Blanchie, I gotta tell you something." Blanche wrapped her arms tightly around his neck. "I'm gonna be leaving now."

"No, don't go, Daddy."

"Gotta."

"How long this time?"

"Ain't say'n. May not be able to get back. You be a good girl for your mama, okay? Take care of the baby too, would you?"

"Daddy, please don't go. Please, please, please." Blanche howled in grief. Junior wailed, his tiny voice wafting out to the living room.

"Great father you are!" Gwendoline said. "Blanche, get your brother to stop crying."

"No! You do it! He's your baby!"

Blanche ran out the door, scrambled down the stairs, jogged for several blocks. Neither parent followed. She returned to her park bench, and panting, she lay down.

The first blush of daylight revealed a teenager Blanche on the bench. She awoke, sat up, and trod carefully to the apartment building. Her hair retained the snow white of childhood and it gently curled downward. She entered the room, and her mother flitted back and forth.

"Hurry up or we'll be late. I have your dress on the bed. Don't forget the ribbons!"

"I'm not going," Blanche said. She went to the kitchen and scooped coffee grounds into a percolator. She poured some flakes and milk into a cereal bowl. Junior quickly scooped his breakfast into his mouth.

"Got a science project due today," he said. "We're learning about sea animals. Look at the pictures."

Blanche smiled as she flipped through the report on dolphins.

"I wanna go to college," she shouted, "to be a nurse."

"Ain't no college gonna take you with an eighth grade education," Junior munched.

Gwendoline entered. "A nurse? Get dressed, now!"

"I'm not trying out for another play. I despise singing and dancing."

"Oh! What a ridiculous girl you are. Hurry!"

Blanche drove Junior to school, and then she and her mother drove up to a theatre. Her mother clambered out, but Blanche remained.

"Hurry up!"

They entered in the back stage door. Girls, primping, tittered, and laughed along the front row of the theatre. Blanche scowled.

"There's Mimi. Let's go over and talk to her," Gwendoline said.

"I'll stay here." Blanche plopped down on one of the wooden seats.

For three hours the hopefuls danced, sang, and acted, tempting the director to choose them. Mothers powdered faces, combed hair, or applied more makeup to enhance their daughters' chances. Blanche pulled out Faulkner's *As I Lay Dying*.

"What trash are you reading now?" Her mother grabbed the novel, but Blanche hung tight, and the two women wrestled for it. The director and his assistants stopped and stared at the two women.

"Would you please be quiet or you'll have to leave!"

"Great!" Blanche shouted.

Back to the park bench Blanche and I went. This time when she awoke, I beheld a woman in her late twenties. She trudged up the flight of stairs. Someone had finally taken out the trash. She let herself into the apartment, went to the kitchen, and began preparing breakfast.

"Is that you, Blanche?" Gwendoline's voice. "Did you sleep on that park bench again? You're gonna get sick or killed one of these days!"

"Do you really care?" Blanche asked impassively as she cracked eggs and popped bread into the toaster. Within minutes, she took the breakfast to the living room and waited on her mother.

"Why ain't you found a man yet?" Gwendoline asked. "You're too old for acting. Never met a girl with your looks who didn't dream about being on the big screen. You could be in Hollywood, but all you do is answer telephones."

"You wouldn't let me go on to school to be a nurse."

"Nurse? They'd send you off to war just like Junior. What you need is a good man, one that will stay by your side."

"Who's going to take care of you?"

"I'm fine. You dote on me too much! Can you pour me some more coffee?"

"I wonder how Junior is doing," Blanche shouted from the kitchen. "Ain't heard from him."

"He's coming back real soon, I'm sure of it," her mother said. Blanche poured herself some coffee and carried both steaming cups back to the living room.

"How come you ain't eating any breakfast? You're skin and bones."

"Ain't hungry, I suppose." Blanche walked over to the television and flicked it on. A cheery weatherman reported rain for the day. Blanche stood up, went to a closet, and pulled out a vacuum cleaner. She was just plugging it in, when the doorbell rang. The women looked at each other, knowing something, yet saying nothing.

Blanche slowly opened the door to reveal a uniformed man and a minister. She slammed it shut, then ran to her bedroom. Her sobs were loud and deep. Gwendoline went and opened the door. The soldier had tears in his eyes.

"I have an important message to deliver to Mrs. Rivers from the secretary of the Army," the soldier stated somberly. "May we come in?"

Gwendoline quietly motioned them in.

"The Secretary has asked me to express his deep regret at the loss of your son, Herman Rivers, Jr. His troop was ambushed, and none of the soldiers survived."

Sweet little junior, dead. He probably was only in his early twenties. My dad's cousin we didn't even know existed. *Why wasn't his last name Rivers*, I wondered, but realized that Gwendoline and Herman probably never married. Back in those day that was almost as bad as murder.

Blanche returned. "Get out of here, you liars! I hate you. Go, get out!"

The soldier rifled through his pocket. "I knew your brother. Herman and I were best friends. This is for you." He handed her a stuffed envelope.

She slit it opened, and out fell a medal and other papers. She began reading the letter aloud.

Dear Mother and Blanche,
By the time you get this, I'll probably be a goner. They're getting
closer and closer every day. I don't think I'm going to survive this.
Donny Patch, well, he might not survive, but I say he has nine lives,
so that's why he's going to bring this letter back to you. I just want
you to know how much I really loved you. I know life hasn't been
easy for you, but you made my life wonderful. Blanche, I hope you
find a husband...

Blanche stopped reading aloud and scanned the remaining words in silence.

"I'll be here if you need anything," the soldier said.

"Yeah, right," Blanche opened the door and motioned for them to leave.

Gwendoline, staring out into space, sat down on the couch. "Go get my bottle."

"There are no bottles."

"Go get me one."

For hours they sat, stupefied, silent. Around four o'clock there was knocking at the door. Oblivious they sat. The knocking intensified.

"I know you're in there. Please let me in." Blanche finally stood up and opened the door. The soldier entered with bags of food.

"I'm the Donny Patch from the letter." He began lifting out cartons of food. "I thought you might need to eat a little something. Where are the forks?"

Blanche stood up and went to the kitchen. There she began to brew coffee and grabbed some flatware.

"How'd you know my son?" Gwendoline broke the ice.

"He had the top bunk, I the lower one. He snored up a storm."

Both women laughed. "Oh, yeah, Herman snored." Blanche smiled.

"Herman got me to stop drinking," that far-away look reappeared on Gwendoline's face. "He said, 'Mama, what you doin' ruining your life and ours too? You chased away Daddy, and you're gonna chase us away.' Oh, I was mad, madder than hell at him, but I knew he was right. But sometimes I get to thinking that a drink is the only thing that'll make things alright again. Now that Junior's dead, that's the only thing." Her body heaved in sobs. Blanche went over and rocked her mother back and forth in her arms. Donny watched curiously, and then went to the kitchen. He returned with the coffee pot, and three brown melamine cups.

Gwendoline drank deeply of the hot brew as if it was cold and refreshing. She lovingly clasped the cup between her hands. "I've been sober now for seven years. It ain't been easy. Couldn't have done it without my kids."

"Dad drank lots," Donny stood up. "Didn't stop in time to prevent the cirrhosis. Died plenty young, my age now, thirty-four.

C. L. Paur

"Herman knew how to make everyone laugh," Donny smiled. "The worst day could become the best with Herman's antics. One day he put glue on the drill sergeant's chair. It was so strong, the sergeant's pants stayed on the chair when he stood up."

"Oh, he did that in school, too!" Gwendoline laughed. "He almost got expelled for that."

"He put pebbles inside our folded socks. He also had this confounded horn and would sneak up behind you and blow. He got into so much trouble, but everyone liked him, so they didn't kick him out."

They talked for hours, laughing, but mostly crying. At midnight, Donny stood up. "I best get going. I can help with the arrangements."

A small crowd stood behind Gwendoline and Blanche at the graveside service. After the gun salute, the flag was folded. Donny ceremoniously presented the flag to Gwendoline, and then slowly saluted.

It looked as if Blanche's life took a ride on the road of happiness. She and Donny courted, married, and enjoyed the life of newlyweds. They bought a house, traveled, and talked about their dreams of having a family.

In the park where she would sit on the bench, there was a playground. Donny was pushing her on a merry-go-round. She was a blur it rotated so quickly.

"Stop!" she would scream.

"Not until you say ten!"

"Ten!"

Donny yanked the merry-go-round to stop it. He lifted her off, and they ran to the swings. Back and forth they'd swing. Donny's foot brushed against a tree branch.

Then I watched another scene. This time they walked hand in hand in a warm, spring rain. Sorrow had no place in their lives, but I sensed it would edge itself between them.

"Six years and seven months is how long they were together," my angel appeared.

"Six? Only six? But they seemed so happy. Does Donny leave her? Does he start drinking? Does Blanche go back to nursing school and find herself?"

"Keep watching, Catharine."

Around the dinner table Donny and Blanche sat, candles burning, both grasping each other's hands.

"I have news to tell you," they said simultaneously.

"You go first," Donny said.

"I went to the doctor's today," Blanche began. "You're going to be a father!"

"And you're going to be a mother!" Donny smiled, but only briefly. He brought her hands to his lips and kissed them hard.

"What? I thought you had wanted a baseball team!" Blanche asked, confused.

"I went to the doctor's today, too."

"I forgot." Blanche looked down.

Donny died before the baby was born. Pancreatic cancer takes its victims fast. Blanche planned another funeral. She also signed adoption papers for the baby.

"Why? A baby would bring us so much joy!" Gwendoline said.

"But what kind of life could I give this child?" Blanche said. "I want the baby to have the best life possible."

I watched the delivery of Blanche's baby daughter, Ursula. The nun held the baby for Blanche to see, then Blanche waved her away, tears falling down her face.

"That baby was Ursula, one of your stories during your trial," the angel said.

"Ursula was adopted? Why did she never say anything about it?"

"Her parents never told her. She was also your relative."

Yes, Ursula would have been my cousin or second cousin. I had never figured out cousins, second cousin, cousin twice removed, and on and on. It didn't matter, Ursula and I were related. Maybe that was why I felt a strange connection to her.

"Okay, so we were related. How did that figure into Blanche's life? Why am I to blame?"

"No one said you were to blame, Catharine."

"But I'm here, in Blanche's past. Surely I did something wrong."

"You're a water bug, Catharine," my angel said.

"What?"

We were in a classroom. People sat on chairs in a circle. I spotted Blanche between two heavy-set men. She stood up.

"I'm Blanche Patch and I'm an alcoholic."

From the classroom to one of the five benches in Wilma Allibates Community Gardens. There sat Catharine Zimmer, drinking cappuccino, and watching a woman walk toward her.

"May I sit here?" a sober Blanche asked.

"Fine," I sipped my coffee, edged a little further away from her, and looked out to avoid conversation.

"I used to sleep on this bench as a little girl," she began. I cringed wondering what would come out of her mouth next. My body involuntary response was to sidle away. "I wanted to be free of my mother."

I want to get away from you, I had thought at that moment.

"You remind me of me, when I was younger," she continued, though I didn't encourage her. "I had blond hair, though. I heard my grandmother had red hair, just like yours."

"Oh," was all I said, hoping I would not age as horribly as she did. I stood up and strode away.

I blushed, if one could blush in death, watching this exchange. I remembered it well. The woman struck me as odd, and I didn't want her problems sucking me into her life. At that moment, however, I realized I was there to share her burden, perhaps even to ease it a little.

Blanche also stood up and walked a different way to the liquor store. She paid cash for her whiskey and then walked until she reached the end of town to a cemetery. This time she sat on a wrought-iron bench, which stood next to three headstones. Herman Rivers, Jr. Donny Patch, and Gwendoline Rivers. All dead, but keeping her company.

More regrets washed over me. My angel was right. I had never plunged deeper than the surface of the water. What does it say about me that I was so concerned about maintaining mental homeostasis that I couldn't even take a few moments to listen to her?

The park disappeared. I was the loser in this encounter. From my neglect, I had lost the opportunity to dive deep into the waters of Blanche's sufferings so as to emerge fully like a butterfly from its chrysalis. Instead, I remained cocooned up only to die still in the larva stage.

Blanche appeared before me, joyous. The edges were softened, and her hair returned to its blond tresses. Standing next to her were Ursula and Donny. We hugged saying nothing. I knew at that moment I would be in this existence for a very long time. My heart filled with dread and I contemplated where I would find myself next.

CHAPTER 14

My new home would be a flattened cardboard box. Next to me was a grocery cart, filled with bags and boxes overflowing with aluminum cans. Though the day sweltered, I was wearing a faded Army coat, slouching tan khakis, and boots with no soles. A stocking cap covered my head.

The angel scribbled something onto another board.

"There. You're all set," she said. She turned it around.

"What does it say?"

"Please help me. I'm homeless," she answered.

"What language?"

"English."

"Why can't I read it?"

"You're illiterate. Do you know how many people can't read?"

"What does this have to do with me?"

"Catharine, you're a slow learner, but all this has to do with you."

I sniffed. Dead fish, but there were no oceans, only a garbage dump. I lifted the lid, but I smelled nothing.

"Where is that smell coming from?"

"Try your armpits," my angel said.

I walked over to a storefront to observe my reflection.

"This is awful!" I exclaimed.

"Not your most hygienic moment, I must admit," the angel frowned.

"Why this?"

"Pull yourself up by the bootstraps, young lady, and stop sponging off the system."

"Will everything I had said while alive return to mock me?"

"Only those times when your heart was most hardened."

She abandoned me, but a heavy man, wielding a broom, exited a store and chased me.

"Get away from my boutique!" He clouted my shoulders.

"Ouch! Assault and battery!" I grunted. "I'm calling the cops!"

"Don't worry, I did already to haul your ass off my front sidewalk!"

I indignantly shook off my shoulders, "It's a free country!"

"Not if you're loitering. You've been begging for the last five minutes."

"I'm hungry. I don't have any place to stay! Show some mercy!"

"Mercy? The government squeezes out enough money from me and my business. Go somewhere else and sponge off them!"

"Hire me," I persisted, yet he held his broom higher. "Please! I worked retail before."

I had become what I had disdained -- a vagabond, panhandler, beggar. Covered with newspapers on park benches, sleeping on heat grates, or simply holding a sign on the corner of the road, their very presence disrupted my equilibrium, but only for a moment. Quickly I'd convince myself they were losers bilking the system, and or drug abusers looking for their next hit.

Whack went the broom over my head. Where was my angel when I needed her? He went back into his store. The police never did show up.

Clink! went some coins into my cup. There she was, bending over my tin can.

"Why don't you get a job?" she asked.

"Very funny. I didn't choose to be here."

"Really?" No pity, just sarcasm.

An image appeared before me. Confident Catharine Zimmer, strutting down the street laden with shopping bags, stopped in front of a large, homeless man. He reminded me of Emmett Kelly, the famous circus clown. I dubbed him Wheezy Bobo, the town clown. He held out his cup, but I skirted around him, ignoring his silent pleas.

"Not once did you stop," my angel again. "Not once!"

"He was going to use it for liquor. Did you see that nose on him? Bulbous, tiny broken blood vessels, all signs of a drunk. I might have gotten lice from him, did you notice how dirty he looked?"

"Did you bring him any food?"

"He didn't look like he was starving."

"Did you ever smile at him?"

"That would mean I'd have to talk to him, give him money, help him. Why didn't he get a job? Why didn't he go to the homeless shelter?"

Panhandler Catharine was back on her cardboard mat.

"I guess you need a little time out here."

"Could you bring me something to eat?"

"There's some money in your cup. Try to buy something with that." Gone.

Guardian angel? She was more like kidney stones than some divine being.

I scooped the money out of the cup. One dollar and thirty-three cents. Probably not even enough to buy a cup of coffee. I lifted my head and beheld a cherub staring at me. Her golden hair cascaded down her back. Blue eyes penetrated mine.

"Mommy, may I give my doughnut to this lady?"

"Cherie, darling, are you sure you want to do that?"

"Yes, and I'd like to give her my allowance. Please?"

"Okay, dear."

I greedily gobbled up the cardboard tasting doughnut and grunted my thanks. It's humiliating as I write this, yet at the time hunger knew no shame. Cherie then touched my head.

"Have a nice day, lady."

As they walked away, the mother said, "That was very kind of you, Cherie. I'm very proud. We must always remember those who are less fortunate than ourselves."

The storeowner came out again. "Hah! Scaring my customers away! Why don't you move to another street? The cops will be here any minute now!"

"Right. I'm leaving anyway. Gonna find me a job," the child and the flat pastry revived me. I began walking away.

"Clean up your mess," he shouted.

I scrunched up the cardboard and threw it in the trash. Bradley's, that's where I went first. They would recognize and hire me.

As I entered the store, people gawked in horror. Though the malodorous aura still lingered, I had forgotten what I must have looked like to others. A security guard grabbed my elbow. I yanked it away.

"What are you doing? I'm here to apply for a job!"

"I'll escort you to Human Resources," he said.

We climbed the stairs. I had forgotten how old the building was. He took me down a long, dark hallway and pushed through a door.

"Hi Frank, who do we have here?" A woman with painted eyebrows asked.

"This lady wants a job."

A fake smile covered her face. "Sorry, but we're not hiring right now."

"I've worked here before."

"You did?"

"Yes, Catharine Zimmer!" I shouted it, hoping she'd recognize my name. Only a blank stare replied back.

She bolted from her desk and entered an inner office. In a moment she returned with an attractive, middle-aged woman, with cropped gray hair and very red lipstick. Her clothes came off the expensive racks of this store. Her woody oriental fragrance overpowered my skanky odor. I sniffed enjoying a little bit of pleasure that had been robbed from me during my journey.

"What fragrance are you wearing?"

She smiled, but answered my question with a question, "How may I help you?"

"I'm trying to apply for a job here, but no one wants to hire me."

"Okay. Why don't you fill out this application?" She handed me a paper. The words were jumbled, like my homeless sign. I stared hard, trying to decipher the strange characters. I assumed the first section wanted my name, so I put the pen to paper and began to write. This is what it looked like: Ш'▨▨8ɔ6ʊjʰ. That is all that showed up. I tried to flare the letters, or the figures, but I wrote nothing, but scribbles. The angel did tell me I was illiterate.

"Come on, Catharine, you can do this," I told myself. Nothing, but scratches. Finally, I gave up.

"Sorry. I have a headache. May I take this home and bring it back?"

"Of course. Please do," Natalie smiled. "Once I get it back, I'll look it over and give you a call."

A call? Where would she call?

"Before you leave, would you step into my office for a moment?"

Natalie and I were alone. "Ms. Zimmer, if you can get a shower and some clean clothes that might help your prospects. Our church is hosting the homeless shelter..."

"Who said I was homeless?"

"Well, you can just go there and get a little job training too. You don't have to be homeless." She wrote something on a slip of paper. "Give this to Frank. He can drive you over there if you want."

Frank set a blanket down on my seat and immediately rolled down the car windows when I entered. He said nothing during the twenty-minute drive.

"You don't talk much, do you?" I looked out the window. The scenery had changed. The houses shrank in size and status. I locked my door.

"Nah. It just gets me into trouble, especially with my wife." He turned into a large church parking lot. "Here you go, St. John's Lutheran Church." He dropped me off at the door. "Good luck," and he drove away.

I pulled on the doorknob. Locked. I tried all six doors to the property, locked. I sat on the grass and began to cry. Then I noticed a house, probably the rectory, and decided to try that.

I pressed a doorbell, and waited.

"Hello! How may I help you?" A cheery woman's voice asked from an intercom.

"I'm here for the homeless shelter," I mumbled.

"Honey, they're all gone right now. Let's get you settled. They should be back in about an hour." She opened the rectory door. I followed her to the church.

Coolness enveloped me as we entered the church basement. The secretary scurried about and soon appeared with bath towels, shampoo, and soap. She also had clean underwear, a bra, top, and bottoms. Not matching, not attractive, but clean.

"You'll have the bathroom all to yourself. When they come back, they'll have lunch. Are you okay by yourself?"

The question seemed to imply if I planned to steal or break anything.

"Don't worry, I'm not a thief," the moment the words were out of my mouth I remembered Dad's money intended for college going for my search-for-a-husband cruise.

"Great. Here's a phone," she pointed to a black, antiquated device hanging on the wall. "All you have to do is press 234 if you need me."

When I turned on the shower, dirt rolled down my body and pooled around my feet. Thirty minutes of scrubbing and finally the water ran clear. My favorite part of a shower was toweling myself dry, but in my present condition, it felt more like a pumice stone rubbing against me. I dressed, then looked around the basement. Cots, thirteen of them, were backed up along the wall. I didn't want to crawl into just any cot. I came up to the thirteenth cot. On it was a note, but I couldn't decipher it. It was probably my bed, so I reclined on it. Sleep arrived only to be chased away with someone jostling my shoulders.

"Hey lazy bones, wake up! It's lunch. You snooze, you lose!" I looked up to see a toothless woman staring into my face. I jumped up.

Chardonnay lunch this was not. Stewed prunes, over-cooked vegetables, and dry mostaccioli. I was reminded again that death demanded the food looked like food, but tasted like plastic or cardboard. Mindlessly I shoved the food into my gullet just to get it over with.

"Hey, slow down. Save some for us," Toothless said. "You're too damn skinny to be eating like a pig. I'm Lucy. Whatta they call you?"

"Catharine Zimmer," I said, chomping on a piece of buttered white bread.

"That's a highfalutin name, girly," she yanked at my tresses. "Think you're some looker with that fancy hair of yours?"

"I'm just here temporarily. I'm going to get a job and find a place of my own."

"Hah, hah, hah," she cackled. "That's what they all say."

The afternoon was job training. On the projection screen were charts, outlines, and graphs. None of it made sense.

"Catharine, do you read?" Jennifer Bittmann, the homeless shelter coordinator, asked.

"I used to," I replied.

"What did you read?"

"Everything. I even used to be a writer." Titters from all the other women.

"A damn writer! Ha!" Lucy said. "Must not be selling too many books!"

"Ladies. Please. Okay Catharine. Just sit and listen for now, and we'll talk later," she said. Back in kindergarten, that's how it felt, but I was a grown woman.

I snoozed through the entire presentation until Jennifer shook my shoulders. I followed her into the kitchen. From the cupboard she pulled out a box and set it on the table.

"Let's sit here," she said. "What's this word, R E D?"

I shrugged my shoulders.

"How about C A T?"

"Nope."

"Did you have a stroke?" She was very kind.

"No, I died. And this is what I get for ignoring Wheezy Bobo," I wanted to say, but only shrugged my shoulders.

Heavy, long sigh. "Well, let's start at the beginning. Today we'll learn a vowel and some consonants. This is the letter A. It is at the beginning of the alphabet. You do know your ABCs, don't you? Can you say A? It's the first word in apple. In many words it actually it pronounced like cat," she said. "Repeat after me."

It took two hours to learn A, C and T and to begin to relearn the alphabet that I had so proudly memorized at age three. I put the letters together to form cat, and learned to write them. She then had me practice my penmanship and gave me homework to study E, B and D.

"Catharine, is like CAT," she said. Catharine starts with C A T."

The next day Jennifer rounded us up after breakfast to head down to the employment office.

The employment manager looked at me while Jennifer whispered in her ear. After some discussion, Jennifer approached me. "Catharine, let's go downtown. I think we have something for you."

Portland Inn needed a cleaning woman. After a brief discussion, Jennifer left. The manager took me into a locked room filled with brooms, hotel carts, and cleaning supplies.

"Take this bin, put the garbage bag around it," the manager demonstrated. He talked loud and slow.

"Just because I can't read doesn't mean I'm hard of hearing!" I retorted back.

"Oh, a little attitude, huh?" he said. "Hey, I don't have to hire you. I can find anyone to take your place. I was just doin' a favor for Jenny."

The entire day I cleaned hotel rooms, the front lobby, took garbage to the back dumpster, and learned how to clean the pool. Five cockroaches in closets, two mice in the hallway, and a dead squirrel floating where it shouldn't have been. The next day I would learn how to put out the continental breakfast, clean the eating area, and launder the bedding and towels.

"You might not know how to read, but I wouldn't trade you for anyone. You're fast, and you're good. And you're not bad looking."

"Keep your comments to yourself. I'm married."

"Married? Where's the man?"

"He's dead."

Never met a good-looking, eligible hotel owner in life. In death it was no different. Arnold Bender, who was probably in his mid-fifties, still had hair all over his head, and a strip of fur over his lips. He stood at eye level, and when his wife came in, she towered over him. He treated me fairly, but if I had seen him on the street, his brown, squinty eyes would have told me not to trust him.

Bad days at the department store held no candle to hotel cleaning. People staying in hotels, especially at the Portland Inn, had, I swallow hard as I recall, putrid habits. I didn't mind the overflowing garbage, crumbs on the counters, or even the bedclothes strewn about. But some of the items left for cleaning caused my stomach, my very dead stomach, to recoil. I demanded plastic gloves. Arnold's wife, who managed all the money, told him no. He went out and bought me some. "Just don't let Norma see these!"

At night, I'd learn my letters. I began reading the Dick and Jane books, the very ones my parents had read as children. Grandma Zimmer had kept an entire selection upstairs in one of the bedrooms. "See Dick run. See Jane run. Run Dick run. Run Jane run."

My career with Portland Inn ended with bedbugs. I spotted the apple-seed-sized parasite on a bed I had been changing. It scurried away, but as I looked closer, I saw droppings and dead skin.

"We ain't ever gonna be in business again," Arnold moaned. "Sorry kiddo, gotta let you go. Don't worry, it warnt your problem. You clean real good. Health department says to close. And I can't keep you if there ain't no one coming in."

From Portland Inn, I went to Millie's Restaurant. Arnold gave me a stellar reference. It was almost embarrassing when the employment agency read it aloud. Did Arnold want to run off with me?

As a wait staffer, I struggled with taking orders, but the cook seemed to understand my crude writing. I worked there for six months. Then that closed. Employment came, employment left. Discouragement hounded me even though I began reading longer sentences. I was moved into the permanent homeless shelter. Between jobs I'd clean the shelter and cook.

Before I knew it, my one-hundred-twenty days at the shelter were up. I read like a second grader, but not good enough to go on my own. I panicked and hid in the bathroom for three hours.

"Catharine! Catharine, come out here. Catharine this is an emergency shelter. Only a short term housing."

"I have nowhere to go!"

"Go back to the churches and if you can't get back on your feet in a month, come back."

Money for a bus ride, and I was on my way back to St. John's Lutheran Church. Locked doors again. I rang the rectory doorbell, but it was past five o'clock. *Why did he send me here if he knew they wouldn't be here?* A man, whom I assumed was the pastor, appeared.

"Sorry, the homeless shelter isn't running any more. Dear Jennifer passed away suddenly. It was a great loss for our church. No one has stepped in to take her place."

That explained why my reading lessons had ended. Why didn't anyone tell me? They just stopped taking me.

"Here, take this. There's a shelter downtown." He handed me a twenty then shut the door before I could tell him I couldn't return.

It would be dark soon. Where would I go? I had never slept outside before, except for camping. I had a tent, sleeping bag, camp stove, food, and coffee. Right at that moment only the baggy clothes on my back belonged to me.

Up one street, down another. People sitting on their porches stared. I stared back, hoping someone would take me in. So intent was I in my search, I failed to notice the sky darkening. When a street light blinked on, I looked up to stars already twinkling merrily, oblivious to my plight. I shambled to Veteran's Park and dropped on the metal bench. My feet hung over and would be numb if I slept there all night. I didn't have to worry, a police car drove up.

"Park's closed," he shouted out the window. "Better get home."

"I'm homeless!" I wanted to shout. I wanted his pity. Perhaps he'd take me to jail for the night. They would have to feed me wouldn't they? I mustered up a little courage to speak, but he drove away before I uttered any words.

Alleys, that's where the homeless sleep, right? I needed to find an alley. But where? I staggered with exhaustion and collapsed. I remember nothing more of that night. When I awoke the next morning, Wheezy Bobo held out a doughnut and smiled.

CHAPTER 15

I had found my alley, or perhaps my alley found me. Alleys are the city's under-the-bed space. No one is allowed to look under the box spring, but it's there, along with the dust balls and lost shoes. Milk crates, lined up in a three-dimensional pyramid, leaned up against one of the brick buildings. Wheezy sat on a lone crate, proffering his doughnut and smiling.

"Good morning," I said. "Coffee. I need coffee!"

Wheezy's grin was painted on his face.

"Hey! Get out of here!" The same fat man that chased me away from his storefront months ago appeared at his back door. "Don't I know you?" Fish eyes squinted behind convex eyeglasses.

"We're not doing anything," I said. "Just leave us alone."

"Going to break into my store, huh? I'm calling the cops."

"Go ahead, they never showed up the last time." Donut crumbs flew out of my mouth when I spoke.

He disappeared. "Angel, I know you're listening," I shouted while Wheezy beamed. "Angel, I sure hope that store owner got some hard punishment, which is if he even made it."

"Hello, Catharooni Macarooni!" My angel bowed deep. "You should never wish ill on a person."

"Where did you get that name?"

"The online clown generator. The same place you found your name for Wheezy."

Such an insignificant little act of revenge, done so long ago, returned to taunt me. It all began one sunny morning. I had just purchased my morning hot beverage and was heading to work. Cappuccino in one hand, phone in the other, I began to cross over his body, resting all over the sidewalk. He lifted up his leg, I tripped, spilt my coffee over me, and my three-hundred dollar suit became a Frankenthaler original. I was still brewing over it late into the evening hours, when I decided to give the vagabond a name.

"I think you and I need to talk," I said to Angel, pulling a crate from the pyramid, watching the rest tumble like dominoes as I sat down. "You and I are hardly best of friends. I think this experience has been wasted on me. I'm not feeling any more, what would you say, any more..."

"Inspired?" She supplied for me.

"Not a very good word, but I guess it'll do for now since I only have a second grade reading level."

Two cups of coffee appeared. A moment of ecstasy filled me as I whiffed the aroma.

"I'm starting to feel friendlier toward you," I said as I sipped. Instead of hot, bitterness, however, I tasted lukewarm, flatness. This wasn't coffee; this was mud with turpentine added for flavor!

"All part of your condition, remember?" Angel smiled.

Wheezy smacked his lips. The brew burned, like it was supposed to. He grinned and nodded in approval as he guzzled the black brew. It was surely not the same blend that was used when I heard the stories. Heat radiated off my face as I remembered my trial where I heard Aleric, the dictator, Ursula, the nurse, and Adrien, Hollywood's beloved son share their stories and learned my connection with all of them. My face burned when Adrien's image worked itself into my mind.

"This coffee is making me warm." I said. Could a corpse blush? This realm confused me. *Was I a ghost, corpse, ghoul?*

"A soul, Catharine, a soul, meandering through her purgatory. Sometimes your bodily functions return, if only to enhance the learning experience. Sometimes you wander as a spirit would wander, faceless, nameless, but still in existence. You're blushing because of a certain person. He's doing fine, if you'd like to know."

"I hope he doesn't see me like this," the tyrant vanity still dictated many of my thoughts. What I would do for some foundation, eye makeup, and lipstick.

"A shower would do wonders," my angel said.

She began to motion with her hands. Wheezy motioned back. They were talking in sign language.

"Eddie says he'll take good care of you," the angel smiled.

"Eddie?"

"Eddie Parker, not Walter Smith, and surely not Wheezy Bobo."

Walter Smith was the name I typed in the clown generator. He had looked like a Walter Smith to me. The angel signed once more, hugged him, and disappeared again.

"Eddie, I think I'll take you to the homeless shelter." He smiled, though he had heard nothing. The tip of his nose expanded like a red beach ball. Broken blood vessels mottled not only his nose, but also his cheeks and forehead. I leaned close to him but could detect no alcohol. "They don't allow alcohol at the homeless shelter," I said. Eddie grinned.

"Catharine, you're back already?" Tony Black, check-in coordinator at the shelter, smiled. "Couldn't find a place? You have twenty-nine more days."

"I'm trying to help my friend, Eddie, here."

Eddie violently shook his head and hands.

"Sorry, Catharine. No can do. Eddie here won't stay anywhere except for the streets."

"What do you mean? What about wintertime? Doesn't he have family? Someone?"

"None that we've been able to locate."

"Try again. Maybe he'll stay because of me."

Tony signed. How did all these people know how to sign? I had watched the interpreters at church sign the mass for the deaf parishioners, but never learned the language myself.

"He says he has to watch over you," Tony laughed. "Let's see if we can accommodate you both tonight." He stood up and walked to the back office. I knew that office. I had cleaned it, chatted with Rosemary, the director, watered and pruned the plants, and read my second-grade books. Rosemary appeared.

"Hello Catharine." Then she signed to Eddie. Once again, he violently shook his head, and backed away.

"Sorry, Catharine, he won't come in. No one can get him to stay anywhere. Chris, over at housing, found him a place, but he refused to move into an apartment."

"He chooses to be homeless?" I said.

"No, I don't think he chooses to be homeless, Catharine. It's very complicated. He was abandoned as a child. He lived in one foster home after another. That's all I really can tell you about him."

"Is he dangerous?"

"Not any more dangerous than you or me. It's against our policy, but you may stay tonight."

"I think I need to stay with Eddie."

Eddie led me away. We walked about fifteen minutes until we reached a church. He led me to the back of the building, and we descended down worn cement steps. I held onto the railing. The light of the cafeteria waited at the end of the dark hallway.

"Hey, Catharine!" Lucy shouted. "Sit by us."

Fraternizing with life's derelicts was only feasible in Catharine Zimmer's afterlife. Yet I found comfort among these people. No new house remodels, no new outfits, no new cars, no new anything for Catharine Zimmer to compete with. Just people in rags, happy for some food and a night's lodging.

Why had I felt as if I had to compete with others? Envy blemished every success story I had read about. Wasn't it enough for me to celebrate the blessings others enjoyed and be thankful for what I had? But I had left my writing undone which had opened the door to insecurity. Others were successful, but not Catharine Zimmer, who longed to write, or would it be more accurate to say, longed for the accolades? Writing for hours would have meant hard work and commitment, two other fearful tasks for Catharine Zimmer.

"Heard you got kicked out last night," Lucy said. "Where'd you stay?"

"I fell asleep in some alley and woke up with Eddie Parker gaping at me."

"Oh," her eyebrows arched. "You and Eddie got a thing?"

"Lucy!"

"Who's Catharine going out with?" A panicking Dudley Duncan interrupted. Dudley had already proposed to me, sixteen or seventeen times.

"Eddie Parker," Lucy supplied.

"Ah, Lucy, he's old enough to be her grandfather." Dudley tapped the bench next to him. "Sit by me."

"I'm going to stick with Eddie for now. I told the ang..." I stopped. Best not mention the angel, and yet these people were all in this strange dimension with me. Perhaps they were reliving their lives. "I have an angel," I started.

"Are you losing your mind?" Lucy squinted.

"No. I meant I saw an angel in the storefront the other day."

"Nice. Hey, let's get in line to eat," Dudley, never a gentleman, jumped ahead of us. Eddie motioned for me to go ahead of him. That night it was tater-tot casserole, salad, fruit cocktail and a chocolate chip cookie. My angel was in the serving line. She smiled sweetly. Eddie waved at her while I scowled.

Eddie and I washed dishes, swept the floor, and hid in the bathrooms. When we were sure everyone had left, we crept out of our hiding places and into the dark basement. Earlier I had spotted some fabric in the corner. Lots of it. I flicked on a light then pulled out the fabric. Enough for two beds! Joy oh joy. I didn't have to sleep on the sidewalk tonight.

Do dead people dream? I did that night. All sorts of strange images flashed through my unconscious state. I was on a train with my family to the Grand Canyon. Then I was trying to get onto a cruise ship, but there were hundreds of bikers on the road eating tater-tot casserole. Each vignette ended with me standing near a grave. My final dream seemed more like a nightmare. Eddie fell off a cliff. I tried to grab him but I let go, and he fell, screaming. The only sound I had ever heard from him. Tears streamed down my face and jolted me awake. I touched my wet cheeks. Eddie stood over me, smiling, and proffering me a cup of coffee.

For two whole weeks, we stowed away in that church basement. Eddie shopped and secreted away the eggs, juice, bacon, meat and potatoes. I didn't question where he got the money to pay for these items, only ate them though they offered no comfort. Only once during the fortnight did we have to hide. The church was having a funeral and luncheon to follow. Once the place had cleared out, we feasted on boiled ham, potato salad, and lemon cake. I say feasted, but for me, it tasted like all the other food in this realm, flat and like chewed-up paper.

The only downsides to living in a church basement were making sure no one discovered us, and not having a proper shower. In the cleaning closet there was a long, black hose dangling from the ceiling, with a drain below it. It was used to fill the mop buckets with water. Dish soap became my all-purpose body wash. I'd hose myself down, lather over the goose pimples, and quickly rinse. I once grabbed Eddie's shoulder to encourage him to shower, but he violently shook his head, "No."

Eddie and I didn't communicate much. I tried gesturing, and he often understood me. I wrote simple sentences, and he wrote back. I tried to ask about his family. He would shake his head, "No."

"Why you homeless?" he wrote one day.

"I can't find job." I wrote back.

"Did you go to college?" That question stung as I recalled my judgement which seemed like a hundred years ago.

"No."

"High school?"

"I can't remember," I wanted this conversation to end. "What about you?" I wrote back.

"No school."

"How did you learn to read and write?"

"Taught myself. Went to library. Found books."

Heading into the third week of our palatial stay, the custodian discovered us. He must have suspected something because he woke us up at five in the morning.

"Ah hah! I thought there was someone living down here!"

My eyes squinted as we ascended the stairs back to the outside world. Two weeks can make a difference in the weather, as I noticed fall filling the air with its presence. The custodian fed us before he kicked us out. He then packed us ten peanut butter sandwiches, gave us a bag of apples, and a box of fruit drinks. Eddie carried it all in his pack. Eddie shook the custodian's hands in thanks. I wasn't so gracious.

Eddie led me to one of the many parks he resided in. He pulled from his bag one of the peanut butter sandwiches and began to feed the pigeons. I shook my head no. *What was he doing encouraging these pesky birds with our food?* The pigeons swarmed us, with one even landing on Eddie's head. I laughed; it was quite comical. Once the sandwich was gone, so too were the pigeons.

For hours we sat on the bench. We watched a mother, pushing a double stroller, stride past us; children playing soccer; people in business attire, coffee in hand, strutted along the sidewalk. A soccer ball bounced off Eddie's head; he laughed. I would have been outraged, but Eddie acted as if it was some special blessing bestowed upon him. All humanity seemed impervious to our presence, except for a police officer, who approached late in the afternoon.

"You two can't loiter here all day," he said. "Go on now, get moving."

Eddie led; I followed along a stone path. It curved down and around the river. Eddie knew where he was going and led me down into a cavern. It was his home.

Inside the darkness was a sleeping bag, a tin can, and a few other odds and ends. This was where he slept. Eddie then took my elbow and led me on another trip to another church. That evening we had spaghetti, with broken noodles, green beans, peaches, and brownies. Lucy and Dudley were our guests.

No church basement stays anymore. Word must have gotten out because the bathrooms were locked. Back to the cave. The sleeping bag was for me, Eddie insisted. He used his coat to cover himself as he slept on the dirt ground. Sleep evaded me, but not insects. It was November, but all night whizzing flies hovered over my face, while the crawling creatures moved in and out of my sleeping bag. Several times I jumped up and shook them out. Eddie snored peacefully.

In the morning he checked his tin can. He held it up over his head and shook. Empty. Another excursion. Where this time?

We approached a well-manicured neighborhood. Self-consciously I looked around. He and I walked past an opened gate, along a tree-lined driveway to reach a white Georgian style mansion. I leaned against one of the columns as he rang the doorbell. A maid, wearing a burgundy smock top and black pants, opened the door and smiled. She disappeared for a moment and returned with a pad of paper and pencil. She began to scribble.

"Garden out back needs to be prepped for winter."

Eddie nodded, and pointed at me.

The maid began to write. "I can hear and talk. Is there work for me?" I said as quickly for I wouldn't be able to read whatever she had written.

Is there work for me seemed so humbling, so groveling.

"Have you ever cleaned silver?"

"Yeah, I did that at the department store."

She gave a start at my comment. "Oh? What department store?"

Quick, Catharine, think. Change the subject. Don't bring up where you used to work when you were alive!

"It was so long ago, I don't remember."

She led me into a dining room, eyeing me curiously. Inside the looming chamber, a long table bedecked with chairs fringing its edges awaited guests. A tablepad over the dark wood looked like bandages. The woman spread newspapers over the white pad. "We don't want anything getting on this table. The owners bought it in Italy. Cost them over thirty-thousand dollars!"

Soon, candlesticks, coffee and tea servers, trays, a gravy boat, ice bucket, and flatware surrounded me. Then she brought out cleaning polish and rags. The silver looked clean to me, but if they were willing to pay me, I would polish it. I hummed as I worked and I was cleaning for about two hours when the owner of house, Mrs. Gaitley, appeared.

"My, you're so young and beautiful. How come you're with Eddie?"

"He needs a helper," I said. *What other prying questions will she ask?*

"Eddie can take pretty good care of himself." She pulled out one of the dining room chairs and sat down. She apprised me from head to foot. What was she thinking? "My name is Mrs. Gaitley, Honoria Gaitley. What is yours?"

"Catharine Zimmer," I said as I continued polishing.

"What a beautiful name. How do you spell Catharine?"

"The usual way," though I had no idea what to tell her.

"With a C or a K?"

What did my teacher say the other week? Didn't it start with a 'k'? The elusive memory refused to surface. "Does it matter?" I gruffly asked.

"Can you read?" Her manner was so gentle, yet I responded as if she prodded me with a cattle prong.

"What is it to you?"

She smiled so kindly that she had reminded me of my mother, whom the pangs of being separated called up tears to my eyes. I had wanted to befriend her, but my pride stood in the way. All my life I had wanted people to think of me as having money, status, and even control of my life. In this realm I was just an illiterate, homeless woman.

"Do you think your life has less value than mine?" Honoria asked. "Sure, we have a beautiful house, but I am no better than you, Catharine. If you'd like, you can return, and I'll teach you how to read."

"Do you think he gets lonely?" I asked, trying to divert her focus from me to Eddie.

"I never thought of that. I suppose he does. They told me at the homeless shelter that he had a rough life. What about you? What's your story?" Mrs. Gaitley wiped her brow and then picked up a piece of silver and a cloth. She began scrubbing away at the clean creamer dish.

Was she asking about my life before death or after?

"Not much to tell, I guess." What could I make up?

"I'm sorry for prying. Perhaps it's difficult. My husband and I were near homeless." She set down the creamer and then picked up the sugar bowl. "We had just borrowed money from the bank to start our business, when the stock market collapsed. Henry and I took any odd jobs we could to help pay back the loan. Back then it was $1,000, but it felt like a million."

She held up the clean pieces for my approval. I nodded, and she continued with the coffee pot.

"My husband invented a little tool that became very important in the automotive industry. We became millionaires almost overnight, but we never forgot our beginnings." She set down her work, then picked up one of the spoons I had just cleaned. "You're very good at this, like a professional."

"I used to clean silver," was all I answered.

"We have offered to let Eddie stay with us, but he won't. Instead he comes about once a month and works with the gardener. When it gets cold, he agrees to sleep in the shed out back. Henry had heat and a bathroom installed. Eddie refuses to stay there until it gets very cold."

Great, I'll freeze with even the slightest chill in the air. Mrs. Gaitley stood up. "My offer is good. You can come next week, perhaps Tuesday?"

"I will check with Eddie," was all I said.

"God bless you," she said. It was as if we were parting forever the pain cut to my heart. She didn't have to tell me her story, but it seemed as if she wanted to show me she had empathy for me. Yet, how could this woman living in such lavish surroundings understand the plight of a homeless person? True, she and her husband almost became homeless, but they didn't, and soon reaped millions of dollars.

"Thank you," I said.

The maid counted every piece of silver before handing me a folded wad of cash. I met Eddie outside, and we opened up the money. Both of us were paid one-hundred dollars apiece. Steak, shrimp, wine. That is what I wanted to buy with my money, though why I wanted to waste money on tasteless food and beverages seemed foolish. I also craved a little makeup and outfits that were more stylish. Eddie shook his head. I followed him as he trudged to the homeless shelter. Tony answered the door. Eddie handed Tony the $200. Then he pushed me inside the building.

"Eddie wants to pay for your lodging," Tony said after reading Eddie's sign. "He thinks he can give us money so you can stay here."

"I'm going to stay with Eddie," I answered. Tony signed again. Eddie shook his head, and pushed out his arms as if he was pushing me away.

"Eddie says the street is no place for you. He doesn't want your pity."

"Tell him I don't pity him. I want to be his friend."

"He is happy for your friendship, but he wants to be alone."

For ten minutes I pleaded, then finally gave up. "Tell him I'll visit him tomorrow."

Eddie signed, "Thank you. I would like that." We hugged, and that sensation of being separated for life resurfaced. My heart skipped a beat. There were tears in our eyes.

That night was worse than the bug cave. What was Eddie hiding? Why didn't he want me along? What did I do to offend him? Why did Catharine Zimmer care what Eddie, the homeless man, thought? On my cot I met with tossing and turning, sweating, chills, more tossing, more turning. The pillow was too soft. It was too hard. I couldn't adjust it correctly under my neck. My pajamas were too big and wrapped themselves around me.

At four-fifty-three I decided sleep had forgotten about me. I scrambled out of my cot and left the homeless shelter. Dawn hadn't peaked over the horizon yet, but I remembered the cave's location. As I neared, something felt different, wrong. I listened, but only heard the chirping of the early morning birds.

I crept down the embankment and entered. Eddie's cave had become his tomb. I touched his body. Rigor mortis had arrived and settled in. I'm not sure how Eddie came into the world, but he departed alone.

"What have you learned, Catharine?" my angel asked, suddenly appeared.

"Homeless is where you live, but homeless can never define a person."

"Anything else?"

Eddie didn't need Catharine Zimmer to fix his life, he only needed her attention. Not the kind that takes over the other person, but a glance, a smile, a friendly nod. Perhaps I had avoided him and others like him because I knew I couldn't set him, like a trinket on a shelf, in a perfect home setting.

Was my life more significant than Eddie's because I had a job and house? Was there greater meaning to my thoughts and actions than those of Eddie?

There were many people in my life I had wanted to befriend me, but I was beneath their social strata. They knew nothing of who Catharine Zimmer was. In my mind I fantasized about how they would finally recognize my importance and seek out my wisdom. Never happened. I was their invisible speck right in front of their faces, but unseen. Eddie had been my visible, but rarely noticed, speck.

The dream finally made sense. So much insignificance in my life, like the tater-tot casserole, prevented me from discovering those around me. The ship sailed away. Real people, like Eddie, were on that ship. Nevertheless, the phonies, the social climbers, like me, remained ashore, watching, waiting. It's a hard lesson to learn, even when you're dead, to discover you were a snob. All the magnanimous imaginings wandering through my mind - I was going to solve all the world's problems - was just a farce. I would deny no one my kindness, but, I had.

CHAPTER 16

My revenant passed through cathedral walls. Inside the massive structure the cool dampness threatened to turn my specter into mold. I shivered and watched florists cart in rose topiaries, tulle encased candelabras, and cartons of bouquets and boutonnieres.

Was that Claire? She directed the florist and Christina as they draped tulle along the edges of the pews. Patrick and Tom, dressed in tuxedoes, dragged a table toward the front entrance. John set a package on top. Father Dominic, from St. Anne's parish where I grew up, was flipping through his lectionary in the sanctuary.

So much flurry of activity in anticipation of a joyous occasion, yet why did regret press upon my soul?

Within moments hundreds of people filed in. A cello's vibrato of Bach's *Arioso*, like a television remote control, set the players in motion. It was Patrick pushing the bow back and forth. Ribbons of the melody fluttered as Christina arm and arm with a man I didn't recognize, ambled down the aisle. Claire and another man followed, with John and his new bride, Melody, behind them. Another couple followed. My mother stood in the left front pew, and a woman, with bleached, over-teased hair, stood alone in the right front pew. For a moment the actors in this drama paused. The arioso began to crescendo, then stopped. Where was I? Why wasn't I invited?

Then Adrien appeared at the front center. He dabbed his eyes with a white handkerchief. I smiled at his endearing image, until it dawned on me that I was at the wedding that never was. The chair was taken from under me. I fell!

The congregation stood up and turned to face the back, staring with hushed anticipation. There, I, Catharine Zimmer, glowing from the windows behind me, stood an ethereal statue, waiting. My gown was pure silk, with a square bodice and capped sleeves. The full skirt began at a dropped V waist. The translucent blusher revealed my unruly auburn hair trying to escape the chignon. Next to me was my father, all smiles. Tom and his son rolled out the white aisle runner.

A trumpet blast, and then the organ played *Trumpet Voluntary*. Dad hooked his arm into mine, and we began the descent down the aisle.

Left at the altar, yet I was the one who didn't show up. While living I had adjusted successfully, I believed, to being single. As the years passed, I even relished sharing my life and home with no one else. I could eat what I wanted, come and go as I wished, travel or not travel, volunteer at church or not. All of my life's decisions revolved around me. After my parents died, the holidays became more difficult, though Claire often invited me, the lonely aunt, to her family gatherings. Her family was delightful, so I looked forward to spending time with them. What more did I need?

It took dying for me to realize what had been missing in my life. I reached to caress Adrien's face, but halted, afraid of what emotions his smooth face might elicit. Then someone took my ghostly hand into his warm grasp. Adrien!

"Let us share this sorrow together," he said, tears coursing down his phantom face.

The ghostly Adrien and Catharine watched as the earthly couple exchanged vows and rings, and the kiss. We rushed down the aisle and out of the church into a chauffeured champagne-hued Rolls Royce Phantom. Pictures at a garden, then to the country club. Toasts, cheers, clinking wine glasses, dancing, bouquet toss, smiling faces.

"I can't believe there wouldn't have been a fist fight!" Adrien interrupted. "All good weddings have some drama in them."

I shook my head, and we continued watching. Honeymoon, then fast-forward to the birth of our first child, that beautiful babe of my dreams that I had met during my judgement.

"What do you think his name would have been?" Adrien asked. "Jacob would have been a good name."

"Jacob?" I laughed through the tears. "I had thought Alexander."

"Alexander Adrien Inveres. Nice ring to it," he said, which released more anguish and tears in both of us. Images, spun quickly before us, like old silent movie reels.

"Hentges House. Look, it would have been our home. There's my mother. She is living with us."

Crystal, the woman with the bleached, over-teased hair, kissed our baby, and rocked him back and forth. More tears of regret rushed to my eyes.

Adrien on the floor playing with Alexander as a toddler, sucking in his cheeks in imitation of a fish. Catharine bathing the baby. More children, more chaos, more happiness. Christmas, Easter, Thanksgiving, summer picnics and parades - the holidays marked by crowds of family, friends, and a nun.

"Amber!" Adrien exclaimed. "Look at her crawling on the floor with her habit on."

Trips, ceremonies, daily existence, the life of Catharine and Adrien Inveres spun forward in a surreal dreamlike fashion. So much life, but only of what life should have been.

Then a sullen young man appeared a carbon copy of Adrien - Geoff, Adrien's illegitimate child from an earlier liaison that I had learned about when Adrien told his story. Catharine and Adrien at the kitchen table in a serious discussion. A room was made for Geoff, and he joined the family, transforming him into a confident man. His wedding, and the weddings of his half siblings, our children, followed.

The moments of sorrow came, but in those times, Adrien and I found comfort in each other. Full-fledged shouting matches, too, often at the kitchen table. The death of family and friends. Broken movie deals, broken book contracts, rebellious teens, illness, and finally, old age.

Gray and wrinkled Catharine sat on an armchair next to a king-sized bed, leaning forward, her face only inches away from Adrien, who shared the same fate of aging as Catharine. They clasped hands together, hers stronger than the weakened Adrien's. She was bidding him good-bye. She kissed his forehead, and he expired.

"I died first, huh?" Adrien always ruining a tender moment.

"I think you died before me anyways, but at a much younger age. Being married to me would have preserved you a little longer."

"I didn't really die of cirrhosis then, but of a broken heart?"

Scientists have discovered a physical reaction to broken hearts – a rush of adrenaline weakens the heart muscles. How could I have answered that but through tears?

"I'm sorry, I shouldn't have said that."

"No, Adrien, I'm so, so sorry."

"Catharine, don't apologize. We share this burden together. How did I know? How did you know if I would have even been interested in a writer, especially a redhead? I always went for blond actresses. Just because Giant-Boy said so, how would he have known? I am sure there would be no way prim and proper Catharine Zimmer would have anything to do with me."

I smiled; stubbornness flowed through Adrien like sap through a tree.

My angel appeared along with another angel.

"It is time for you both to part," she said.

"I'm not ready," Adrien said. "Can't we have another hundred years or so together before we have to part?"

"Nope," my angel said. "You'll have an eternity once you're finished. This journey isn't about fun and games."

"Tell me about it," Adrien said. He turned to me. "Catharine, I lied. I fell in love with you the moment I met you up there. I know I would have fallen for you on earth. Can you believe that?"

"No," I smiled. "I know I didn't feel any love for you at our meeting."

"Who would?" he asked. He wiped the tear off my cheek. He kissed my forehead. "Man, this is harder than I had expected."

"You promised you wouldn't give me any trouble if I let you do this," said the other angel.

"Do I really have a choice in the matter?" Adrien asked.

"Nope," my angel answered. "Catharine, say good-bye."

CHAPTER 17

Did I know Shannon Lamb? I asked myself, looking down at her gravestone. Death snatched her at thirty-seven. "Loving Daughter and Mother." The words rested next to an image of her face etched into the stone. Smiling, long curly hair, probably brown, though I couldn't tell. It was a warm face. It was a familiar face.

Sunny's. Shannon waited on me every Thursday morning.

"Hey, honey," she'd say, pouring steaming java into my mug. Sunny's had the best coffee in town. It was a superior blend they didn't let sit for more than twenty-minutes. Fresh and dark.

I inhaled the aroma and sipped before speaking. "Hi, Shannon. What happened to your eye?"

"Ah, bumped it on the door. Damn clumsy. Shroom om-let?"

"Yep. Good memory!" *Another bruise? How can she recall what I order after bumping her head so often?*

She pulled out a wisp of hair from her ponytail to cover her eye. "You order it every week, honey. Rye with no butter?"

"Wheat." I took another sip. "Did you put an ice pack on it?"

"Sure. It's Benny who's the rye guy. Rye guy! Hey! Me a poet!"

She began walking away when I asked, "How are the kids?"

With her back to me she answered, "Ah great. Both doin' real good in school. So, you found yourself a man yet?"

"I'm getting too old for that."

"Well, they ain't always what they're cracked up to be, that's for sure." She rushed back into the kitchen to place the order.

Variations in the conversation might have included speculations on the weather, holiday shopping, or our parents. That's it. Once the omelet was delivered, she'd stomp from table to table, place the check discreetly under my plate, and walk away. I'd pay and forget about Shannon Lamb, and her many bruises until the following week.

Thursday mornings at Sunny's began as manager meetings with our then store manager Audrey Brown. All the department heads would enjoy the breakfast on the store's account as we discussed upcoming sales, merchandizing, or problem employees. Once Audrey moved on, the breakfasts ended, but I had grown so used to the weekly ritual, I had kept it up for years later. Changes were common at Sunny's

- new cook, new furniture, and new owners. The only permanent fixture in the establishment was Shannon.

Breakfast deteriorated with the new and improved breakfast menu, thus when The Breakfast Cup opened, I dumped Sunny's. Shannon Lamb was no more. Occasionally I wondered how she was doing, especially on Thursdays with the myriad of incompetent wait staff at the other restaurant. I remember being so outraged at The Breakfast Cup that I had decided to go back to Sunny's. When I arrived, a different woman took my order.

"Where's Shannon?" I asked.

The woman standing at my table reminded me of the black and white optical illusion that could be seen as an old woman or a young woman. The waitress's looks favored the hag with her long, wide chin, slit of a mouth, and black hair clumped to the front of her head. "Shannon's been gone for a while," the woman said, pushing back her silver-framed glasses.

"Did she get a different job? Oh, I hope so!" Then I ordered forgetting Shannon while hoping my breakfast would be served correctly.

As I looked at the headstone again, snow fell from the gray pregnant clouds, the icy flakes drilling into my skin. Across the cemetery, a black limo followed by a long line of cars, pulled next to a chapel. People exited their cars, slamming their doors. The snow, however, muffled the sounds.

"Shannon Lamb was murdered by her husband," I jumped at the angel's sudden appearance.

Here it goes again, the blame game. "What did I do this time?"

"You're catching on."

"Was it an article I failed to write? Did I entice her husband to murder her? What?"

In answer, she waved her arms turning on an invisible television, where I became the star of my own show. I pressed the keypad on a phone and put it to my ear.

"Immaculatta? This is Catharine Zimmer. I'm fine. There's this waitress I see every Thursday. I think she might be getting beaten up by her husband. She always has bruises on her face. You have information I can pass along to her? Great. I'll pick it up tomorrow."

I hung up the phone, sauntered into the living room, and plopped down on the lazy chair. The scene faded into Immaculatta's office, where the brochures and informational packet sat. In the background, the seasons changed outside the window. Rainy spring, sunny summer, and windy autumn.

Snow was falling in Immaculatta's window when she finally put the brochures back into their respective file folders.

"Never made the time to pick those up, did you?"

C. L. Paur

I squirmed not from the cold, but from the guilt with edges that had sharpened with the passing of each year. "I forgot."

"Right back to your television. No notes, no reminders. You made the call. It was off your conscience." She was dropping gram cubes onto a balance. She dropped the last cube, and the balance sank.

With the ping of the scale, I was transported to the inside of a house decorated with strong manly accents. The head of a buck hung on one side of a long window, and the head of a black bear on the other side. Both lifeless creatures' eyes warned me to escape or suffer their demise. The chandelier dangling above the leather ottoman was comprised of antlers. Dark paneling covered the walls, but hid behind the massive, stone fireplace, which roared with flames. An eggshell-colored sectional nestled all its pieces together to face a large television. Cozy throw pillows in contrasting colors rested on the sofa. Comfort and wealth tried to speak over the din of the evil lair, but they were drowned out.

A stretching bungee cord squeak directed my attention to the front door. In walked my enemy wearing a worsted wool dark suit, set off with a crisp white shirt underneath. His straw-colored hair was stylishly cut with longer locks in the front combed neatly to one side. Shadow of whiskers hung below his lips and chin. There was nothing about his appearance that looked threatening. He was that bottle of poison little children mistook for soda pop.

"Whatta doing?" He asked.

"Thinking," I said.

Slowly, like a hunter creeping up to its prey, he moved toward me. "Why you look so guilty?"

"Guilty?" I backed away into the ottoman, falling onto it. I looked up as he neared, his countenance convulsing.

"Yeah, guilty. Where is he? Where ya hiding him? I knew I'd catch you if I got home early." He stormed out, and his footsteps crashed through the rooms downstairs and then he mounted the stairs to check the bedrooms. Then silence. I panted knowing what awaited me, but terror glued me to the chair. Slowly he descended, each rung mounting more horror in my soul. *Why can't I move?* Then he appeared, his weapon in hand. I crossed my arms over my face, but they did nothing to ward off the smash of the metal bar. Like a carpenter banging a hammer, he pummeled my face, arms, legs, and torso. Crack, my ribs splintered inside me.

"Stop," I cried. I fell to my knees.

"You whore," he screamed. "I'm taking you in to be check for VD! I ain't sleeping with a whore!"

"I haven't slept with anyone!" I whimpered.

"You lyin' cunt!"

128

Oh, those words hurt almost more than the beating. I was like a mongrel, ready to sink my teeth into anyone who came near. He kicked my body, and it rolled over, like a barrel. I remained there, motionless, panting, waiting for the next blow. He left. Sleep consumed me.

I awoke to rocking back and forth. He cradled me in his arms. My brain recoiled, my body acquiesced. Confusion roared. I despised him, yet wanted to forgive and forget what had just happened.

"Baby, baby. I'm so sorry. I had a bad day at work. Ain't no reason to take it out on you. You're just so beautiful. I can't stand to think of anyone else touching you."

Thirty-seven times I relived this torture. Planted in the middle of the living room I stood, he'd stalk in and beat me. I'd fall asleep and awake to his cradling and apologizing.

"Angel," I said as I stood waiting for my thirty-eighth beating. "Angel, why? Can't you make this stop?"

"You must make it stop."

Make it stop? How? I scrambled through the house, opening closets, cupboards, desk-drawers looking for a gun. When he walked through that door, I would put a bullet through his heart. There was nothing in this house, but furniture and appliances. I even looked inside the refrigerator. An expired gallon of milk offered its limited abilities as a weapon. I figured a gun would not be an option. Instantly my body was placed back in the middle of the living room. The door opened. I looked up, and the terrible ritual began.

The vase. I grabbed the vase.

"What ya doing?"

"Cleaning," I lifted the porcelain higher.

"Why ya hold 'in it like that?"

"Don't come near me!"

He ignored me, his footsteps menacing.

The heavy ceramic vase shattered upon contact. His body slumped onto the bear rug. I searched in his pants pockets and found his pickup keys. I had never driven a standard transmission, but I pushed in the clutch, and released at all the right times. My eyes scanned the rearview mirror, searching for some vehicle that might follow me. Where is the police station? I wondered.

In front of a gas station, I pulled up. I ran inside and patiently waited until the clerk checked out the three customers before me. An elderly man, using a walker, tottered up behind me.

"You look like you're in a bit of trouble, ma'am, if you don't mind me say'n," he said.

"I need the police station," I turned toward him.

"Should we call them here?"

"Nope, just get me the directions!"

The clerk stopped ringing, and the customers turned toward me. One of them spoke, "I can drive you there miss!"

Angel spoke in my ear, "Complete strangers, all willing to come to your aid. Wish you had learned from them."

In front of me stood a beacon - the police station. I parked the pickup truck and ran inside.

"Help," I leaned into the dispatcher's window. She was knitting, but dropped her needles when she saw my face.

"What the hell happen to you?"

"My husband's been beating on me."

She leaned around her desk and shouted, "Donald, come here, you need to take down a report." She turned back to me. "My name is Renee, honey. Donald will take good care of you, then we're gonna take you to the hospital."

Donald asked all the questions, and then drove over to the house. A woman police officer, Dorothy, drove me to the hospital.

"It's gonna be alright," she said. "Once the doctor checks you over, we're going to Bethany's."

"I don't really need a doctor," I said. "I'm fine."

"Just a little check-up. We do it for all our domestic cases."

Bethanys, that home for beaten women and children with the mysterious address. I donated some old sheets to it once. I had to drop them off at the police station because the address was a secret. Now I was going there as a client. More like victimized animal than client. Client sounded too neat, too in control of the situation.

"My ex beat the hell out of me," Dorothy said. "We're going to get you all better and back on your feet. But you gotta to be strong. You gotta press charges, throw the bastard in jail, and get some counseling. Ain't no goin back no more. I assumin' you ain't got any kiddies?"

"I could never leave them in the house," I replied in horror at the thought. What happened to Shannon's kids? I wondered.

"Do ya have any schoolin'?"

"Not much."

"Whatta ya think ya might wanna do?"

"Right now, just get some sleep."

"Yeah, sorry for rushing you. I just wanna make sure you don't change your mind and go back to him. You might find yourself gettin' killed."

We stopped in front of a two-story, brick building. In the 1900s, it had been Hardts' Grocer and Liquor Store but it had closed in the 70s when bigger and better grocery stores opened. It occupied most of the block. While alive I had driven past it often wondering why no one bothered buying it or razing it for a new building.

Because it was the best hiding space in town.

Dorothy took my elbow and gently led me to the front door. She tapped three times and then pressed the doorbell two times.

"Secret code. Every day it's different."

A plump woman looked out before fully opening the door. Feeling safe, she let the door swing completely opened, and we stepped in. She wore a brown sweater that extended below her thighs, tan leggings, and brown knee-high boots. At her neck, hung a wildly patterned scarf that reminded me of Africa. Though I guessed her age to be somewhere in the sixties, her smooth complexion and soft brown hair lessened the effects of age.

"I'm the house mother here," she said. "My name is Juliana." She looked at me, all bandaged and broken. "I give free hugs, but only if you want one."

We wrapped our arms around each other. She reminded me of Robbie, my stuffed reindeer I had as a child. He was so round and soft. I squeezed him whenever I felt afraid. She was like that, but only smelled better, like the honeysuckle bush in our front yard. Though soft, the hug had the effect of a bracing cup of coffee. I felt renewed at that moment.

"Let me take you to your room," she said, taking my hand.

Dorothy and I hugged and said our good-byes. "Thank you, Dorothy."

"It's my job. Take care and be strong."

Juliana led me to what appeared like the inside of an Arabian tent with blankets and royal colored pillows strewn upon a double bed, and rugs scattered all over the floor. Purple and pink silk curtains concealing the metal bars on the windows. On each side of the bed were matching lamps with camels painted on the lampshades.

"I hope you like it," Julianna said. "If you feel it's too much, we have a simpler room."

I gazed and slowly turned to absorb each of the images painted on the walls, a genie lamp, a star within the arms of the crescent moon, a flying carpet, and intricate floral designs painted on the wall reminiscent of Queen Mumtaz Mahal's tomb. Above the bed was a picture of the long deceased empress of the Mughal Empire. I had visited the tomb while alive, its marble beauty leaving me speechless. My bruised spirit wondered about the intentions of the Shah Jahan. Did he really love her, or was the tomb just a way to salvage his conscience? I was about to tell her I wanted a different room when she spoke up.

"Asiyah, one of our clients, decorated the room after she left. It was her way of saying thank you. Asiyah is still saying thank you! She brings us all sorts of wonderful gifts. Some I like to eat," the woman said, patting her stomach.

"The room is gorgeous; I'll stay," I said, changing my mind. A native daughter would know, wouldn't she?

As a young girl, I had begged my mother to read the tales of One Thousand and One Nights. It was the cunning Scheherazade who managed to save her life with these tales. Sitting in the room and battered, I despised the emperor for killing all his wives.

"Scheherazade managed to stay alive with her stories," the angel appeared, lounging on an overstuffed, round chaise chair. "Perhaps if death were facing you every day, you would have written your books."

"Very funny. I want to be alone."

"This isn't about hating men."

"I don't understand."

"Rage. You're feeling rage toward all men. Not all men are monsters. In fact, some women beat on their husbands, though not as often."

"Why do they do it?"

"Evil has no answers."

"Great way to evade a question." I grew thoughtful, but wrath simmered. "Why did I have to go through the beatings thirty-seven times? How horrible!"

My angel also grew thoughtful and said nothing for a long time. Finally she spoke, "Shannon was beaten thirty-seven times and died on the thirty-eighth try,"

"Why did she keep going back to him?"

My angel stood up from the chair and neared me. "Sickness. She needed more than medical treatment. Something inside her wasn't right."

"Did her parents beat her?"

My angel shook her head. "Nope. Fortunately they had the children when the terrible deed was done."

"What happened to the guy? What was his name?"

"His name is not important, and you're not to know everything about everyone on this journey."

"Journey," I scoffed. "Cruelty. Where is the mercy I expected?"

"Where was your mercy while on earth?"

Bethany Home boarded me for six months. It was humbling to have to take classes on nutrition and finance, since in life I had managed my health and home very well.

"Why do I need these classes?" I groused to the angel one day.

"Why not?" she responded. "Are you better and wiser than these women?"

"I ran my own house very well."

"As did many of these women. Listen, Catharine, listen to their stories."

Laura was a successful interior designer, Rochelle a lawyer, Martha, a stay-at-home mother, who volunteered at her church. There was also Stephen, who was a car salesman. He slept in different quarters, but attended all our classes. Flesh and blood covered the bare statistics.

Every morning at seven o'clock, Juliana left on a short trip. The weather never deterred her. Some of us discussed it, and I decided to question her about it one day.

Her face grew wistful before answering. "Why don't you join me tomorrow? It's not really a secret, but the pain is too much for me to bear."

We drove for twenty minutes. Julianna drove into a cemetery and up to the familiar headstone.

Shannon Lamb: 1954-1991. She died the year I was promoted to store manager. I celebrated by traveling to Asia. At Christmas the store awarded me a nice bonus. I bought new furniture, had my floors redone, and renovated my downstairs' bathroom. I had enough money left to purchase a new Christmas outfit. Catharine Zimmer, academy award winner of her own life!

Julianna faded away only to be replaced by my angel.

"No one begrudges your successes, Catharine," the angel placed an orchid on top of the stone.

I dropped my head in shame. "I had left her stranded, alone on the highway. No directions, no assistance, just alone."

"Her husband killed her, not you."

"I was busy climbing the ladder of success, while she struggled to stay alive." I brushed snow off the stone and saw her smiling face. "I never followed through." The sting of watching Immaculatta return the brochures back into their folders returned. They were there, waiting, but I had never taken the time to collect them to pass along to Shannon. Good intentions never fulfilled are sometimes worse than bad intentions. There had been moments when I remembered those packets of paper, but brushed the memory aside for another time. I had been too tired from work or didn't want to pay the downtown parking meter. I didn't even bother to call Immaculatta back to have her mail them to me.

"This journey was not so much about accusing you, Catharine, for your apathy, but to teach you empathy. Reading about it is never the same as living it."

"But I had failed to pick up the baton, and it was Shannon that had lost the race."

She placed her hand on my shoulder. "You're learning, Catharine."

"How much more of this must I endure?"

"More awaits. There is still much you don't understand."

CHAPTER 18

For most, this next narrative may be difficult to grasp. It was for me. As a young girl, I checked out at my school library the biography of Helen Keller, at least fifty times. Young Catharine Zimmer was fascinated by the spoilt, Neanderthal-type personality tamed by Anne Sullivan. At this moment of my death's journey, however, all fascination for the blind and deaf woman ceased as I entered what must have been a sound-proof and sight-proof booth.

I dared not move lest I crash or topple over something, or worse, fall over a cliff. It didn't matter how many times I told myself I was dead. The Grim Reaper still held his grip of terror over me.

A strong hand grasped mine. *At least I have the sense of touch.* I sniffed, nothing, it coincided with the blackness around me. The hand led me. I followed. The hand gently pressed my shoulders down. Would I fall onto the ground? A soft chair received my body. For a long time nothing happened. I sat. I sat. I sat.

Would I spend the next four hundred years like this? Panic swelled up inside, my heart pounding. I wanted to spring forward and abscond from this madness. Pushing my arms against the chair arms, I stood up, slowly. My right foot extended, then my left. Cautiously, with my arms outstretch, I proceeded. Where? I do not know. As I gained confidence, my steps quickened.

Bam! My right shin crashed into what felt like a brick. Why wasn't there a layer or two of fat around the shin? I bent to rub away the throbbing, yet only succeeded in cracking my head onto something. Where was that chair when I needed it?

I dropped to my hands and knees and ambulated, dog style, touching everything around me to figure out where I was. Some creature with hundreds of legs crawled over my left hand. I scrambled to my feet, stomping, stomping, stomping, and hoping to kill whatever borrowed my hand as a bridge. With my right hand I brushed my left one to erase that crawling sensation.

Another hand touched me. It was different, smaller, and more feminine. Was it my angel? I couldn't tell, but I tried to speak.

"Get me out of here!" I shouted, but the sound waves did not reach my eardrums. The feminine hands also led me to a rigid chair, sans armrests. Panic enveloped me. I bolted once more and tried walking away. Crash! A wall halted my progress. The feminine hands again let me back to the chair. She pressed an eating utensil into my left hand. My right hand felt the fork tines, sharp and prickly. She then took my left hand and led it to a plate. The rim felt cool, as if it were metal. She guided my fork to scoop up the food and steered it to my mouth.

I spat out what I felt were worms squirming around my palate. Neutered taste buds, like my neutered sense of sight, sound, and smell, provided no clues as to what I was eating. The hands guided my fork again. This time, when my teeth clamped down, it felt like blood bursting over my gustation factory. Again, I spit out the offender.

The experience generated a long forgotten memory. It was my Halloween party. Mom and I filled three bowls with zombie intestines, werewolf eyeballs, and vampire brains. Of course they were only spaghetti noodles, grapes, and gelatin. The unsuspecting party guests had to insert their hands, blindfolded, into each bowl. It was gross, and we loved it. At this moment, however, I was not loving it.

I crossed my arms unwilling to eat any more. The hand pried them apart and opened my left hand, grabbing my forefinger. Repeatedly it guided the finger over a hard surface. What was she doing? After about ten minutes, I discerned that she was spelling words. C, I made out a C. A, came next. She was spelling Catharine. Then she wrote EAT THE FOOD.

I wrote back, NO, IT'S GROSS.

THAT IS PART OF YOUR MISSION, she fingered.

IT WON'T TASTE GOOD ANYWAY, I replied. Back and forth, painstakingly we argued. Finally I wrote, WHERE AM I AND WHY AM I HERE?

YOU HAVE TAKEN MUCH FOR GRANTED.

HOW LONG?

AS LONG AS IT TAKES.

I GET IT. I REALLY DO. I'M SORRY. NOW CAN I GET BACK TO NORMAL?

WHAT IS NORMAL, CATHARINE?

She really didn't need to spell out my name since it added another three minutes to the fingered conversation.

My angel dropped my hand. Obstinacy forced my arms to cross again. As I stewed, images of my past, long forgotten, flowed through my consciousness. I stood behind the cash register as I watched Wolfgang Holleder, stick in hand, head in the air, ascend to my floor.

"Wolfgang, Wolfgang, what do you want today?" I asked as I watched him swing the stick side to side, guiding him ever closer to my register. We were having our semi-annual sale, and the customer line was ten people deep. *Why are you here today, Wolfgang? Can't you see I'm busy?* Of course he couldn't see, but his presence elevated my irritation. Customers had complained all day, and Wolfgang would only add to my miseries.

"You forgot to give me the extra ten percent," a woman, with gray roots seeping through her dyed red hair, complained as she looked at her receipt. I grabbed it, and pointed out the discount.

"It's right here." Impatience simmered under my calm voice.

One by one, I rang, bagged, and bid, "Good-bye," while Wolfgang clicked his stick, back and forth, waiting. Finally, he was in the front of the row.

I NEED SHEETS. He typed on his Screen Braille Communicator.

You need a shower.

WHAT SIZE? I typed back.

TWIN.

I gently led him to the bedding area, leaving the rest of the customers waiting. For a long time it seemed, he fingered and touched each sheet set as if they were silk.

I WANT THESE.

THEY COST $75.

ARE THEY ON SALE?

THAT IS THEIR SALE PRICE.

ANY CHEAPER SHEETS?

I guided him to the less expensive bedding. He wasn't happy. He wanted the $75 sheet set. His crumpled gray jacket and greasy hair told me he probably couldn't even afford our less expensive sheet sets. Wolfgang continued to guide himself back to the $75 sheets. I looked back at my register; the line expanded like foam insulation. Diane, our new store manager, walked past.

"Catharine, do you need some help?"

"Wolfgang is here and he wants the $75 sheet set, but can't afford them."

"Find out how much money he has," Diane went to my register and began ringing up the customers.

HOW MUCH MONEY DO YOU HAVE?

Wolfgang pulled out a wad of crumpled ones and searched for my hands. I took the wad, sorted, and counted $17.43. Not even enough for our promo set at twenty-five.

WAIT HERE, I typed.

I set the money onto the counter as Diane rang the customers.

"Give him the sheets he wants, and I'll cover the rest," she said.

After ringing him up, I thought we were finished.

LET ME TOUCH THE SILVER.

"Diane, he needs more help," I moaned, as she continued to ring up the customers.

"Just help him," she said. "Don't worry; I'll stay as long as you need me."

As in the past, I took down candlesticks, coffee sets, trays, salt and peppershakers, frames, and other silver trinkets. Wolfgang would take the items and touch them to his right cheek then his left, then onto his neck. Some of the items were too big, so I had to press those items onto his face. The customers watched with odd curiosity. This continued for about forty minutes. Diane said nothing, just rang up customers.

WATERFORD CRYSTAL, he typed.

I led him to our crystal shelves. Lovingly he fingered each facet on each goblet, on each vase, on each candlestick. Why today?

WOLFGANG, I HAVE TO HELP OTHER CUSTOMERS, I typed.

THANK YOU FOR GIVING ME THIS JOY. He communicated differently than others. His phrases were odd, but still nice.

THAT IS WHAT I AM HERE FOR, I typed, feeling very proud of myself.

I AM AN ARTIST, a phrase he typed every time he came to our store.

YES, I KNOW, I replied politely, yet knew in my heart of hearts this poor man had all he could do to just survive, let alone create art.

"Thanks for taking over," I said to Diane as I approached the register. At that moment, the area was free of customers.

"You're very patient," Diane said. "I couldn't do what you do. It's important we take time with him."

"He always tells me he's an artist," I laughed a little.

"Never underestimate anyone, Catharine," Diane said. "That reminds me, have you given any more thought about entering our manager training program?"

"Yes, I have. And I'm very excited to tell you that I'm accepting your offer." A strange sensation washed over me, as if a door had slammed shut.

My angel spoke inside my mind, "You know what that door was."

A forlorn red barn appeared inviting me inside. A menagerie of artwork crammed itself inside the vast space. Wrought-iron sculpted trees, flowers, and birds towered over me. Splashes of colored landscapes and seascapes, portraits and still lifes, on never framed canvases, leaned up against rotting wood. The ethereal museum stood in silence, yet also accusatorial.

"Wolfgang's art. The world has never seen," my angel said, appearing again from out of nowhere.

"Since I felt impatient when he showed up taking up my time I'm to be punished? Isn't this getting scrupulous?"

"You never wrote his story."

Damn, damn, damn. I was caught up in the never-ending wave of my deceit, unable to extricate myself, as if caught in an undertow, pulling me deeper into its murky depths.

"Only his mother beheld some of the world's greatest art."

"Why didn't she do something about it?" I tried shifting the blame.

"She did, but even her friends doubted, so his work remained invisible. If Catharine Zimmer worked at the newspaper, she would have been curious enough to, at the very least, investigate."

IF. That word IF. Minute word, prodigious consequences. Still, I persisted. "It's hard to get editors to agree with your story pitches."

"And that's supposed to allay your guilt?"

I stepped carefully through the sculptures, canvases, lamps, vases, and other lovely objects d'art. "Does the barn still exist?"

"Bulldozed. No one ever looked inside. At least your family found your novels in the back of your closet."

"I suppose they're garbage."

"Nope."

Imagine a priceless gift, a family photo, an heirloom object, lost forever. For the entire world I carried the acute pain of loss for Wolfgang Holleder's priceless, yet missing works. What wall stands empty, what museum holds a bare spot, what hollow fills someone's heart, what inspiration is missing for a child? What ugliness has taken its place?

An eight foot by twelve painting hid behind another, smaller one. I pulled it out. Silver candlesticks, two crystal wine glasses, and a glowing figure of a woman. An odd picture, but I knew instantly the woman was I, the *Woman at the Store*, the title of the piece.

My knees fell on straw while my eyes spilled out tears. I hadn't displayed much emotion in life, but on this journey, my emotions pushed the cry button at almost every juncture. Wolfgang stood next to me, but he was no longer the pauper I had waited on. His eyes were round and blue, fringed with dark lashes. His face was square, yet held the hint of a smile just waiting to surface. His brown hair differed from the long, greasy locks he wore on earth. A black t-shirt revealed a muscular form.

"Don't cry, Catharine. You showed me kindness when so few ever did."

"I didn't feel kind. I did it only because I had to."

"I never sensed it," he replied.

"But all your artwork. It's gone forever."

"On earth, yes," answered my angel. "But here, all beauty is restored."

"I could spend my eternity here," I said.

"Yes, but you must continue on your journey. When you have completed your mission, you may visit the museum as often as you would like. The best part? It's free!" She smiled. "Yet, before you leave, Wolfgang will finish his story."

"My real name was Nyles Boerner. My mother, or should I say, the woman who raised me, gave me her husband's first and last name. She found me, abandoned.

Somehow she convinced the State to let her adopt me rather than put me through the foster system."

As he spoke, we walked through the museum.

"Anne Boerner, everyone called her Anne Sullivan, raised me, taught me, and loved me like a mother should. She knew I had a talent and taught me my colors and shapes. She would give me a green crayon, then she would let me touch anything that was green; grass, leaves, her green walls. Then she would label the colors in a way I could identify. When I dabbed my brush onto a prepared palate, I knew I was painting with green, blue, violet, or any color."

We stopped at a wall filled with portraits,

"Anne would take my hand and run it down her nose or along her cheekbones. That is how I learned faces. For the horizon lines, she'd fold a piece of paper somewhat in half." He pointed to a wall filled with landscapes.

"Anne read to me, took me to museums, to the ocean, even city gardens. I touched anything I could, which is why I would come to your store. The cold silver and crystal, the soft sheets, they were my inspiration. Outside I would finger the bark on trees, climb them, and count the number of branches that led to twigs, and then count the leaves."

I looked at his trees, so perfectly aligned with nature's rendition. The grass on the mountains, the water in the seascapes. These were the images he painted from his mind, more perfectly depicted than any work I had seen painted by an artist with vision.

"My mother died suddenly. I painted for a while then sank into depression. About a year after her death, I died too, alone."

That explained why I had stopped seeing Wolfgang. Shortly after I had sold him the sheets, he stopped coming in. I had forgotten him, like so many people who had come and gone from my life. He was never a three dimensional person, just some flat, cardboard image of a blind and deaf customer who took up my valuable time.

"Wolfgang..."

"You may call me Nyles. I no longer need to be named Wolfgang."

"Nyles, it is. Will you accept my apologies?"

He kissed my hand and forgiveness washed over me. We hugged our goodbyes, and he disappeared.

"Angel, I guess I am ready for more."

"Are you?"

"Do I have any choice in the matter? Why torment me? Just take me to the next punishment."

"Is this what you call it, punishment? Do you feel remorse or just chastisement?"

"Pain."

Little things that I had brushed off as insignificant were sources of misery and anguish for others. It was like a tiny bug bite that festered into some malignant infection. Could I ever atone for the loss?

CHAPTER 19

Why did I find myself in a cemetery, its long forgotten gravestones teetering to their demise? What is the significance of this necropolis? Trees, thousands of years old judging by their width, joined the gravestones in their macabre dance, leaning so close to the earth that they seemed themselves ready for the grave. Each headstone, in a language I didn't understand, announced the person's entrance and departure.

A tidy row of seven stones stood in a line. The surname Araya was carved into each stone. Birth dates were different, but all seven died on September 15, 1873. I began to notice another pattern. Entire swaths of markers were etched with the year 1999, the year following Aleric's coup d'état. I had thought that listening to the dictator's story would be enough, but I began to wonder if I would have to experience his rule as part of my judgement.

I sat down on a tree stump and looked around. I spotted a tiny spider which had captured an insect ten times its size in its web. For several minutes I watched the arachnid crawl up its rope and down to the insect, poking at it. Finally the insect was coated in white webbing, and the spider hauled it up to a crevice in a gravestone. We fear large predators, but the tiny ones seem more deadly.

For a long time I pondered the insect's grisly demise, waiting for something to happen. I stood back up and began to pace again. Then I noticed a marble mausoleum, its metal door flapping back and forth in the wind. *Who's buried in there?* I approached the building, but held back. Rodents and poisonous creatures probably waited.

I held back, but siren bellowed, fissuring the dead air. I responded as if I were the fugitive and the sirens were for me. No time to hesitate, I precariously entered the tomb. My eyes adjusted and I noticed names carved into the wall. A movement. I jumped. Over in a corner a large lump moved. What was it? Why did I feel brave enough to edge near it? I was dead, what could really happen to me? Yet, my journey so far had only brought me danger and woe. Why would I expect otherwise? Vipers? Alligators? Would I feel the crush of those reptiles' seventy-plus teeth on my limbs?

A child's whimper? Was there a child here? I rushed to the mound and lifted a dirty canvas to reveal a family, hovering in sheer terror.

"Ayúdame! Ayúdame!" A man's voice shouted. He rushed to the door and slammed it shut. He used a skeleton key to lock it from the outside.

"Shh!" I whispered. "They are in the cemetery." I spoke perfect Spanish, surely not my mother tongue.

"We run from the general. He seeks my husband," the wife spoke. "My husband spoke out against the regime. They take enemies and incinerate them. Me esposo could not tolerate this evil."

What time was I in? I wondered. Before Aleric, during or after? I thought San Xavier became a Republic after Aleric left.

"Does it matter?" my angel spoke in my ear. "They need to go to the mountains, where Sister Veronica waits to take them over the border to freedom."

"During," I answered for myself. "Will I meet the evil tyrant?"

"Perhaps," she answered evasively.

"But, history is done, it has been recorded."

"You forget, this is not about history, this is about your judgment."

"So I can just sit here and wait? Can't my judgment allow me to sit and wait?"

"That is not how it works, Catharine."

"Mountains? Danger? What kind of purgatory was this? I had gone as far as I wanted in this so-called adventure. Metanoia worked on other people, not me. I was dead! Dead, I tell you. Couldn't I have just waited around like a rock until my appointed time to go through the pearly gates?"

"Suit yourself." She disappeared.

The family stared at me as I sat down in a corner. I leaned against the cold wall and closed my eyes. Something with eight legs crawled upon my shoulder. A spider! I screamed and brushed it off or I thought I brushed it off. It landed on my shin and instantly stung me. Searing pain coursed through my tendons, ligaments, muscles and bones in no way I had ever experienced while alive. Wooziness enveloped me. The culprit scuttled up my leg, onto my torso, up to my chest. I looked down to see a scorpion. Combined with the pain, the horror of its image thrust me into unconsciousness.

I awoke to a pain akin to someone gnawing at my shin with metal teeth.

"Señorita, Señorita! You have been bitten by a scorpion. We must get you out of here."

The man tried to pull me to my feet, but I stumbled as the stabbing seemed to kick my leg out from under me. Nausea erupted in response to the pain. I retched, and retched.

"She is hot," the woman stroked my forehead. "How will we move her?"

"We must," was the man's only answer. He went to the door and looked out. The police had left. The key went into the lock and soon the door opened again.

"I, I, musth heelp you," I slurred, drunk from the pain. "Lead you, you..."

"No talk. You must save your strength." The woman pushed my right arm over her shoulder, while her husband took over on the left side. Each step brought about a new affliction. I wanted the leg cut off, anything to stop the stabbing. Dripping from perspiration, I fell onto the soft grass when we left the mausoleum.

"Kill me," I thought. Nothing would be worse than this. Maybe if they caught me, they'd rush me to the hospital.

The man scurried about, pushing aside bushes and plants. Finally, it appeared he found what he needed, a little black box. He opened it, and began treating the wound. Different syringes appeared, and one injection in my arm and another in my thigh. He then leaned me against a large stone.

"You need hospital but for now rest," he said.

"Me esposo es medical doctor," the woman spoke.

"Mama, I'm hungry," a girl, about five years of age, said. "Can we eat?"

"We have nothing, sweet bambina, but God will provide."

I wasn't feeling too religious at the moment. I wasn't sure God was going to provide anything but more pain. I knew I brought it on myself, my obstinate self. If I had only acquiesced we might already be on the way to the mountains.

Mountains? Which way? Geography, map reading, directions were all left for others to figure out. How was I, the woman who got lost in her own house, going to find where they needed to go?

Through the pain, I tried to recall Aleric's words. I think he said north. I beheld the landscape. Mountains surrounded me. Which way was north? Where was the sun? It was overcast. Tonight, if the clouds continued to shroud the earth, I would not find the North Star.

"Which way is north?" I asked.

The man pointed.

"We need to go north. You will all be free if we get there."

"Alive?" A ten-year-old boy finished the sentence into a question.

They continued talking, but I dozed off. On and off I dreamt of stars, pointing, leading me and this family north.

Once the scorpion stupor faded, I could no longer be the patient; I had to be the tour guide in a country as foreign to me as car mechanics. From the cemetery we crossed over a grassy valley meeting up with the foot of the mountains. We would take the mountain path north. Jungles met us. Nocturnal animals, deadly animals I was sure, awaited, salivating before the kill. Which would be worse, capture by soldiers or teeth clamping down on my flesh, cracking my dead bones? I hesitated entering into the arms of the teeming foliage. Dr. Carteñes nudged me.

"Let me go first," he said. "I will lead the way."

Dr. Carteñes stopped and his arms swayed backwards to halt our movement.

A jaguar gnawed at the carcass of a peccary. Sensing us, it stopped, its topaz eyes glowing out into the darkness.

"Are we more appetizing than that?" I asked.

"Shh!" Dr. Carteñes whispered.

Fatigue and terror erased all my childhood dreams of living the existence of Jane Goodall. A bubble bath, thick towels, juicy hamburgers, and warm blankets, those were what I craved at that moment. Leave jungle living for the jungle animals. The jaguar returned to its kill. We plodded on with Dr. Carteñes pushing back the vines and ferns. That night I saw more animals than a trip to the zoo. Sloth, vine snake, anteater, and a foot long centipede eating a baby mouse. My empty stomach revolted.

The angel appeared. "Houses, with candles burning outside, are safe houses," she whispered. She pointed to a clearing. "There you will find food and shelter."

She was right, because we found a hut, with a candle burning on the ground, waiting for us. I led the family to the clearing. I knocked and knocked, half guessing no one would answer. The door opened to reveal a man and woman waiting.

"Come in," he said. "Dr. Carteñes. So glad you've escaped."

"You must be so hungry and tired," the woman said. She began meal preparations. The Carteñes children dropped on the mats and fell asleep. "Poor babies." She looked down at my leg.

"Scorpion bite," said Señora Carteñes. "Our friend needs rest too."

"I'm hungry," I said, the stab of hunger resonating throughout my body.

I don't know why I looked at the chicken floating in cumin and cinnamon sauce with excitement since it would only be flat and miserable. I swabbed up the food and ate anyways, but the starvation pangs continued.

Whispers around the table, almost inaudible to my ears, kept me awake until spikes of sunlight bored through the windows.

"How much more can we take of this?" Señor Abaroa moaned. "My nerves are frayed to the point of snapping."

"Imagine how Dr. Carteñes feels, running from Regallito like a roach running from exterminators."

They were of course talking about Aleric, the dictator. I wanted to say I knew all about him; his childhood, his military life, and his death. They would think I was crazy.

"Señorita, what brings you to San Xavier?" Señor Abaroa asked.

"Just visiting," I said to a round of laughter.

"Who would visit our country during such turmoil?" Señora Abaroa asked.

"I'm a writer and I'm trying to gain more information about your country."

In the corner my angel appeared and shook her head. Too late.

"Writers have been banned, or so I thought," Señora Carteñes said. "Only those who feed into the ego of Regallito are allowed to stay."

Any camaraderie that was built between me and these people fled in an instant. Who was this woman, they must be wondering. Instinctively it was natural to distrust in a country where any misstep could mean torture and death for you and your family.

"Are you helping or only leading the Carteñes family to their destruction?" Señor Abaroa quizzed, studying my expression for any telltale deception.

No, no! I was thrust here as part of my judgment, my mind screamed out, but could not be heard. "I was sent to help them," was all I said.

"Who sent you?" Señor Abaroa scraped his chair as he stood and backed away from the table. He opened a cupboard and pointed a gun at me.

The angel whispered in my ear.

"Sister Veronica sent me," I answered, quickly. Señor Abaroa returned the gun to the cabinet. Señora Carteñes began to weep.

"So sorry, so sorry. I can't take this anymore."

"Sister Veronica is north?" Dr. Carteñes asked. "I have heard about her, but didn't know where she was hiding. Please accept our apologies."

"What is she like?" Señora Abaroa asked.

"I don't know her personally, only of her," I stammered. Please, memory don't fail me. "She's very beautiful. Her mother was from San Xavier and her father from the States. She's a writer like I am a writer."

My angel rolled her eyes. "Writer, indeed."

"What do you write?" Señor Abaroa asked.

Nothing, I thought. I finished nothing as an adult, only childhood plays and stories. What will I tell these people?

"Revolution is coming soon." Señor Abaroa changed the subject. I sighed inwardly with relief.

"That's all this country has had! When will we have peace? One evil tyrant after another, each more loathsome than the one before him." Dr. Carteñes snorted.

I fell asleep before Dr. Carteñes shook me awake.

"Time to go. But first, let me do this."

He spread ointment on the scorpion wound and wrapped my leg. Outside darkness had arrived to shroud our journey north. Guns, food, and prayers, we were ready.

Night in and night out, that is how we lived. A sheath of anxiety waxed all my nerves, each insignificant noise, each insignificant movement becoming significant in the shattering of my composure.

Safe houses were hard to come by, so we often hid deep in the jungle during the day. We were accompanied by burning bug bites and itchy bumpy skin. Dr. Carteñes stood guard as sleep sequestered our daylight hours. Stoic describes the Carteñes children. Not one word of complaint as they silently obeyed and followed. They were fearful too, but years of terror seemed to temper their childish whims.

We had found some ruins to rest in one day. Typically, I would have studied the structure, but this was no sightseeing trip. Inside a cavern we hid and fell asleep. Gunshots thundered. Dr. Carteñes touched his fingers to his lips. We squeezed tightly together. As still as possible, we waited. The ancient structure was well hidden, but if we had found it, so could the soldiers. Snapping branches, heavy footsteps marched in closer and closer. Adrenaline flooded my bloodstream.

My angel appeared and motioned to me. She was guiding us to a hiding place.

"Over here," I pointed.

"No, no. We must not move from here." Dr. Carteñes said.

"Yes, yes. Please listen." The urgency in my voice persuaded him. About one hundred steps later we dropped into furrowed dirt. Enough to cover us. We held our breath as we watched the soldiers stop and listen for any sign of their prey. Thud, thud, thud, my heartbeats overcoming my eardrums. Would the soldiers hear it? Five of them stomped inside the ruin where we had just been. Could I hold my breath even more? Could I be even more still? Cement seemed to glaze over us as their footsteps neared. One booted foot kicked dirt into the hole. Still. Silence.

"They're gone! Check the trees!" They sprayed bullets above their heads. Animals, dead, fell out in response, but no humans.

"We're wasting time!" The man's voice reminded me of Aleric's.

We could see nothing in our hole, but we waited it seemed for an eternity before they were satisfied we were nowhere in the vicinity. I wanted to climb out, but Dr. Carteñes held us back.

"Nighttime is coming soon. Let us wait."

Seven more days, a full week, not the shortened workweek we have in the U.S.A., but a full seven days we continued like animals, on the run, sweating, panting, and starving.

"I'm dead! I'm dead. This is just pretend," I tried to psyche myself out cycling the phrase continuously. Nighttime of the seventh day, Sister Veronica's sanctuary came into view. For the living, it was relief. For me, it was just a continuation of my purging.

Aleric was right when he described the beauty of this mountain retreat, though it could bring me no joy. The stone building was nestled within flowering shrubs. Standing on the summit, I beheld the river that separated the two tiny countries and more green. Sister Veronica rushed down to greet us. She, and several sisters, led us to the inside of the convent. The Carteñes family quickly ate, and Sister Veronica gave a pack to the doctor. "This will have all your paperwork. You'll find food too, though someone should rescue you quickly."

I stood watching Sister Veronica, stunned by her beauty. Perfection had directed all placement of her facial features with perfect symmetry. The white habit, though of plain cotton, could have been a bridal gown.

We waited and watched until a light flickered in the distance. Sister Veronica and I followed the Carteñes family as they descended down the mountain to the river. Going down seemed so much easier than the ascent. A boat waited for them. I hugged the children.

"Come with us," they pleaded, tears streaking their too skinny faces.

"You must go on without me," I said.

Señora Carteñes cried. She did a lot of crying on our journey. "You have been so sweet for helping us. I will pray to God for you. Please be safe."

Tears welled up in my eyes. Again, I felt the pangs of missing my own mother and family. I wanted to go home to our brick house, but it seemed like this tour of duty would never end. My heart ached as the boat pushed the Carteñes family away forever.

Sister Veronica led me back to the convent without speaking. Her beauty could not disguise the torment etched onto her face. We went silently to our rooms. A tiny cell, with a crisply made bed and a crucifix hanging above the window, would be my temporary lodgings. I leaned out the wooden frame to sniff, but it seemed like anosmia overtook my olfactory senses. The flora and fauna mocked me as all my redolent memories evaporated. It was as if I was watching a movie, with the brilliance of colors and noises bombarding my vision and hearing, while disregarding my sense of smell.

I rest on the cot, but screaming and crashing doors quickly awakened me. A military man rushed into my cell and snatched my hair dragging me off the cot and out of the room. Spikes jammed into my scalp would have hurt less than the violent tugging at my locks. Judging by his appearance, I was relieved my sense of smell had been robbed.

Once out of the convent, he threw me on the ground and began to undress. Suddenly Aleric appeared.

"No! Leave the women alone!"

"Come on!" The soldier complained. Aleric lifted up his pistol, the soldier buttoned his shirt immediately. Relief flooded through me. Like cattle we were shoved into the back of some military vehicle reminiscent of a jeep, but with a longer back. We sat on wooden benches, and held onto each other for support. A quiet hum emanated from the sisters. They were praying. I wanted to scream, to cry, yet somehow their prayers calmed me.

An opened window between the front and the back revealed that Sister Veronica was squeezed in the seat next to Aleric. She was praying too. The lewd soldier continued gazing at me; my skin crawled in revolt.

"You, pelirroja!" He shouted as he began to unzip his pants. The sisters, in complete unison, screamed. The jeep halted.

"Have you no decency?" Aleric shouted. "These are nuns!"

Aleric pointed his pistol through the window and shot. The soldier slumped over onto my lap. One of the nuns quickly drew a cross on the dead man's face. Then a few of them took his body and rested it on the floor between all our feet. The sisters returned to their prayers. We were followed by two more trucks as we continued the jostling journey down the mountain. The soldiers sang as if returning from a successful hunting trip.

I knew the rest of the story. We would be incarcerated and then executed at dawn. For these men, that was their entertainment, their thrill. We were no more human to them than a cage full of rats, except for their evil designs on our virtue. Thankfully we would be spared the horror of that degradation.

We slipped down worn steps as we descended to the hell called prison. Stones, the size and shape of skulls, encapsulated us into the dank cellar. No smooth cement walls, just these skull looking rocks, eyeless and faceless, yet conveying the message of death.

The sisters were housed two to a cell, yet for some reason, I was alone. They quickly slipped to their knees, while I walked around examining the skull rocks to see if indeed they were human remains. Then I stopped. In the prison across from mine, Aleric knelt, his torso leaning over his cot.

"Aleric! What are you doing here?" I whispered.

"Señorita Zimmer. You are to spend time here too?"

"But you're upstairs, you're about to have us killed!"

"You and I, we each must live out our punishment. I rot here until they free me. For you I can only guess you have been immersed in the distress produced by your inaction."

"We will be shot at sunrise."

"Is she here?"

"Yes, of course. But are any of us really here? Are we all not dead?"

Ignoring me, Aleric continued, "I have not seen her since that day."

"We're reliving that day right now."

"I must see her."

"Can you escape?"

"From here, no. Every moment I roam the cells. They say theese preeson ees haunted." His accent thickened as he slipped through the bars and found her cell. It was empty. Except for our two souls, it appeared that no one had lived in this dungeon for centuries. It was abandoned soon after Aleric was deposed. Would I be shot at dawn or did I reach the end of my Purgatory? *Temporary, this is only temporary.* I tried to soothe myself.

My angel appeared. "You have much more to endure here."

"No! How can one little deception be the cause of all of this?"

"You still don't understand, do you?" In an instant, she was gone, I back to my cell, watching Aleric on his knees, and the Sisters humming in prayer. Back and forth surreal swirled into a different sort of surreal like a rippled ice cream cone.

Back in my cubbyhole with the skull rocks, I tried to pray. What was a dead woman to pray about? I could only remember Mom telling me that dead people couldn't pray for themselves, but for others.

"God, I don't know if you're listening, but I want to pray for peace in our world. I also pray for my nieces and nephew still on earth." Once I began, I couldn't stop. The needs of the world were great, and I began to understand how some orders of nuns pray every hour of every day.

Marching feet, the clang of bars opening and shutting, the clutching of each one of us and pushing us up the stairs. That is how I met the morning, the morning of my execution, the execution I must undergo for my crime of apathy. I had already experienced death, so fear should not have accompanied me, but it did. "Rat a tat tat, rat a tat tat." With the drumbeat, my heart kept rhythm, loud, pulsating, and prepared to burst through my chest. Sweat rolled down my brow.

The soldiers pulled tendons I had no idea existed when they snapped my arms behind my back. A soiled bandana, probably used multiple times for executions, squeezed my eyes shut. I am assuming they led us into a line, but I cannot be certain since I couldn't see. Words in Spanish were shouted, perhaps to shame or to gloat over us. Then the counting, "Uno, dos, tres!" Explosion of shots, then a searing pain through my chest as if a bucket full of glass shards were heaped upon it. Then nothing.

When I awoke, I was back at the cemetery. Why was this my meeting place? I guess it was the best location since I was dead, twice dead now. I tried to find the catacomb, but it was gone. The tree, the ghastly headstones, they were still there. An obelisk caught my attention because it stood taller than any of the other markers. I looked down to read Sir Frederick Caswell of Wiltshire, 1569-1648. Why would an English headstone be in a graveyard thousands of miles across the sea? Who was Sir Frederick? Did he have family? I searched for more Caswells but found none.

The obelisk leaned forward slightly, and weather and time had faded the lettering. Strangely, geraniums, three in a row, flowered below its base. Around me a riot of grass slapped my hips and thighs, but here, at Sir Frederick Caswell's grave, the grass stood in reverence, almost afraid to move with the promptings of the wind.

"Pardon me, lady. I beseech thee to inform me what dost thou stand at my grave for?" I beheld a tall figure of a man, very tall. Something was familiar about his countenance. I knew him, yet how could I have known a man born hundreds of years before my time?

CHAPTER 20

Pray, prithee tell me," he continued.

The Giant! Sir Frederick Caswell was the Giant, my judge, my jury. We didn't part on very happy terms, as he imposed upon me this long, tortuous, nomadic life. What now was I to learn from the Giant called Sir Frederick?

"You're the Giant! I'm Catharine Zimmer. I had to listen to three stories, and you were there too. You showed me how my writing, or perhaps lack of, destroyed lives."

"No, no. Please don't say that! That is why I am doomed, doomed, doomed to tend my own grave and more." He stopped, his doleful stare sending waves of grief over my dead body.

"What? You too were a writer?" I asked incredulous, recalling how the Giant besmirched me. This young man, however, had no recollection, no idea of our previous meeting. Chronological time had no place in this altered dimension. Forward, backward, sideways, flip flop. The year 2000 to the beginning of time, to the year 1950, back to the 1600s and forward again, like the motions of a wash machine. "What time are we in now?"

"Long before your death, Catharine," the angel appeared. "Sir Frederick has yet to reach his appointed time."

"Why me?" I asked, but why did I bother? Her answer, if she even bothered to answer me, would not satisfy.

"You will see." That Cheshire smile appeared again on her face. I was a dog person, myself, especially since I was allergic to cats' fur and their attitude. Her feline smile did nothing to endear me to that species.

"Each day, if you call it that, I return to this very site where I am buried." Sir Frederick knelt pulling at imaginary weeds.

"What do you do the rest of the time?" I asked.

He replied by standing up and trudging away from the polyandrium of sorts onto an unmarked path. I followed in silence. Miles we walked, my feet still sore from my life as a run-away in the jungles.

It appeared on the horizon, a large timber structure, a home for its dwellers. Four stories up, and about one city block wide. Mahogany trees flanked both sides of the stone walk, shielding us from the sun and any joy that might be derived from the blue sky. As we neared, I spied the other smaller buildings on the property; a blacksmith, corn grist, cotton gin, shoe shop, kitchen, and a long, low building, probably for the workers of this farm.

"Slaves," the angel said. "Sir Frederick was a plantation owner and had over 200 slaves."

Indignation seized me in my tracks as I recalled the Giant's derision during my heavenly indictment. Holier than thou was his attitude, but he had left a legacy far more loathsome than Aleric, Ursula, Adrien, and me combined! A slave owner! Who would have guessed?

"Why must I travel to his past? What has this to do with anything in my life?"

"You are still learning, Catharine."

"But I am dead. And I already know the scourge of slavery, its ugly blemish defiling all of history."

"You've read about it in your history books, but did you ever write about it?"

"What?"

Again I was transported, but this time to a more recent period of history, on a continent far from my own. A kiln? Men, women, and children stirred clay, shaped bricks, and set them into the fire. Heat escaped and whorled around anyone as close as twenty feet away. Sweat poured down my face. Their skin shined as if it was oiled.

"Where am I?"

"Does it matter?" she casually replied. "Did you know there were more slaves during your lifetime than any other period in history? Children, men, women, all kidnapped to serve without freedom or dignity. This would have been one of your writing assignments, but you were too busy traveling the nicer parts of town to notice."

Mountainside retreats, medieval cathedrals, markets, bazaars, cafés, pyramids, walls, more cafés, more shopping, spas, skiing, safaris, golfing, climbing, wine tastings, cruising, gambling, swimming, more cafés, more savoring of each country's delights. But my itinerary never included this, never the witnessing of human bondage. Babies, broken down before even reaching their youth, worked alongside the near-to-dead grandfathers and grandmothers. Starvation ruled over these people like an unmerciful tyrant. Hope was squashed like a spider on the wall.

"How can this be?"

"How can it not be? Catharine Zimmer dallying around with her own pleasures to alert the world of this evil."

"I already found water for a dying village. Why this?"

I leaned over the baby, wanting to carry him, bathe him, feed him, and clothe him. But we were separated by the dimension called death. And yet I knew the gulf would be broken soon, as death ebbed nearer and nearer to this cherub, ready to snatch him away from life.

We were back at the plantation. I was different. Instead of pale skin, my arms were brown. I was wearing a cotton gown, and a rag tied over my spiral, black locks.

"Woman! Come hither!" It was Sir Frederick's voice. "Did you spill this sugar?" He accused.

I saw nothing, but Sir Frederick grasped my hand and swiped it on the table. Grains, invisible to the eyes, became visible to my skin.

"Waste!" he shouted as he lifted a switch and swatted me like a fly. Five times the leather minced my skin. Blood trickled into my eyes. "Stop bleeding or you'll soil the food!" As if I could turn on and off my blood like a faucet. I kicked him in the shin. "Insolence!" He shouted, striking harder and harder.

I tried to shield my face with my hands, but the whip, like bolts of lightning, seared across my flesh. It seemed he was never going to stop, when suddenly a young woman appeared.

"Frederick! Stop!" She confiscated the switch and hit him hard.

"How dare you interfere!" he challenged.

"Each flaying of her, is a flaying of me!" A tiny right arm went over my shoulder, and the woman guided me away from Sir Frederick.

"Leave the affairs of the house to me!" He shouted after her. She led me up the stairs, down a long hallway and into a sitting room outside of a bedchamber. There she set me down on a cushioned settee and wiped away blood, the stinging sensation somewhat soothing.

Light toffee-colored, wavy hair cascaded over her shoulders. A periwinkle blue ribbon held the tendrils off her face. It matched her satin gown, which looked too regal for this setting. Unusual for women of her time, sun had tanned her face and arms. The beaches of California seemed a better setting for this woman than a slave plantation.

"You poor dear," she crooned. "You about to have a baby."

He followed us and stopped in the doorway. "You let this animal into our rooms?"

"She is a human being, Frederick, not an animal." She finished salving my wounds. "Let's go back to your house," she said gently lifting me to my feet. Our hands were clasped in friendship; her love endeared her to me. She turned her face back to her husband. "I'm returning back to the motherland." The words chilled the air.

"No!" he shouted

"In a fortnight."

His fist punched the wall and then he disappeared.

The slave quarters were unfit for rats, let alone human beings. Straw structures were our beds, and I watched as fleas jumped up and down on them. Dirt covered the floors. Rags served as blankets. Mongrel dogs roamed through periodically searching for weakened human flesh ready to die.

"I am sorry. I wanted to make it all better for you, but failed," the mistress of this plantation apologized. "I loved him, once, but now I am not so sure." She gently leaned my body onto the straw. "Sleep. I will take care of dinner."

When I awoke, I was at a port, standing behind Sir Frederick. He stared for hours after the ship faded in the distance. Then back to the geraniums in the cemetery.

"I took my inheritance overseas to build a farm for my wife and family. I would write and farm, and she would look over the children and the house. Greed settled into my heart. I was quite prosperous when she arrived to marry me. I was unwilling to give up the money. Writing was a waste of time. People were like animals to me, to be used and discarded at my whim.

"Then she left. Oh to be sure her heart had already left when it discovered the coldhearted plantation owner. She wrote, beseeching me to leave this horrid occupation, but I had ignored her."

The ghost of Sir Frederick threw himself onto the ground, sobbing. I still couldn't get over that my judge, so to speak, was once a slave owner.

"You still don't understand," my angel's voice whispered in my ear.

"I understand well enough," I replied. "How dare he act as judge and jury of my simple life. I killed no one. I did not beat anyone like he had. People were like machines to him. Expendable with no soul."

"No one died because of your inaction?" The angel evaporated before I could answer.

I was back in the slave quarters. Next to me slumbered an infant, a beautiful baby with wiry black curls, chubby cheeks, and petulant lips. I was Josiah's mother, and love flowed from me to this baby, much as I had felt for Chibueze while in Africa.

Scooping him up carefully so I would not topple onto him, I rocked him back and forth, the warmth from his tiny body penetrating through to my skin, and into my heart. In this tender moment, I kissed his forehead. He seemed to smile. I laughed.

Then I heard footsteps heading inside. Instinctively I clutched Josiah closer to my breast. My heart knew those footsteps meant danger. I had seen it with the other slave mothers. It was about to happen to me.

"Grab the child!" Sir Frederick commanded.

"No!" I screamed.

Sir Frederick backhanded me in the face. I relinquished the baby to prevent me dropping him.

"Get back to work, woman! This is of no concern to you!"

As Sir Frederick and his evil henchman left, I heard them talking. "Got a pretty price for this one. We better get mama sired again. She produces a good litter."

I rose up in a rage and hurled myself out of the building and onto Sir Frederick's back. He tumbled into the dirt. I pummeled him in a murderous rage. Soon, more white men appeared and peeled me off his back. It would be the pillory again for me. My head was thrust into the wooden opening and they clamped down the splintered wood over my neck and arms.

Sir Frederick ripped open the back of my blouse, and then grabbed the proffered leather whip. I knew what was coming, this moment transporting my memory to summer camp. Catharine Zimmer was only eleven-years-old. The camp counselor forgot to put sunscreen on my back. Six hours later, with my back searing in second-degree burns, I fell into a bees' nest. Hundreds, thousands of bees angrily poked their stingers into my already flaming back. I spent the rest of summer camp in the hospital.

"Lash!" I heard the crack before I felt it, my body steeling itself for the pain, my teeth pitting themselves against each other. "Crack!" The whip relentlessly seared my flesh. Sir Frederick was crazed. When I thought he was done, "Crack" again went the whip. My back bloody and raw, wooziness and nausea were my only comfort. In my confused state, I thought I heard horses' hooves clamping down toward us.

"Stop!" A man's voice shouted. I looked up to see the horseback rider seize the whip and raise it above his head menacing Sir Frederick.

"Who are you?" Sir Frederick demanded.

"I seek food and shelter for the night," the man responded. "I was told to come here."

"By whom?"

"Madame Caswell," was the answer.

"Is she here?" A light flickered in Sir Frederick's eyes.

"No. She remains in England."

"She sent you here to stop me?"

"Yes or your soul will perish in Hell."

Sir Frederick began to laugh. I was still caged up, bloody and in pain. "Please, would someone get me out of here?"

In an instant, the man jumped off his horse and released me from the pillory. "My name is Father Peter," he said to me, and offered his hand. I shook it, amazed at the strength of it. Father Peter then led me toward the slave quarters.

"Get me some water and clean cloth!" He demanded. Sir Frederick hesitated, but the glower in Father Peter's eyes convinced him to obey.

After a fellow slave woman bound up my wounds, I got up and returned to the kitchen to prepare dinner. No hospital stay this time. No soda poured over ice or fruity popsicles, just subjugation.

I began to serve the two men their dinner. Sir Frederick sat at one end of the table in front of Madame Carswell's portrait and two wall sconces. His head was positioned in such a way that the candles looked like horns jutting from his scalp. Father Peter sat to his right. Behind Father was the buffet loaded with a sterling tea set, candelabras flickering, and silver vases filled with the flowers that I had picked that morning. The placement of the items posed as if in a still-life painting.

The men ate in silence. Sir Frederick wiped his lips and set down his fork. He paused for a moment, thinking of what he was going to say.

"Why did she send you?" Sir Frederick mocked Father Peter.

Father's black stringy locks circled his face as if someone had placed a bowl over his head to cut his hair. His brown eyes, framed by crow's feet, were the color of a monk's cassock. He wore a black robe, belted by a rope. "She is sick."

Sir Frederick dropped his fork onto the floor. I scurried to pick it up and take it to wash it, but he grabbed it from me.

Father Peter stood up, pulled a chair to the table, and tapped on the padded seat. "Sit here," he said. I looked at Sir Frederick, his stare challenging me to disobey him. I sat.

"Damn you!" Sir Frederick stood up, spilling his food onto his lap. "I will not eat with that filthy animal!"

"I will," Father Peter casually placed some of his food onto a smaller plate and pushed it toward me. Sitting was a luxury. We slaves usually ate coarse bread and salted pork while standing. This dinner was roast beef with a myriad of vegetables grown on the farm. Father buttered a piece of bread and handed it to me. It wasn't the brown kind we ate, but white and soft. I knew it would be good, for I spent yesterday kneading and baking it in my hundred degree kitchen. I glanced at Sir Frederick, but hunger prodded me to eat. I remembered what butter tasted like. Little Catharine Zimmer, no more than two-years-old, would crawl on the kitchen table and scoop it into her little mouth. It was amazing I grew to be so thin. Damn, I forgot! Enjoyment of the textures and flavors were denied me in my present state. The bread swirled in my mouth like car oil over cardboard. I wanted to spit it out. That would not be acceptable. I stood up, curtseyed, and left the room.

Father Peter stayed for a little over a month. During the day, he would work side by side with us, and at night, he would teach us math or how to read. After lessons, was music. We taught him our songs and he taught us his. Sometimes he'd play with the children or tell them stories. Before breakfast he and Sir Frederick would engage in a dueling match of words; Father's fire-and-brimstone voice warned Sir Frederick of the dire consequences of his stubbornness. Over time, the arguments grew fiercer. One morning I was churning the butter and making bread. They were in the parlor, but their voices trailed into the kitchen.

"Damn you to hell!" Sir Frederick seemed to have the final say. Finally, Father Peter spoke, but so quietly I creaked opened the kitchen door to discern his words.

"Sir Frederick, I only wish for your eternal happiness. I pray that even if you are not reunited with Charlotte here on earth, that someday in heaven you two will meet again."

Before departing Father gathered us all in the slave quarters. He had been crying.

"I want to personally apologize. Things have not gotten better for you. In fact, I pray and hope that I have not made things worse for you all. I plan to return again but I need to move on."

He hugged each one of us and thumbed a cross on our foreheads. Many of my family began to cry. Sir Frederick had lessened his evil punishments while Father Peter was here, but we guessed they would intensify when the priest left. We were right.

For about two months, Sir Frederick released his anger onto all of us. Beatings, isolation, food deprivation – we all suffered under his wrath. Twelve of my family members died. Then came the letter.

Whispers traveled from one slave to the next. "She is dead."

There was no official mourning except that Sir Frederick hid in his rooms. We dusted and swept, but there was very little to do inside the house. Since the food would go bad, I began to serve the other slaves what I had been preparing for Sir Frederick.

We were forbidden to go into his rooms. I would bring up a tray of food and would return later to see it untouched.

Many of the slaves had tried to escape, but had been returned by fellow plantation owners and sympathizers. Though they were willing to capture us and bring us back, none came to offer condolences to Sir Frederick. Over two hundred people lived on the plantation, but Sir Frederick was alone.

One morning, as usual I prepared his breakfast and knocked on his door. "Sir Frederick, your breakfast is ready."

"Come in," he said this time. His words startled me.

I stared in shock at his form. It was as if he powdered his body, his skin was so pale. His clothes hung on his skeletal frame. A shaggy beard grew from his chin. His eyes had lost its fire of arrogance. I dutifully set the tray before him and turned to leave.

"Stay," he said. "Sit." He pointed to the settee I had sat on when Charlotte nursed my wounds. We looked at each other, neither knowing what to say. He cleared his throat. "She loved all of you. She saw your humanity, while I was blind."

He stood up to go to the window. "I had done this all for her, or so I pretended I had done this for her. Money was opium. I couldn't get enough. Back in England, my family existed in poverty. Here, I ruled like a king. But for what?" He turned back toward me. "You may go now."

After that conversation, I had expected him to be over his grief, but the home had remained a tomb for another month. We lived in temporary relief, unsure of when he'd come back to life and begin the torture. Then one day he stepped outside and called us all together.

"As of today you are all free. I will write up a notice of freedom. I hope that the other plantation owners will honor it. If you wish to stay on and work, I will pay you a wage and provide proper food and lodging. Husbands and wives may live together. I will sell no one."

When he finished his speech, a parade of men galloped onto the property. A black carriage followed.

"Sir Frederick," a voice called from within the carriage. "I believe you have some slaves for me." A bloated man descended from the vehicle. He wore a white wig, and his breeches looked ready to snap like a rubber band pulled too tightly. At his neck rested a frilly white cravat. His black boots carted him over to me, and his fat hands fingered my hair and caressed my face. Leeches crawling all over me would have disgusted me less.

"How much for this beauty?"

"Nothing. She is not for sale. None are for sale. In fact, as of this moment, they are no longer my property."

A raucous guffaw exploded from his too pink lips. "Sir Frederick! You amuse me!"

"Charlotte has died," was Sir Frederick's only response.

"Oh, I heard. Don't you believe you're overreacting? What will happen when all this rabble is let loose? They need to be chained down. Before you know it, they'll be infecting the other slaves, and they'll all rise up in revolt! Who knows how they can kill?"

"Sir Chad, I suggest you remove yourself from my property."

Sir Chad's blood-shot eyes bulged. He huffed and then turned back toward his conveyance. The entourage left to our cheers.

Many of the slaves departed that very day from the plantation making plans to board the next ship heading back to Africa. They were hoping to be reunited with their families and not be recaptured by other tribes and sold again. Others took their papers north, trying to find some freedom in that strange land of fur traders and Indians. Sadly, the papers meant nothing to the other slave owners. Those who had left often suffered worse fates than with Sir Frederick. He often rescued them.

I also fled the plantation, alone, but in the wood where I hid, I became Catharine Zimmer. *Great! Let's move on.* But I didn't. I was forced to watch Sir Frederick's life unfold until its completion. Nights metamorphosed into morning while Sir Frederick furiously wrote letters and speeches for sympathetic ears. Tirelessly he'd meet the slave ships, alongside Father Peter, and buy as many slaves as possible, then grant them their freedom, handing them pouches of money. Broken ribs, ostracism, and death threats were his only recompense.

Age crept up on him as he neglected his body. His straight, haughty gait was replaced by a dragging left foot and a hump growing out of his back.

Then his deathbed. Gabriel Joseph Smith, once a slave, stood by helping lead his once owner, now friend, to death. Gabriel had been baptized by Father Peter a year before. Once life departed from Sir Frederick, I watched as the man prepared the body and placed it in a mahogany box. Father Peter appeared and prayed over the deceased. He, Gabriel, and four other men carried the box along the melancholy distance to the cemetery. Next to the opened earth, the obelisk waited. They carefully set the box deep into its final resting place, and they faded away. The Giant, as I knew him, appeared.

"Over four hundred years I relived those painful moments of my life. For the pain and suffering I caused, four hundred years was not enough."

"Did you ever write? Did you write a book?"

"Nope. Only letters imploring people, begging them to stop. But to no avail."

"In your time, yes, but by the time I lived, slavery had ended."

"Really?" His eyebrows arched. "That's not how I understood it."

"Well, the African slave trade ended, at least to the Americas."

"Catharine, do you understand why you lived a part of my existence? How lives, hundreds, maybe thousands of years apart, are connected by some unseen thread?"

"This journey already is too long. Will I have four hundred more years?" I said, not fully grasping his meaning.

"I cannot answer that, Catharine. All I know is you must walk away a changed woman from each experience. If not, you will go back until you do."

"No, no! Please I cannot go back."

"But you must."

And I did, seven more times. Seven times Sir Frederick stole my infant Josiah, the pain growing exponentially. Seven times I stood in the pillory, beaten bloody. Seven times I watched the grieved Sir Frederick release his slaves.

As I immersed myself in the misery of others, I became less fearful of suffering and more regretful at my neglect. All my life I feared failure, I feared disease, I feared calamities. I lived my life in secured comfort so completely oblivious to the wretchedness around me.

For the very last time I stood in the cemetery. It had befriended me, and I it. The Giant stood next to his grave, I across from him.

"You're ready, Catharine."

"Will I enter heaven now?"

"That is not for me to say. But you will no longer see me on this side."

He engulfed me as we hugged. When he left, I was suddenly in complete silence and darkness. Gloom settled over my soul, as I remained motionless, afraid to move in this obscurity.

CHAPTER 21

Remorse and I continued on an invisible treadmill, moving yet going nowhere. As my legs moved, however, terror encased my entire being. I had already been assassinated, chased by a dictator, stared down by a jaguar, and beaten by a loser husband and slave owner. Why did I tremble? What more was there to fear? Because fear had trailed behind me like my shadow while I was alive.

In the morning, upon waking, it was anxiety, not caffeine that jump-started Catharine Zimmer. This addiction to worry began at an early age. Questions swirled in my sleepy mind.

Will anyone tease me, today? Will I flunk a test? Will I trip when I walk to the front of class? It didn't really make a lot of sense since no one teased me, my grades were great, and I was somewhat graceful. Aging increased my fear, much like a fun house distorts the thin to the corpulent. *Will I get fired? Will I get invited to the party? Will I make a fool out of myself at the party? Will they like my food? Will I get into a car accident? Will I get cancer?*

I trusted my anxiety. It told me to avoid anything that might cause pain or suffering. After I confidently followed its advice, however, I felt tenser. The daily anxiety was unpleasant, yet familiar, much like the feeling of cutting your fingernails way into the nailbed. My world also began to shrink. In the back of my mind, I knew fear kept me from college, but I was still able to work and travel. Eventually, however, trips overseas, parties, seeking new friends, and grocery shopping all ceased.

I was getting old, I had justified to myself. Yet long before I had retired, I based all my daily decisions off the weather newscast, road construction, or the police radio that sat on top of my refrigerator. Snow, any snow, meant no additional driving, leaving me home often on holidays or birthdays, alone. Road construction meant adding another half hour to my travel plans just so I wouldn't get into an accident. I had stopped attending plays, movies, and the opera because I was afraid to enter my house at night. What if someone was waiting for me when I returned home? Sometimes I had lived in my basement for days anticipating a tornado.

My doctor offered me an anxiety pill, which deadened the fear, as well as all other sensations. Years of therapy did nothing, though it wasn't the many therapists' fault. I didn't want to do the exercises proscribed, so never progressed out of my chronic misgivings.

Now dead, I resented fear, and its control over my every thought, my every action. There was no reason to fear, was there? Through the stories, I had learned how fear had crippled my capacity to live, which had changed the course of history.

"You were dependent upon your worries," my angel said.

"Yes, yes, I know. It seemed as if I couldn't live without them. Peace - that word was for other people, not Catharine Zimmer. If I had a happy moment, I had to destroy it with some gloomy premonition."

She nodded. "Addictions are hard to overcome."

"But they can be overcome. It just takes determination, guts."

"What was your excuse? You greedily fed off the drug of worry, allowing it to dictate your life."

"God made me this way," I said, still muleheaded.

She smiled for only a moment, then a tear rolled down her brown cheek. We were in an apartment denuded of furniture. In the middle of the living room floor, a young woman rocked back and forth on the floor. Brandy Robinson! We had worked together at the department store, but she moved away to pursue modeling. It hadn't worked out as she had planned, and I met up with her one day on the street. Her eyes looked different, but I couldn't figure out why. Brandy invited me to her house that night for a party.

I remember spending over an hour just deciding on what to wear. The party started at eight, and when my wall clock read 8:45, I decided to put away my clothes and go to bed. Comfort and ease typically won out, but my nosiness nudged me to get dressed.

Brandy Robinson managed the cosmetic counter when I was first hired. She offered to make up my face, and I bought everything she used that day. We chatted amiably, and I listened with rapt attention when she told me she was leaving soon to go to New York for modeling. A little tinge of jealousy prickled, but I smiled and wished her good-luck. She stood about six-feet tall, her straightened champagne tinted hair hung to the middle of her back. Her features were perfectly spaced apart, but not necessarily striking. A plain palette that could be painted into different moods or settings.

Driving to her home, I imagined luxury and style, but the address led me to plain, low-income apartments.

"Hi!" Brandy said when she opened the door. There was no wind, but her body waved like branches in a breeze. I stepped into the entryway and fumes of cannabis overpowered my nostrils. On the floor, sitting around a coffee table were men and women sniffing white powder.

"This is illegal!" I exclaimed loudly; some of the guests' heads popped up.

"Catharine, honey, sit down, and try it." Brandy pressed her arm over my shoulder.

"No, I don't do drugs. Well, maybe wine, but not this stuff that can ruin your life."

Brandy shrugged her shoulders. "Suit yourself. There is wine in the kitchen."

"Hey, honey," said a man wearing a black turtleneck sidled up to me. "Come sit by me, and I'll show you a good time."

"I gotta go," I said, pulling away from him. "Brandy, can we talk for a minute?"

"Okay," she said, her figure still waving in the breeze. "Let's use the bathroom."

She slid down her pants and sat on the toilet, "Hope you don't mind."

I did, but said nothing and turned away. "Brandy, these drugs are terrible. Now I see what is wrong with you. There is treatment out there. Just kick everyone out now and start a new life."

She had finished her job and had the sense to wash her hands. "You don't know everything, Catharine. How can you just come in here and judge?"

"I don't need to know everything. Isn't it clear to you? Is this the life you wanted for yourself?"

"That dream disappeared a long time ago."

"I tried to stop her," I said to my angel. "What more could I have done for her?"

"This isn't about your apathy, Catharine, but about your pain and guilt. You hung on, unwilling to let Brandy go."

"It was terrible," I said, remembering. "There had to have been something more I could have done for her."

The next day I had returned to her house hoping to confront her again about her problem. It was nine o'clock. I figured she'd still be in bed so I could reach her before she left for the day.

I knocked and waited. There were cars parked in her driveway so I knew someone was home. My hand reached for the doorknob and turned. She was probably so stoned she hadn't even bothered to lock the door. I walked in, and bodies, were strewn about, sleeping. I found Brandy on her bed, alone.

Then I heard a television and children's voices. *Children?* I followed the sounds and discovered three kids — two boys and one girl. They looked as if they walked out of the pages of a fashion magazine. The boys had wiry black hair, jade eyes, and soft tan skin. The girl also had black ringlets, but wore her hair right above her shoulders. Her eyes were chocolate colored.

"Hi," I had said to them.

They looked at me suspiciously. The older one picked up a baseball bat resting by his feet.

"You better get out of here or else." He poked the bat into the air.

"I'm a friend of your mother's."

"Are you from Social Services?" the girl asked.

"Nope. Are there any adult supervisors, you know, people to take care of you?"

"Have you looked around this mess?" The younger boy spoke. "We're supervising ourselves."

Piles of dishes stacked themselves on the television, bookshelves, chairs, and the floor. Shoes and jackets joined the fray. I was relieved to see that the drug paraphernalia of the night before had disappeared.

The girl spoke, "Did you attend Mama's party?"

"Just for a short while."

Terrence nodded. "So you don't do drugs like all of Mom's friends?"

"We worked together, but I lost contact with her. She went to New York City to be a model. When I saw her yesterday, she invited me to her party. I didn't know it was going to be that kind of party."

The words I spoken had the same effect as if I had just told them their mother had died. The girl began crying.. Terrence set the bat down to comfort his sister.

"I didn't see any of you last night. Where were you?"

"Mom's boyfriend locked us up in the bedroom."

My face crinkled in disgust. "How did you get out?"

"Terrence climbed out the window and came around and freed us." The younger boy must have trusted me because he stepped forward and shook my hand. "I'm Tobey, that's Terrence, and she's Wendy."

From her sorrow arose suspicion. Wendy asked, "Are you going to take us away from our mother?"

"Do you like living like this?"

They looked at each other, a secret pact had been formed, and each wanted to make sure the other would not break it. Terrence spoke for the small group, "This isn't the life we want to live, but we lived away from our mom once before, and she almost died."

A verbal rock struck me. Terrence couldn't have been any older than eleven or twelve, yet he and his younger siblings had foisted their mother and her problems onto their shoulders.

"I want to help," I could only say. Food seemed to be a good starting point. "Have you had anything to eat this morning?"

They looked at each other, wondering what kind of ruse I was using to capture them.

"Let's go out for breakfast, and then maybe get some groceries? I promise I will return you here."

They all climbed into my car without asking any more questions. I was amazed they trusted me, but they were hungry. At the café, each child dutifully ordered fruit, milk, and oatmeal.

"How old are you?" I laughed. "That's a senior citizen breakfast!"

"Mom said all the other stuff is bad for you."

I didn't want to undermine their mother, but I also wanted them to enjoy themselves a little. The waitress held her notepad patiently as I spoke. "Do you all like oatmeal?"

All three heads shook in the negative.

"Please, I am sure just this one time you may order anything on the menu."

What a dichotomy. It was okay to sniff and smoke all sorts of drugs to get high, but food was bad for the body! Treating food as if it was lit dynamite seemed a bit ludicrous to me.

The children sat with their hands in their lap as we waited for our meals without speaking.

It was time to break the silence. "Where's your dad?"

Terrence spoke, "Don't see him too much. He has a new wife, younger than Mom."

Probably not as beautiful as Brandy.

"Daddy got tired of Mommy and her drugs," Wendy said. "He's trying to get custody, and that's why we're hiding from Social Services."

"Do you really believe if you leave your mother she will die?" I don't know why I felt so bold with these children.

They nodded, and Terrance added, "We also don't want to end up being the babysitter for Dad's new kids."

We all ate silently with our own thoughts. I paid for their breakfast, and then we drove to the crowded grocery store. Terrance pushed the cart. The first aisle was the cereal aisle. I grabbed three boxes of kid cereal.

"Mommy never lets us buy this kind of cereal," Tobey, the youngest boy, said. "But we'll eat it anyway!"

Brandy was still sleeping when we returned with the groceries. A few of the party stragglers had awakened, and stood around the coffee pot almost as if it were some god.

"Food!" One of them said.

"Nope. Get your own damn groceries!" I shouted at them. "This is for the kids. Move out of my way so we can put them away."

"You were pretty angry," my angel interrupted my thoughts.

"Yes. Get a job is what I wanted to tell those losers."

"Mercy, Catharine, mercy," my angel remonstrated.

How could I be expected to show mercy when these people were sponges who had no concern for anyone but themselves? Didn't they see there were three children trying to thrive in that horrible existence?

"Just because people refuse to live up to their humanity doesn't mean we have to throw our towel in with them. Every one of those people needed someone to minister to them in some way."

"Was that my job?"

"Catharine, the children were your mission."

The mob cleared out of the kitchen while I unloaded the packages. Once the groceries were packed away, I began washing dishes. The children brought in the plates and cups that were strewn about. Terrence began singing *We Three Kings*.

"We three kings of Orient Are, bearing gifts we travel so far..." he stopped when his mother entered, leaning against the doorframe.

"Oh, my head. Noise! Quiet."

The children froze and watched their mother. I took their dishes and plopped them into the sink. "Good morning, Brandy," I said loudly. I refused to pamper a drug addict who neglected her children.

"You were sure throwing in the judgement," my angel said.

Brandy rubbed her eyes and focused them on me. "Catharine! Did you end up staying last night?"

"I returned this morning. I had no idea you had children."

"You're not going to rat me out, are you?"

"What should I do, Brandy? Is this the life you want for your beautiful children?"

She sat on a kitchen chair. "Did he send you here?"

"I had no idea you were married, or even had kids. Brandy, what has happened to you? You were going to be a big-name model, but look at yourself now! You're just a drug addict." I couldn't believe I had blurted out those words, but that is what she had become. Her eyes were hollow, she must have weighed only a 100 pounds, and her beautiful hair was dry and tangled.

"Thanks to the modeling," she said. "Had to keep pushing, pushing. Lose another five pounds. No sleep. Entertain the clients. Here's a little something to keep you going."

"Brandy, you can stop. Let me help you." The poor children watched us, their eyes so hopeful.

"Would you? Would you help me?" Did she really want help, or was she playing me along? I had wanted to give her the benefit of the doubt, but I was unsure.

"Addiction is hard to overcome, but it can be done!" I said. "Are your parents alive? Can they take care of the kids while you get clean?"

"We don't talk." Another sorrow pushed down her head.

"Oh, but they must want to see their grandchildren," I pleaded, my heart breaking more as each second passed.

"They don't know I have kids."

"Brandy!"

"And they surely wouldn't want grandchildren from a black father."

Terrace dropped a dinner plate, the ceramic scattering to every corner of the kitchen. "You said it didn't matter, Mom."

"It doesn't!" I fell to my knees; not caring if the shards ripped opened my flesh. I steadied myself and looked into his beautiful green eyes. "Listen and listen well. You are all so beautiful. No one, do you hear me, no one has the right to put you down because of your heritage!" I remember shaking in such anger.

Wendy tiptoed over the glass and patted my shoulder. "It's okay. We're used to it."

"You don't know my parents, Catharine. They were social climbers. This would not look good to them."

"Then they're horrible people. But you don't know that for sure. Please, let me talk to them. Give me a chance." My heart burned to fix this problem, to make it all right.

"Mom, can't she try? Just let her try." Tobey said.

"I just don't want them getting disappointed again."

"And you don't think seeing their mother like this isn't disappointing?"

The words struck. A new resolve filled her vacant eyes. Brandy rifled through some papers inside a kitchen drawer and handed me her parents' name and address.

"You really don't have to do this." Was there hope in her eyes?

"Will the kids be okay for the next couple of days?" I asked, worried about their fate.

"I can take care of us," Terrance said, puffing out his chest. "I flushed down the drugs this morning."

It took three different phone messages before someone called me back. It was one of their employees. He said they were too busy to meet with me.

"Do they know about their three grandchildren?" I asked.

The next day I drove up a long drive that curved up to a prairie style home securely surrounded by fir trees. I parked my car, and a woman opened the front door. I followed her along the long corridor to a great room that overlooked Lake Beulah. Arthur and Ruth Robinson sat stiffly on a leather couch, but rose when I entered.

Ruth spoke first, "Tell me about our grandchildren. How old are they? What are their nam..."

Arthur glared at her.

"Terrence, Tobey, and Wendy." I looked to see what effect my words had on them. "Unfortunately your daughter, Brandy, is addicted to drugs and wants to come clean. The kids need somewhere to live while she goes through treatment. She had hoped you would take care of them." I said nothing about the children's father.

"Her name isn't Brandy," her father said. I looked at Ruth, imploring. She stared, impassively.

"Do you want her to die?" I has asked.

"She made her..."

"Made her bed, crap!" I interrupted. "Some people don't know how to make their bed properly! And some people make it, then realize it's all wrong." Where was I getting this stuff? "Brandy is..."

It was her father's turn to break in. "I said her name isn't Brandy, dammit! It's Stephanie! Where the hell did she pick up that awful name?" He rifled his hands through his fading gray hair.

"We tried counselling for her," Ruth spoke. "She's been in and out of drug hospitals, but she goes right back to the drugs! Arthur! She has three kids!" She crumpled onto an oversized ottoman and began to sob. "Arthur, listen! She has three children. Our grandchildren. Can't we help them?"

I had never been comfortable sympathizing with others, but I had rushed over, and put my arms around her shoulders. She hid her face into my chest and cried. Finally, she looked out, her face resolute.

"We're going to pick up the children," she said.

"You're walking into another nightmare," he responded.

"You don't think it's not a nightmare wondering day in and day out whether she's dead or alive? And now we know she has three children? We are not monsters, Arthur. Those children need us."

"And then when they start up with drugs like their mother, are you willing to go through that hell again?"

Ruth began adjusting the items on the coffee table. A slight move to the right went the crystal candleholder, a little forward went the music box, and to the left went the candy dish.

"Catharine, will you go with me?" was all she said.

We drove in silence, but our thoughts kept us company. Stephanie's addiction had already destroyed her parents' lives and it would soon trampled over her children's. I so wanted to erase the problem like bleach removes stains.

I finally spoke, "I'm sorry."

Ruth's hands gripped the steering wheel.

"I thought you two were monsters who neglected their child."

"We did."

"But..."

"We gave up too easily. Stephanie's drug problem was ruining our comfortable existence. We thought our lives were not meant to include such pain, that we had to rid ourselves of it. 'This is Stephanie's problem,' we placated ourselves."

"But at some point, it is Stephanie's problem."

"We slipped too easily back into our lives without looking back."

At the apartment, Stephanie must have been looking out the window because the door opened upon our arrival. Her mother rushed to her, and they embraced, sobs racking their bodies.

"Are you two going to hug all day, or are you going to come in?" Terrance asked.

Stephanie turned to the children. "This is my mother, your grandmother." Her eyes were swollen and red.

Wendy approached first. She held out her right hand. Ruth shook it very professionally, and smiled.

"Can we hug, instead?" Wendy asked.

Ruth looked at each child carefully before speaking. "When did you marry?"

"Martin and I had a small wedding in New York. I was pregnant with Terrance."

"But he divorced Mom because of her problem," Tobey spoke. "He's trying to take us away from her."

"Your children are beautiful," Ruth said. "I wish we had known about them."

Ruth helped the children pack while I sat in Stephanie's room, trying to convince her to come with us. I found her suitcase in the closet and set it on her bed.

"You can leave this all behind," I said. "Make a fresh start. Live a life the children can be proud of."

"I can never recapture that," she answered. "I'm a drug addict. What is there to be proud of?"

"To overcome such an obstacle as drug addiction? Stephanie, that would be a great accomplishment for anyone."

"What they must think of me now?"

"They love you, that is all they are thinking about. They want you to get better. They want you to be happy."

My words seemed to bounce off a steel wall. Then suddenly she began pulling open the drawers and emptying clothes into the suitcase. Victory surged through my veins.

"If I can just get away from the drugs. I can do this," she said more to herself than to me.

"Yes!" I said, encouraged.

"We can start a new life. Maybe we should move away from here." She stopped packing for a moment, holding a blouse in her hand.

"One step at a time."

"One step?" she asked.

"Yes, start small."

She sat on the bed, pensive. "I want to come clean, now!"

"And you will! But we have to get to your parents' house, then." I stopped myself. I didn't want to scare her. "It'll all work out."

She snapped the suitcase shut and dragged it to the floor.

We loaded the luggage into the trunk. The kids climbed in. Stephanie opened the passenger door, then stopped.

"I forgot something," she said, and slammed the door. She ran back to the apartment. Wendy began to shout.

"Mommy, come back here. Come with us."

I followed Stephanie, but she had locked the door. I knocked.

"Stephanie, are you coming?"

"Have them go without me. I have some unfinished business."

"I'm not leaving without you!" I shouted back.

"No, Catharine. I will follow later. Really. Just send them off."

I hesitated, and then headed back outside.

"Catharine!" Stephanie shouted.

I turned back, hopeful.

"Thank you," were the last words she had ever spoken to me.

The entire car mourned as it drove away. Terrance, Wendy, and Tobey wailed for their mother, reaching their arms outside the car windows. I stood watching, wondering if I had done the right thing. In my heart I knew Stephanie would probably destroy herself. I had wanted to force her to come with me, to change her life, but I couldn't. Never had I felt so full of despair than at the moment.

We were back in the empty room with the whimpering Stephanie.

"Except for her angel, Stephanie died alone. Humph, so much for all her parties."

"Did I do this?"

"No, Catharine. This was your shining moment. You forged ahead in a hopeless situation, and brought forth more hope."

"The children? What happened to them?"

"They all lived drug-free lives."

"That's all you're going to tell me?"

"For them in their circumstances, that was a big step. Terrance became a lawyer; Wendy married and stayed at home to raise four children." She stopped.

My heart skipped a beat. What had happened to Tobey? Why did she hold off in telling me? She took my hand, and we were standing in the front of Arthur and Ruth's home. There stood a large plaque surrounded by bushes and flowers.

"Stephanie Robinson's Home," was all it said.

"It is here where Tobey opened a research and drug rehabilitation center. He began cutting-edge research into drug addiction.

"Stephanie's parents, Arthur and Ruth, though deeply saddened by their daughter's life, died knowing they had rescued their three grandchildren."

"But I couldn't save Stephanie," I said, my shoulders drooping.

"No one could have, Catharine," but it wasn't my angel's voice that spoke. I looked up and beheld Stephanie, a glowing, beautiful image. Her brown hair, smooth and silky; her blue eyes, once vacant, full of life. She took my hands. "You held onto a guilt that was never yours. You were so noble and brave in saving my children. For that, I will never be able to thank you enough. You must understand that you did not kill me, I did. I carry that guilt."

We embraced, and all the remorse I had held in my soul for Stephanie had fallen away.

"You were able to overcome your addiction, Catharine," my angel said. "See what you can accomplish when you face your fears?"

CHAPTER 22

The next experience revealed that I hadn't quite gotten over all my fears. I found myself, green-gowned and hunched over on the hard, paper-encased semi-bed in a doctor's office. A light tap, and then a young man entered. Doctor Rogers was on his name badge.

"Clara, we got the results."

"Cancer," I blurted out.

"Yes, Clara, I am sorry to say, you're right. The good news is we found it early, and your prognosis is very good. I'm referring you to Doctor Westwind, an oncologist." He regarded me with compassion. "Do you have any questions for me? Do you have anyone you'd like me to call?"

"No," I said.

"Are you okay?" He looked me in the eyes.

"I think I'll go home, lie down, and wait to die," I responded.

Doctor Rogers laughed. "Clara, you'll have to wait a long, long time. You're going to miss out on a lot of life. You have many years ahead of you, even if you didn't get treatment, which I wouldn't recommend."

Could cancer bully a dead woman? I was willing to acquiesce, roll over, and let it take me captive. I feared chemotherapy more than the multiplying cells inside of me. Nausea, baldness, ports in my vein.

"Isn't there a vitamin supplement I could take to make it all go away?" I asked.

"Clara, the treatment has improved. There is anti-nausea medication, and there are many attractive wig options out there."

"A wig?" I shouted. "Wig? They're scratchy and blow off with the wind."

Doctor Rogers shook his head. "I'll have Nurse Nancy come in and talk to you about setting up an appointment with Dr. Westwind. I'll keep tabs on your progress too." He shook my hand.

Within a few minutes, I found myself sitting on a blue chair with the dreaded portal taped to my arm, dripping mysterious fluid in my veins. Around me I noticed other cancer patients, old people, middle aged, and even a few children. I reached under the cotton bandeaux and felt only scalp. I grimaced. A nurse appeared. Did she have any idea what we were going through? Did she go home at night and worry about getting cancer?

"You're just about finished." She examined the tubes. "Do you have someone to take you home?" She wore a jungle print front-button smock. Her nametag said, "Marlice."

"I don't know," I replied, touching my scalp again.

Another nurse, working with a different patient, looked up at Marlice and me.

"We usually call the taxi for her," the nurse said.

"Okay. Let me do that. Do you want to stay here or follow me?"

I felt queasy, but sitting on the chair was depressing. I stood up and swayed back and forth.

"Easy now," said Marlice. "Here, hang on and we'll call for you."

When she finished making the call, Marlice led me out to the waiting area. The taxi would arrive in twenty minutes.

He dropped me off at an apartment complex, built probably in the late '60s or '70s. Two stories of cream-colored brick, interrupted with windows and a black strip cutting the two floors in half. Bald spots covered the entire front lawn, and weeds, not flowers, flourished in the flowerbed.

"Here you go," the driver said. "That will be twenty-dollars."

I handed him some cash that I had found in a brown paper bag that I had been carrying around.

"No need to give me a tip, ma'am."

"Please take it."

"Do you need me to help you get to the door?"

"I think I'll be fine."

He left, and I stood looking at the apartment names next to the door buzzers. Clara Johnson, apartment 207.

A combination of stale smoke and ammonia offended my nostrils. Mottled fabric, which was once orange carpeting, clung to the wooden stairs. I climbed, tripped, and heaved in and out, each step near insurmountable.

The recliner. That is all I wanted at that moment, to ease my feet up and rest. Wan springs tried to push back under my weight, but my frail body sank into the chair's folds. I didn't care. I was tired.

"Here, drink," my angel appeared.

"I'm not thirsty."

"It's good for you."

I drank the water then handed the glass back to her. "Let me sleep, please. I'm tired."

"You have to go to work at two," she said.

"Work?"

"Cleaning bathrooms."

My stomach rose up in revolt. "Bathrooms? Where?"

"The Fiesta Mini Mall. You clean all the bathrooms for the seven businesses. There used to be eight, but Fiesta lost a tenant."

The clock on my television said 1:16. "How far is Fiesta? Do I drive or have to take public transportation?"

"You'll find money for bus fare in your brown bag. You better head down, it's a block away from the stop, and the next one is coming at," she looked at an imaginary watch on her wrist, "1: 26."

"Can't I just float from one trip to the other? You make it look so easy." Her answer was to disappear.

It felt as if I was climbing up the Grand Canyon. I panted as I crawled onto the bus. I stood waiting and watching two young teenagers gyrating to the music blasting at their eardrums. They were oblivious to the "Reserve Seat for Elderly or Disabled," sign. Reminded me of another bus ride so long ago. I stood, grasping the bar above me, muscles aching. The bus driver heaved off his seat and yanked at the boys' shirt collars.

"Get off and let the lady sit!" he growled.

The boys glared. Everyone seemed to stare at me. A little girl pointed at my head, her mother shook her head and said, "Shush."

Another girl, probably about ten, watched. Waves spun out from her head. She wore a faded jean jacket and slacks with holes revealing scabby kneecaps. I wasn't sure if that was the fashion of the day or what the girl's family could afford. She smiled, revealing yellow, crooked teeth. "My classmate in school wears a scarf like that. She has cancer."

"So do I," I turned toward the window and watched the landscape skid away.

She stood up and stood next to my seat. I reluctantly slid over. "Do you have lots of friends?"

What a strange question, but in this existence I felt abandoned, like some mongrel roaming the streets. "No. No, I don't have any friends."

"That's sad. I don't either." She sighed a long, sad sigh, and then she smiled. "I'll be your bus friend. Where are you going?"

"Fiesta Mini Mall." I returned her smile. A little hairpin tried unsuccessfully to tame the frizz. She wore owl stud earrings and pink rectangle glasses. "Why don't you have a lot of friends? You are a very friendly girl."

She looked furtively over to her distracted mother, and whispered, "We move around a lot."

"Do you like to travel?"

She shook her head. "Mom is running away."

"From whom?" I asked in shock.

"Dad. We're going to the mall too. Are you shopping?"

"Nope. Cleaning bathrooms. Won't your father find you?"

"Sure. This is just a game they like to play. Then he takes us out for dinner. Nothing fancy, you know, but it's a night out. We do it maybe once every few months." She studied me for a moment.   "Aren't you sick? Should you be doing that?"

I smiled at her concern. "Bathrooms get dirty even when people are sick."

"Sometimes I have to clean the bathroom at home. It's yucky." She looked around the bus. "Hey, I can help you."

"Bathroom's are yucky, didn't you just say?"

"Sure, but when you got two people, it makes it better."

"Honey, you could have a crowd cleaning some of these, and it wouldn't make it any better. Thank you, though."

"What's your name? My name is Aria Cromdon." She pushed her glasses up the bridge of her nose and then twisted her owl earrings around until they were upside-down.

"Catharine Zimmer," I said. "Nope, wait...huh I'm Clara."

"I guess the cancer got to your brain a little bit," she said. "Are you married?"

"Nope."

"Ever? Dad met Mom at the restaurant she worked at. Not the most romantic, but at least they got together."

"Aria! Please don't pry into other people's business," a woman, probably in her thirties said. She sat across from us. The state of her clothing matched her daughter's.

"I should have married, but I blew the chance."

"Was he cute?"

"Aria!"

"More than cute, he was handsome." I looked toward the back of the bus, and was surprised to see Adrien smiling and waving. "But he had an attitude, a big, bad attitude." Adrien frowned. It was my turn to laugh.

Next stop, Fiesta Mini Mall. Aria slid back to her mother. The passengers slogged off. I clutched the railing and teetered down each step. Passengers behind waited in polite silence.

"Thanks for talking to me," Aria said. "I hope we see each other again." Her mother politely smiled and nodded her head. Then they faded in with the rest of the crowd.

If one could have a favorite public bathroom to clean, it would be Samantha's Sewing Senter, with only one toilet and one sink. Since most of its clients were women, the bathroom took only twenty minutes to clean. Nija's Bar and Grill, however, took the longest. Men and Women's bathrooms, six stalls of each, and two large sinks. Bar patrons were not tidy bathroom users.

"Hey, Clara. How ya doing," Nija asked as I waddled in. "Ya lookin good."

"Thanks."

"Don't work too hard. The rush won't in be until around six."

"No problem, Nija." Paper towels and soiled toilet paper adhered themselves to the wet floors. Stall six in the women's bathroom looked as if it had never been flushed.

"Nija," I called out. "Stall six needs a plunge."

I finished Tony's Vacuum by 8:57. Buckets, mops, rags, and cleaning supplies were stashed in the back of the mall. The door locked, I headed down the wide parking lot toward the bus stop. I sat on the bench.

"You're gonna be here a long time," my angel said. "Last bus left at 9:02. It's," she looked at that imaginary watch again, "9:07. You're gonna have to walk."

"Can't you just fly me home?"

"Nah."

Couldn't she understand I had cancer? I had to pretend I was living like a normal person while my body was doing all sorts of abnormal things inside of me. I crumbled to the ground, my legs caving in under me. Nausea was replaced by hunger.

"People do this all the time. Get cancer, get treatment, and get to work. You're not any more special than the rest of them."

One hour it took to creep home, dizziness and wooziness accompanied me.

"Hey! Watch it you old woman," some guy shouted when we collided.

Kids, who should have been in bed, shouted out, "Dime bag over here, dime bag!" Since they got no response from me, they threw rocks at my back.

Blackness, then sharp lights, blackness, then lights. No two streets were the same.

"Angel, how much more? I'm lost."

"Keep going," I heard her voice, but she didn't materialize.

It was the longest walk of my living and dead existence. Finally, like a beacon, Lincoln Apartments appeared. Feebly I crawled up the worn stairs to apartment 207. Inside I opened the refrigerator. It was empty! One by one I flipped open the cupboards. Empty, except for a can of sardines. Sardines?

I passed the all-night grocer just minutes before. Back down the stairs, into the night air. A neon sign blinked. The door jingled when I opened it.

"Hi Clara. Late night, huh? You should have called, I would have brought something for you."

"Thank you. I didn't realize I had nothing in the house." I leaned over a cart as it skidded up and down the aisle. "I think this should do the trick," I said, placing the items on the conveyor belt.

"I'll carry it to your apartment," the grocer said.

"Are you sure?" I hesitated, wondering if he'd cheat me out of the few items.

He followed right behind and set the groceries on the table.

"How much?"

"No, Clara. It was my pleasure. Now go get some rest."

In bed I looked at my arms. Only the port where they plugged in the I.V. indicated that something was different. Were these the arms of a cancer patient? I touched my toes. They felt normal. My face, nose, eyes, ears. All normal. My scalp. Not normal. But its baldness was only a response to the chemotherapy.

Who did I know, while living, had cancer? Claire had breast cancer, but she licked it. Aunt Jane had brain cancer and died two years to the day of her diagnosis. Andy, my old boss from the department store, died from pancreatic cancer. Father Uhen died of throat cancer. Mom would almost weekly tell me of a friend, church member, or nursing home resident who contracted the harrowing disease. Imagined toxins crawled over my skin as I learned of a new casualty.

It was what I feared even more than roller coasters or tornadoes, those two-faced, double crossing cells producing masses and tumors all over the body, yet a healthy cell lived such a short life. It was like that backstabbing friend, creating chaos in your life, while you, unbeknownst, blithely carry on a relationship with that person.

I had avoided contact with cancer at all costs. My life consisted of antioxidants, exercise and filtered water. Even at eighty, I walked on my treadmill forty minutes a day. Doctor Laura said I was the model patient.

I had also avoided cancer patients at all costs. Once the dread disease struck, they were no longer Claire, Andy, Aunt Jane, or Father Uhen. They were teeming with flagitious cells. Cancer was the modern leprosy. Funerals of cancer victims were also taboo. I had envisioned the dead cancer cells resurrecting and finding a new host. Claire was the only survivor that I had known with cancer.

"She could have used your help," the angel sat in the chair across from my bed. "She had four little ones under the age of ten."

"I couldn't get off of work."

"Yeah, yeah," she mocked. "I told Him," she jutted her chin upward, "that He should have given you cancer with six little kids to care for. No, you just had to be Clara Johnson."

"I thought you had told me never to wish ill on another."

"I am your guardian angel. I can offer suggestions for your treatment."

"Good thing He," this time I looked up, "didn't listen.

"Get some sleep. More chemo tomorrow."

For two weeks, the potent liquid dripped into my veins, searching and destroying the evil cells. Three weeks off. In the morning I'd watch the news, then some soap operas, have lunch, nap, and then prepare for my cleaning job. News, soap operas, lunch, nap, work. News, soap operas, lunch, nap, work. This existence was fine for the first week, but the next two weeks in isolation seemed more deadly to my soul than cancer to my body.

No phone calls. No visits. Sundays I went to mass, anonymously. No one turned to greet me; no one said good-bye. At least I got a few smiles and nods. I still went. I attended mass while alive, it was something I had never missed. Going as Clara made me realize that Catharine Zimmer talked to no one she didn't recognize. Neither did the parishioners at St. Adalbert's Catholic Church.

I was starting to look forward to treatment week. There I'd chat with the nurses and other patients. Stanley Quinley talked the loudest, but listened the most. He had seventeen grandchildren and four great grandchildren. He never told me how many children he had.

Lunch was usually served after our treatments, something I didn't know the first day. Stanley and I usually finished our treatments about the same time, so he, "treated" me to lunch. Once his wife, Sylvia, found out I was taking a taxi, she insisted on driving me home.

"Dear, is someone picking you up?" She peered down at me while I sat in the waiting area.

"I'm taking the taxi."

"Oh my goodness. Let us take you home."

For fifteen more minutes I'd have some company. Then alone to my apartment until heading off to Fiesta Mini Mall. There I'd smile at people, trying to gin up some conversation, but for the most part, it didn't work. Nija was talkative if he didn't have too much work. And Tony at Tony's Vacuum was friendly. He didn't have too many customers so we'd shoot the breeze for a good twenty or thirty minutes. I made sure I finished cleaning before nine o'clock, to catch the bus.

Week two of treatment would start in less than twenty-four hours. I bathed, found a presentable outfit, and was in bed by eight. Tomorrow I'd hang out with the rest of the gang.

An odd sensation greeted me when I reached the clinic. My blood was drawn, I waited for the results, waited for the pharmacy to fill the prescription, and then headed to my chair. Marlice grabbed the port, and began connecting the tubes.

"Where is Stanley?" I asked.

She didn't answer me.

"Marlice, did you hear me?"

"Stanley passed away last week," she whispered.

All forms of human suffering ground out any joy at that moment.

"Stanley!" Then a floodgate of tears. Why? He and I had only known each other for a week, and then parted ways for three weeks.

"The tears you never shed during your life," my angel said, invisible to all, but me.

Marlice patted my shoulder. "I'm so sorry, Clara. Stanley was a great patient and a great guy. I didn't want to tell you, but I knew you'd keep pestering me."

I sat with my drip, saying nothing, wondering who would be next. Who would break the chain of our quixotic friendship forged in the minefield of cancer? Then there was a disturbance in the hallway heading toward the treatment room. Sylvia, dressed in a royal blue pantsuit, was standing next to me.

"Clara!" she said. "I'm here to take you to lunch. Stanley made me promise. He told me, 'Sylvia, that poor Clara is all alone. Can you make sure you drive her home, and take her out once in a while?' I couldn't disappoint my Stanley. He'd haunt me, you know! "

She leaned down to hug me and we both began sobbed and hiccupped.

"Oh Clara, I miss him so much." Her body shook mine, but we embraced for a long time. She wasn't afraid of me, wasn't afraid of catching my disease. Shame and sorrow chastised me as I remembered the distance I had placed between myself and those family and friends that needed me.

"He lived so much longer than we had expected. He was waiting for grandchild number eighteen to be born. And he made it just in time."

Sylvia and I grew close outside of the clinic. I visited her home; she visited my apartment. She often treated when we went to restaurants. Sylvia decided to host their annual Fourth of July party, even with Stanley gone. There I met the family and friends of Stanley and Sylvia Quinley. I was isolated no more! Sylvia treasured our friendship as much as I did. Who would ever guess that in death friendships could flourish?

After my treatments and the waiting period, my doctor said I was cancer free. The same day I had received the good news, I had received the bad news.

"Clara, this is Sylvia." Her voice sounded tired on the phone. "I have some news to tell you."

She lasted only three weeks and then she was gone. Sylvia's funeral was the first cancer funeral I had ever attended, though not as Catharine Zimmer, but Clara Johnson.

Flowers perfumed the air and lightened the gloom. Each of Clara's four children hugged me. Her youngest, Cheri, walked me over to the photo board.

"There you are, with Mom! And there's another picture of you holding Baby Jeremiah."

"Cheri! Who took these pictures?" I asked, looking at my wigged image in disdain.

"I did, while you weren't looking."

"You're very sneaky!"

Sylvia was eighty-three years old, but I wouldn't have guessed her age to be past seventy. I had often assumed greatness was measured by fantastic accomplishments

– such as writing a novel. Sylvia's greatness resided in her ability to love without measuring the consequences.

"Are you ready?" my angel asked as I stood at the bus stop outside of the church.

"Yes."

"Did you learn anything?"

"Yes."

"Are you going to tell me?"

"No. You know what I have learned."

"Yes, but it might be better to talk about it."

"Sometimes it's best to say nothing." A bus appeared. "I was a jerk, if that's what you want to hear."

"That's all?"

"It's too painful to put into words right now," I said as I climbed into the bus. We were the only passengers. The vehicle rolled forward toward utter blackness. After several hours, I had begun to see mountains. Oh joy!

"Don't get too excited," my angel said.

"Where are we heading?" I shouted, feeling an oppressive weight bear down upon me.

"Where do you think?" she asked.

CHAPTER 23

The landscape provided no clues. I approached the massive mounds imbued with browns, pinks, and white, trying to recall the different geography I encountered on earth. There was nothing like this. Then I halted and screamed. Tucked inside each other were arms, legs, heads, torsos, hands, and necks. It was a junkyard of body parts. The expanse of this sordid mountain lay beyond my vision. Mile upon mile, body upon body. How could one begin to count -- to fathom the numbers?

"The Mound of Abomination. Its depths grow from the bodies of the unloved." My angel returned to my side. "There are many on earth that go through their lives spurned, but this is the most ignominious. No hatred is greater than this."

My left eye began to twitch. Then my right. I grasped at them trying to stop the nerves. The odor of decaying flesh wormed itself into my nostrils. I pivoted away from the fulsome knoll.

"Why must I be here?" My eyes twitched violently.

"You have seen, Catharine, how your life impacted the course of history," my angel spoke. "Here lies the greatest toll on humankind. Brilliance, bravery, truth, and beauty all gone from earth to be tossed into a forgotten heap. And each day people are filled with more loathing for humankind."

"What do you mean?" My inquiry did nothing to still the twitch of my eyes or the revolt of my stomach.

"You still don't understand?"

"No!"

"Then this will be your home until you do."

Her words were like a rogue wave crashing and carrying me out to sea. Every muscle within my body fell prey to atrophy. There was no help for me, as I stood, both my eyes convulsing.

Then I began to notice something even more horrible --weeping. It was no cry of a child, but the moan of rejected humankind. Its cadence descended as if to Hell, and then reverberated against my eardrums. To block out the noise, my hands clutched my ears, but there was no muffling the cacophony.

"I had nothing to do with this, ever!" I said.

"Pontius Pilate wiping her hands," my angel answered. "Come, we will walk together, but only for a while."

As we traveled, images of people appeared, standing and weeping at this rampart of human refuse. United Nations they stood. Every race, every age, every creed -- all mourning their lost heritage, their lost generations, their lost souls.

I recognized none, but they all assumed a familiar appearance. Then I spotted her blond tresses and mournful eyes. In her arms she held the remains of an unloved one.

"Catharine," she said, her lilting voice weighted with grief. "Why are you here?"

"Tell her, Catharine," my angel answered.

"I don't know," I replied.

"You do know, Catharine. You have only touched the surface of your emotions," the angel prodded. "Ursula, let Catharine hold your baby."

"No!" I shouted when I saw the raw, acid eaten flesh, and the blood oozing from its nostrils. More twitching. I wanted it to stop.

"Give him to her!" the angel demanded.

Ursula held out her baby, but my arms remained at my side, my head turned away. I recalled at that moment during my judgement a part of Ursula's story. It had seemed so insignificant at the time. She and Ty had gotten married, and then she became pregnant. When Ty found out that the child might be born with Down syndrome, he had convinced Ursula to have an abortion.

Why must I touch that horrible thing in her arms? She had the abortion, not I. My eyes twitched so much I became blinded.

"Years, Catharine, you are adding years to your punishment," the angel admonished.

The angel touched the broken body in Ursula's arms, and instantly it became a resplendent child of about two. He had that tiny slant in his blue eyes, that tilt all children with that extra chromosome have. His hair was blond, like his mother's, and he grinned at me.

My arms immediately reached out to touch him. I wanted that joy, and knew I could have it if only I could touch him, hold him in my arms.

"This child is beyond your grasp," my angel said. "Catharine, you are unfit to move beyond this journey. You will remain."

"Here? Me? No, no, no. Take me out of here. I'll go crazy!" I fell to my knees. To my horror, I was seeped in blood. The morass gripped my kneecaps, preventing our separation. Like the water in the well, the sanguine fluid drew me in deeper and deeper. "Agh!" I screamed.

My angel held out her hand. I reached for the warmth and was immediately at her side.

"Forward," she commanded.

"What?" I didn't understand.

"More stories await you. Good bye."

"That's it? Don't go!" She vanished. Ursula, too, had departed. I was alone with the cries of the unloved, and the horrible twitching eyes. I stepped forward, only one step. What would that bring? Nothing. Another step, then another. I was tired before I even began this excursion; some mysterious oppressive force weighted me down. Yet what else could I do? There were no lovely stones to rest upon nor trees with birds whispering their secrets. I held my head erect, unwilling to look to my right or to my left. Was I heading north, south, east, or west?

A man in a gray-green military uniform appeared. I could not tell you his nationality, but his eyes spoke the universal word of sorrow. He touched my arm, and we were transported to a village filled with gunshots and screaming. There I watched this same soldier, in his younger days, standing at the doorway of a thatched roof hut. Soon, more soldiers poured out from within, grabbing and pushing a young woman. Her midnight black hair was coiled in a bun. Her tiny body bulged with pregnancy. A young man clawed at the rushing soldiers, but the leader struck him with the butt of his rifle.

Immediately the image morphed into a dingy operating room. The same pregnant woman was hoisted onto a table. Her legs were pushed open. A woman wearing blood-stained surgical scrubs appeared. I could look no more, yet no matter where I turned, the image followed me. I closed my twitching eyes, yet it remained.

I cannot put into words the abomination that followed. The patient was given no anesthesia, and malevolence directed the doctor's every move. As the doctor scraped, the pain assaulted me as well. I crumpled over, and blood poured out from me.

"Stop!" I screamed. Instead of obeying my commands, the scene repeated itself; my insides battered me with pain. Blood ascended around me.

"Round up the women; that was my job. I was a proud soldier, doing my duty for my country." I had been so submerged in the woman's torture as well as my own, that I had forgotten the soldier standing next to me.

Another tiny hut emerged as the surgical room dematerialized. The blood around me disappeared. Inside this hut sat an elderly man sitting on the floor with a table set with a teapot and cup in front of him. He poured a golden liquid into the cut and lifted it to his lips. The young man stood watching him.

The father slowly returned his cup to the table before speaking. "You have shamed the family." His voice cracked.

"I have a duty," the youth stated, his voice cold.

"Your duty is family, but you kill family."

"Too many people. How can we be a strong country with so many mouths to feed?"

"People are its strength. People, not some crazed government."

"You speak treason!"

"I speak truth!" The old man hobbled to his feet. "I would much rather die speaking the truth, than living a lie."

Another soldier crashed onto the scene. He roughly seized the old man and savagely pushed him out of the hut. Soon I saw a row of people, eyes covered with rags, standing in front of a grove of trees. Soldiers were poised to shoot. I recognized the father next to the trees, and the young man, gun in arms, standing with the soldiers. Bullets rang out, and the bodies crumpled to the ground.

"Every day I must relive this," the soldier said. "My own father I killed. I will be here till the end of time."

He disappeared.

"Angel! I must leave this horror!" I shouted.

She was once again at my side. "Catharine, in life you cared not for the plight of others."

"Was I to be there for everyone?"

"Do you remember Doctor Chen? He spoke at your parish. You shook hands with him, left church to go out for breakfast, and gave no more thought to the horrors he revealed. The little envelope you picked up so you could write a donation check to his organization became a slip of paper you wrote your packing list upon."

I wanted to throw myself down in shame at that memory. Doctor Chen had spoken after Mass one Sunday. I sat in the pew wondering when he'd finish droning on and on. I was going on a cruise the next day, so instead of envisioning the pain and suffering he painted with his words, I had envisioned the outfits I would pack. Then I was hungry, and this doctor seemed to talk forever. All I could picture was the mushroom omelet waiting for me at Sunny's. I became blinded by the convulsing of my eyes.

Trumpet blasts startled me. Brilliant beams of sunlight crashed through the desolation. I squinted and shaded my fluttering eyes. Through my hampered vision, I detected angels descending upon the mound. From the heap arose tiny glowing infants. They looked like the cherubs in the old Victorian Valentine's Day cards. Their innocence crushed my soul with an anguish I had never felt. I craved their caresses, their smiles. It was not to be. The angels scooped them away. The rescue was quick, and I was submerged back into the misery.

An elderly woman stood waiting for me. She held out her hand, to which I clasped with my right hand, and covered my twitching eyes with my left.

"You remind me of my daughter," she said.

My eyes stilled themselves. "Why are you in this awful place?" Such a lovely woman, with cropped white hair, rosy cheeks, and a smooth complexion. Surely she couldn't be guilty of anything!

"I killed my daughter and grandchild."

My hand recoiled from her grasp.

Inside a living room I stood, with a younger version of this woman, and a teenage girl. Sunlight streamed in from the cathedral-sized windows. Soft, mahogany-dyed leather furniture nestled together in a cozy, yet fashionable formation. On end tables stood Matisse-styled sculptures. A thick Fereghan rug carpeted the polished wood floor.

"You will go through with it," the woman demanded. The same one standing at my side, though younger. "You will throw your life away if you have this baby."

"I can give it up for adoption," the girl pleaded.

"I could never bear my grandchild in another woman's arms!"

From that scene we were transported to a cemetery, next to a flower-bedecked casket waiting for burial. Pouring rain pushed through my garments. My body joined in the spasms of my eyes.

The woman at my side disappeared, leaving me alone with the casket. Like some terrifying nightmare, the casket squeaked open. The flowers fell into a heap as I was physically compelled to look inside. The corpse sat up, and her eyes opened like a doll. Then they bulged in accusation.

"Why didn't you stop me? Why didn't you stop me?" It was a chant. As she cantillated, my being was transported back to an clinic, the one squeezed in-between my favorite coffee shop and the department store where I had worked. There I saw the young teen, walking toward the facility along with her haughty mother.

I, Catharine Zimmer, was marching quickly from the opposite direction, returning back to the department store after my lunch break. The memories of that day, I had so successfully tucked away, rushed into my consciousness. Twitching eyes again.

"Hi," the young girl had implored. She was trying to catch my attention. I had ignored her. I knew what went on in that building, and I wanted nothing to do with it, or the people streaming into it, or the crackpots, I believed, stood outside.

"Hi!" She repeated, louder. Her mother tried to push her into the clinic without me noticing them. There were no crazies that day. I was relieved. I was running late. Often the people outside handed me brochures or began offering help as if I were pregnant. The experience had always left me feeling indignant while compunctious at the same time. I'd return back to work, surly. It would take several days to shake off that contemptible sensation, which was why I would often walk the extra two blocks to avoid it.

"All I asked for was one voice, just one person. You pretended I wasn't there. Pretended. Pretended." More chanting from this dead ghoul.

"It was not my place!" I shouted over the din.

"To let your fellow sister die with her child is of no concern to you?" Her face lost its ghoulish appearance. "Would you also have walked past a burning building while someone cried for help? Would you have also watched a child drown in water? Would you? Would you? Would you?"

"You are not talking about the same thing!" I justified myself.

"The lies of earth that sedate humans into apathy are irrelevant here. They are peeled away to expose the truth. Where a child resides should not decide his or her fate, even if that place is the womb."

Was it my job to stop her? I was already late for work, but I knew she needed a voice of conscience. I had sensed that what she was about to do was wrong, but I wasn't about to tell her what to do with her life. It was a topic that splayed itself in the news and politics, but I hadn't felt it was my place to say anything.

Back to the Mound of Abomination I returned. Grandmother and mother knelt down and woefully kissed it. Another radiant child appeared and floated into the young woman's arms. Joy lifted the sorrow from their faces, and they all vanished.

Alone again with my twitching eyes I advanced slowly, looking down at the beaten path. Many must have journeyed here. Loneliness replaced my horror. I couldn't decide which was worse. Another sound interrupted my musings. Beep, beep, beep. Dump trucks in reverse. This time there were no luminous lights or angels, just more desolation as I watched the trucks dump more body parts onto the horrific pile.

Years passed. My eyes continued to twitch, sometimes one at a time, often both simultaneously. I had become accustomed to it. My angel said my stubbornness had cost me many years, but she gave me no numbers. I would roam, hear the wailing, watch as angels rescued some, while the dump trucks deposited more. Tragedies continued to unfold as I began to understand the angel's words of the toll this atrocity played on humanity. Musicians, artists, doctors, nurses, garbage collectors, teachers, farmers, stock brokers, mothers, fathers, brothers, sisters, cousins, aunts, uncles, and on and on and on and on it went. All taken in the secret of their mothers' wombs.

One day a child began to follow me. He appeared from nowhere. He had reddish hair, blue-green eyes, and a plump little body. When I'd stop, he'd stop. One funny thing I noticed was when I'd put my arms behind my back while walking, he would do the same. I didn't say anything because I was afraid it would scare him away, yet I also craved conversation.

"Who are you?" I broke the silence.

"I was given no name."

"Why do you follow me?" He was just a child, but I felt he would speak painful truths to me.

"You would have been my godmother." Each syllable, vowel, and consonant were pronounced clearly, though he was probably only three or four.

"How?"

"Madison," he said.

I blinked wondering what my former state capital had to do with all this. Then I understood: all our laws were created underneath that big, white dome! This entire mess was a political issue. My mental mercury rose. Why weren't all the dead politicians who created and voted for those laws forced to experience this travesty?

He broke my reverie. "My mother worked for you." As I tried to remember anyone with the name of Madison, he spoke again. "Mom wanted to talk to you one day after work, but you had some appointment."

Hair appointment! The day's memories thumped into my consciousness. Madison Royal, beautiful, but tortured and needy. I didn't have time for her problems. It had nothing to do with the fact that she was more beautiful and stunning than I was, I had tried to convince myself. Nor that she had been dating the same manager I had a crush on. What was his name? His name didn't surface, but the images of that day did.

I was tidying up my desk and kept looking at the wall clock. I had skipped lunch for this appointment. My shoulders slumped when I heard the knock on my door. Jason probably needs something done before I leave, I had thought. "Come in."

Madison closed the door behind her and studied my face. "May I talk to you?"

The drive to the salon was thirty minutes without traffic. I mentally calculated if time would be on my side. My expression had revealed my true intentions, so she turned back toward the door. "That's fine. I'm okay." She grabbed the doorknob.

I tried to recover and said, "Oh, I have a few minutes," but, the tone of my voice said, "No I don't have a few minutes. I don't want to miss the hair appointment."

She quickly scampered out, her shoulders hunched over. Then I left without giving it any more thought. It was a lovely fall day; the trees waved at me with their scarlet and copper scarves. My car windows were down; the leafy smells of fall rode alongside of me. Inside the salon, smiles and welcomes greeted me, then my shampoo, cut, and style. I cringed as I recalled all the compliments I had received the next day at work barely noticing Madison's absence.

"Your hair turned out very lovely," the child's voice worked into my thoughts.

I barely heard what he had said. "Were you the one I saw in the shadows?"

In life, occasionally I would see someone pass beyond my peripheral vision. I would be sitting in the living room, and it would cross over to another room. At parties I would see it too. It was my imagination, I would tell myself, and yet I sensed there was someone extra in my life, someone that wanted to know me.

"Yes. I was lonely and wanted to be with my mother, but she had abandoned me."

I dropped my head, "But I had abandoned your mother. I suppose she wanted me to stop her."

I probably wouldn't have tried to stop her. I would have said it was her own business. "She wouldn't have listened to me," I spoke. Oh, how I wanted to justify myself before this tiny judge.

"She wasn't looking for your opinion, just your compassion."

Opinions. I had plenty of them while on earth. The environment. The pope. The president. World leaders. Senators. The Congress. News media. Hollywood. What people should wear. What people shouldn't wear. How people behaved inside church. How people behaved outside of church. The choir. The lack of a choir. The sermons. The family in front of me. The family behind me. The slutty looking woman who should have never showed up at mass. My co-workers. My bosses. Opinions. Opinions. Opinions. All truths because Catharine Zimmer espoused them.

"While you sat in the salon, my mother went home and scheduled the appointment. She drained herself of tears before she died."

Did Madison die while still working at the department store?

The people in this realm all had the ability to read my mind. "No. She quit. You forgot all about her, but she never forgot you. Mom looked up to you. She felt you had a strong faith. That was what she was looking for as a godmother." When he spoke, he had lost that angelic quality and became a monstrous ventriloquist doll. "Mom married and had a good family. Cancer found her, and she died when she was only thirty-five."

"Why haven't you been reconnected?" The only highlight within this grim abode had been the witnessing of the mothers reclaiming their lost children.

"She is near the end." His angelic expression returned. "Soon we'll be reconnected. Come, let us continue walking." He spoke with the wisdom of seeing horrors, yet not letting them destroy him. I followed him, and we walked.

After that, every day he and I walked along what looked like the same path. I had never known earthly life with this child, but realized the gaping hole his death had created. He often told silly jokes, especially when the oppressiveness weighed hard upon me.

"What do angels do all day?" He waited for my response for only a moment before giving me the answer. "Harp." He laughed at his own joke.

"What does that mean?" I asked.

"Well, angels are known for playing the harp. And the word harp also means to talk. Get it?"

Sometimes he would whistle. "This is a parakeet. This one is a finch."

But the thing the boy did that made me laugh the most was the Irish Jig. He'd tap his right foot, then jump, and then move it in front and behind his left leg. He'd repeat the steps with his left foot. Sometimes he'd dance for hours. It was such an odd, but delightful thing to watch in this miserable land.

"Who taught you that?"

"My angel," he said.

"Why?"

"I asked him to. It was something I had wanted to learn on earth." He turned away, put his arms behind his back, and began whistling.

Sometimes he walked up to the pile of mangled bodies and spoke to the unloved. They would shout out questions or requests.

"Boy, where is my mother? Boy, soothe our pains with your songs! Boy, we are lonely."

Time existed differently in this dimension, but there still seemed to be a beginning to the day and an end, and then it would start all over. At the conclusion of the strange day, the child never failed to press his lips on the mass of bodies, often stepping away with blood on his bow-shaped lips.

"Come, kiss them with me," he would plead.

I held back, repulsed, the spasm of my eyes blinding me. He would never force me, but would say, "You keep missing the keys."

It meant nothing to me, but fear grew inside of me, especially as we reached the end of each day. Would someone force me down to make contact with those gruesome bodies?

One day it seemed as if the mound had begun tapering off.

"Where have all the bodies gone?" I asked the child.

"I am drawing near the end of my time, godmother." How could he call me godmother? He called me that every day, his words stamping the brand of guilt onto my heart. "Mother is coming!" He smiled, but quickly resumed his solemn expression. "The rest of the journey you must finish on your own." I picked him up and hugged him. He pecked me on the cheek. Madison appeared. I blinked and covered my eyes from the rays emanating from her. "Mother!"

He scrambled into her arms, and then they left me alone, sad.

I studied the mountain wondering when I could leave. The image of my godson kissing the dead bodies flashed into my mind. It was the key he was talking about. I had spurned the mountain for its hideousness, but it was my actions that were detestable. These poor infants had only asked for love.

Down on my knees I fell and strained to find the courage for my next action. The incessant crying seemed to stop as if waiting for me. I leaned forward and touched the mound with my lips. At that moment, I felt connected to each abandoned soul.

The twitching stopped. I blinked a few times, to make sure, but my vision cleared.

"Took you long enough." Next to me stood my angel.

"So? Am I ready for heaven?"

"No, Catharine, not yet." She was not smiling.

CHAPTER 24

No one is ever ready for this next stage of the sojourn," the angel said, her dark eyebrows furrowing in distress.

"What?" Could anything be worse than living among hacked apart and chanting limbs? I wiggled my feet trying to rid themselves of the feeling of blood seeping between my toes.

"Do you remember Jonathan Flyce?"

I blankly stared into space, trying to recall the person behind the name.

An image from the department store appeared. I stood behind the cash register, and there stood Jonathan Flyce, who was not nice. There was a poem I had made up about him. We would recite it after he'd leave the store.

"Jonathan Flyce, who was not nice, fell in bed, woke up dead."

I was very proud of my prose, and after saying it, all of us tittered uncontrollably. We had to, because an encounter with Jonathan Flyce was like crashing into a semi-truck and denting our entire psyche. I'd have to go home and sit on my balcony for several hours just to recover from a Flyce encounter.

"What kind of sales clerk, are you?" he'd demand. "You again. I thought they fired you long ago!" "You're so incompetent!" "You should get a job as a monkey at the zoo!"

He said senseless things, but Jonathan Flyce owned most of the town I lived in. Money excused his behavior. His wife, Tina Flyce, must have come from the same mold as her husband. When she floated up the escalator, we hid. Ding! Ding! Ding! We had to replace that bell several times because of Tina Flyce. The person feeling the bravest would timidly appear at the register.

"You wanted to push her down the escalator, didn't you?" the angel asked.

"More than once," I replied without any hesitation. "She put the b in the word..."

"Yes, I know," the angel sighed heavily. "Catharine, despite your last journey, your heart is still very hardened."

"But those children, they were innocent of all wrongdoing. The Flyces had no excuse for their behavior."

"Did you ever pray for them?"

Pray for them? They tried to get me fired - not only once, but multiple times. Their lies almost prevented my ascent into management.

"Why are we even talking about the Flyces? Isn't this about my life, my eternity?"

The angel pointed downward where I spotted, between the flickers of flames, two rotted out corpse screaming in torment.

"Mr. and Mrs. Flyce are not looking so nice," the angel quipped with no mirth.

"Am I also to blame for their demise?"

"They chose freely." A look a sorrow washed over her face. "But your hardness of heart for them and their damnation is an unacceptable attitude for heaven."

"I was expected to pray for those awful people?"

"You know your catechism. Because of their attitude you felt justified in your persistent antipathy toward them."

"My prayers would have done nothing for them."

"But they would have done much for you. Are you ready?"

"For what?" My eyes bulged in terror. Was she asking me, telling me to go...?

"I am not permitted where you are going," the angel said soberly. "Suffice it to know, your stay is temporary, even though one millisecond in there is too long."

"You're my guardian angel! You're supposed to be with me at all times! If I go, you go." I yanked on her arm, but she dissipated.

My body slowly descended as if in a malfunctioning elevator.

"This is their just punishment, not mine!" I recalled the relish I had felt while watching the bad guys in movies getting shot up by the hero.

My words were engulfed in flames. Suddenly my body imploded from within, and I was this horrible cavernous corpse. My mouth seemed only capable of emitting screeches of terror.

Nothing on earth, nothing anywhere could compare to the compounded explosion of misery that consumed my being. Fear, desolation, despair, sorrow, nausea, headache, muscle spasms, anger, hate, and distrust poured into me. There was no room for joy, peace, love, faith, hope, nor comfort. This far exceeded the horror I lived as April Morris or on the Lake of Desolation.

Maggots wormed themselves in and out of my ears, nose, and mouth. My skin had caught on fire, as if I had fallen into a volcano. Even my toes blistered from the furnace of hell.

"Get me out of here!" I screamed, but everyone around me was in his or her own misery to notice. Then I spotted him, the Prince of Darkness. He swaggered over to me.

"Catharine Zimmer, the big-mouth. You're one of the temporaries, aren't you?" He snarled.

"I want out!" I responded, horrified once again as I had encountered him face to face.

"Shut up or I'll make sure your stay is permanent." He walked around me. There was no flesh on me or I would have had goose pimples crawling up and down. "A lost opportunity. There were so many chances. You were so self-righteous, judgmental, yet neglected so many around you. You were ripe for the picking, but that damn priest had to come and give you last rites! I tried a flat tire, engine problems, but he still showed up."

"I would never have chosen this!" I replied.

"No one ever chooses this! Why do you think I'm so successful?"

"But there is no love."

"Love? Money, power, control. Those are what people really want." He shook his head in derision. "Go learn what you're supposed to learn, and then get the hell out of here." He roared at his pun, flames flickering from his mouth.

He disappeared, but the agony remained. I gasped and coughed trying to rid myself of the scorched sensation searing my throat. Heartburn on earth was mild to this. Water is what I craved at that moment, but I knew that even if I had drank the equivalent of the seven oceans, the thirst would never be satiated. Then I noticed something that suspended any thoughts of my own comfort, the souls of the damned, the people who had chosen freely this eternity. This is where Adrien might have ended up. Who is here? I wondered.

The cacophonous moaning and groaning far exceeded the cries of the Unloved. Instead of deafening, however, the noise sickened me to the point of uncontrollable revulsion. Every few moments I had the horrible sensation of the digestive system defying the force of gravity, and returning the food partially digested back into my mouth. On earth I had tried to avoid retching at all cost, but here, in Hell, it is what everyone did between the cries of horror and dejection.

I recognized people even though they appeared in ghastly forms. I cannot divulge their identities, but suffice it to say no one class of people escaped this wrath. Among the damned were the rich as well as the poor, those who had scorned religion as well as those who had worked for religious institutions, celebrities as well as the homeless, the powerful as well as the weak. What I found most startling, however, were the small numbers actually dwelling in this horrible abode. Indeed, one soul was too many. The course of human history is long, but fortunately, many, many souls were spared.

"They got their just reward, right?" Another dark angel appeared. "This is what they deserved."

"Yes," I agreed with him, yet something stirred within me, an emotion outside of the despair and horror engulfing me. I would be released, but they were here forever and ever and ever. There was no finite to eternity, only infinity. It's a concept that is not understood on earth because most things have a beginning and an end. The sun rises; the sun sets. We start work and end work. We start a project, we finish the project, or at least should finish the project. We are born, we die. It is hard for us to completely understand that life on earth is very short, and that it's only a testing ground for our eternity.

Empathy began to seep into my soul. True enough by their lives they had chosen this final destination, but my heart pounded in intense sorrow for their ultimate destruction. What could I have done or said to spare these people? My angel was right. I should have prayed for the Flyces and others like them, but I was too busy nursing the wounds they inflicted upon my self-image with their cruelty. I should have been more humble and tried to extend love and kindness to the Flyces, if only through my prayers. Nevertheless, my ego was fanned by the laughter of my co-workers. I got more positive feedback when I made sarcastic remarks. If I had said nothing, and quietly prayed for the Flyces, no one would have known.

I remembered a co-worker's desire for Hell. He would tease me about my faith (little did he know how little faith I really had). "I'm going to Hell," he'd boast. "And I can't wait!" I cringe thinking of that moment because I find it hard to believe anyone would choose this.

Sorrow gripped my heart like a sixty-ton metal chain clamped tightly around my soul and dropped into the ocean of sorrow. A parent grieves the loss of a child, but I was grieving for the eternal loss of all these souls. Oh, how I longed to rescue them, or at the very least, bring them comfort.

The pain swelled and I literally burst like a water balloon. My body became a sprinkler, the damned rushing to the cooled waters. When it touched them, it spat and hissed, and they shrieked in more pain. This only increased my anguish, and the sprinkler was replaced by a life-sized water fountain. Every pore of my body released a torrent of water. The damned crowded even closer despite the pain the water inflicted upon them.

Another demon approached. "It's too late!" He sniggered. He tried to shove them away like a security guard pushing away screaming fans, but the damned only pushed in closer. I thought I had reached the summit of mourning, but it had climbed to another height, and more and more water gushed from me.

"Dear God, spare others this horror," I prayed. I recalled the Bible story of the rich man and Lazarus. Riches saturated the rich man's life to which he had no care for anyone but himself. Hell awaited him, and in his misery, he begged to have Lazarus bring him some water and for his brothers to be warned. It was too late for the rich man, it was too late for all those people who were damned, but could others be spared? Couldn't I return to earth to tell others Hell really does exist?

"If they will not listen to Moses and the prophets, neither will they be persuaded if someone should rise from the dead," my angel, who appeared on the other side of a partition, quoted Abraham from the Bible.

These words released yet another surge of grief. This final stream, however, was soothing and cleansing. My angel beckoned. I walked past the souls, through the wall, and emerged on the other side whole and renewed.

"Your journey is completed," she said.

"How come I feel as if there is more to do? I don't feel quite ready."

"Catharine, you have been stripped of your self-love. You are finally ready to do what you had been created to do."

CHAPTER 25

My angel had fled once more, and I found myself engulfed in a desolate prairie of wild flowers, weeds, and thistles. Surely this wasn't hell, but it didn't come close to my visions of heaven. What had the angel said? I needed to finish what I was created for? Writing? If that was my final job, why had I been sent into this deserted grassland? Wouldn't it have been more practical to place me at a desk? In the distance was a crimson brick manor. Maybe that was where my computer waited. I tripped over mud clumps hidden in the overgrown vegetation as I approached the structure. Dusk began to descend as I approached the dwelling.

Six dormers burrowed into the mansard roof. Four chimneys, perched on each side, emitted faint wisps of smoke. Gargoyles peered over the eaves. The overhang sagged above the porch, which was strewn with hay. My foot felt its way up the collapsing stairs. Dim rays escaped from a window. I began to doubt the existence of a computer waiting for me to begin my stories, but curiosity prodded me forward.

I turned the knob. Locked. I knocked. The door squeaked opened to reveal a woman in a herringbone black woolen gown. It was cinched at the waist and cascaded to the ground. Tiny buttons, beginning at her neckline, traveled in a straight line down to her rib line. Her sleeves were gathered in a black bow at her upper arms, and then flared out at the wrists. Underneath the black were white eyelet cuffs. Around her neck was a black silk tie.

"Come in, we've been waiting for you," she smiled and ushered me into a once magnificent library. Along three of the walls stood ceiling high, mahogany bookcases. Chunks of wood were missing, along with the plaster on the walls. Several people or spirits resided in this room, all dressed in costumes from different eras in history. Most of them stood, tightly packed in the library. Others sat in Jacobean-style armchairs that rested between the bookshelves. "Sit there," the woman pointed. It was the same chair I sat on during my judgement.

"Is the giant here?" I looked around, but didn't find him mingling with the crowd.

"Your writing," the woman peered down at my old journals. How could she have retrieved them from the back of my clothes closet? I had assumed dust and neglect destroyed my meager beginnings.

"Nothing is ever lost forever," the woman looked up.

"What is the purpose?" I didn't really want the answer.

"So," a man abruptly interrupted, "you called yourself a writer, huh?"

"I liked to write." I pushed my shoulders deeper into the brocade chair.

"But you didn't write," he stated.

"I did."

"But you stopped."

"Yes, I know. I know that already. Why must I go through this again?"

"Do you know who I am?" A British accent laced itself through his words.

"No."

"Listen." He pulled out a book.

This was very uncomfortable, and I was half afraid. However, the only thing to be done being to knock at the door, I knocked, and was told from within to enter. I entered, therefore, and found myself in a pretty large room, well lighted with wax candles. No glimpse of daylight was to be seen in it.

"Charles, this is not your time," the woman continued reading my work.

"*Great Expectations,*" I answered. "Pleased to meet you Mr. Dickens," I held out my hand.

"Catharine, Catharine, wherefore art thou Catharine?" The Bard dramatically pushed past Dickens. Like all the pictures I've seen of him, he wore a goatee. He stood shorter than me, and when he smiled, it looked as if he had wooden teeth.

"I never understood that line," I replied.

"Fie! Merely seven hundred years have passed and death unto the English language."

Can a specter break out in hives and a clammy sweat? I did. The greatest writers ever were going to study my feeble attempts at prose.

"I can't go through with this," I reached to grab the boxes filled with papers and notebooks."

"You mustn' reach. It's rude," who was this woman? "I'm sorry," she proffered her hand,

"Emily Bronte."

"And, is that your sister, Charlotte?" I nodded toward a fair woman with her light hair pulled back away from her face.

"Of course, and there is Jane Austin and Louisa May Alcott over there. I must ask, why did you stop?"

"She feared the bromidic," a man, dressed from the 1950s, stepped forward. "Some overcome it, others it overcomes them."

"Fie! Bromidic. What art thou saying?"

"Boring, commonplace. She feared being mediocre, not unusual, nor unique."

"Is that why you committed suicide?" I asked him.

"I didn't kill myself. It was a gun accident." Hemmingway was handsome with dark hair and proud stance. He drew deeply on a cigar and slowly exhaled the smoke. In his hand, he clutched the play I wrote in high school.

"You can't want to read that," I said, reaching.

"Grammar! Who taught you grammar?" Mary Shelley asked. She too held my writings in her hands.

"Let us begin," Dickens' voice rose above the rest. "I have her very first poem, written in first grade.

I am home in bed; With a cold in my head; I feel very sad; For being sick makes me mad; Why can't I play instead of being sick all day?

They chuckled. I winced in pain.

"Here's a cute story, it's about a toothpick. In the tale the toothpicks tells how he came to be."

"'Mr. Johnny Toothpick.' I wrote that when I was only seven. Really, don't waste your time."

"Another one about an angel who couldn't sing in the Christmas choir. Quaint." Code word for boring, I was sure.

"This poem, *Bowtieden*, is extraordinary," Another writer, one I didn't recognize, spoke. "You were thirteen when you penned this. It was quite good."

"Yes, it was a fine piece," Percy Bysshe Shelley spoke up. "I almost wished I had written it myself."

One by one they pulled out the stories, the articles from high school, the poetry. Finally, four boxes were held up.

"Your novels," Jane said. "All started, but never finished. You told the giant you had stopped writing after high school. This one was penned when you were twenty-five, this one thirty-eight, this one, fifty-nine, and this one, seventy-two! Look everyone, she had her own printing press!"

"Typewriter," Hemmingway said.

"Computer," I piped up.

"What?" Their voices spoke all at one, but their different pitches created a discordant tune.

"Oh, never mind," I said and pointed at the boxes. "These were all false starts! Just a waste of time for a fanciful woman. I couldn't bring myself to believe that Catharine Zimmer was a novelist," I tried pleading my case. "Each time the black splayed itself onto white my inner voice warned me to stop wasting my time. No publisher would touch it. No one would read it. Fame would never be mine."

"Fame? Is that what you sought, fame?" Another man, one I didn't recognize, stepped forward. "If fame was what you wanted, you could have found it in many other places than at the writing desk. There were many in your generation who discovered *fame*," he emphasized the word in a derogatory tone, "with many doing ignoble things for a chance to have the spotlight shine upon them. Writers seeking fame are not really writers."

"The word is infamous," Hemmingway stated.

The writers broke out in chatter.

Radulf appeared too. "Hello Catharine. How has your journey been?"

They say a mother forgets the pain of childbirth, but I had forgotten the horrors of the previous centuries. "It is almost finished," I replied.

"Yes, but this next and final step will be your most challenging. You had put off writing for so long; the chasm created by your neglect will be difficult to bridge."

"I don't understand," I puzzled at his words.

"You're terrified of it," Radulf said.

"Of what?" Did Radulf know he was talking with me and not one of his companions from his novel?

"Your writing. In your mind it had become larger, more dangerous than any sea monster I had ever written about. The words will wrap themselves around your neck and strangle you. They will torment, tease, harangue. They will show no mercy. Or so you believe." His braids flipped onto his neck as he gave his impassioned speech. He flicked them off and continued.

"The terror ends when you sit down, alone, and write."

"Write what?"

"Write anything, just write," Mary Shelley stepped forward. "Just write, and soon the words will flow. You will compose a story."

"But, but..." I sputtered.

"And you will have to go back to it, and back to it again, until you find the right words, the right meanings." She wiped her brow. I tried to find signs of the evil monster that she had depicted in her novel. High cheekbones, aquiline nose, and large expressive eyes seemed more fitting to write a children's book than a horror story.

"Have you ever painted, Mistress Zimmer?" A man, dressed from the 18th century, spoke. His German dialect accentuated his serious demeanor.

"Never. I scribbled, doodled..."

"Doodled? I don't understand," he said. "Painters may paint an image on their canvases, but they are not done until they go back and add the tints, the shades, perhaps an outline. Many mistakenly believe that one swipe along the canvas is enough, but it usually isn't." He adjusted his cravat. "Have you seen my *Travelers in a Landscape*?"

I stared hard, trying to figure out who this man was.

"Johann, thank you," Emily interrupted. "Catharine, his words ring true, don't they?"

"But what if you have no talent? What if you're just deluding yourself, like I had done?"

"The words don't lie. There is no pretending in these boxes." Dickens shouted. "Even so, if the desire to write was placed in your heart, you were to write."

Who had said that to me before? The Giant. He didn't say I would write beautiful prose, but I would write. I had wanted to be a master, like Mozart with his symphonies, like Michelangelo with his genius. Instead, writing felt clumsy, awkward, contrived. I was afraid to keep chiseling away at those seemingly innocuous words. I had walked away before I had sculpted the image from my mind to an image for the world to see. The lump of marble remained just a lump.

"You're lying. It's easy to say this when we're all dead," I rushed over to the boxes and grabbed my notebooks from the writers' hands.

"I admit, no one will ever write like me," the Bard stated. "And, yet Mistress Catharine, tears and laughter came to me with your words."

"How could I have made a living out of it?" Practical Catharine Zimmer. "And the critics? They would rip my writing apart."

Dickens began to laugh. "My dear, my work is still being scrutinized and disparaged."

"Some have the audacity to believe the Earl of Oxford wrote my plays! Indeed!" The Bard strutted like a peacock. "Even the Queen knew I had written those plays. She was one of my most avid admirers."

"The problem is, as I see it, you never took it seriously. Oh, to be true, there are plenty out there who claim to be writers, and those who claim a desire to write, but the endowment of this gift is not liberally applied," another writer, again, I didn't know his name.

"See, I didn't have the talent to write."

"Please don't interrupt. As I was saying..."

"Get to it!" Was that Samuel Clemens speaking? "Miss Zimmer was sleeping at the helm. She could not even lift a stylograph to write a *Letter to the Editor*. Father died when I was twelve, and I began working at thirteen. Still had time..."

"We're not here to discuss your life, Samuel." Emily said. "Don't mind them, Catharine. Many of them, even though they have died long before you, are still stuck in this dimension. Judging from their comments, you can probably guess why. The rest of us came to help you see a path to finishing your works."

"It confounds me no end to see good talent go to waste, and most certainly it was wasted on her," Samuel's mustache twitched with his words.

Denunciatory eyes bored through me.

"What does this have to do with anything now? I'm dead."

"We're your peers, Catharine." Hemmingway snuffed out his cigar. "You felt your writing couldn't measure...."

"She was lazy, I tell you!"

"Samuel!"

For a long time the writers argued. A tennis match, I watched, back and forth. Silence.

Emily stood up and placed the cartons before me.

"You have some work to do," she said.

"What do you mean?" I gasped, horrified at the prospect before me.

"They're unfinished."

Samuel procured a feather and ink well, no typewriter, no computer.

Emily hugged me with her final words. "Your journey will never be finished until these novels are complete. Godspeed to you,"

Each of the authors followed and either hugged me or shook my hand. The Bard, however, kissed my cheeks, and Samuel, shook his head in derision. Then, like a winter day, when night comes too quickly, the authors faded away.

"Angel! Angel!" Emptiness. Just the boxes staring at me in the macabre manor house.

Behind me stood the bookshelves, my sentinels. My body refused to sit, so I scraped my chair against the cracked wooden floor. I tripped over a tattered Indian rug, grabbing the edge of the table to rescue me.

"Angel. Please. Get me out of here."

Her voice answered back, "You have four books to write. Then you must find a publisher."

"A publisher?"

"I'm just joking. But, finding a publisher is often more difficult than writing."

"How can anything be more difficult than writing?"

"Catharine, Catharine," she shook her head. "In this realm you will remain until their completion."

"Whatever for?"

The boxes mocked and tormented me. I could no longer be in the same room with them. I escaped from the library into a hallway pointing to rooms everywhere, their archway-entries draped in cobwebs. Upstairs? What secrets did it contain? I climbed the steps, my foot plunging into a gap. I yanked it out and stepped onto the first floor landing. An odd menagerie sprawled itself onto the matted carpet. Cobwebs coiled themselves around a gray pram with a broken shade. Above it I peered out the two-paned, cracked window. Blackness. It was as if a spotlight was on the inside, with all the surrounding area enshrouded in obscurity.

I stumbled over the rubble toward a rusted birdcage. Inside a skeleton of a feathered creature reposed.

The darkness began to seep inside. I looked for light switches but found only wall sconces with consumed candles. Stumbling to the stairs and clutching the bannister,

I crept down, trying to avoid the gaping step. My hands groped in front of me in the darkness.

"Angel! Angel. Help me." Complete opacity absorbed me into the darkness. Was that panting I heard? Animal footsteps? It was coming from the library. Then light. The only light in the haunted manor was in the same room as the waiting beast and those horrid boxes. Dare I enter?

Something fell on me and writhed between my blouse and skin. The beast on me or in the room? I had to choose. I rushed into the library. Adrien stood next to the table with the boxes.

"Here is your monster," he handed me the first page of the first chapter of my first book.

"Get the spider off of me!"

"There was no spider. It was the only way I could get you in here."

"Adrien!"

"It's pretty bad that you have to be dead and spooked before you face your writing."

"Shut up." I didn't need any sanctimonious lecture.

"What can't you face, Catharine? Just write!"

"I can't."

"You must or you will never leave."

"Will you stay?"

"Nope. I still have a long way ahead of me. Here," he handed me the quill. "It's not the same one as the stories. This one you have to dip into the inkwell." He set the paper in front of me. No typewritten words, only Catharine Zimmer's cursive handwriting on aged parchment.

"What happened to them? They were neatly typed?"

"If you wait much longer, you'll have to make your own paper, like the monks. So get to it!" He began to fade. "Oh, I forgot. Here is your supper." He pushed forward a board with a small loaf of brown bread. "Bon appétit!"

CHAPTER 26

I fixed my gaze on the boxes. I pulled the bread closer and tore off a piece. It was something to while away the time. Crumbs spattered over my lips as I munched down on cracked wheat probably older than the house. There were no decks of cards to play solitaire, a game I had found so handy on my computer during my self-imposed writing times. I went back to the mirror. I beheld myself this time dressed in a brown brocade gown, buttoned up to the neck. Black velvet trimmed the cuffs and the collar. *This fashion suits me.*

After admiring myself, I turned to the bookshelves spanning from ceiling to floor in this ancient library. *Let me read for inspiration.* Gargoyle statuettes resting on the top of the shelves, glared. Dare I touch a book? The books, however, lured me, and spoke, "Open and read!"

Dust swirled as I grabbed a leather bound book and flipped opened the cover. As if to torment me, the words had fled. Like a useless witness at the scene of a crime, only the white vellum remained. Again, I reached for a book as if on a desperate hunt, but found only emptiness. I should have stopped, but like a gambler that keeps losing at the slot machine, I cranked again. Every book stood void of words. After an hour of this futile pursuit, I spied, in the lower right corner of the last rack, a tiny book. It would also be empty, but I still took my chance and opened it.

"You will be here for an eternity if you don't begin to insert your own words in your own book."

Slam! Down I tossed it to the floor. The gargoyles smirked. I turned back to the boxes of Catharine Zimmer's unfinished literature. Book one. *Catharine, start where you began so many years ago.* I pulled out the first sheet, and the words drew me in. I read, but then dampness hovered disrupting my concentration. That's how it always was with my writing. I would carefully set all my implements in front of me - a glass of water, chewing gum, and a thesaurus. Then I would look at the blank computer screen. Time to flex my fingers. Crack. Wait. Nothing. I'm hungry. I would go into my kitchen and make a sandwich. I marvel I didn't end up weighing more than I did, but then my little writing exercises were as sparse as plants in a desert. Back to the computer I would wait like some oil baron waiting for the black liquid to gurgle to the surface.

Then the computer games lured me away for hours. When social media arrived, Facebook embezzled my time. I was just keeping up with the nieces and nephews I had convinced myself. There would be no computer in this odd dimension. I crossed my arms and rubbed my hands up and down my shoulders, hoping the friction would warm me. My eyelids weighted by an unseen force, began to close, and slumber shoved my face onto the table.

"How dare you defy me," a voice awakened me. My eyes blinked, trying to focus. "I explicitly forbade you from this!" A man, probably in his forties, took my manuscript and tossed it into the roaring fireplace.

"No!" I rushed toward the blaze, but his grip detained me.

"No daughter of mine will do the work of the devil!"

Years and years of writing gone in an instant. How could this be? I would have to start from scratch. I will be here forever! I began to sob.

"How could you?" I pounded my fists into his chest. He slapped my face.

"Go to your room and prepare yourself. The carriage is waiting."

A maid ushered me upstairs, but I was no longer in the haunted mansion. Bright sunlight streamed through clean, clear windowpanes dressed in heavy damask draperies. Carpeting covered the wide staircase.

"Much sorry for your loss, ma'am," the maid curtsied. "Your mama was special. No reason why your papa needs to send you away to school. You're near grown now. You can begin to take care of the house matters."

A manservant entered and carried my trunk down the stairs. My maid bathed me and brushed out my hair. In this realm I no longer felt fear of water, but it held no warmth. I shivered.

"Oh, you poor thing." She draped a towel around me and scrubbed me dry. I wasn't used to having someone put clothing on me, but that she did. I wore a long gray pinafore with a ruffled skirt and a white, long-sleeved blouse underneath. She then braided my hair and coiled it atop my head.

I wanted to ask her name, but thought it would be odd since she knew me and assumed I knew her. "Do you mind if I write to you?"

She laughed. "You know I can't read."

"Then you should go to school with me."

"Oh, but it's for ladies, not me."

"You're a lady! Mistress..." I wanted her to fill in the blanks.

She ignored me and said, "Here is your cloak. Come on."

I followed obediently down the stairs. My father tried to hug me, but I turned from him. How could he so cavalierly toss out my work and then expect me to return any affection? He pecked me on the cheek then pushed me outside.

"Be a good girl. I'll be travelling overseas."

He held out his hand and helped me into the carriage. My maid rushed forward and tucked a fur blanket over my lap.

"Tis cold," she said. "Don't know why you can't buy a carriage with walls," she scowled.

Crack of the whip, and we were gone. I loved horses and dreamed of carriage rides, but this was a somber road. I had read countless novels about the English moors, not fully understanding their gloom. Today, as the black phaeton ambled on, I comprehended loneliness as I beheld hilly scrubland, dingy, scudding clouds, and desolation. We traveled for hours, no words exchanged between the driver and me. I tried, but he wouldn't respond.

Finally, he pulled up alongside an inn. He helped me out.

"Go ahead and eat without me," he said. "I will feed and water the animals." He led the horses and carriage back to the stable.

Inside I entered a paneled, red-carpeted room, with tiny tables and chairs. A woman led me to a table next to a roaring fireplace. I recalled the terrible incident of the morning, the flames devouring the pages in contumacy. Wearing a dirty white apron, the innkeeper appeared and took my order.

"Meat pie and ale," I said. The innkeeper darted me a strange look.

"Ya mighty young to be drinkin' ale," he said. "How about some nice tea?"

"Ale it is. My father allows it at home."

He walked away grumbling, but returned with the meat pie and ale.

"Would you happen to have any bread and butter, as well?" I had hoped it was better than the crust of the night before.

"You're not the only patron here," he remonstrated, though all the other tables were empty.

I slathered the bread and ate the entire tiny loaf. I washed it all down with the ale. It was tasteless like the other delicacies that had passed through my lips in this domain. Why had I expected it to be any other way?

The innkeeper hovered as I ate. When I finished, he took up the dishes, and left. My angel appeared.

"Finally! The angel returns! I had thought you found a new person to torment."

"Writing is something you must do alone," she replied. "It is a voyage you have avoided all your life. Even now, when you're dead, you can't face it."

She left. I paid the innkeeper and gave him a little extra. He literally leapt for joy at the shillings. I smiled and some compulsion led me to hug him.

"Come back again!" he shouted as we pulled away.

More hours slipped by. Dusk was followed by blackness. I pulled the fur around my neck. Then, in the distance, I beheld a lone manor atop a hill, its silhouette even darker than the night sky. Pinpricks of mottled light contrasted against the black, but not enough to overcome the darkness. The horses heaved forward as we traveled up the mount.

A man waited for us when we pulled up the long drive. He helped me down took my baggage.

"She's waiting for you," was all he said before disappearing.

Inside, a woman, probably in her sixties, stood as gray as the manor house.

"It's about time! Take her bags to the room on the west end of the third floor. You have missed dinner, so must go without. Go to your room and wash, and return to the parlor for evening prayer."

My father brushed his lips against my cheek. "Be a good girl." He then left.

I followed the manservant up the stairs and down the dark hallway. Inside he led me into a room with eight beds, four lined up on the north wall, and the other four on the south. How I knew the directions in the dark room, you wonder? There were, posted on each wall, its cardinal direction. North Wall. South Wall. East Wall. West Wall.

"Madame had me paint these plaques and hang them," the manservant must have read my mind. "Here, my wife saved you some supper. You best hurry. The Madame don't like dalliers."

He left me alone in the dark room. Fortunately, the moon came out of hiding, its rays shining on my bed. I ate the meat pie. I was shivering so was reluctant to remove my cloak. No fuzzy robe or booties waited to comfort me. I felt my way back to the main floor.

Inside the parlor sat several, somber looking young girls. They wore gray woolen smocks, and their hair was severely pulled back. The Madame stood in the center, a prayer book in her hand. When I entered, she stomped forward and ripped off my cloak.

"I told you to wash."

"It's too cold in here," I answered. "Why don't you get a fire started?"

Titters. She turned to face the girls. The smiles vanished instantly.

"For your insolence you will scrub the kitchen floor when we finish with night prayers."

She turned back to face the girls. As her voice cackled and droned on, I felt my eyelids drooping.

"Wake up!" She shouted. "Here, you read," she handed me the black book. I looked it over and realized it was a John Calvin book of prayers.

"These are very nice, but I'm Catholic," I said.

Her eyes bulged. "Go to the kitchen at once!"

A kitchen in a manor house is not like a kitchen in the modern 21st Century. A small house could almost fit inside. Along one wall was the hearth, its soot smearing its ashes onto the stone. A timber table, which could probably seat thirty people, ran along another wall. A larder stood off to another side. Dead chickens hung from the ceiling, blood obeying the laws of gravity, forming pools underneath the deceased fowl.

"I ain't' gonna let you wash this floor," the cook appeared from the shadows. "You stay down here and keep me company. Madame don't need to know." The cook, her name was Hilary, pulled out a bench for me to sit.

"I don't mind washing the floors. Just get me a mop," I said.

"A mop?" She gave me a quizzical stare. "Sit. I'll make you some tea first."

After settling me in with tea and some scones, she began scrubbing, on her hands and knees. It was too much for me.

"I can't sit here and watch you. Get me another bucket, and I'll start on the other side."

House cleaning was another distraction for Catharine Zimmer. As I sat staring at my blank pages, a litany of chores sang in my mind. Clean the bathroom. Wash the kitchen floor. Fold laundry. Clean out the refrigerator and the cupboards. Vacuum. Change the sheets. Mop the bedroom. Dust the house. Clean the stove. Of course these things needed to be done, but every time I sat down to write? I became so proficient at cleaning I thought of taking on a second job. My mother dissuaded me.

"Catharine, you make enough at the department store, why would you want to clean people's houses?"

"I didn't know you were such a snob?" I tried diverting the significance of her comments away from the neglected authoring.

Mom parried my remarks with one of her own, "Catharine, when you stop running, you will find happiness."

I shook my head at the memory and watched Hilary return with a bucket and rag. The frigid water bit as I plunged my hand inside. I recoiled. Why had I ignored my mother's wisdom? My knees winced as they encountered the cold stone. Back and forth I scrubbed, but my body twitched from the chill.

"I knew you was too much a lady for this," Hilary said.

"No, no. Let me get used to it." Again my hands entered the icy depths. I squeezed out the rag and began scrubbing. "Don't you have hot water?"

Hilary laughed. "It is hot, dear."

We both scrubbed our respective areas, bumping only once. I hummed. Madame's black boots stood on a clean, wet spot.

"Singing is reserved only for music instruction and church," she remonstrated. "Not for work." She marched away.

"Take off your shoes," I said to myself as I rewashed the area she had sullied.

Hillary and I finished the floors about an hour later.

"The tea must be cold," she said. "Here, let me make you some more."

It wouldn't matter, but I didn't tell her that. "Only if you join me."

For two hours Hilary told me her story. I knew I had to write about it. When I returned back to the dorm room, I searched in my bag for the paper I had stashed away. There were no writing utensils, so I fumbled around in the shadows, opening and closing doors. Finally, on the second floor, I found what must have been a classroom. The quills and inkwells were lined up along a table. I snatched one of each and left. Madame must have been a heavy sleeper, for she never awoke.

The clock struck one o'clock when I finished writing. I hid the papers under my mattress. I fell onto the bed, without changing. Before I knew it, someone was shaking my shoulders.

CHAPTER 27

Wake up; you don't want to wash the floors again!" A meek voice spoke. As I opened one eye, then the next, I beheld my roommates. "You sure told her off last evening!" They all began to laugh. I smiled.

"It's a dreadful place here. Where are we, debtor's prison?" I asked.

They laughed again.

"No, it's Madame Brimstone's School fa Young Ladies," a dark haired lass, with a strong cockney accent said. "But I'm naht a lady. At least dat's what Ma'am Brimstone says. She's been workink on me talkink."

"She puts soap and rocks and thistles in poor..."

"Thistles?" I interrupted. "That's child abuse!"

"How old are you?" A petite flaxen-haired child asked.

"Much older than I look," I answered. We stared at each other, they and I. Not having time to waste for introductions, we splashed ice water onto our faces and tried to sponge bathe ourselves. Up went our hair, pulled so tightly my head began to throb. Then we donned gray, woolen frocks, that we called our uniforms. My skin broke out in a rash.

We marched down the stairs, for that was our duty. Then we continued the drill outside, into the cold November, minus coats and boots. Around the stone edifice we strode, ghostly shapes of mist levitating out of our mouths.

Back inside we took our bowl and spoon and waited for the cook to scoop porridge or some horrid concoction into our bowls. It was like hot maggots squiggling down my throat. In my condition, I understood that food would be horrible, but for these young women, why were they made to suffer? The look of disconsolation on Hilary's face when she served us seemed to comfort me. She was our ally! Her heart desired to serve delicious food, but Madame Brimstone refused to use tuition money to feed us anything better than pig refuse.

We ate in the kitchen, away from the schoolmaster and the teachers. It was preferable since the heat emanating from the burning hearth warmed us. Footsteps sounded, and we paused with spoons held in the air. The head mistress, her locks of hair wrapped tightly at the nape of her neck, stood next to me. As she exhaled, cold air descended upon my neck and shoulders. Chills resonated throughout, freezing even my soul.

"Ladies!" Madame Brimstone began. "Before we begin our studies, I have discovered something missing in the classroom. Would anyone care to confess?"

I didn't want to wash the floors again, but I also didn't want the other students suffering.

"Yes, Madame Brimstone. I apologize, but it was I. Father is lonely," I groveled, though my inner constitution rebelled.

"May I see them?"

"They have been dispatched already."

The stone floor vibrated as she stomped her foot. "Liar! I found these!" She flung the pages into my face, while I heard a collective gasp of the other students. "Your father warned me of this!"

I tried scooping up the pages, but she moved faster. She shredded as she collected them. No burning because there were no fires in any rooms, except for the kitchen. Madame Brimstone thrust fresh parchment in my face.

"I'll give you something to write." She quickly scribbled something on the top of one of the sheets.

"*If we regularly beheld the glory of Christ, our Christian walk with God would become more sweet and pleasant, our spiritual light and strength would grow daily stronger and our lives would more gloriously represent the glory of Christ. Death would be most welcome to us.*" *John Owen (1616 to 1683).*"

"Five hundred times. But not until you finish your classes and chores."

French, grammar, sewing, pianoforte, and etiquette classes, all fitting for girls of nobility or people with wealth.

"My, you're quite proficient," Mistress Winkerly, our instructor, said to me once the girls had left.

"Thank you." My hands cramped as I wrote, "If we regularly..." I had already written it over one-hundred times. I looked up only to watch her quickly push a book under her seat. "Do you teach science and math too?"

"Mistress Catharine, those are not appropriate lessons for ladies," she answered. "Yet," she hesitated, "come look," she stood up and pulled out more than one book. "These are mine."

A book of astronomy and mathematics. There were Arabic letters on the outside of the books.

"I don't dare let Madame Brimstone see these, for she would surely have them burned and me also!"

"I won't tell anyone. I'm a writer," I confessed.

She let out a gasp of surprise. "Writer? At your age? Well, I guess Jane Austen had one novella published when she was only nineteen."

"Madame Brimstone ripped up my writings. That is why I'm here still writing this quote. I probably won't be done in time for you to leave."

"Poor dear," Mistress Winkerly said. "We must find someplace to hide your work. Let me ponder this."

Eleven o'clock and I was finished with John Owen. I had it memorized. It was hard to think of anything else, but I knew I had to start anew on my first novel. Hilary, the housekeeper, had brought me paper and I began writing. The words flowed smoothly, but it all felt futile. Who would destroy my work next?

"Follow me," Mistress Winkerly appeared in the dark classroom. It was past midnight. I thought everyone would be asleep.

We walked down a hallway to another set of steps leading to another floor. Our feet padded silently to an attic. On one of the inside walls, she tapped gently and a wooden panel popped out. I handed her my papers, and she tucked them inside. She readjusted the panel.

I hugged her and went back to the cold classroom.

Henry had started a fire in the room, and my black cloak rested on the chair back.

"I'll get too cozy and fall asleep," I protested, but the little comforts were like a hug. I wrote for five hours, something I had never done in life. I tiptoed upstairs, locked away the pages, put the ink well and quill in their places, and retired. The next morning was Sunday. *Perhaps we will sleep in.*

Shocked into consciousness, I awoke to the ritual of the frigid bath, scratchy clothing, and a march around the manor. This morning we would go to church instead of doing our studies.

"Since Catharine is a Catholic, she'll have to eat her breakfast after her church," Madame Brimstone spoke as if discussing some contagious disease. "We'll drop her off at her church before we go to ours."

"I ant yur religion," Hannah, the cockney girl said.

"There are no temples in the area," Madame Brimstone said.

"I wanna go with Cafarine," Hannah replied.

"I want to go with Catharine," Madame Brimstone corrected. "Say it correctly, and then you may go. I have no idea why anyone would want to go to *that* church."

Hannah and I rode on the top of the carriage with the driver. The bitter cold scratched our cheeks, but bliss filled our souls.

The angel appeared.

I swiped my dribbling nose with my sleeve and asked, "Did she make it?"

"Make what?" My angel's eyes squinted.

"To heaven or is she burning in hell?"

"Did you see her when you visited it?"

"I don't know."

"And that's all you need to know."

The carriage halted in front of a stone cathedral. Both Hannah and I strained our necks looking to see where the tip of the structure met with the sky.

Madame jut her head outside. "Hurry on, you two!"

We quickly jumped off, and the carriage sped away. A few of the girls waved from the back of the carriage window.

I yanked on the wooden door that must have been at least twenty-feet tall. Hannah and I entered the empty, massive edifice. Centuries ago church services had taken place here, but at that moment it was a catacomb. Large, empty holy water fonts in the shape of shells, rested on each side of the door. Several stone columns shouldered the weight of the building.

"I don't think they use this church anymore," I said. *Madame Brimstone knew the area, why did she bring us here?* I didn't really need to ask myself that question.

"Sorry, Cafarine." Hannah shivered and reached out for my hand. "It's scary in here."

"Scary? No, Hannah. Let me give you a tour." *All those years traveling have finally paid off.* "Right now, we're walking over the tombs of the dead."

"Agh! You mean we walking on bones?" Hannah shivered.

"Look." I pointed down to a large etched out rectangle. Duke Albert we could make out, but the rest of the stone had been rubbed smooth. When we finished our tour, we waited outside for two hours. We forgot the cold and played tag, hide-and-seek, and just frolicked as we waited. I laughed, a simple pleasure I had taken for granted during life.

"It's comink!" Hannah shouted when she spied the carriage. We both assumed our solemn manner.

As the carriage returned back to the boarding school, Hilary and Henry, lugging large trunks, passed us going the opposite direction.

"They are no longer in our employ," Madame Brimstone said. "They've been fraternizing with the students." She bore holes into me. "No hired help will defy me."

Waiting for us was a dour looking woman and a tall, quiet man.

"My sister Helga, and our brother, Mundy will take their place. Now freshen up and come down to prayer."

Could a building ever be more desolate? The stone manor, void of two kindly people, became such a place. It was indeed Purgatory or even worse.

No Sunday nap, snuggling in bed with a book, I guess. Downstairs we trudged, ever dutiful. In the hearth a fire roared. A fire? We scrambled to have the seat nearest the blazing warmth.

"Ladies! The fire produces enough heat, we don't need to throw ourselves into it, unless one wants to," Madame Brimstone's eyes searched me out.

Helga was setting the dining room table with fine linens and china.

"We are to have a guest for dinner," Madame Brimstone said. "We must all be on our best behavior."

Guests meant a half-decent cooked meal, I had hoped though I had to remind myself that was a futile request in this existence. I recalled when Hilary had told me when she had arrived she was very careful about preparing the food.

"Madame Brimstone didn't like the way I cooked. 'Take out all sweetness,' she said to me. I hated it. Once she dumped out an entire kettle full. Ah, it's a shame."

Judging from Helga's looks, food around here was going to get even worse. Sir Fretwell, our guest, arrived. Madame Brimstone's face actually cracked slightly into a smile. We formed a line, and as he passed us, we were to curtsy. I tripped in the endeavor and toppled over him.

"Mistress Catharine!" Madame Brimstone shouted.

The girls stifled giggles.

"Ah. Madame Brimstone has written about you, the redheaded she-devil," he stated formally, with consternation in his voice. "Later I must have a word with you alone!"

As I contemplated my fate, Sir Fretwell and Madame Brimstone droned on and on about the monarchy, the lazy poor drivel crowding the streets, and the New World.

"It's fa of Indians, ya know!" Hannah spoke up. The two older persons turned and stared at her.

"That's sort of racist," I said. "We don't use that term any longer."

Everyone turned to stare at me; Madame Brimstone's eyes were drills rotating furiously into me.

"We don't speak, Catharine, unless spoken to."

I mustered up as much defiance I could and returned the glare. She turned away, so I returned to carving tunnels through my pasty potatoes.

"I'll eat them if you don't want them," Hannah whispered.

"What are you two discussing over there?" Madame Brimstone demanded.

"The potatoes are delicious," I lied.

After dinner, Madame Brimstone marched the girls into the village to visit the ill. I was to remain with Sir Fretwell for our little talk.

Too pampered, too pale, and too fleshy and white like a pillow. This was one cushion I would avoid. Sir Fretwell discarded his earlier dignified air and goggled in lust at me. He lounged on the settee, while I stood before him, like a chastened child. Mundy entered to pile more logs onto the fire. After completing his task, he stood up and lingered.

"You may go now, man!" Sir Fretwell said. Mundy remained.

"He can't hear you," I said. "Why don't you let him stay?"

Sir Fretwell heaved his large body off the couch and stormed over to Mundy. Through hand motions, he directed Mundy out of the room. Mundy peered carefully at me and then backed out of the door.

Sir Fretwell returned to stand behind me. He extricated a pin from my hair, and it dropped down onto my back. Then he touched my shoulder. I still cringe at the horrid memory.

"Mistress Catharine, I sense a fire in your blood." His hand roamed down my back.

"Do you want to make love to a corpse?" I blurted out.

He stepped away for a moment, but then neared me to undo my top. Goose pimples of horror popped out of my skin. Suddenly my shoulder was bare. He bent down to kiss it.

Fortunately, he did not have his grip on me so I escaped and scurried behind a table. A large brass candlestick invited me to use it as a weapon. It weighed heavily in my hand as I lifted it. "Don't you dare come closer!"

"Hah, you a mere child," he edged in toward me. I lifted the candlestick higher. Suddenly Sir Fretwell slumped to the ground with Mundy behind him, a wooden mallet dangling from his right hand. Blood oozed from the head wound. Helga rushed in.

"You killed him," she glared at me. "You will die for this!"

CHAPTER 28

Cockroaches roam in darkness and remain undetected, and that was how Constable Richard, a good friend of Sir Fretwell, decided to convey Catharine Zimmer to jail, in the darkness of night without detection of the law abiding populace. Mundy tried to convince the rabble of accusers, but Madame Brimstone and Helga's testimonies held greater weight than that of their deaf brother's.

While they were crowded together in the front hallway, Hannah pulled me aside. "Wha ya wan me ta do wif your book?" she whispered.

The novel! How was I ever to finish it in jail or worse? Affliction in this realm never ceased, yet grew like fervent yeast within the perfect conditions. "Run up and get it!"

She scurried up the staircase, but Constable Richard grabbed my shoulders. "Gotta take you down. Will I be safe in the carriage or do I need to bind you?"

"I want my father," I said.

"Father? What a disgrace! Who would want their father knowing of their misdeeds?"

"I didn't kill him."

"The fine ladies disagree."

I climbed into the dark carriage and he followed and sat across from me. He pulled a pouch from his inner pocket and inhaled a pinch of tobacco.

"That cause cancer," I said.

Cancer studies were more novel than cars in this century, so Constable Richard glowered. "Be quiet, you!"

Ignoring him, I said, "How much are the two sisters paying you to whisk me away in the night?"

"I beg your pardon. I'm not that kind of man."

"Then why didn't you heed the words of Mundy?"

"He's deaf. How can you trust that?" He pulled out a rumpled rag that probably served as a handkerchief and held it in my face. "I'm warning you!"

The deaf were untrustworthy? Loss of hearing did not mean the loss of scruples or decency or intelligence. I fought the urge to argue and instead turned to look out the tiny windows. At least he didn't suffer from the same proclivities as Sir Fretwell, I consoled myself.

The ride was short, and he led me into the jail, in which its architects borrowed the template from the Tower of London. Inside blocks of stones had squeezed together centuries ago to create the barricade to the outside. Barred, pane-less windows gave prisoners a whiff of the outdoors with gusts of wind whistling through the squares. The constable shoved the skeleton key into the keyhole and cranked it. The heavy metal door swung aside, inviting us in. My dainty shoes tapped silently on the dirt floor.

This was not to be solitary confinement. Five other professional women stood in various corners, shivering while contemplating their own troubles. A man, sobriety escaped from, pushed his face into the squares of the outdoor windows.

"Gad evenin' ladies! Promise you'll come home with me, and I'll rescue ya!"

The women ignored him, but the constable rushed toward the window and waved his stick. "Go home, scoundrel." he shouted. "I'll come right out and arrest you."

"If ya gonna put me in this cell, come an' git me!"

"You'll be staying with the Slasher in cell five!" The women shouted in horror at the utterance of the serial killer's name.

Prostitutes and serial killers. Could my travels get more interesting?

My angel appeared, but only to me. "These people are human beings too." She sat next to me on the cot and crossed her legs. Her costume reminded me of the old-fashioned Christmas carolers, with her teal, satin gown, and black velvet jacket.

"Your outfit is lovely." I wanted to think of something else besides the characters sharing a home with me.

"Look ee, we got ourselves a baby who is talking to herself!" one of the women exclaimed. Blond curly tendrils spilled out from her bun. Rouged lips and cheeks heightened the blue in her eyes, but her appearance surely was not angelic. "Wha ya here fa," she asked, smoothing my hair in a motherly fashion.

"They accused me of killing Sir Fretwell."

"Agh!" A raven-haired woman exclaimed. "He was one af me regulahs! Mean buzzard. He'd..."

"Shh! Not in front of the baby," the golden hair woman said. "Who ya talkin' to?"

"My angel. But no one can see her, except for me."

They roared loudly. The drunk fled, and the constable looked back at me. "Maybe we got you in the wrong place!" He scurried out and quickly locked us all in.

"Sah ya keelled him, hah?" Another woman stepped forward. "The world's a betta place now."

"I didn't kill him. Mundy, our manservant, did. Sir Fretwell was going to attack me, but Mundy hit him in the head with a hammer."

"Then what's ya in ere fa?"

"His sisters accused me. Mundy tried to convince the constable of my innocence, but they were determined to pin the guilt on me."

"The chopping block for ya, mah lady! Maybe you and Slasha will share the platform togetha'!" The women tittered. They had troubles of their own. One more or less victim of a corrupt legal system was none of their concern.

"I can't die! I must finish my novels!" Delirium tainted my countenance and verbiage.

The angelic one peered deeply into my eyes. "Maybe Mr. Constable was right. Ya loony in the 'ead!" She jumped off my cot. The rest of them hovered in a corner.

Disorders of the brain seemed to frighten them more than the murderer in cell five. I was thinking of how to clarify to these women the situation, when Mundy appeared, his arms clasped behind his back. A different officer pushed him forward. Constable Richard appeared looking dejected. How did this all get cleared up with the two wicked sisters?

"You're free to go, ma'am," he said.

"She's not safe!" the pale-haired woman said. "She's speaking all sorts of nonsense."

"Mind your business, ladies. Move back!"

Still fearful of me, they pressed themselves against the cold walls. My angel had disappeared. I followed Constable Richard to the front of the building, where Mistress Winkerly, in her a heavy black cape and black bonnet, waited.

"Mistress Catharine!" She grabbed my hands, and her eyes traveled up and down my shaking body. "Are you okay?"

"Did you know that Tibbetts is here?"

Everyone in England, even the students at Madame Brimstone's school, had heard of the monstrous Tibbett, the Slasher, who preyed upon the nocturnal population.

She nodded solemnly. "I just found out when I arrived."

"How were you able to convince the Constable of my innocence?"

"Your father is a very influential man."

She signed some papers, and we quickly left the precinct. A man's baritone voice shouted, "Death to all who enter this place."

The serial killer's voice rattled me. I was in cell three with the prostitutes, only two doors away. His talent had been wielded mainly on women lurking in dark streets seeking employment, which might have explained the trepidation simmering through my cellmates. A few drunks had also caught the edge of his axe. Would he have attacked us if he had escaped?

"Your father will not be happy when he finds out you spent the night with those horrible women and evil murderer," Mistress Winkerly spoke up. "I quickly dispatched a letter to your father when Mundy appeared."

"Mundy?"

"We'll talk at home."

Talk? Will she tell me who my father is? I only know of a beleaguered man determined to destroy my writings. I called him father, but I didn't even know his name or his profession. Judging from the interior of the mansion I had resided in for a short period of time, wealth and prestige buffeted the family from the hardships of poverty. Despite the protection from worldly despair, his money could not inculcate him from losing his wife to death. Was sorrow fueling his antipathy to my writing? On the other hand, was he just a player in my drama and his only job was to thwart my writing?

The carriage stopped at a tall metal gate. We tiptoed along the long narrow sidewalk to a redbrick, three-storied home. Smoke rose out of the chimney. Inside we removed our cloaks. I watched as she touched a stick into the blazing fire to extract a flame to light the candles throughout the room. Like the movies, when the room is black, and candles are lit, the room magically appeared.

For a woman instructor she lived in finery. Portraits, with gilt frames, hung throughout. Sterling candlesticks stood on the fireplace mantle. I spied a large tapestry hanging regally on a wall. When she finished, she sat down and tapped the settee cushion next to her.

"When Mundy came home, he told me everything." She spoke so quickly her words ran into each other.

"Home? Mundy?"

"Mundy is my husband, but we have kept it a secret. Late at night, he comes home, and early in the morning, he returns. He is a scientist, of sorts," she seemed to apologize.

"He was willing to save my life?"

"Mundy, so unlike his two sisters, knew he had to save you."

"But the constable wouldn't listen to him."

"That was why I was there."

"But that means..."

"Oh, Mistress Catharine, I can only surmise death. Sir Fretwell was a prominent man."

"He was lecherous," I interjected. "Apparently he had a reputation with certain ladies, or so I was told tonight in jail."

"Really?" Mistress Winkerly's eyes widened.

We talked late into the night. She told me of Mundy's inventions, and how some of them had made them very wealthy. They kept it a secret. If Madame Brimstone and Helga knew, they would try to extort money from them.

"Unfortunately, I am sure they will soon find out more about us than we wish. They will only be too happy to see their brother executed, and then they'll find a way to get rid of me so they can steal our money."

"Do they know where you live?"

"They will tonight. I had to provide my address before Constable Richard would release you. Let us go to sleep. We will need to be prepared for when they appear."

She slept while I roamed through the gloriously decorated home worried it would all be soon sucked up by her criminal sisters-in-law. I had thought deceit and fraud only resided in the 21st Century, but they were antiquities carried into the future. Back in the guest bedroom, I tried contacting my angel.

"Angel, how am I to help Mundy and Mistress Winkerly? This all feels so futile."

"You obviously don't understand the lesson, student." There she was again, fully dressed like a Victorian woman, complete this time with a velvet bonnet fastened under her chin. "Are you more interested in my fashion than your plight?"

The words diced, leaving my thought in shards. "Isn't this all about my writing? Why did I have to get arrested? For that matter, why did I have to have that sleazebag touch me?"

"Had you done the work given to you while alive, you would not have had to experience this."

Blah, blah, blah. How could so much rest on an abandoned vocation? Lots and lots of people gave up too easily, forgoing risks and sacrifices for a more practical existence. They didn't get punished, did they?

"You don't have to worry about the others." She faded away.

The next morning, as to be expected, Madame Brimstone and Helga made their appearances.

"Agh! So this is where Mundy goes at night!" Madame Brimstone's eyes coveted every square inch of the home. Her attention froze onto the silver candlesticks. "How long have you two been married?"

"Fifteen years." Mistress Winkerly spoke quietly.

"And we didn't even get an invitation to our brother's wedding." Helga plopped down on a wingback chair as if she belonged there.

Madame Brimstone's arms reached out to grab me. "Her father will be angry that you took her from the school. She must come back with us."

"She will be in my care, now," Mistress Winkerly began showing a backbone.

"And who gave you permission?" Helga asked

Mistress Waverly held out a letter sent early that morning from my father. "I notified her father last evening. He has replied and given me permission to care for her while the authorities investigate you and your awful school for girls."

"Permission, you say?" Helga's nostrils flared, increasing her likeness to a swine. I half expected to see a tale poke out of her bustle. "She's coming with us." Helga brandished a pistol so close to my face the metal nicked my cheek.

Could this existence become any more bizarre? One obstacle after the other seemed to impose itself upon me, circumventing any opportunity to write.

Mistress Winkerly backed away and picked up the fire poker. She prodded it between the two women. Helga pointed the pistol at me.

"Put it down, or I'll kill her," Helga threatened.

"Don't listen to her!" I shouted.

Mistress Winkerly hesitated and then gently set the heavy metal stick down.

"Come, you little wretch," Madame Brimstone seized and shoved me outside. "I'm sure we'll get a pretty price from her papa for his little brat!" She stared hard at Mistress Waverly. "And when we're finished with her, we'll come back for you."

Inside the carriage Helga fastened a rag around my mouth to muffle any screams. Another rag went over my eyes. They shoved me below the seat so I wouldn't be visible to any onlookers. Off we went.

As we rode further and further away, it became apparent that the gulf between the novelist and the novel was becoming almost insurmountable to bridge. With no writing implements, but only terror to feed my imagination, the book was dead. Gothic - the genre of my four novels had become the dungeon of my present existence. I winced at the irony.

"It was all my idea," Helga crowed. "Madame Prim and Proper would hear nothing of it, until I convinced her we could make more money off of you, than teaching a bunch of spoilt brats."

"Be quiet," Madame Brimstone said.

"You just don't like my bragging. You're the one that got us into this mess in the first place, inviting that incorrigible Sir Fretwell to dinner."

"He offered to help us financially."

"That's after he'd had his way with all the girls! Now you're going to listen to Helga."

I began gagging from dry mouth.

"Shut you up!" Helga demanded.

How could I stop an instinctual reaction to a filthy rag jammed down my throat? The retching continued until Helga slammed something on my head, and I lost consciousness.

I awoke to my arms popping from my sockets, as the two dragged me across a gravelly road to a round, stone farm building. Inside a sow lay, while her piglets suckled. The two sisters shoved my body next to the mother. Squealing and scurrying of little pink bodies welcomed my intrusion. The sow stood up, a minacious glare from her red eyes. I scrambled to my feet, but the two sisters shoved me back onto the ground.

"Tie her up!" Helga shouted.

"I don't have anything," Madame Brimstone complained.

"You were supposed to be responsible for that!" Helga said, and then bopped me on my head with her pistol, benumbing my brain yet again.

A headache awakened me, the throb pulsating as if counting down a rocket blastoff. My body was sprawled with my wrists tied together and over my head. I shifted but soon realized they had bound my feet tightly together. Little bodies, I hoped were not rats, pushed up against me. In the blackness, I could make out three little curly pigtails. *My three little pigs.* I smiled in spite of the roaring pain.

"Finally awake," Helga was there also.

"You almost killed her!" Madame Brimstone yelled. "What good would she have been if she was dead?"

Madame Brimstone pushed a plate of swill in front of my face. I ate it like a dog would slurp up its food. It was gummy and stuck around my lips. I turned my face toward an arm and swiped as best I could. The food did nothing to assuage my hunger, but my headache lessened somewhat.

"Here, take this too," Madame Brimstone held a steaming cup of something toward my face. It smelled like tea. "This should help your headache." She lifted the cup to my lips. It scalded, but surprisingly in this realm, it offered soothing consolation.

"Can we have lights?" I asked.

"No! We don't want anyone to know we're here," Helga said.

"We're miles and miles away from civilization," Madame Brimstone said. "You're over-reacting."

"We've never kidnapped anyone before," Helga answered. "We cannot be too sure of ourselves."

They disappeared. I shivered, unable to bring my arms to my side as they were still tied up above my head. The stinging pins and needles had long disappeared, leaving my extremities without the flow of blood coursing through their veins. Only my torso had life, as it shook from my lonely sobs. The cold air evaporated the tears on my face, leaving a chill on my cheeks. Pity for myself consumed me. No novels, no eternal happiness!

CHAPTER 29

A strange sensation awakened me, nibbling at the rope that bound me. A mouse scurried away after it finished its task. The pain of sleeping limbs coming to life almost prevented me from easing them down to my side, but I did. I untied my legs, and stumbled as I rose from the dirt. A piglet dropped to the ground.

"Oh, you poor little creature," I picked it up and placed it back on its mama. The sow snorted in her sleep.

Outside a jagged crack of light separated the black terrain from the midnight blue sky. I rubbed my arms hoping my captors were still asleep. Another wooden structure stood next to the barn that held me prisoner for the night. I tiptoed over to it, praying they were not in there, but discovered only horses and a carriage. I had ridden horses, but never tacked one up. I stared stupidly. The movies had made it look so simple. I tried climbing on one of the beasts' back, but it reared, and I fell off.

"What good is it for me to be free if I can't escape?"

I looked around for a different conveyance, but finally decided the only means of escape depended upon my own two feet. My eyes scanned the fading stars and fell upon the Big Dipper. North. Should I go north? South? Where would freedom be waiting?

I found a woolen horse blanket and wrapped it around my shoulders giving me new resolve as I stepped on the gravel trail. My tight, dainty shoes were not intended for walking along the English countryside. What felt like hours later my feet begged me to stop. They pulsated with blooming blisters. The bullying cold weather thwarted any temptation to remove the kid leather. I pushed myself up and continued walking. For added effect, I tripped from the pits in the dirt.

For hours I traveled like this. All life seemed to have migrated, the birds to warmer climates, the furry animals to their burrows, and the leaves from their trees to become part of the soil. The sky, a moth gray, warned of winter's ensuing approach. Crunching leaves seemed to echo in the hollow silence.

Then I beheld a blessed image, a man, with a horse cart, riding toward me.

"Sir! Sir! Please help me! I am lost and trying to find Madame Brimstone's school!" I shouted, hoping he would hear me. No response, but the wagon drew nearer.

"May I help you?" He was dressed in a brown hooded, woolen jacket, much like a monk.

"I need to get to Madame Brimstone's school. I'm lost!"

"Sorry, but it burned to the ground through the night."

"No! Could you take me there? I had left some valuables there."

"They are ashes, I tell you, ashes."

At every intersection, the enemy was one-step ahead of me. Yet, I began to consider who the real enemy was. All my life I had forsaken my profession, treating it like an afterthought, then disregarding it completely. Now it wreaked its vengeance on me, its negligent keeper.

"Take me!" I pleaded.

"Market is not in that direction."

"I was kidnapped! Please, I left something at the school."

"Then that too has burned."

"How far is it if I walk?"

He sighed. "I will take you, but after I take my wares to market."

The young man entered a little village. People looked up at me and arched their eyebrows as they crowded around us. For about an hour, the man sold off his chickens as well as the eggs. After this diversion, the man returned to the front, and we were on our way, I had hoped, to the school. Should I have trusted him to take me to my destination? I pondered my fate as we drove in the cold November day. I had to remind myself that death didn't excuse me from pain and humiliation. In fact, this present condition seemed to heighten misery. Maybe this young man would try to rape me like Sir Fretwell. My eyes darted in search for something to protect me. A gun rested on the floor between the man and myself.

He turned toward me. "You don't have to worry, ma'am. I am a monk. I took the vow of celibacy."

"That hasn't stopped people before." I studied him closer. His head was closely shaved. His brown cowl was actually a monk hood. The wind painted his pockmarked face a fiery red.

"Indeed. When I first entered, the abbot there had several mistresses. It was a terrible scandal. Now Abbot Thomas is very devout. In fact, I probably would not have taken you, but the abbot has instructed we needed to be more merciful."

"Is that why everyone stared why you were selling your chickens?"

"I am sure they thought I had taken up with a beautiful lady."

Should I take that as a compliment from a chaste man or a prelude to seduction? The question faded as we approached the ruins of the school. The monk helped me out. "I need to get back. Sorry to leave you here."

I wanted to shout stop as the carriage faded into the distance as I stood next to the rubble of ashes. Heat radiated in mirth over the destruction of the furniture, the building, and the work of Catharine Zimmer. The wind liberated the ashes, and they flew about merrily like a snowstorm. What tiny pieces held the remnants of my book?

The place was deserted so I was free to wonder about. I would have melted if I had stepped into in the hellish debris, so I repeatedly walked the perimeter, trying in vain, to reclaim for myself the thoughts, the words, the pages. What was the beginning? Where had I ended? Only evasiveness, yet I continued like some lab rat scratching for the cheese on the other side of the cage.

That I did for hours, but then I regarded the moors staring down at me. It seemed they wished to reveal a secret. I climbed the mossy inclines. Panting from exertion, I sat on top of a weather-battered stone. After catching my breath, I realized there were more like it, all strewn about like some tiny graveyard, vines masking their faces. I ripped away the decaying vegetation on the boulder I sat upon, and beheld a dissolving word, *Home*. That is all it said: *Home*. What did that mean? I cleaned off another stone to read, *Neglected*.

After clearing all the boulders, these were the words: *Neglected, A, Home, Find, New, Will, Tales*. Riddles were never my forte. I arranged and rearranged the words for hours, but no translation arose.

My angel materialized and spoke, "Neglected tales will find a new home."

I was not sure what this meant, but I forged ahead. "That means I'm finished here. Some more talented and dedicated writer will salvage my words and create the tome that was meant to be."

"You must love this realm!"

My shoulders slumped. "Can't you see it's obvious that completing my novels is impossible?"

"Suit yourself." She was gone again. Those were not the words of comfort I desired. She could have provided advice or even given me hints for this scavenger hunt. Instead, she ignored my feelings and foisted the responsibility for my demise back onto me. This would be my final resting place, this continuous battle of my desire to write, and the words evading me, all in some posthumous cat and mouse chase, with the mouse claiming victory at every turn.

On the hill, I remained as if some epiphany would erupt from the frozen stones, but they only pressed their icy fingers through the woolen blanket. My body quaked as tiny pebbles poked fun at the sores growing on my feet. My stomach growled angrily. My body said retreat, my mind, however, demanded a fight. The physical elements were about to declare victory, when resolve sputtered to life. I found a stick and carved words into the mud. It was an ephemeral home I was sending my words to, but I continued.

About five paragraphs later, the clip clop of horses nearing me halted my crazed pursuit.

"Catharine! Catharine!" My father. "What is wrong? Look at you!" He pulled me up from the dirt.

"My writings are gone, all gone." I sobbed into his shoulders. "I stole the money you had given me for college. I should have written like you had told me. I lied to you. I lied. I'm a scoundrel, a vile scoundrel."

"Catharine! Stop!"

I continued this tirade the entire ride through the countryside until we reached the estate. My vocal chords were raw from the exertion. Father said nothing.

"Oh, my goodness!" our housekeeper exclaimed upon opening the front door. "Let me take her to her room! Bring the doctor!"

"Mimi, fetch me paper." I said as she unbound my hair and began to brush it out. *Mimi, that was her name. How did I know that?* "My book, it's all gone! Ashes, ashes, they all float away!" I chanted the hideous nursery rhyme.

"Shush. Quiet. You must calm down." Mimi touched my forehead. "You're sick with fever." She bathed me, the cold initiating more convulsions. She quickly covered me with my warm nightgown and tucked me in bed. "You poor baby never got over grieving for your mama. Sleep now. Madame Brimstone should be hung!"

As if tacks held them stationary, my eyes were unwilling to acquiesce to slumber. Even though my body was convulsing, I hopped out of bed, opening drawers, searching for paper and some writing utensils.

"Mimi! Mimi I need you!" I rang my bell.

"You should be sleeping!" She returned.

"I can't sleep until you get me paper and pen!" My father had rushed in, watching.

"Give it to her," he said. "Go to my library and get her some."

I began scratching away and for hours, I sat. Mimi brought me some tea. I left it cold. The doctor arrived, but I would not allow him to see me. I continued into the night and fell asleep on my words. Mimi came in and led me to my bed.

"No! Give me my book!" I folded it and hid it under my pillow. Safe and secure, I fell asleep. For how long I slept, I do not know, but I awoke to an arm sliding under my pillow.

"Father! No! Don't touch!"

"I can't approve of this!"

"No!" I clutched the pages but not soon enough. He had them in his hands and fled the room. I pursued him, pummeling him.

"You can't! No, give them back!"

Mimi rushed out of her room, dressed in her nightgown.

"What is the commotion?"

He threw my work into another roaring fire. The effect crumpled my body to the floor. He carried me back into my room, and I must have slept.

I do not know for how many days I remain unconscious, but when I awoke, it was night. It was time for me to leave and find a haven where I would be free to compose my novels. I dressed and donned a black, heavy cloak. I crept down the stairs and into the library. I felt like a thief, but after searching, found money stashed inside a vase. After placing it all into my pouch, I left this home forever.

A town clock tolled midnight. The flames from the street lamps flickered near extinction; darkness was overtaking the light. Forms, shapes, images melded together. I hesitated and spun back toward the house.

"Whatta we got here?" A gruff man seized my shoulders. "A right pretty one, all by herself."

I tried to shrug him off, but his hand was like a vice.

"Come. It ain't right to have you alone, and me alone. Let's keep each company."

I screamed, but his other hand muffled me. He dragged me into a grove of trees.

"Just give me all your money, and we'll part friends," his liquored breath waxed over my face.

I twirled around and lifted my knee to the only place that counts.

"Agh!" he shouted and seized my hair. A knife appeared too close to my neck. "You gonna be a good girl?"

Was this to be another punishment for my negligence? What was this to prove?

Anger fueled a strength I never knew existed. My right arm flung back at the knife, releasing it from his grip into the darkness. My knee repeated its motion and perfectly hit its target. The villain curled up in pain, allowing both my legs to thrust all my force onto his face. Pulling myself up, I spied what looked like a log on the ground. I clouted his head. He was the second man that died after attacking me. This time I was sure I would not get off so easily. Where would I hide? Where had I planned to go in the first place?

Fortunately, stars provided some light to travel along the countryside, but I could not stop shivering from the recent ordeal. Each noise, each twitter of a branch cast my body into stone.   In the distance, I beheld the young monk driving the horse cart. I wondered how close the monastery was.

"You again!" He shouted. "Do you have a home?"

I wanted my own answers. "Why do you keep showing up when I need you? Aren't monks sleeping at midnight?"

"Aren't young ladies sleeping this time of night?"

"You're not really a monk are you?"

In answer, he grabbed a rope, tightened it around my body, and tossed me into the back of his wagon. A burlap drape disguised me while a chicken pecked at my scalp. Shouting would only call attention to the woman that killed the thief, so I rode quietly.

I began to sweat under the gunny bag. The wagon wheels crackled over the rocky terrain. My stomach growled. Then I must have fallen asleep because I only remember waking to the lurching forward of the halting cart. He pulled off the bag. We were parked in front of some type of hospital. A man stood on the stairs.

"I found this lass roaming the countryside," the horse driver said. "This is the second time within the month that I have found her."

"Bring her in," the spectacled, gray-haired man said. "We will examine her."

"Isn't she one of yours?" the monk asked

"Never seen her, but it looks as if she is, you know, suffering." The elderly man handed over a pouch to the young man. "I am sure the good abbot would appreciate a little donation."

I wondered about the strange situation of a monk roaming the countryside looking to capture people for this man. Did he conduct strange experiments on the people in this building? Was this my next job, to save these people?"

The monk bowed and quickly left.

We entered a drafty hallway, but the man led me to a brightly lit room which looked like a cross between an library, office, and parlor.

The elderly man turned to me. "Welcome. What is your name?"

I remained silent.

"Do you have a name?"

"Of course! Catharine Zimmer!"

"Do you know where you are?"

"Some place where you do experiments on vulnerable people without anyone knowing your evil plans!"

He looked taken aback by my comments. "A funny one," he said. He pulled his feather quill out of the inkstand and began writing.

"You can't experiment on me. I'm dead." I said to him.

Gold brocade drapes covered the tall windows. The wallpaper and the pictures on the wall also seemed to emanate a golden hue. A settee and two wingback chairs were placed behind us, as if they were part of another room. Between them stood a white table with gilt edges. The furnishings had a shabby French provincial feel to them.

He rubbed his chin and opened the right top drawer of his desk. "So, Catharine, that is your name, correct?"

"What are you going to do with me?"

"Well, I hope to figure out what is wrong with your mind and then find the right treatment."

"My mind is perfectly okay."

"That's what most of my patients say."

"You're a doctor?"

"A doctor of the mind. I'm not quite respected by the medical community, but I believe that disorders of the brain can be treated, and people can lead happy lives."

What did he mean by treated? Cutting out chunks of their brains? Giving them terrible shock treatments?

I tried a different approach. "My parents are dead. I have no place to live."

"Hm," he did not sound convinced. "You obviously are not an orphan." He stood to walk around his desk. He peered into my eyes. I shivered.

"I fled Madame Brimstone and her horrible sister."

"They were hung last week."

"They were?"

"It was all over the newspapers."

"I've been sick in bed."

"Really? What kind of illness?"

"Can I eat something? I'm hungry." I had hoped it would buy me some time.

The doctor, however, ignored my plea and continued scratching the paper.

"I need that! Please give me some paper and a pen! I must write!"

He continued scribbling.

"I'm stuck in this realm until I finish my novels. Every time I complete something, my works burn up in flames." He eyed me skeptically. This approach was not working. I changed tactics. "I'll show you what a good patient I can be if you'll just give me some paper!"

"What kind of writing?"

"Novels."

"Forbidden!" he said.

"But what about Jane Austen and Emily Bronte? They wrote! Why can't I?"

"Lord Wellington forbade this practice in our town. Why are you unaware of this?"

"What? That is nonsense."

"His wife has recently died and he joined up with some strange religious cult. Unfortunately they have no use for women doing anything but having children or serving." He walked around me, studying every aspect of my body. I shivered recalling Sir Fretwell. "Why do you think your writing is burning up?"

"It's not burning up! My father throws it into the fire."

"I thought you said your parents were dead."

"My mother is gone, but Father still lives. But he thinks it's wrong for women to write." The minute my words fled my mouth, I realized I was the daughter of Lord Wellington. I laughed, a crazy maniacal laugh. I was supposed to complete my novels being the daughter of a man who believes women shouldn't write? *Wait until I see my angel.*

"You're Lord Wellington's daughter!" The doctor exclaimed.

"No, no."

"But it all seems to fit. Let me contact him"

"So you can extort money from him for my so-called care?" I had to figure out how to prevent this doctor from sending me back.

"How dare you imply I..."

"I have just recovered from being kidnapped by Madame Brimstone and her sister, Helga. My father is still grieving over the loss of my mother. Couldn't I just rest here for a little while until things settle down?"

"Are you talking sense or trying to manipulate me?" He pushed his face close to mine; his gray eyes bulged behind thick lenses. I spoke nothing, hoping my silence would convince him in my favor. "That experience must have damaged your mental capacities." His chin was red from his hands rubbing it. The brown leather chair behind his desk squeaked when he sat upon it. "Tell me more about your writing."

I packed as much panic into my voice as I could muster. "I must write or else..." I looked away; my eyes beheld the dawn seeping into the windows. "You know the law. Even Lord Wellington's own daughter will be put to death for writing, and yet it no longer matters!" My hand flung over my eyes.

His need to care for me as a patient weighed more in my favor than returning me back to my father. "Tell me about this realm you speak of."

I sighed heavily. "This place I am caught in," I shook my head. "Between life on earth and eternity of heaven or hell."

"What do you mean?"

"An angel visits me now and then. She tells me what to do."

He squinted his eyes as if trying to fit into mine. "What does she say?"

"Write. That is what she tells me."

"Interesting." He popped back up and continued his habit of smoothing over his jaw. "You're suffering from all this trauma. Let me reach out to your father and ask him permission for you to stay."

"Do you think if he's forbidding all sorts of things, he's going to say yes? Can't we keep my stay a secret? I am of age, you know." *Actually much, much older than you can imagine.*

"I don't want to be hung like Madame Brimstone."

"No, no. You won't. You need to hide me from everyone in this building so no one can reveal our secret."

He spun around and spied me carefully as if he missed some important detail. "You're hiding from something, aren't you? There is nothing wrong with your mind."

"I told you I'm running from my father. I am trying to write my novels, but he keeps throwing them into the fire. Please, please, let me stay here."

We both jumped when someone knocked at the door. A tall, gangly man with a mosaic of pockmarks coating his face, entered. He quickly strode over to the doctor and whispered into his ears. The doctor watched me carefully as the aid spoke.

After the aid left, the doctor spoke. "A man has been found dead right outside of Lord Wellington's estate."

"Thank God I wasn't killed either." I innocently fluffed my skirt.

"You do know I will have to contact the authorities about you?"

I jumped out of my seat, groveling. "No! Don't! I must find somewhere to write. Somewhere my father won't toss my work into the fire. Somewhere I won't be attacked. I must get this done. I'm so tired. I want to leave."

"But I thought you wanted to stay."

"This realm. I want to leave. I've been here it seems the longest."

"Realm. Do you know what year it is?"

Great, I died in 2013, but I have no idea what era I was in.

His mind seemed to play tug of war: should he contact the authorities or should he treat this strange woman? He finally spoke, "Perhaps a stay here will benefit you. I don't usually take patients on with no pay, but I am sure Lord Wellington will reimburse me for my services, that is if he doesn't behead me first."

"No. Don't tell him I'm here." I pulled out my satchel. "I have some money. How much will it cost to stay here?" I tossed pound notes onto his desk.

He slid the money toward him. "It's not a hotel. It will all depend on your treatment."

"I don't care. You can run all the tests you want on me, but please let me stay."

"Okay, Miss Catharine. You may stay, but if your father shows up, I will have to turn you over. Also, since I wish to keep the other patients safe, you will need to be locked up on the third floor."

I had to agree to this or be thrown to the authorities. "Do you fear me?"

"A dead man and a strange woman showing up at my doorsteps? I am not willing to take any risks."

He rang a silver bell that was resting on his desk. "Please take Miss Catharine up to the Blue Room."

"But the police?" the man questioned.

"This young lady has convinced me of her innocence. However, she will need some treatment for the shock she experienced. She was one of Madame Brimstone's students."

The man tried whispering in the doctor's ears. "Is she safe to have in the house?"

"Abraham, you know the procedure for those in the Blue room."

"Yes."

Procedure? I nervously climbed the stairs up to the third floor trying to ascertain escape routes. When he opened the door I gasped in pleasure. It was a room I would have liked to spend my wedding night in. A large canopy bed with a dark wooden frame rested in the center of the bedroom. Dressers, chairs, and nightstands accompanied the bed in the tall room. Off the bedroom was a large sitting room fitted out with bookshelves on each wall. Large windows overlooked the countryside. Snow cascaded from the clouds.

I turned back to Abraham, "There are no secret entrances in here, are there?" I didn't want the doctor sneaking in at night trying to get patient privileges.

"Nope. I aren't supposed to say, but the Doctor an' his wife lived up here. Now he stays downstairs. He has a small bed in a room by his office."

I shivered. Was this their love nest? Did she die up here? Did he kill her?

"It war a pink room when she war alive. After she died, everything war changed. No you warry Miss, no one comes up here."

"Is it haunted?"

"Yar's a funny one, Miss. Do yer want yer meals brought up or will yer be taking yer meals with the others in the dining room?"

"Tonight I'd like to dine alone if that is okay."

The click of a lock confirmed I was a prisoner, but no sooner had he left than a light knock brought me back to the door, only to have it opened by the previous housekeeper at Madame Brimstones.

"Hilary!" I had thought her departure from the school meant I would never see her again. We hugged tightly.

"Mistress Catharine. What a terrible time you have had of it. We heard all about it. Those two horrible women got what they deserved. Good thing we left when we did. Would you like me to draw a bath for you?"

"Do I need to go to the kitchen?"

"No, no, Henry brought up buckets and so did I." I followed her to a bathroom, a very modern convenience in that era.

I quickly scrubbed myself in the ice water. I was almost getting used to the chilling baths.

"Can you stay and talk?" I asked as she began to leave. "So much has happened since you had left."

For an hour, I told her my ordeal.

"Oh, dear. We must keep a lookout for you. We must have a plan for your escape," Hilary said. "There is a tunnel that runs under the house to the barn. They will be checking the countryside for you. My sister lives in the next county. Perhaps we should take you there tonight."

"So soon? I like this place. I feel I can write here."

"Let me talk it over with Henry. See what he says. Now sleep and I'll bring some supper later." She left, but I wanted company.

"Angel! Angel, you have been gone so long. Why did I get placed with a father that doesn't allow female writers? That is ludicrous! Do you expect me to remain her for an eternity?"

There, at the writing table, she sat, in a Damask Pelisse gown.

"As I said before, writing you must do alone."

"Fine, but put me somewhere that allows me to practice this art!"

"Excuses, excuses!"

I decided to change the subject. "Did you choose me, or did He choose you for me?" I asked. How could two entities, so apparently at odds with each other, be united?

"He chose me, of course. Yet when I guarded you in your mother's womb, until this very moment, I have felt nothing but the utmost love and pride in being your angel."

"Pride?"

"Yes, Catharine. You're a beautiful soul."

"But, but..." I stammered. All through this odd expedition, she had only doled out sarcasm and belligerency. How could she call me a beautiful soul?

"No one likes to be chastised," she said. "My job was to guard you and to bring you safely to heaven. Your temperament often needed a little emotional scouring job."

I frowned but let her words soak through my stubborn exterior. Had I been perhaps a little more humble, each of these journeys might have been completed quickly, and the lessons learned more palatable.

"Will we see each other in heaven?"

"Of course. Like they say on earth, I can't be gone that easily."

"I think the phrase is, 'You can't get rid of me that easily.'"

"Correct!" She leaned over toward me and we hugged. It was a delightful surprise, one of the few sensations of joy I had experienced in this world. "I have confidence you will complete this task. I will always be at your side, all you just have to call. Your task, however, must be finished before I take you home." She left again.

Love discovered in an unlikely place wrung unshed tears from my eyes. I also realized that I had loved her all this time. It all began as a child, when I spoke to her about everything. My nickname for her was Toothbrush. What a silly name. "Angel Toothbrush, look at this ladybug. Angel Toothbrush, listen to me sing *Twinkle Twinkle*. Angel Toothbrush, watch me dance." I stopped talking to her around age seven, when the kids at school began teasing me.

Sun poured into the bedroom, giving the impression of warmth, though I knew ice formed outside. The snow had stopped, but it outlined the trees' charcoal limbs. I sat at the desk, which was outfitted with vintage writing utensils. I wrote without ceasing. Hours later, when night cloaked the sun, there was a light tap on the door. Hilary poked her head inside.

"Mistress Catharine, word is out that a man has been killed and the authorities are looking for Lord Wellington's daughter, the prime suspect."

CHAPTER 30

Once again I became a fugitive. Under the tunnel, to the barn, and into the carriage. Hilary bundled blankets around me, and crack, went the whip. By the way I careened inside the carriage, I knew Henry was driving the horses beyond their capacity. After jostling my brains around, I decided to squat on the cold, hard carriage floor. The horses' panting seeped through the thin carriage walls. We drove like this for maybe twenty minutes until the carriage screeched to a halt. My head knocked into a black leather seat.

"Oh no!" I heard Henry curse from outside.

I was about to speak when I heard an authoritative voice ask, "Why travel so late at night?"

"My daughter, she is very ill. We're off to the doctor's."

The man's horse was restless as I heard hooves cutting into the dry earth. "But Doctor Hedwig is that way."

"Doctor René, the French doctor in Dover, will see her. He deals with contagious conditions. Night is the only time we can travel."

The hooves brushed backwards.

"That's quite a nice carriage," another voice said. "Who employs you?"

"Dr. Gustave. He knows of my daughter's condition."

"Does she live in the home?"

More questions. Could they just let us move along?

"We live in the stable, away from everyone."

"Have you caught it?"

Henry began to cough, loud and hard.

Horses backed even further away. I gasped when I noticed a mouse scurrying across my lap. The action caused me to inhale my spit; the effect of that was I began choking.

"Listen, can't you hear her? That is why we must go to Dr. Gustave."

"I thought you said you were seeing Dr. René."

Stuck in fearful gridlock, my heart stopped, waiting, anticipating the next words.

"Sir, I am so tired and the condition is quickly setting in. I am very confused."

"Be gone with you!" the voice commanded. "Watch yourself for a murderer is on the loose."

Off again, bouncing, jostling, my head crashing into anything nearby. The mouse had disappeared, but I quivered wondering if it would find a home in my bags. A new concern entered, this time from my stomach. Motion sickness gripped me and soon I emptied my already emptied stomach. It reminded me of April Morris. Packed into my carpetbag was writing paper, but it would need to clean up the mess. The acrid odor overcame the horsey scent of the conveyance.

"Henry, can we stop for a moment?" I shouted.

I tripped off the steps and swayed toward the copse of trees. The retching continued mercilessly. How could this persist if there was nothing inside me? My stomach finally found peace. I patted my chin, and then stood, staring at the carriage. I did not want to go back to its cavernous insides. They call it the Garcia effect, when you are afraid to eat the last food you ate before you got sick to your stomach. It was not food I feared this time, it was that macabre fun house on wheels.

"You must hurry, my lady," Henry coaxed.

"Do you think I can ride up with you?"

"Suit yourself, but if we see anyone, you must hide."

The bracing wind slapping my face seemed to placate my stomach, but my extremities revolted. Drip, drip, drip went my nose. Tears coursed down my cheeks. Pinpricks of icy cold stabbed at my baby toes, and it seemed as if the wind whisked off several layers of skin on my hands.

For hours, we seemed to ride, only stopping for the horses. Rolling scenery, like in the movies, passed us. Same trees, same fields. Same rivers. Same desolation. Only the black sky seemed to change as it lightened while the stars paled. A ribbon of pink and gray stretched across the horizon line. As we neared the ends of the earth, a complex of buildings, formed in a t-shape, waited for us. The vanguard was the tallest structure, a red brick church, with a cross on top of it. Behind this were its arms, shorter and sprawling to the east and west. Behind the arms was the back building, taller than the arms, but not as lofty as the church. As we neared, I discerned headstones to the east of the building.

"No, Henry, not another school for young ladies."

"It's for ladies, but not the kind you're thinking of."

I sniffed while my lips pressed themselves into a straight line. *Angel, this scenario of evil intents to destroy me and my writing are getting old. I get the point. Can't I just move on?*

"Really?" I jumped when she appeared to my right, floating.

"Yeah, really. Inside those buildings is some evil henchman or woman waiting to terrorize me and forbid any writing!"

Henry turned toward me and gave me a quizzical look. "This ride has taken a toll on your mind, Miss."

I thumbed to my angel, "Henry, this is my guardian angel."

He looked, but of course saw nothing.

"Angel, would you mind showing yourself to him so he doesn't think I'm crazy?"

"Does it matter what he thinks?"

"Yes, now show him."

In answer, she disappeared, but her words floated toward me, "Good-bye. Persistence will pay. I won't be able to help you in your next endeavor."

"When did you ever help me?" I shouted to the air.

Henry gaped at me as he pulled the coach up to the front door. Women, wearing long gowns and dark veils appeared. One of them held out her arms to assist me down.

"Come out of the cold," she said. "Henry, thank you. Will you be staying?"

"I'll take my usual spot in the stable," he said. "Might need to do a bit of doctoring with this one. Things coming out of her mouth, but they're not making sense."

I ignored his comments and smiled recalling Adrien's story of his sister and the nuns he had met at her convent. Inside we squeezed into the vestibule with about one-hundred women waiting.

"You can all retire," the one who seemed in charge said. "Thank you for your prayers." She turned to me. "Follow me," she said.

We settled in a large, dark room, with a heavy oak desk, and a life-sized crucifix behind it. Mother Superior, I had assumed, spoke, "Most novices appear in the day."

"I don't plan on joining the convent."

"Fleeing?"

"From becoming a nun? Of course not. It's just not for me." I brushed off an imaginary speck and fluffed my skirts. A remnant of the vomit seemed to be resting in the side of my lip. My fingers swiped that away.

"I meant fleeing from the law."

I began to tell a fabricated tale when her emerald eyes, glittering with truth detectors, scanned me for any incongruities. My hands rubbed together, my frost bitten toes wiggled, but my lips refused to budge.

"It is good you are not a military spy for your demeanor tells me you've killed someone."

Up I stood. "How can you gather that from just looking at me?" She is from this realm, I reasoned. The angel probably clued her in that I would be showing up. This is probably just a test of my honesty.

As long as she guessed the truth, I filled in all the blanks. When I finished, she stood up and began to pace back and forth, whispering. Talking to herself or in prayer, I could not deduce. Back to the desk she returned, and folded her hands.

"It was self-defense," she acceded. "But you have still killed a man. Hiding a fugitive may put our convent into an unpleasant predicament." She opened a desk drawer and looked through its contents. She then closed it. "Henry says you're from west of here. Tell me the town you hearken from."

What should I tell her? I wondered. From Wisconsin, should I say, or the region between earth and eternity? She was a spiritual woman, or so I assumed, and they believed in those things.

"I'm dead and waiting for my eternal reward," I pronounced, watching her face and waiting for her response.

"How long have you been?" She did not seem fazed by my comment.

"Centuries, at the very least. Each destination I have entered is a consequence of my reckless and careless behavior and words I spoke while alive. Since my death, I have lived in chronic suffering. Worse, due to the neglect of my vocation, I am stuck in this existence until I finish the four novels I had started in life."

She arched her eyebrows and stood up to walk around me. "Hm," she would say every few moments. I leaned further back into my seat trying to escape from her penetrating glances into my soul.

I wanted to fill the silence with something besides her contemplating comments, so spoke, "I have written in this realm, but each time I've completed some work, it's burned up."

"The desire is still weak," she replied.

"Weak? The aspiration is there!" I stomped my foot.

"Is it? We will see. Catharine, you may live here, but each day you must produce 3,000 words."

"Three-thousand? By hand? No Spell Check?" My mouth stood agape as she continued speaking.

"At the end of each day, which will be eight o'clock, you will hand over your work for my review. On Saturdays we'll discuss your writings, and Monday you'll do rewrites if necessary."

"Rewrites? What if I feel they don't need rewrites?"

"I'm sure they will," Mother Superior chortled.

"Are you qualified?"

"Of course, I'm Mother Superior."

She had the habit, if you'll pardon the pun, of pushing invisible hair up further into her wimple. Then she would fluff the back of her veil as if she was pushing her long hair off her shoulders. I guessed her hair to be black because her eyebrows were charcoal. Her large, oval green eyes contrasted with her ivory skin and blushing cheeks. She was beautiful despite her habit.

"You think nuns are supposed to be ugly?" She read my thoughts.

"I don't think the outfits are very becoming."

"Beauty shines from the soul, Catharine, not from the exterior." She pushed up more of her imaginary hair. "You will reside as if no one else is here. The day you fail to produce is the day I contact the authorities. I am sure that even though you are dead, being hanged will not be a pleasant experience."

"I've been assassinated already," I bragged.

"And, did you enjoy the experience?" she asked.

"I mistakenly believed I would have no feelings in this existence, but the pain was far more excruciating than anything I had experienced on earth."

"Describe it to me," she said.

Was she sick? Did she enjoy gratuitous violence?

"It was as if someone stabbed me, and then poured acid over the wound."

"Is that what you want again, Catharine?"

I fidgeted in my seat. She was right. I did not want to go through that again, and yet she was asking for an impossible feat. I barely wrote one-hundred words a day, let alone three-thousand.

Her habit swooshed as she stood back up. She floated toward me. "The sisters awake at four, and I expect that from you as well. In your cell your meals will be served. A table and writing utensils will be provided. Is that agreeable to you?"

Hanging or stuck in a cell until I finish my four novels? *Perhaps if I was hanged it would be done and over with.*

"Catharine, I assure you the sensation of hanging will only be more harrowing than the shooting. Imagine a rough cord squeezed against your neck. Pop! The bottom falls out and you're dangling, gasping for breath. Who knows how long it will take before you die?"

She left the room with that cheery thought, and another younger nun returned to usher me to my jail cell. There would be no argument or trying to cajole Mother Superior into a different, more amenable arrangement.

"I have an extra blanket for you," the novice whispered in an Irish accent. Tendrils of blond hair floated over her forehead. Her royal blue eyes shone in purity. "I also plumped up your bed a wee bit. We sleep on straw, but I..."

Mother Superior drifted by. "Catharine will get the same treatment as the rest of us." She confiscated the extra blanket and removed the cushions from my cot.

The novice frowned and looked sorrowful.

"Your intentions were noble, Sister Agnes, but Catharine has coddled herself for too long, which is why her work remains undone. Good night, Catharine. Don't forget your prayers."

Blackness enveloped me in the already enclosed space, but it was comforting, not stifling. There was no use calling for angel, since she and I had said our good-byes at the gate. I missed her and wanted to chat with her.

"You're just looking for an excuse not to write!" she said, illuminating my black box. She was floating like she had been when I was on the carriage.

"Why do invisible entities only show themselves to certain people?" I was still feeling miffed.

"When you get to heaven, I'm sure someone will answer that for you." She snapped her fingers like a magician, and brightness entered. "Why don't you try this chair for size? You'll be using it for a *long* time. She patted a wooden, three-legged stool that belonged in a milking parlor not under the delicate bottom of Catharine Zimmer. I rubbed my rear end. Next to that, stood a roughly hewn table. The four legs attached look more like blocks than apparatuses designed to hold up a table. Slivers were waiting to slither into my skin. My angel pointed to a large feather, an inkstand, and parchment. "Here are your writing implements."

"You mean to tell me pens haven't been invented yet?"

"You're just a few years shy of that!"

I sighed in disgust. *Why did I wait so long?*

Down I plopped, my heavy skirts providing some cushion. My hands seemed to cramp in anticipation of torture when I picked up the quill. What was left of the feather had lost its stiffness. There was no point at the end, only a rounded edge. I dipped and scratched, but the effort was like writing in the sand. "She wants three-thousand words? I can barely write one with this lousy instrument."

I threw it to the corner of the room.

The angel set an hourglass onto my desk. It was no more than two inches tall. "This represents a thousand years."

The sand began to fall like snow in a snow-globe.

Over the corner the quill waited for me to pick it up. "What happened to the novels I had already started?"

"Burned! Don't you remember?"

I picked up the quill. Sigh. "Don't remind me." Tap. Tap. Tap went the quill on the desk. "I could sure use some gum."

"You're in luck. That's been invented already. Bad luck, Mother Superior forbids it in the convent." Oh, she loved to torment me, my angel.

Back into the inkwell dipped the feather and I began writing gibberish. "Why am I a writer? What is the purpose of all this? I can't write. The thoughts have fled away. This is boring. I want to dance. Give me something to eat."

"Let me see what you've written so far." She grabbed the parchment and scanned the words. "Catharine!"

"You didn't tell me what to write."

"You're right. So, keep going. What do your psychologists call it, free association?"

"My angel is beautiful. She has wiry, black ringlets that bounce with each of her movements. She and I don't always agree, but she has been with me since my very conception. I had no choice in the matter, but I think she was a good fit for me, for the most part."

"For the most part?"

Then another idea popped into my brain, and I began to write again. This time the words flowed, and I felt a story growing. The writing guided me into the next day, but I would not retire onto my cot. Yet, I must have fallen asleep because I had awoken to Sister Agnes tugging at my shoulder.

"Would you care to join us for Morning Prayer?" she asked.

No instruments, only a heavenly euphony as the voices reverberated against the cold, walls. One hundred strong, the voices, not necessarily beautiful, echoed the answers I had been running away from all my life. Right at that moment, I accepted my calling.

A chunk of coarse brown bread and tea awaited along with more parchment. Ignoring breakfast, I took up the pen. Instantly I continued where I had left off. The images, phrases, metaphors, similes, alliterations crowded, vying to be first on the paper. Faster, faster I wrote. My hand cramped, but I continued, the words gushing out. I stopped when I heard the knock.

I reluctantly handed the sheets to Mother Superior. She glanced through the pile.

"Catharine, I believe this is far more than my requirement. You are quite prolific if you choose."

"You haven't read it yet." I wanted to seize the papers back from her clutch.

"Trust, Catharine, trust." She hugged me, kissed my forehead, and left.

Each day that followed was the same. Morning prayers, writing, and a goodnight kiss from Mother Superior. Then the arrival of Saturday, the day I dreaded more than any other. Mother would be perched at her desk, and I would meekly enter. Perhaps meekly is not quite correct. I entered ready to do battle, prepared to fight for every word, phrase, or sentence.

"Catharine, this is quite good, but what do you think about this?" Or, "Catharine, what were you trying to say here?" Worse, "Catharine, I think you need to go back and start over."

After the harrowing sessions, I would curtsy, and lie, "Thank you, Mother Superior. These are good suggestions."

On the way back to the cell, I would fume and mimic Mother Superior.

"Catharine, what about this?" Or, "Catharine, take this back." On and on I'd rant, until one day, after a few minutes of my caricature of Mother Superior, I realized she was immediately behind me.

"Are you finished?" she asked. "Good, here are a few more notes I wrote down. Tomorrow is Sunday, Catharine. No work for you."

The tiny hourglass continue crying sand, but I believed I would be done long before a thousand years. However, it would take me more than a decade. I had begun to look forward to the meetings with Mother Superior, as she offered sage advice, and actually complemented some of my writing! The stack of completed pages grew higher and higher. I had long shed the excuses I had used in life to avoid composing. Three completed manuscripts sat in Mother Superior's room. I was quite proud of them yet felt disappointed they would not be shared with the world. I had mentioned that one day when I was in one of my meetings with Mother Superior.

"I am not sure, Catharine, if the value of this exercise was all about showing off."

Chagrined, I stormed off to my cell to finish the fourth book.

One day I took a moment to look out my cell window. Spring had once again returned to the convent. It was a warm, wet day when I inscribed the final word onto the last page of my final novel. I had thought after writing the four books that the ideas would dry up, but I had opened up the dam, and the ideas flowed continuously. At that point in my journey, however, the four books would be enough.

I set the last sheet onto the parchment mountain, a victory over my lifelong insecurities and anxieties. It was long before Mother Superior's nocturnal visit, so I escaped the convent and strolled through the gardens. Back from their winter's sojourn, birds chirped while others tweeted back. Lines of white, purple, and yellow tulips bordered the walkways. The sisters were at their chores. Mother Superior ambled toward me.

"I'm done," I said.

"Congratulations! I believe a celebration is in order, though it is only Thursday!"

"Aren't we going to discuss all this on Saturday?"

"Did you enjoy our sessions, Catharine?"

No, I did not enjoy them. I grew accustomed to them, yet does anyone enjoy dental visits?

"Catharine, your visit with us is soon coming to a close. We will feast tonight."

Those words are hardly joyful for anyone with food allergies or stomach disorders, or to the dead Catharine Zimmer whose taste buds had fled during this entire experience.

"Where do I go next?" Trying to get my mind off the idea of eating cardboard.

"Your angel will come when you are ready."

She permitted me to walk some more through the grounds, and I was struck by the smell of baking bread. I sniffed. It was bread! If you have ever fasted, you know the sense of smell grows keener when the stomach is empty. For this entire voyage, my senses were on a fast, but I knew at that moment that fast had ended.

In the large dining hall, voices echoed. Three wooden planks stood for tables with benches resting on each side. When I sat on one of the long wooden benches, Sister Agnes handed me the breadbasket, which emanated heat from the bread.

"Help yourself! Here, we have some butter too."

Another sister pour a glass of wine into a pewter goblet.

"To Catharine," Mother Superior toasted. "To the success of her books and reclaiming the gift she had been bestowed with at birth!"

Clink went the glasses, along with laughter and talking. "Speech! Speech!" They shouted.

"I have only to thank you for your patience and kindness. You will all hold a special place in my heart." I raised my glass. "To you, my dear sisters!" More clinks, sniffling, and laughter.

Mother Superior seemed wistful as she led me back to my cell. We spoke no words until we stood at my door. She pecked my forehead, "Good-bye, Catharine." She walked away, leaving me alone at my door. I trembled. What awaited me?

"Are you coming in?" Angel's voice echoed through the wooden planks.

When I opened the door, my angel, in white with magnificent wings, stood waiting next to a tunnel streaming with brilliant rays of light.

"I thought you said angels don't dress like that!" I said, marveling at the gilt tinging each white feather.

"The occasion calls for some dramatic effects, don't you think?"

I frowned. "This is my eternity. Don't you think the moment deserves a little solemnness?"

"Where you're going there is only joy."

"Before I leave," I began, "did I do anything right on earth?"

She enfolded me in her arms. "Catharine, Heaven isn't about doing things right, but choosing love. Though there were cracks, your choice to love God and others was stronger than your self-centeredness."

"What will happen to my novels?"

"We do more than float on clouds," she said.

I looked up in shock. "You mean people up here might read my works?"

"Catharine, relax. There are no critics from *The New York Times* up here."

I gasped as I remembered the fate of those in hell. "You mean, they all went..."

"Still can't take a joke, Catharine." She winked and motioned toward the waiting passageway. Streams of gold bathed my face. I began walking toward some glowing figure with arms extended, waiting in the distance. Few get to write about it. Yet insignificant Catharine Zimmer, a no name in the annals of great literature, had the privilege of putting to paper the mystery too powerful for the pen.

I was alone, but I wasn't alone as I felt the presence of the billions of those who went before me; those dearest to me, and those I had yet to meet. How can I even begin to describe this experience as you read, still mired in the human condition? It would be like trying to detect a sub-atomic particle with the naked eye. For now, take hold of your happiest moment and magnify it at least one-hundred-billion times. You would still not be able to comprehend the complete joy awaiting your arrival.

As for me, Catharine Zimmer, my journey here has ended.

Acknowledgements

Special thanks go to Doctor Andrew Seddon, author, and Elizabeth Meier, president of Women of Christ - Milwaukee, who thoughtfully read over the manuscript and offered meaningful suggestions.

ABOUT THE AUTHOR

WAVES IS C.L. PAUR'S second novel. She graduated in 1998 with an MA in Communication from Marquette University. Since then she's been writing freelance articles for secular and religious publications. Paur writes screenplays and children's stories as well as produces and directs children's plays.

Paur lives in Wisconsin with her husband and four daughters.